RETURN
OF THE CLOTH

An Easter Parable
for All Seasons

LOUIS A. TARTAGLIA, M.D.

Even your mistakes give God the
opportunity to bring you back to Him.

RETURN OF THE CLOTH
Last Gift of the Magi - Part II

For permission requests, write to the publisher, addressed "Attention: Permissions Coordinator" carol@markvictorhansenlibrary.com

Quantity sales special discounts are available on quantity purchases by corporations, associations, and others. For details, contact the publisher at carol@markvictorhansenlibrary.com

Orders by U.S. trade bookstores and wholesalers. Email: carol@markvictorhansenlibrary.com

Creative Contributor - Amanda Morsch
Cover Design and Book Layout - DBree, StoneBear Design

Manufactured and printed in the United States of America distributed globally by markvictorhansenlibrary.com

New York | Los Angeles | London | Sydney

ISBN: 979-8-88581-138-5 Hardback
ISBN: 979-8-88581-139-2 Paperback
ISBN: 979-8-88581-140-8 eBook
Library of Congress Control Number: 2024900687

"Christ's light was so powerful that His image was burned into the Shroud of Turin forever. Dr. T illuminates the story in an omni-delightful, easy-to-read, easy-to-understand, and irresistibly compelling way that you will love and want to share with everyone you love. Happy reading."

Mark Victor Hansen, World's Bestselling Author, Co-creator of *Chicken Soup for the Soul*®, *ASK!*, and *One Minute Millionaire* series.

Dedication

To my wife Jeanne Civello-Tartaglia, the Italian American firebrand, gift from God, a delightful being who exemplifies carrying Christ around in all that she does. *Thank you for your encouragement and support.*

Without her love and backing, I would not have had the stability or peace of mind to do what I do.

ACKNOWLEDGMENTS

Thank you:

To Carol McManus my editor who is easy to work with kind and understanding and most of all patient with me.

To my great friend Les Brown who has encouraged me to write about character and got me started on that path with his radio show many years ago. That led to my book *Flawless: The Ten Most Common Character Flaws and What You Can Do About Them*, which outlined the principles that Heba used to teach Jamil that character can truly change. Without his help I would not have published the Last gift of the Magi.

To my great friend Mark Victor Hansen whose help and encouragement has been constant through this whole project. Over the years we have had so many outrageous conversations!

Thanks to the late Og Mandino who encouraged me to build a sequel into the first story, 'Last Gift of the Magi.'

To the copy editor Amanda Morsch, whose fine work is appreciated and from whom I've learned a lot about improving my writing skills.

And lastly, Thanks to the Sisters of the Visitation Monastery, Toledo who have prayed for me and my family as well as encouraged me to include deeper spiritual concepts into my writing.

NOTES OF HISTORICAL INTEREST

When I started writing in the genre of religious historical fiction, I did not even know that category existed. My purpose was to tell a story that was a little more historically accurate that I could leave to my children.

Gradually the book became a venue for teaching character transformation. I received feedback that my readers wanted more in-depth lessons about character transformation and more in-depth explanations about the spiritual dimensions of character transformation.

When I started working on the sequel to *Last Gift of the Magi,* I discovered that the Coptic church in Egypt had a 2000-year tradition of where the holy family traveled. Please forgive me for taking the liberty of embellishing the story.

During this period of time my friend Les Brown kept asking me to write another book on Character as a sequel to *Flawless.* The problem with that was that I was no longer able to practice Psychiatry due to an illness and I did not have the patient vignettes that would make the book interesting. I chose to use a fable because fables can teach lessons and get past conscious resistance to change.

Les Brown, who is a great example someone what has changed his character for the better and lived his purpose in life, understood that there was a process. We talked about it through the years. I didn't want to write a self-help book with a process or a formula for change.

Finally, one of the sisters of the monastery of the visitation suggested that I include more information about the power and influence of Grace on the process.

Last Gift of the Magi started the process. It focused mainly on the identification of one's defects in character but needed to stress more about how Grace influences letting go of the defects or flaws and using your will to practice the virtues that are opposite of your flaws. Return of the Cloth delves deeper into the process. The process always involves transformation through suffering, which increases faith. Gradually, one understands that virtue is the staircase to heaven. Forgiveness is always associated with each step you take. And eventually you realize that you are grow in love and joy.

Summed up by St, Paul in Colossians... Brothers and sisters: Put on, as God's chosen ones, holy and beloved, heartfelt compassion, kindness, humility, gentleness, and patience, bearing with one another and forgiving one another, if one has a grievance against another; as the Lord has forgiven you, so must you also do. And over all these put on love, that is, the bond of perfection. And let the peace of Christ control your hearts, the peace into which you were also called in one body.

And be thankful. Let the word of Christ dwell in you richly, as in all wisdom you teach and admonish one another, singing psalms, hymns, and spiritual songs with gratitude in your hearts to God. And whatever you do, in word or in deed, do everything in the name of the Lord Jesus, giving thanks to God the Father through him.

Now for my personal definition of character:

Character is the blend of virtues and flaws that your soul wears as presents itself to the world. Character is destiny and may your character transform to eventually model the character of Christ. Then you will live your destiny, the destiny God created you for!

FOREWORD BY LES BROWN

Doctor T and I go back nearly 40 years. Most people don't know that he was part of helping catapult my speaking career. We met through serendipity in a parking lot at the Church of Today in Detroit. He introduced me to the church founder Jack Boland who subsequently brought me in to speak 52 times, as word spread and my audience grew. Doctor T has been an inspiration to me, and I am convinced he will be an inspiration to you as well.

Indeed, life takes many twists and turns, with various ups and downs. As we go through life, we sometimes find ourselves yearning for purpose, struggling to unearth our inner potential, and standing at the brink of despair. It is in these moments of introspection and uncertainty that we seek not just guidance but a beacon of inspiration that lights the path to self-discovery and character development. Doctor T's latest book, "Return of the Cloth" is the sequel to his book "Last Gift of The Magi." It will bring you just that. It is wonderfully written like the classic fables that have stood the test of time.

Dr. Tartaglia's first took us on a journey with the Magi to baby Jesus and the holy family. The protagonist, Jamil, is a camel with very flawed Character. If Dr. T would forgive me, the camel reminded me of Dr. T when we first met those many years ago. "Last Gift of the Magi" was a primer in character development. It has a wonderful surprise ending.

The sequel is a marvelous story that will take you through the Holy Family's travels through Egypt. Finally, it brings you back to Jerusalem 33 years later in time for the Passion

of our Lord. The trip back, however, is a much deeper look at character flaws, spiritual direction, and transformation.

Whether you are facing a difficult challenge or simply looking to grow and improve, this book offers valuable perspectives and practical advice that can help you achieve your goals and live a more fulfilling life. If you are looking for inspiration and guidance on finding purpose and meaning in your life this book by Doctor T is a must-read. His special insights provide a unique perspective on the power of hope and perseverance and the importance of finding direction and developing character in life.

Doctor T's message is universal and can inspire anyone looking for guidance or struggling to find their way. Get ready to take the next step on your journey. Dive into this inspiring book and discover the power of hope resilience and the human spirit and you will be transformed.

Contents

1

A Promise Made

A Long Time Ago, East of Beersheba

The two nomads pushed their camels eastward at a grueling pace. They were running on a direct line from a point east of Beersheba in the desert toward the southern tip of the Dead Sea. It led directly away from a mass of dark angry clouds in the distance. They could smell the storm, though it hadn't reached them yet.

The desert sometimes gave warning that a major storm was brewing. In that sense it was kind. When the storm hit, however, it would be cruel. Only camels were really prepared to withstand it. Nature had provided them with all the necessary equipment to survive. It was programmed into their instincts. Living in the desert was part and parcel of their being.

Nemir and Abdul, the two nomads, on the other hand, were instinctively afraid. They wanted desperately to reach the land of Moab on the southeastern shore of the Sea of Salt, or the Dead Sea. There the mountains of Moab would protect them. There were caves that they could use for shelter if they could just move a little faster.

"Hey, Nemir!" yelled Abdul. "We need to hurry. This is going to be a bad one."

"My beast can't go any faster."

"You're too fat, Nemir! Such a little short body, but so much weight!" yelled Abdul.

Nemir reached back and touched the bolt of fine linen that he was carrying. He thought about throwing it off his camel to lighten the load. Then he thought that he better not. The linen was not his. It belonged to the Magi they were pursuing. It would be wrong to discard it. The linen must be returned.

Abdul and Nemir both looked back and watched anxiously. The storm was still building, but it seemed to hesitate as though deciding whether to pursue them or not. Their beasts marched forward unperturbed and confident. They could only watch and hope.

"Do you think it has stopped?" asked Nemir.

"No. It is deciding when it wants to hit us," said Abdul with a laugh.

Sometimes a big storm would appear to stall. That was the case now. It hadn't really stopped. They were ascending a rough mountainous terrain and could see much further than usual. This made it easier for them to spot the far-off clouds. As they got higher, they could see further. This storm was so large that its presence was felt long before it struck, giving the impression that it had stalled. It was coming, they just didn't know how big it really was.

They reached the southern tip of the Sea of Salt. Nemir and Abdul both noticed the camel droppings indicating that a caravan had passed this way. The droppings led to the well-marked trade route toward the Southeast. They would

not descend down the steep grade that led to the Dead Sea but were going to swing around and enter Moab. The terrain became more barren as the elevation diminished. Going down into the valley helped hide the tempest from their view.

The storm was closer, but they still had time.

†

Up ahead, traveling at a slower, but nevertheless steady pace, was the caravan of Magi. There were twelve Zoroastrian princes in this caravan which was heading home after their visit to the newborn king. They had fulfilled the prophecy of the Oracle of Hystapes. They had delivered the gifts to the special child foretold by the scrolls handed down from Sem, the son of Noah. This had been a long trip for them and yet it was only half over.

The Magi were from three different areas. Three were considered kings. There was Gaspar from India, Balthasar, who had come from Babylonia, Persia, and Melchior who hailed from the southern tip of Arabia. Each of the kings traveled with three other lesser Magi and an entourage of assistants.

One of the Magi, the king named Gaspar, was said to be a direct descendant of Sem. He was heading back to the Indus Valley, to India, land of great riches and fragrant spice. Gaspar's life was fulfilled. He had carried out the main task of his destiny to present gifts to the child king that was foretold in the scrolls from the ark. Many years before, a party of Zoroastrians traveling through the mountains near a peak called Ararat were trapped in a storm. Disaster struck in the form of an earthquake and landslide. The scrolls had come

rumbling down with the debris from on high. It was said that the ark was still on that peak. Gaspar's ancestors had read the scrolls and understood the Messiach Command. It was a duty entrusted to the Zoroastrians to honor the incarnation of God in the form of man. Gaspar's family was given custody of the scrolls. It was Gaspar's duty to carry out the command.

Not often does a man know that he has fulfilled his destiny. Gaspar was grateful for that. He sat high and majestic in his saddle, unperturbed by the storm that seemed to pursue them. He recognized that all was part of God's unfolding plan, both the storm and the calm, the chaos and the tranquility. He was filled with gratitude. Man's obligation and duty is to always and everywhere give thanks to God for the present moment.

Gaspar had the longest journey home. It would take a couple of months of travel. He was accustomed to long journeys. They were a chance for him to contemplate and study the heavens. Two other princes were traveling with him. All of them were Magi or high priests in the order of Zoroaster. They had accomplished their sacred mission of the Messiach Command and were returning home.

Melchior, the youngest of the three Great Magi, was on a camel next to Balthasar. His polished black skin glistened in the twilight sun. His huge smile beamed as he listened to his newfound mentor Balthasar.

The pair rode along side by side, calmly discussing the unusual terrain. The Dead Sea's water faded behind them. It was a giant ocean of concentrated brine.

"Did you know, Melchior," said the elder Magus, "that there was once a powerful city on this side of the Dead Sea."

Balthasar pointed to the eastern part of the sea.

"How could that be? As far as the eye can see there is only water now," said Melchior.

"Legend has it that this is the area of the great city of Sodom."

"And the sister city of Gomorrah?"

"Yes, Melchior. Have you heard tell of the story?"

"I have heard mention of it, but if you know the whole story, would you be deigned to tell."

Balthasar laughed at the compliment. They were equals in status, but his age afforded him respect.

"Gentlemen, do you see the expanse of the Dead Sea off in the distance?"

He turned in his saddle and swung his arm in a huge arc indicating where he meant.

"Here was once a plain, flat and verdant, that extended over this portion of the waters. Once there existed a beautiful, but fatally corrupt city. Tonight, by the campfire I will tell you the story of Sodom and its sister city Gomorrah."

The other men smiled. They were delighted at the prospect of listening to one of Balthasar's stories. They looked out over the expanse of dark blue water. It was so placid and calm, seen from the hills where they were. The terrain next to the Dead Sea was barren. No vegetation grew there because of the salt in the soil. It gave a clean swept look to the shores, more like the ocean than an inland sea.

"First we must continue to run from this storm and find appropriate shelter," said Gaspar. He turned in his saddle, looking backward toward the dark clouds in the far-off distance. They were heading for safety near the foothills of the land of Moab.

Abdul, whose vision was sharp, was the first to spot the caravan winding its way through distant countryside. Because they were further east and sunset was approaching, it was hard to make them out. Neither Nemir nor Abdul was aware that the caravan had already spotted them highlighted in the sunset where it broke through the tall columns of clouds of the approaching storm.

Seeing the caravan gave the men incentive to continue with their rapid pace. Riding on a camel that is moving quickly isn't as difficult as it seems. After a while staying on comes naturally, but after a long ride a man was tired and needed rest. These two would need rest when the caravan stopped for the night. They had been left behind by the caravan and had traveled a greater distance in less time. They were both quite fatigued.

There was also a great incentive to travel together. Neither rider relished the thought of traveling back to Persia without the rest of the party. There were dangers in the desert. There was safety in numbers. They pushed their animals harder.

†

The caravan had just pulled over to make camp for the evening. A camel driver hailed them and announced their arrival to the group.

Gaspar was the first to speak to Nemir and Abdul when they arrived.

"Were you able to get the two camels into the well?" he asked, referring to Makhtesh Ramon. This was a large chalk basin, miles wide, south of Beersheba in the desert. Legend

had it that the swirling receding waters of the great flood of Noah formed the basin. Perhaps somewhere in the labyrinth of chalk and stone was a drainage hole that led to hell.

"Yes, sir," said Abdul. "I went into the basin with both animals."

"And you were able to leave without them following you?" asked Gaspar.

"Yes. I tied the two beasts together so neither could climb out on its own."

"Actually," said Nemir, "The older camel looked as though she wanted to stay. She seemed to know that this was what she was supposed to do."

"Yes. It was the little one that seemed bent on getting out of the basin," said Abdul. "He was scared and tried desperately to climb out."

Melchior handed the reins of his camel to an assistant and said, "But the little one was securely attached to the older?"

"Absolutely. There was no leaving for him without the older letting him," said Abdul.

"We watched for quite a while after he came back out of the basin and took a route that enabled us to see them for some time," added Nemir. "They stayed there."

"Good," said Balthasar who noticed the bolt of linen still attached to one of the saddles. He gave a questioning look to the other Magi.

Melchior asked, "Why was the cloth removed from the seat? Was it not to be given to the Holy Family for their use?"

"It was too large to allow the child to fit so I put the Zoroastrian caps in its place," replied Abdul as he handed over the luxurious material.

"This belongs to the child," said Balthasar.

He held the bolt in his powerful arm for a moment and looked at the fine fabric. He turned and handed it to one of the other priests who secured it safely on a pack animal.

"One day it will have to be returned to its rightful owner. I sense the cloth will have purpose in his mission. You will have to return it. It was not yours to remove."

"Yes, sir, I understand," said Abdul.

"You and your families will be held responsible for the return of the cloth," added Gaspar. There was a solemn tone to his voice.

Abdul and Nemir understood the gravity of the situation. In their custom, it was a man's duty to carry out the orders of the Magi. They were not often allowed to change plans as they had done in Makhtesh Ramon. The bolt of fabric was a gift and now it was their responsibility to one day return it.

"When would you wish that we return the gift of fabric, sire?" asked Abdul.

Gaspar looked at Melchior and Balthasar. He was not sure.

"We will pray about when. For now, let us make camp and secure the animals against the coming storm.

For the men on the caravan, preparing for a storm was not an uncommon affair. They worked efficiently together helping one another get their animals settled and their supplies safely positioned away from the dangers of nature's fury.

The caravan had selected a small rise that was ensconced in the hillside of the leeward portion of the foothills of the first mountain that they had approached in Moab. This was ideal because the walls embraced and protected them while at the same time safely set them above the runoff areas for the rainwater.

The camels were camping. Camels camped in an instinctive way. They had the tendency to form small groups together in tight circles when storms struck. Their tough hide and double lidded eyes allowed them to survive high winds, dust, and sand without too much difficulty. Each of the Magi had a group of camels forming up a camp. The animals would lay down during the storm. First, camels went down on their knees, and then they rested their bodies, chests, and bellies directly on the ground.

"Do you think the camels realize that Heba and little Jamil are gone?" Nemir asked.

"Probably," said Abdul. He pulled on the reins of his camel and the camel knelt. "I think they are a lot smarter than we give them credit for."

"Sometimes I think they are as smart as I am," said Nemir. "But then I think, no they're smarter. They're like Abdul."

Everyone around them laughed. Nemir was at it again. His teasing could go on for hours. He was usually a worrier but around Abdul he would relax enough and his personality would shine through.

Abdul handed his reins to the man who was assigned to this camp of camels. Each little circle had its own watchman, who would stand guard for a few hours. Someone would relieve him during the night.

†

The warm fire at the campsite danced in the wind as though it had a life of its own. The dance increased as the storm approached, giving a visual warning to those sitting nearby. The flames flickered wildly before the storm hit. Its fury built slowly, allowing the men to continue to check their

baggage and their lashings so that everything was secure.

Melchior was the last one into the tent. Balthasar and Gaspar were waiting for him, along with a few of the other Magi; Merodak from Melchior's group, Hormidas from India, and Akreho from Persia. Melchior was the youngest of the three kings and had stayed out in the elements the longest. They would weather the storm's high winds together and tell stories throughout the night.

"Melchior, a man's eyes are precious portals to his soul. You must not be about in a storm like this too long. The sand will scratch your eyes," said Gaspar. He was a kind man, whose gentle demeanor allowed him to comment on a man's behavior without feelings of offense or reprimand.

"Only a camel has twin eyelids," said Balthasar. "One is for shutting out the world so that sleep may come. The other is to keep blowing sand out, yet it enables the animal to see."

"I stayed out long to make sure that everything was fastened and secured. Now isn't there an old man in this tent who promised me a story?" said Melchior. It was more of a playful challenge than a question. He nodded to the others and added, "These old men still treat me like a child."

They all laughed. The wind howled and shook the tent as Melchior tied the closure tighter.

"So, you wish to hear the story of the city of Sodom?" said Balthasar.

"We wish to hear it told too," said Akreho who was part of Balthasar's group.

Balthasar nodded to them and waited for absolute silence. He hesitated a moment longer before he started.

"A long time ago, many centuries perhaps," said

Balthasar, "two cities existed on a plain that extended into what is now the Sea of Salt."

"Balthasar, how could such a dead sea support two cities?" asked Merodak who was part of Melchior's group.

Balthasar looked at him. It was a good sign to be interrupted so early. It meant that the men were curious about his tale.

"A good question," said the old man, Balthasar, with a twinkle in his eye. "It indeed would seem impossible to have that sea of brine sustain life, and yet back in antiquity the sea was not filled with salt. There, cities flourished. The waters yielded wonderful catches of fish and the land along its banks was fertile."

"So, what happened?" asked Melchior.

"The twin cities of Sodom and Gomorrah were lulled into the belief that because of their material prosperity they could do whatever they wanted. They became centers of immoral pleasure and delight. Things were common in those cities that Magi would disdain to speak of. One would certainly not speak of them in mixed company. It was a time of uncontrolled licentiousness and immorality."

"Not unlike the Romans of today?" asked Melchior.

"Far worse. The city was more like a brothel with walls. Every form of human deviance was practiced. People with various—how should I say this with dignity—obsessions, depravities, and deviant lusts, flocked to the twin cities to act out their secret cravings."

"So where did the cities go?" asked Akreho. "Were they destroyed by their king?"

"Heavens no. The leaders of the city were just as evil as anyone else. The cry of outrage against Sodom and Gomorrah

was so great by the few good people there, that God sent two angels to the city to investigate."

"Was it so bad that one angel wouldn't do?" asked Gaspar with a smile.

"It was worse than that. The two angels arrived at the city of Sodom. The angels intended to spend the night at the taverns, among the people. They wanted to investigate for themselves, to find proof of Sodom and Gomorrah's wickedness. During the day they met a good man by the name of Lot. He begged them to spend the evening in his house rather than outside in the debauchery. He was worried for the angels' safety. They refused at first, but eventually Lot persuaded them to stay in his house with his family."

"If they stayed indoors at night, how where they able to prove that there were wicked things going on in the city? Didn't they have to move about at night visiting the brothels?" asked Melchior.

"Ah, the evil was so great, and the shame was so small that evil found them. A large group of men, young and old, heard that *new* men, strangers to the city, were at Lot's house. This group demanded that the angels be given to them so that they might know them with their lust."

Balthasar waited for the enormity of Sodom's folly to sink in.

"Unbelievable!" said Melchior.

"They were fools," said Merodak.

The others nodded in agreement.

"They tried to break into Lot's house to attack the angels. They still thought that the angels were men," said Balthasar. "Can you imagine how arrogant they were, that they wanted to sodomize angels?"

Balthasar paused to let the idea sink in.

"They attacked. When they did, they were blinded by the angels, who told Lot to gather his entire family so that they might leave the city."

"I'll warrant you that his sons must have been terrorized and wanted to leave immediately," said Melchior.

"No, to the contrary Melchior. They thought their father foolish. Only his two virgin daughters and his wife were willing to leave."

"Foolishness is often the prelude to disaster," said Melchior. The other men nodded in agreement. Melchior was young but very wise.

"As they were leaving, the angels commanded that no one should look back at the destruction wrought upon these cities, or risk being turned into a pillar of salt."

"I would have been curious to see the destruction," said Merodak.

"Yes, that would have been a great temptation, and in fact, Lot's wife did look back. She was turned into a pillar of salt very near our camp," said Balthasar.

He pointed down to the ground. Then he raised his eyebrows as if to say that the pillar might even have been outside.

"Here on this ground once stood the village of Zoar, but Lot chose to go live in the caves above us."

"What happened to the two daughters?" asked Akreho.

"The licentiousness and disobedience of the cities of Sodom and Gomorrah stayed with them. They wanted desperately to be good, but it infected their souls with disastrous results. They plied their father with wine on consecutive nights and lay with him. Later they bore his own

children. The first was named Moab, and it is his name that is given to these lands. That name Moab, for the Israelites, means son of my father."

"Did the other daughter have a son too?" asked Melchior.

"Yes, and she named him Ammon. Which means son of my kin."

"That refers to the tribe of the Ammonites from this region?" asked Melchior.

"Precisely."

"So how did God destroy the city?" asked Merodak.

"He rained down fire and brimstone upon it."

"But it disappeared completely," said Merodak. He looked at the others as if to ask how it was possible.

"There was a gigantic cave of salt under the city and beneath that a pocket of bad air or natural gas. When the city started to burn, the cave collapsed in and the bad air exploded. The entire plain sank to the bottom of the inland sea. The salt so contaminated the waters that all life died."

The wind outside howled and rain started falling upon the tent. The men looked around silently checking if the tent was secured properly.

"And what happened to Lot's wife?" asked Melchior.

"It was storms such as this one that dissolved the pillar and washed it down into the sea of brine where it belonged. To this day, her remains are part of the salt in that sea of brine."

The men laughed.

"How could the men of Sodom and Gomorrah be so foolish to believe that there would be no price to pay for their licentiousness?" asked Melchior.

"They were prosperous, knowledgeable, and living in

peaceful times. Those three together often convince man that his good fortune is due to his own ingenuity and not to God's grace."

"We are prosperous, knowledgeable, and living in peaceful times," said Melchior.

"Yes, but we are grateful to God for our prosperity. They were proud of what they had created. We are grateful for what God has created through man. That makes all the difference."

†

In the morning when they awoke, the men methodically checked their animals and started re-packing to continue their journey east.

As was the custom for the Magi, they paused to eat before they left and discussed what dreams they may have had during the night.

Gaspar was the first to speak.

"I was told to leave the bolt of cloth with you Balthasar," said Gaspar. "Did you dream of it too?"

"I did," said Melchior. "I too was told that it was yours to keep. The child must first ascend to his throne."

"I dreamt that I should hold it until it was time to give it to his servant. I would be told when," said Balthasar.

"That settles it. You are the keeper of the cloth until that time when it should be sent to them," said Gaspar.

"It is only fitting that you keep it. Your kingdom is the closest to Judea and you will be the first to hear that the young child has become their king. You should hold onto it for a while and then send it back."

Nemir and Abdul were listening.

"You two come over here," ordered Balthasar.

The two camel drivers hurried over to the Magi.

"Where are you from?"

"North of Babel, on the banks of the Euphrates River," said Abdul.

"I will send my emissaries to you when it is time to return the cloth. You will deliver this bolt of linen on our behalf," said Balthasar.

"When would that be, sir?" asked Abdul.

"It will be some time in the distant future. I think the babe will be at least a boy before his kingdom comes to pass."

"You have our word that we shall make ourselves available to return it," said Nemir with a bow.

Abdul joined him in his bow.

They both retreated to their animals.

The command to break camp and leave was given. A few minutes later they were underway.

"How did we get involved in this?" asked Nemir. He was fighting with his emotions, trying not to show that he was upset. Nemir was not a worrier. He usually just stuffed his feelings and made jokes when he was worried.

"What do you mean?" asked Abdul. He was smiling at his friend's anxiety. It was so like Nemir that it delighted Abdul.

"You volunteered us for another long trip," said Nemir. He was upset. "We get home and then we have to leave."

What was really bothering Nemir was that he saw the trip as a reprimand for having made a mistake. He made mistakes like everyone else, but he enjoyed charming his way out of the consequences. With the Magi, it was impossible to use charm. They saw through people and demanded

righteousness and responsibility.

"It's worse for me. I have young children and a very headstrong wife," said Abdul with a laugh. "When we started it was I who was the one afraid of leaving. When I return home, my wife will have borne me a young child. Do you think she will want me traveling all across God's creation to deliver a bolt of cloth?"

Abdul paused and then answered his own question.

"No!" he said loudly.

Nemir laughed.

"It won't be that bad, though," said Abdul thinking out loud. "We'll be invited to dine with a king, a royal family."

"We're ambassadors," said Nemir.

"That's right," said Abdul.

"We're ambassadors from the house of Balthasar of Persia!" exclaimed Nemir.

"That's right. Dignitaries!"

"They'll feed us wonderfully!" said Nemir.

"You would think about that," said Abdul with a laugh.

2

A TIME FOR PATIENCE

Egypt

A splendid entourage of angels accompanied the two camels and the Holy Family. Mary sensed their presence but said nothing.

"What a feeling of profound peace I have atop this beast Mary. I never thought I would be riding a camel, let alone feeling so…" Joseph hesitated.

"Have such a sense of trust in the Lord's goodness and protection." Mary finished the thought for Joseph.

"I was so nervous when we started. The dream… the warning… the animals… and now I am so peaceful."

"It must be the Lord's grace," said Mary.

They were traveling along the Via Gaza, near the sea, bypassing the small city of Gaza and taking the Via Pelusium to enter Egypt through Farama. The Romans renamed the city Pelusium. It was the first settlement inside Egypt. In just a few more leagues, they would be safe from Herod. It was situated on an eastern branch of the Nile.

The Angels smiled knowingly. They had been safe the entire journey.

This time there was room at the inn. They quickly stabled the animals and got their welcomed rest… Mary, Joseph, and baby Jesus wrapped in swaddling clothes.

✝

When dawn broke, Joseph said his morning prayers. "As for you, you meant evil against me, but God meant it for good; to bring it about so that many people should be kept alive." As he recited these words, he couldn't help thinking about his ancestor Joseph who was kidnapped and brought to Egypt.

Joseph went to the innkeeper to purchase some provisions and pay for the night. While he was gone Mary happily attended to baby Jesus, telling him about the journey and the fact that they would have to take a barge across the eastern branch of the Nile, to get to Leontopolis.

✝

When Joseph returned, he announced that they would stay for the midday meal.

"The innkeeper said it would be best to cross the Nile during the afternoon since the first barge is leaving in a few minutes," said Joseph. "He claims his wife is an excellent cook and the meal is included in the price of the room. We could then travel in the afternoon and would be in Leontopolis by early evening. The roads are safe and patrolled by Roman Legions who keep a strict peace."

Mary was pleased with the decision and welcomed a nice meal before the next leg of the journey. "He understood that we are Jewish and need to keep our dietary laws?"

"Goat and okra with rice pilaf."

She smiled at Joseph. He probably could already smell the meal cooking and it convinced him to stay. "Good, since it was already included in the price of the inn," said Mary.

†

The meal was delicious and uneventful. Jesus was the center of attention with the innkeeper's wife fussing over him and holding him so that Mary could eat. There were only a few other travelers, but each got the chance to see the precious little traveler. Soon it was time to get onto the barge and take the next leg of the journey.

†

"Heba, do you see what I see?" said the young camel, Jamil.

"Yes, I do, Jamil, that is the largest river I've ever seen," said Heba. They had passed by the Mediterranean Sea, but the water was not alluring because it was salty and had an odor that was unattractive to camels.

This water was different. It smelled heavenly. There were many boats; some with fishermen and nets, some with sails, and some with oars. They were heading toward a dock with a barge. It was large and there was a depression up front for the animals to stay in and not tip the boat to the side.

"Follow my lead, Jamil. We will walk right onto the barge and then go down into the hold and kneel down. The water is deep enough that we would immediately drown. Also, try to stay still to not rock the barge," cautioned the older camel.

"I understand," said Jamil. He was surprised at how little stress there was being around water this time.

†

The captain called to Joseph, "Do you want to blindfold them or are they well trained and will lie down in the hold?"

Joseph had no idea.

When they reached the barge, two bargemen held the camels while Joseph and Mary, with Jesus, got down from the animals. They walked them right up and then down into the hold.

Mary and Joseph had never been on a river and were surprised at how peaceful it was. The crossing was shorter than they would have liked but they were anxious to get on the road to Leontopolis.

†

Joseph saw a glimmer in the distance. He pointed it out to Mary, who was on the camel named Jamil, with baby Jesus.

"Look Mary," said Joseph. "There is light in the distance. We must be nearing Leontopolis. Let us make haste so that we can find a place to sleep for the night."

What Joseph saw in the distance was the effect of the huge candles burning in the night. Leontopolis was an ancient settlement in Egypt, now under Roman control. Like most Roman cities, they burned large candles to illuminate the city. These candles, known as Roman candles, could be seen for many leagues. Leontopolis had a large Jewish population. Inside the walls of Leontopolis there was a magnificent synagogue with a Jewish temple that, although much smaller, rivaled the beauty of the temple of Solomon in Jerusalem itself.

Mary looked down at baby Jesus. They had been traveling for two days, nearly sixteen hours, on camels. This was the same desert terrain that Moses had traversed thousands of

years ago. The infant Jesus slept most of the time that they had traveled. The gentle rocking of the camel lulled him into a sweet sleep.

Mary looked up from Jesus toward Leontopolis. She secretly hoped that they would find a room in the Jewish quarter. She knew that most of the Jews who would normally be on the road traveling for the census had gone to Judea.

Mary was not worried about what kind of people they would encounter in Leontopolis. People were basically the same everywhere. The descendants of Abraham who they would meet in Leontopolis would be similar to the families that she knew in Jerusalem and Nazareth. Not only was Leontopolis a big city with a large settlement of Jewish families but she had distant cousins there. The climate was similar to the kingdom of Judea. The water was clean and the food was basically the same.

Joseph on the other hand had worried most of the first day of the trip. It was a father's duty to be concerned for the welfare of his family. Travel was not a luxury, but a necessity filled with danger. Their travel to Leontopolis, however, was more than a necessity. Herod was sending his men to find and kill their baby. This was a personal exodus. It was the start of a life that would symbolically express the relationship between God and Israel. Jesus was born in Bethlehem and would come out of Egypt, both in fulfillment of the scriptures.

Joseph listened to the rhythmic slap-slap of the camel's hooves on the road. The stones that the Romans used to build their roads were large blocks of granite buried upright into the ground. They looked like small blocks about a foot

wide and two feet across but were actually four feet deep. This made the road very solid. One thing the Romans did well was build roads. The magnificent road that the Romans built along the southern tip of the Mediterranean shortened the travel time to Leontopolis.

Joseph was concerned about protecting Mary and Jesus. Joseph had been on guard for most of the time they spent traveling. Even though they had encountered no bandits and Roman soldiers were patrolling the road, there was little rest for him until he arrived in the city. The safety of civilization afforded them consolation, while the size of the city afforded them anonymity. They would quickly blend into their community.

This leg of the journey had been easier, but both Joseph and Mary were now hungry and tired. Only baby Jesus was content to sleep peacefully in the pouch. He was as well fed as any infant, warm, and dry. His only concern was an occasional bit of air that he swallowed. Mary looked down as he rested tranquilly. He was comfortable and content and didn't have a care in the world. It was as though he had a divine sense of his own destiny, that nothing bad would be threatening this trip.

†

Heba noticed the glowing light on the horizon long before Joseph had mentioned it. Camels have a sense of what belonged in the desert and what did not. She knew that this light meant that human beings were somewhere in the distance. She recognized that they were rapidly approaching an area where there would be water, comfort, and food. Soon all their needs would be taken care of for them. She was

perfectly comfortable with traveling even longer without food or water but was delighted that the journey was coming to an end.

A camel's life was a series of caravans, often with the same friends. At the same time, life for a camel was an individualized journey. Just like every life, every journey was different. Every journey was an exploration of self-potential and a discovery of latent talent. This had been a special journey for Jamil because he had not only discovered untapped potential, but also because he had learned his purpose of life.

Discovering one's purpose in life was a monumental task. For Jamil the task had required a long dark night of the soul. A night where Jamil was forced to understand what gifts God has given him in order to survive in the desert. A night where he was tested by God to trust without any reassurance that he would survive. The young camel that Heba looked at right now was far different than the little one who had left on the caravan many months before. Understanding one's purpose gave a great sense of fulfillment. Jamil was not older in years but was a much older soul. Wisdom was the fruit of a soul's maturation.

The now much wiser Jamil had an air of confidence that was no longer based on the need to pretend, to be secure, or the desire to prove that he could overcome adversity. His confidence was now based on the experience of having survived, having overcome. Arrogance often substituted for confidence in the young. Jamil was no different. In Jamil's case his initial arrogance was used to mask a deep fear that he carried with him. He was afraid that he would not survive his first journey into and through the desert. He was afraid

that he would not find the necessary substance within to overcome the adversity that the desert thrust at him. But as with all survivors, when Jamil overcame adversity, he developed a self-assured, rugged confidence and lost his arrogance.

Jamil and Heba were traveling quickly now with the Holy Family seated on their backs. The lights in the distant city served as an impetus to move even quicker; to pick up the pace so that their arrival would be sooner rather than later. The faint glimmer in the distance was slowly becoming a soft light. It was a beacon of hope for the young family. Hope was a spur that could temporarily wipe away the fatigue of a long trek.

Camels sensed a human's emotions in many ways. Heba felt the reins tensing in Joseph's hands. She felt him pulling and wondered if it was out of nervousness or anticipation.

They continued to move on toward the city. Their brief but intense journey was drawing to a peaceful close.

†

"Joseph, where do you think we should go when we arrive at Leontopolis?" asked Mary.

"Surely someone at the city gates will be able to direct us to the Jewish quarter," said Joseph. He looked nervously at his young bride and child. Then he looked back up at the city looming in the distance. He didn't know what the future would bring for his little family. He was not sure what they would find in Leontopolis, but it certainly was safer than being on the road.

"We are likely to find someone from the House of David

living in that city who could help us find temporary lodging,"
said Joseph.

"My mother Anna used to speak of a certain Saul of
Leontopolis, who was a distant cousin of my father, Joachim,"
said Mary.

"Then there will be someone who will know Saul and
direct us to him," said Joseph with conviction.

As the Holy Family made its way along the road the gates
to Leontopolis loomed larger in the distance. Small clusters of
houses lined the road to the great city. They were almost like
little villages. Fertile fields of wheat and vegetables separated
the clusters of homes. The fields were irrigated by canals that
had locks on them to divert the flow of water. Everywhere
they looked there was evidence of man's amazing ability to
reap the harvest of an extremely fertile land.

When the Holy Family reached the massive doors to
the city Joseph found them locked in for the night. A small
window slid open with a loud clang of metal against metal.
A face looked through the opening and a voice asked the
tired couple what business they had in Leontopolis.

"I am Joseph, and this is my wife, Mary, who has just had
a baby. We are in search of our cousin who lives in the Jewish
quarter. His name is Saul," said Joseph. He knew that the
guard had already determined that Joseph and Mary were
Jewish by their clothing.

"You must fully dismount from your beasts," said the
guard. "You will have to unburden your animals and bring
your belongings in first in order to pass through the needle's
eye."

The Roman guard at the gates to the city was referring
to the small door cut into the main portico of the city. It was

commonly known as the eye of the needle. It was customary for a late traveler to either spend the night beyond the city gates or to unburden his beast of all its belongings. He would then hand them over to the guard and try to get the unpacked camel to fit through the small door. This sometimes presented a problem because some camels did not like to bend down to pass through the narrow passage. Joseph had no idea whether his camels would pass through, but he didn't want to spend the night outside the city.

The Roman legionnaire knew that a dishonest man or someone carrying contraband preferred to spend the night outside and wouldn't have approached at this time of night.

Mary handed Jesus to Joseph. He cradled the babe in one arm. Then Joseph helped Mary dismount from Jamil. He handed her baby Jesus. Joseph then reached up and unstrapped the elaborate contraption sitting on Jamil's hump. The guard, seeing that they were alone, came out and helped Joseph carry the bundle in through the eye of the needle. Mary walked through the door and stepped to the side with baby Jesus. The guard waited on the inside of the door for Joseph to bring in Heba's saddle and the gear.

Now the fun began. The Roman guard called one of the other legionnaires and asked him to stand by. He quickly recognized that Joseph was not accustomed to handling a camel and was going to need assistance getting the beast into the city. Out of respect for Joseph's authority as head of the family, the Roman soldier did not offer assistance until he was asked.

"Sir, I am not very experienced at getting an animal through the eye of the needle. Would you advise me as to how it should be done?" asked Joseph.

"Young man, the trick is in getting the head of the animal into the city first. Once the beast sees what's inside his curiosity will get the best of him and cause the rest of him to enter. So, the trick is getting the head."

"The proverbial nose of the camel under the tent," said Joseph.

The legionnaire laughed.

The other Roman guard nodded vigorously in agreement. He had seen many caravans enter the city late at night. Generally, however, caravans preferred to stay outside the city limits until daybreak because it was much easier to get the animals to enter the city when the large doors, or porticum, were open. One or two camels invariably refused and caused a commotion.

The first Roman guard looked at Mary and at baby Jesus and then confidently stepped through the small door. He helped Joseph pull Heba through. She came through remarkably easily, but Jamil was another story. He stepped back at the first attempt. Joseph held the reins firmly in his hands. He had difficulty trying to get Jamil to stick his head through the small door.

The Roman guard raised his eyebrows for a moment and watched the struggle and then pulled Heba around to face Jamil. As soon as the younger camel saw that Heba was all right he stopped fighting and stepped through too.

The Roman soldier shut the door. He moved a beam across the needle's eye and threw the bolt over it to lock it. The second soldier helped Joseph repack his animals.

Mary decided to walk rather than ride. It felt wonderful to be off the swaying beast while holding her baby in her arms.

The soldiers helped Joseph tether the two animals together so that he could lead them through the city. Candles and lamps were burning everywhere as people moved through the streets finishing the day's activities.

"The Jewish quarter is in that direction. You can't miss it because of the temple. It is a major landmark," said the soldier to Joseph. He was pointing toward the south end of the city.

Joseph and Mary knew that the Temple of Leontopolis rivaled even that of Jerusalem. They were thrilled to be able to see it.

"Do you think it is too far?" asked Mary. "I would prefer to walk for a few minutes."

"It's less than a tenth of a league," said the Roman legionnaire.

Joseph and Mary saw where he was pointing and started walking. They were impressed with the great white buildings made of marble and limestone. Statues of Roman leaders, as was the custom, adorned the front of many of the imperial government buildings.

†

Jamil sniffed the air. There was the smell of water everywhere. A fountain bubbled in the center of the Piazza. It contained the figures of young women pouring water pots into a garden. The water flowed out of the water pots and then drained into a cistern. Women were carrying water back to their homes from the fountain.

Heba motioned to Jamil. She was looking at a water trough where horses were drinking.

"I see it," said Jamil, who turned toward it without consulting Joseph.

Heba followed suit, which left the Holy Family to watch as the camels refreshed themselves.

The water was cool and fresh, but after only a two-day journey they had little need.

†

Mary smiled at Joseph and then attended to baby Jesus who had stirred in her arms.

"These animals are stubborn," said Joseph. He was frustrated and tired, but still treated the beasts well.

"They have a mind of their own," said Mary. She was smiling at his frustration. Her thoughts drifted back to the visit by the Magi and how she had refused to accept them as gifts.

"We are fortunate that they had left them in the desert," she added. "They made the voyage much shorter."

"We'll sell them to someone who will appreciate them once we find your cousin," said Joseph. "They are good animals, but then again what do I know about camels?"

"You did just fine for your very first time on a camel," said Mary.

Joseph was beaming with pride. The journey had been difficult and using camels had made it more cumbersome for him. He was used to donkeys and horses but recognized that the camels had made the journey quickly. They had taken chances, traveling late into the night, but instead of a three-to-five-day journey on a donkey it had taken them two.

"Even if riding a camel is a talent that God has given me—one that I didn't know I had—I still think it would be best for us to sell the beasts and journey back to Judea by other means," said Joseph.

"Perhaps," said Mary.

"Do you doubt that this would be a wise choice?" asked Joseph.

"No. It is just that the camels were a convenient way to travel across the desert," said Mary.

"We shall see, Mary. Strange, though, you were the one who didn't want them," said Joseph. He was still filled with pride for having done such a fine job on the camels. He watched them dip their heads deeply into the trough to get the water.

The animals finished drinking and backed away from the water trough. Joseph's look of satisfaction was matched on the faces of the camels. He noticed that they seem to be easier to handle once they had been watered. He realized that he had a lot to learn about handling camels, though. He preferred to ride horses back to Judea, however, but wasn't sure if he could exchange the camels in an even trade for horses.

Mary walked beside Joseph as they headed toward the great temple. She could tell that they were entering a Jewish quarter, since all the men in the area were now wearing yarmulkes and phylacteries and the women were wearing veils. Seeing the Jewish community was reassuring for Mary. Two days of running from unknown harm had left her worried for the safety of her child. Now that she was among people from her own tribe, she felt reassured and comforted. The Jewish community was known for taking care of its own people. They would find safety and anonymity here.

Joseph felt comforted too, by being in the community of his people. He, along with Mary, wondered about when they would be told to return to Judea. An angel in a dream had told

him that they must flee from Israel to Egypt. Joseph presumed that he must wait until an angel told him to return before he could travel back to his home in Nazareth. The safety of his new child and that of his wife was of paramount importance.

Joseph and Mary were not certain where they would stay. They knew that there were numerous Jewish settlements along the Nile River. They presumed that Mary's cousin would bring them to a place that was safe for the time being, but they didn't know if they would stay in Leontopolis itself or move off to a small village.

A young boy walked up to Joseph and stared at the two beasts.

"They are magnificent animals, aren't they?" Joseph asked the little boy.

"Yes. They are so big," said the little boy.

"Could you tell us where the temple is from here?" asked Joseph politely. He was treating the young boy like a knowledgeable man.

The boy pointed to the obvious. Joseph thanked him and then he and Mary continued to walk.

When they arrived at the temple, they spotted an old rabbi. He was walking briskly down the steps. He had a shawl over his shoulders and a Torah in his hands.

"Rabbi," said Joseph.

The man looked up and saw the couple and child with the camels.

"Yes?" replied the rabbi.

"We belong to the House of David," said Joseph.

"We are looking for my cousin. The family used to live in Beersheba but were from a lineage in Nazareth. The father's name would be Saul," added Mary.

After a few minutes of questioning the old man knew exactly who Mary and Joseph were talking about. The rabbi walked with them a few blocks until they arrived at a modest home, where an elderly man was just sitting down to supper.

"Good evening, rabbi," said the old man.

"Shalom," said the rabbi. "These people are looking for you."

"Who are they and what can I do for them at this hour of night?" asked the man named Saul.

"My name is Joseph, and this is my wife, Mary. She is the daughter of Joachim and Anna from Jerusalem," said Joseph politely.

"Anna's daughter?" said the old man. He stepped forward, reached out, and embraced Joseph as one would a close member of the family. He turned and embraced Mary.

His wife, Tarah, had come out. She was wondering what the commotion was. When she realized that this was Anna and Joachim's daughter, she pushed him away so that she too could embrace Mary.

"You have a baby with you. He is so young! Hurry, come in," said Tarah.

She rushed Mary and Jesus into the house.

Joseph and Saul stood watching for a moment and then realized that the rabbi was still there.

"It is fortunate that they are here," said the rabbi.

"Why is that?" asked Saul.

"We have reports tonight that the Roman Herod has ordered the death of all male babies two years old or less. You wouldn't have known about it because you've been traveling, but word just reached us tonight that the blood of many Jews is flowing."

Joseph shuddered. They had made a personal exodus and by the grace of God, their first born had been spared from the jaws of death.

The rabbi bid them goodnight.

The two men unpacked the animals.

"I know a fine caravansary for these beasts," said Saul.

"A caravansary?" asked Joseph.

"Yes. It's an inn for caravans. The stables are attached and there is plenty of room for the animals.

He called a servant out and gave him instructions. He first moved their belongings into the house. Then the young servant walked off with the two beasts in hand.

"So, I see that you are a carpenter," said Saul.

"Yes, you saw my tools," said Joseph.

"If you are good, I can find you work. How long will you be staying?" asked Saul.

"I don't know," answered Joseph. He really didn't have any idea.

✝

"Now we're off to a fine stable at a caravansary," said Jamil. "I sure hope they have fine food there too. I am hungry."

Jamil couldn't help looking back toward the mother and child. For some strange reason, he was sad that the burden of carrying them was over.

"You're always hungry," said Heba interrupting Jamil's thoughts. "It's a reflection of your youth."

"If I recall correctly, we haven't eaten well in three days. I don't know about you, but I am a very hungry camel," said Jamil.

"Well, my young friend, I'm not very hungry. I am more interested in seeing what this city is like rather than staying in a stable the entire time," said Heba.

Staying in a stable was not a lot of fun for a camel. Much like horses, camels liked to roam. They preferred to be out in the desert under a starlit night. Being cooped up in a stable might be good for them in terms of eating, but it was not good for the soul. A camel needed to journey into the heat of the desert. A camel needed to be on a caravan with a destination in front of them. Heba understood this better than Jamil did.

Jamil, on the other hand, knew that life in a stable provided for all of one's needs. He knew that living with security was easier than being tested in the desert. The problem was that after the caravan with the Magi, Jamil understood that he needed to push himself in order to test his mettle. There was a part of him that now wanted to move off into strange lands and mysterious journeys.

There was also a part of Jamil that didn't want to be pushed, tested, or uncovered. It wanted luxury. It longed for a life of ease. He was looking forward to the stable. Even the sound of it—stable—brought a sense of peace and tranquility. The word created images of security in Jamil's imagination.

"Is it nice in a caravansary?" Jamil asked absentmindedly as the servant of Saul walked them down the street.

"You'll like it for a while," said Heba.

"What does that mean?" asked Jamil.

"Well, for the first few days, I always feel comfortable and pampered. There is plenty of feed, and you are sheltered from the elements."

"That sounds just about perfect," said Jamil.

They were handed over to the stable boy who talked to

the servant for a few moments. Then they were led to a very large stall with fresh straw on the ground.

"Nice straw," said Heba.

"So, what's wrong with all this?" asked Jamil. He looked around at the stall and saw a water trough and a feed bucket.

"You're a camel. You were born to live outdoors, under the stars," said Heba.

"This isn't so bad."

"It will become boring soon. It will become scratchy to your soul," said Heba.

"Scratchy to my soul?" repeated Jamil. This time it was a question though. "My soul feels pretty good with warm straw, fresh feed, and water."

"Luxury is not always conducive to peace," said Heba. "For tonight enjoy it. In time your soul will beckon you to the desert. It is as inevitable as a child's birth."

Jamil knelt down. Camels were the only animals besides man that went down on their knees prior to going to sleep. While on his knees, Jamil said a short prayer to God as he understood him to be the Sustainer of the desert.

"Father, grant me peace and understanding of Your will in the day to come," said Jamil.

"Beautiful prayer," said Heba. She went down on her knees too.

3

A TIME TO WAIT AND A TIME TO RETURN

A Few Months Later

Babies grow quickly at a loving mother's breast, and soon baby Jesus was reaching to hold his mother's thumb as she nursed him. He was a strong, healthy, and vibrant infant. His hair came in thick and curly. His complexion was smooth and clear. The little baby had that sweet baby's smell that comes from nursing on a mother's milk. As the months passed his cry changed from that of a tiny infant to a healthy baby boy's.

The months passed quickly for the Holy Family. Soon, baby Jesus was sleeping through the night. This meant that Mary was much more rested.

Joseph had adjusted the baby seat on the camel for more room. Mary had taken the gold clasps and jewels from the contraption and modified the fabric. There were two small sapphires behind her seat that couldn't be removed without risking breaking them. They were well hidden, however.

The family stayed with their cousins in Leontopolis for the first few weeks and then found a small house to live in

while they waited for news from the land of Israel. During the waiting period reports came back of Herod's cruelty. They were horrified by what they had heard. The despot had apparently ordered the killing of hundreds of little babies during the first few days of their absence. Herod's decree mandated the death of every Jewish male baby two years old or younger in and around Bethlehem and east as far as the Mediterranean Sea.

Suddenly there was a knock on the door. Cousin Saul was quickly let in. He had a look of concern on his face. "Mary, Joseph, there are some travelers from Bethlehem who have arrived and someone told them about you. I am concerned that they will realize you have the child who has been spared Herod's wrath. Worse yet, one of the rabbis told me he believes they are spies from Herod looking for you and the child."

"What shall we do? asked Joseph.

"We have family in Tell el Basta a small city south of here and you could stay there a few months until we can determine if they are looking for you," said Saul.

They hastily packed and left. Only the camels were happy to be on the road.

✝

Two Years Later

Joseph knocked on the door and Saul yelled, "Patience please, I am an old man."

When the door swung open, he called out, "Tarah! Mary, Joseph, and Jesus have returned!"

Tarah stepped out and shouted with delight, "Praise

God, you have returned. Jesus, you are so big and you are walking!"

"And talking," added Mary as kisses and hugs went all around.

"I sent word that Herod was sick and it was safe to return," said Saul.

"We were no longer in Tell el Basta," said Joseph.

"Yes, a well sprung up while Jesus was digging in the sands. We had to leave because it drew too much attention to us," said Mary.

"And Herod had been sending spies into Egypt to find you," said Tarah.

"Then we moved on to Bilbays," Joseph said.

"Our family in el Basta sent word to you. They were told you were there for a while but there was a miracle of a young boy coming back to life at a funeral procession," said Saul.

"The family thought Jesus had something to do with it," added Tarah.

"Correct, but we didn't know how that was possible. We had to leave and traveled to Samannud," said Joseph.

"We only stayed there for a few weeks," said Mary. "I was baking bread at a communal oven when I was approached by a couple who started asking questions. I got the distinct impression they were spies from Herod. I took my bread and left," said Mary.

"She left her granite bowl and came and got me. We left for Sakha immediately," said Joseph.

"You didn't want the bowl?" asked Tarah with a laugh.

"I did and wished I had taken it," Mary replied.

"We stayed at Sakha for a number of months. I liked it there," said Joseph.

"Jesus took his first steps in Sakha," Mary remembered fondly.

"We stayed there until they started having problems with their wells and cisterns," said Joseph. "We headed west across the western branch of the Nile."

"Yes, we got word that you were in Wadi El Natroun," said Tarah. "We heard stories of a well springing up and some of the town's people thought it had something to do with the child."

"That forced us to leave and we wound up in Matariya," said Joseph.

"That sounds terrible, moving from place to place," said Saul.

"It wasn't so bad because there were small communities of the children of Abraham who were welcoming and kind," rejoined Mary. "It was peaceful, and we spent many afternoons under a beautiful sycamore tree letting Jesus play in the shade."

"We moved to the Babylon quarter of Cairo and stayed in a cave for a while because the rabbi had visitors from Jerusalem who were asking questions," said Joseph. "That's when we boarded a boat and headed back down the Nile and came here."

"You will be safe here. We have word that Herod is very ill. He apparently has lost his mind and is given to episodes of rage and confusion," said Saul.

†

The news of Herod's death reached Leontopolis. His son, Archelaus, had succeeded Herod on the throne as the king of Judea. Since his death the persecution and oppression had

stopped. Now it was probably safe for them to return, but Joseph was waiting for a sign. After the visit by an angel in a dream and the knowledge that his obedience had saved Mary's child, he was not willing to move without a sign.

✝

"Mary," said Joseph, who was already up.

He was looking for an indication that his wife was awake. When Jesus—now three years old—stirred in his bed, her hand moved to calm him. The little boy got out of bed with a burst of joyful energy and hugged his mother.

Joseph smiled at the scene. Jesus ran over to him and gave him a big hug as Joseph lifted him high into the air.

Mary looked over at Joseph. Her face said, *what is it?* but at the same time, told him to speak softly.

"Mary, I had a dream. An angel of the Lord of Hosts said, 'Get up, take the child and his mother, and set out for the land of Israel. Those who had designs on the life of the child are dead.'"

"Jesus, we return to the Promised Land," she said. Then she looked up at Joseph sweetly. "Thank you so much for listening to the word of God."

Mary was right. Joseph's willingness to listen to the word of God to guide his decisions was responsible for keeping the child safe.

For both of them thus far, life was about surrendering to the will of the Lord of Hosts. Mary had heeded the call of the angel Gabriel and bore baby Jesus. Now Joseph heeded the call of an angel and was bringing Mary and her child back to Israel.

"I must go secure our beasts," said Joseph.

"And you were going to sell them," said Mary, with a smile.

"Yes, just last week there was a man who wanted to purchase them. He wanted the special saddle for the smaller camel and for some strange reason, I didn't want to part with it. Consequently, he decided not to take the animals."

"The Lord moves in mysterious ways, Joseph," said Mary.

"Yes, we have the saddle with its contraption and the camel that was trained to carry it," said Joseph.

He marveled at the thought. For the past few weeks, he had been doing small jobs as a carpenter. They were able to sustain themselves adequately, but the cost of keeping the two camels in the stable had made life more difficult. He actively had tried to sell the animals, but somehow the deals that he made all seemed to fall through. Now he understood why. They would return to Israel on the camels. It was a trip made far more secure with the right animals.

"When we get to Jerusalem or even Beersheba, we might be able to trade the animals for a horse or livestock," said Joseph. He was thinking out loud.

"Do we risk going right back to Beersheba or Jerusalem?" she asked.

"I don't know, but you have family in Jerusalem, so I thought it would be a good idea. Besides, it would be easier to sell the beasts there. We could travel to Nazareth from there."

"It would also be easy to sell them in Jericho, where the road leads out to the desert," Mary said.

"Perhaps, Mary. For that matter the road to Moab starts in Beersheba so we should try to trade them first," said Joseph.

"I have family there too. They will know," the young mother said.

Mary looked around the small room that they lived in. They didn't have many belongings, so the trip wouldn't be encumbered by baggage. What little they had they could pack on one animal. Her eyes wandered around the room. She realized that it would not take her long to pack. Her eyes settled on a large cap that had been left in the child's seat with the camels. She smiled fondly.

Jesus was still a toddler. Joseph had adjusted and enlarged the seat on the side of the camel's saddle. She was going to attach the cap as a headrest. The saddle had been modified and early on they had taken the gold clasps off and used them to purchase provisions.

Joseph saw her move the hat and said, "What are you going to do with it?"

"You'll see. Would you like to wear it?" she said with a laugh.

"No, I'd look like a Bedouin camel driver instead of a Jewish carpenter."

†

"I am so bored," said Jamil. His voice was pained and gloomy.

"You've told me that a hundred times," said Heba. "I am getting bored listening to how bored you are."

"Can a camel die of boredom?" he asked.

"I don't think so. No, there is nothing to worry about," she said.

"It feels like that for half my life I have been a prisoner in this stable," said Jamil.

"It has been a lot less than that. We only got back here several months ago," said Heba.

"It seems like less to you because you're so old."

"Yes, it does. Maybe that's the benefit of being old."

"We were almost out of here a few days ago, and then we weren't sold to that Egyptian merchant," complained Jamil.

"Be patient. All things work together for good. The Sustainer has put us here to wait. A lot can be said for learning patience. Did you know that patience is the only virtue required to learn the others?" asked Heba.

She looked at Jamil and realized that she had been lecturing and he had tuned her out. She wondered if she hadn't already given him this particular bit of wisdom.

"I've been going out on caravans for many years now. They never stop coming to you until you are too weak to journey. Another one will come along soon."

"I sure hope so. You're certain that a camel can't die from boredom?"

"I'm certain. It's not the boredom, it's being under a roof. Camels were not made to be in a stable, under a roof," said Heba. She looked up at the thick wooden beams.

"That's got to be bad for one's health. You can't just stay inside all day and all night for weeks on end," said Jamil.

Heba knew they'd had this discussion before and simply smiled.

Neither of them bothered to pay attention to the stable boy who had entered a few moments before. His presence was a constant. This time he reached over the gate, grabbed a mouth bit, and put it over Heba's face. She accepted easily, not questioning where she was going or even why. Jamil watched without enthusiasm.

They both had been through this all too familiar routine. The stable boy would take them out of their stalls, bring them to the fenced-in corral, and let them get some exercise. There were other camels, of course, because this was a rather large caravansary. Every few days a new caravan would come through, stay and trade, and then be off. They had met dozens of new camels who had been to so many exotic places. After a while, even the stories of travel started to sound the same.

Jamil took the bit. It was better in the small corral than in the stall, but there still wasn't enough room to run in the corral. He wasn't ready when the boy tethered the reins to a post and walked over to get the saddle.

"Heba, he's getting my saddle!" said Jamil excitedly.

"Yes, and if you look next to it, there is mine too. I told you a caravan would eventually call us," said Heba.

They watched each other get prepped for a journey. When they were both ready the stable master came in and nodded his approval. He told the boy to take the animals to Saul's home.

†

"We are sad to see you leave," said Saul. His wife Tarah nodded in agreement at his side.

"We must return. We are sad to leave you and your family. Your hospitality and graciousness will be forever appreciated," said Joseph.

"Are you certain that you will be safe?" asked Saul.

By now everyone in the Jewish quarter was aware that Herod had searched for a newborn child said to have been of royal birth. Saul, more than anyone except Joseph and Mary,

suspected that baby Jesus was the child that the Roman soldiers had been searching for. He had heard about the visit by the wise men of the East from Mary and Joseph. He had also heard a story from others that Herod was incensed when the wise men had not returned to Jerusalem after meeting the child. Saul hoped that the young family would be safe. He was a discrete person and wouldn't share his thoughts with anyone. In times like these, families knew it was wise to keep quiet.

Mary gave a big hug to her cousins, who each took a turn kissing Jesus and admiring him one more time before she put him in his travel seat. Jesus kicked his legs enthusiastically as she placed him in the seat. He waved and said, "Shalom," to Saul and Tarah. He loved to ride with his mother on Jamil.

Joseph packed his tools.

Hugs went all around. The men kissed both cheeks, as was the custom. Tarah made sure that the food she had packed for the family was secured and then gave Mary a warm hug.

"You and your child have blessed our household. I will never forget you," Tarah said to Mary.

Saul and his family stepped back to watch them mount the animals.

The younger camel knelt down and Mary mounted effortlessly.

The older camel did the same and Joseph mounted him. When the animal stood up Saul's family made more room. Joseph was now high in the air looking down at them.

"We are off to the Promised Land," said Joseph.

"Next year in Jerusalem," said Saul, repeating the ending prayer of the Seder Feast.

†

"Isn't life grand," said Jamil.

It was a balmy morning. The slowly rising sun had burned off the mist of the Nile River. A cool breeze blew in from the Northwest and refreshed them.

"The sun feels good, doesn't it?" asked Heba.

"Perfect. We have a burden on our backs and a destination to carry it to. Life is good."

Unlike most animals, camels needed a burden to carry. With a burden and a place to go, they had a purpose. Most animals don't need a purpose, but camels were more like humans in that respect. They needed a place to go and something to do on the way there. For camels, life had direction and the burden gave the journey meaning. Certainly, they could enjoy the journey by itself but the accomplishment of carrying one's ordained burden made a great difference.

Without a purpose, a camel didn't feel fully alive. It didn't matter what the terrain was like. The barren desert was no barrier. As long as a camel had a destination to focus on it would carry its burden across the desert. That was purpose enough. Purpose gave direction. The challenge to fulfill that purpose by marching the distance to the final goal was the meaning. Too often it was thought that the final goal was the meaning. It wasn't so for a camel. The steps taken were the meaning.

No camel is ever guaranteed that he or she will arrive at the goal. The ideal was meant to be discovered in the advance toward the goal. The ideal in and of itself, however, was not definite. How often has a camel started out on a journey, only to arrive somewhere else? That had been Jamil's experience.

He had started out on a journey to visit a newborn king in Israel. Instead, he wound up visiting a humble family who had taken up lodging in a stable. They were good people, but they were extremely unlike the kings and queens that Heba had talked about.

The destination didn't turn out to be Israel either. It was Egypt. It was not far away, but a different culture within the vast diversity of the Roman Empire. This led Jamil to wonder about what the final destination of this journey would be.

"It is more important to watch your steps along the way than get hung up on the final goal. The master that guides us knows the goal but also knows when to change it and go somewhere else. Our job is to carefully mark our strides to get our precious cargo there," said Heba to Jamil.

They traveled along the same road that they had used when they were coming to Leontopolis. Now, however, it was daytime and the sunlight made the large granite blocks of the Roman road glisten, polished by the hooves of horses and the wheels of fine chariots. The camels' large hooves reached out and slapped the stone creating a gentle beat that added to the swaying rhythm that the camels naturally had when they walked.

The two-camel caravan moved steadily to the northeast. By evening they were approaching Pelusium, a large Roman settlement in the hills above the southernmost part of the Mediterranean Ocean. For the last two hours they had traveled closer to the shores of the Mediterranean Ocean, because the road moved to the north to approach an area where ships found safe harbor and unloaded their cargo.

The Mediterranean shores in and around the area of Pelusium were washed clean by eons of waves pounding a

gentle rhythm on the sandy beaches. It looked peaceful and serene. It had a clean, pleasant fragrance that rode the cool breeze and perfumed the small caravan.

The ocean smelled strange to the camels. The mist of spray that reached them had a pungent aroma so well known to sailors, but unfamiliar to them. It was the smell of the water's edge and meant the approach of land. When one was far out to sea the water had no smell. Jamil took a deep breath and let the aroma bath his senses.

†

"Shall we rest for the evening?" asked Joseph. He was looking off into the distance at the white stone of the buildings of Pelusium.

"I think we should," said Mary.

Joseph was a wary man. He wanted to avoid confrontation. He did not want to attract attention to himself or to his family. He realized that the news of a young child returning to Israel would incite the curiosity of some. So, the question of resting for the evening was more about whether they could find lodging in a Jewish quarter.

As they approached the city, they could see the imposing walls with their open gates beckoning them to enter. Joseph and Mary were silent for a few moments, each praying in their own way for guidance. They looked at each other and smiled. It was a smile of reassurance that they had faith in the God of Israel to guide them and protect their child.

"We enter," said Joseph with determination.

The camels continued to march forward past the Roman legionnaires standing guard at the gates. The men looked at the three travelers and only when they noticed the child, did

they manage a smile. Romans rarely fraternized with Jews. The guards at Pelusium were no exception.

A young centurion, probably a commander of the guards, looked at them for not more than a second before he turned away. He then looked at the animals and their possessions. Seeing the Yarmulke on Joseph, and Mary's shawl, he motioned in an easterly direction.

"The Jewish section of town is there," he said. He was polite, but not very interested.

Good, thought Joseph. He was relieved that the man could care less.

The centurion, however, did notice the camels and the saddles. There were accouterments and fine silk woven between the leather straps. These were not ordinary Jews, he thought to himself. They must be people of means, traveling back to their homeland. Their garments didn't match the luxury of the beasts, so he assumed that they were pretending to be poor. That was a useful strategy when on the road. Showing one's wealth was an invitation to danger.

Mary and Joseph had no trouble finding a place to stay. There was a simple inn filled with travelers from Judea, Galilee, and other areas. They ate quietly, alone in a corner of the inn and then retired for the night.

†

"This is not much of a place," said Jamil. It was more of an observation than a complaint, but there was a complaint hidden within it, nevertheless.

"Were you so used to being in the other stable that this one doesn't feel right?" asked Heba.

"I guess the other one was feeling like home," said Jamil.

"The open road, the desert, and the star-filled night are your home."

"Yes, you're right. It felt better out on the road than in here," said Jamil.

"Home is where you feel most fully alive. It is where your soul is given its greatest freedom. Home is what the Sustainer has created for you to let your soul soar with the eagles and shine like the sun."

"Where is that for you, Heba?" asked Jamil.

"Ah, for me it is the moonlit night, filled with shimmering stars and a cool breeze that allows you to walk for hours in a state of peace. It gives me a feeling of such profound peace that it is beyond my ability to understand it."

"I know what you mean," said Jamil. He remembered a time when he had felt that profound peace. "That incomprehensible peace has only occurred to me during the great storm."

Jamil was referring to the storm that they had weathered together in Makhtesh Raman, the mammoth chalk basin in the Negev Desert. He silently wondered if that was the only time that he would feel such profound peace. A small fear entered his mind. *Would he only experience deep peace when confronted by terrific storms?*

Heba sensed that Jamil had fallen silent and wondered what he was thinking about.

"A piece of straw for your thoughts," she said softly.

"I only felt that profound peace once, when we were in the storm."

"Yes, and?"

"I am worried that I might never feel it again," Jamil admitted.

"You felt it for some time afterward, didn't you?" she asked.

"Yes, but I never quite felt it like that again." There was worry in Jamil's tone.

"You are afraid that you might be one of those who only feel at peace in the midst of turmoil?" she asked her younger friend.

"Yes, I've heard stories about them."

"There are those unfortunate camels who need chaos to feel at home. They are the ones whose lives have always been in turmoil. They feel almost normal in chaos, but they are not at peace in the way you were."

"Why do they feel normal?"

"They feel normal because they have lived in chaos so long that they know no other way. It is sad because chaos is where they live, but they are not home. They need peace more than chaos, but they never find it."

"What happens to them, Heba?" he asked.

"They create chaos when things are calm and wind up being sold off to others. It happens repeatedly. It's a lifetime of gradual devaluation. They wind up losing friends, but eventually wind up on caravans of others like them."

"Do you think I am like that?" Jamil asked.

"No, you are not," she said.

She was convinced, but Jamil was not.

"How can you know for sure?"

"You felt peace in the midst of chaos because you surrendered your will to that of the Creator of the universe. You found a peace beyond understanding because of surrender, not because of the chaos of the storm. When you start to feel that surrender again you will feel the peace return."

"I hope so," he said.

"Trust me. I have seen a lot of young camels in my lifetime. Your destiny is not chaos, it is adventure and journey perhaps, but not chaos."

✝

Joseph and Mary awoke early to a nudge from Jesus who climbed into bed between them. The first glimpse of light on the eastern horizon hinted that a glorious day was at hand. Joseph opened the shutters to their window and looked out while Mary attended to their child.

They quickly set about to their morning prayer rituals and then prepared themselves for the day's journey. By the time they had packed the animals, the sun had risen on the eastern horizon. It was going to be a hot day. Mary made sure that she carried enough water for Joseph, Jesus, and herself.

They left the small inn and headed for the east porticum of the city. The guards hardly paid attention to the small family as they left. To the Romans, they were simply Jews returning to their homeland using the road to Rhinocolura.

"We are on our way," said Joseph softly to Mary.

She smiled back to him and then checked to see how Jesus was doing in the seat on the side of the camel. He was swinging his feet a little faster than the walk of the camel, kicking at the air with delight.

It would be a long day of travel, but the pace would not be rushed. Rhinocolura was an outpost in the desert, not a large city. They would stop there for the midday meal and head out when the sun's rays started to diminish. The ultimate goal of the day was a town called Raphia, though

Joseph would have preferred to push the animals and make it to Gaza.

✝

"It's such a beautiful day. I feel like running," said Jamil. He picked up the pace somewhat and started pulling ahead of Heba.

"Don't get too far ahead or you will frighten the mother," said Heba. "Humans don't like their wives frightened."

"But this is fun. There's a cool breeze and a warm sun."

"Trust me. It's not a good idea to create fear," said Heba. She picked up her pace to stay alongside him.

Heba looked at Mary to see how she was doing. The young mother was smiling at Joseph and watching Jesus kick his legs and clap his hands.

"The husband is pulling on my reins to slow down," said Heba.

"So is the mother," said Jamil. He was somewhat disappointed as he slowed the pace down a bit. Something inside was urging him to run full out as fast as he could. The quicker he moved the more peaceful he felt. One of these days when no one was on his back, he was going to let go, to really let the speed out. For now, however, he had to obey the reins.

"Sometimes it's hard traveling at the pace dictated by someone else," said Heba.

"Especially these humans. They are so hard to understand," said Jamil. The urge to take off and chase the wind welled up in him again. He fought the urge to take off. He was feeling his oats, ready to run. The day was gorgeous, and the surface of the road was comfortable.

"I still get the urge to run like the wind," said Heba. "This family isn't so accustomed to riding on camels that we can cut loose and fly."

"This is a perfect setting for speed. I could really tear up the sand today," complained Jamil. He was referring to the fact that it was warm, but not too hot of a day; and there was plenty of water. Normally there wasn't enough water around to warrant racing. It did merit complaining though.

Jamil let out a noise that sounded like a cross between a creaky old door and a horn.

Heba gave him a knowing look. She understood but was past the time in her life when running delivered a pure sense of joy.

The noise that Jamil made was a complaint to the humans on board. He hoped that they would understand and let him pick up the pace. He tried making noises again and speeding up for a few paces.

"These humans won't get it, no matter how much you complain. Sometimes you don't get to run as fast as you would like, no matter how good the conditions are."

"Why should a human decide how fast I can run?" asked Jamil. He turned his head back and looked at the smiling woman and the joyful child. It had a calming effect on him.

"The task before you is to carry the mother and child. You accepted the responsibility of carrying them and you need to follow through to the end. If we were alone right now, I would be running with you just to experience the fine day," said Heba.

"Sometimes, though, we need to slow down to carry out our duties," said Jamil. He was letting Heba know that he

understood what he was supposed to do and didn't need a lecture.

"A great camel is one who serves others well, not just manages to get across the desert fastest. Greatness comes to one who takes care of duty and responsibility to others. It comes as the secondary gain for doing a job well. Only a fool strives for greatness as an end unto itself."

Jamil knew Heba was right, but he was in the mood to argue. He let his feistiness get the best of his mouth.

"A great camel is a swift camel," said Jamil.

"True, sometimes," said Heba.

"I think I might have been bred for racing," said Jamil.

"Probably, you are certainly swift enough. I was impressed when you ran away from the desert wolves coming through Persia," said Heba.

"See what I mean? This slow pace is going to bore me to death. The frustration will make me sick. It's definitely bad for me."

"Jamil, you never cease to amaze me with your excuses. Self-control will not harm you. It will empower you. A great racing camel has to be able to run when directed to, not just anytime it wants."

"But it's a part of my nature."

"Yes, and it's a part of your nature that you must learn to control. Just because the Sustainer has given you a talent, doesn't make it valuable. A talent becomes more valuable as it is controlled and fine-tuned."

"Frustration is a bad thing. It's not healthy to be frustrated," said Jamil seriously. The muscles of his powerful flanks twitched with his words, almost in anticipation of a gallop.

"Now you have finally said something that I can disagree with," said Heba. She was smiling.

Jamil hated it when they disagreed, and Heba made it worse by smiling. It made him feel like he had already lost the argument. He hated losing arguments. He loved being right. He dug in a bit more with his legs and slowly increased the pace. He hoped that she wouldn't notice.

"Still in a rush, are you?" she asked. She knew that he loved being right more than being happy.

"What did I say that you disagree with?" asked Jamil. His curiosity had gotten the best of him. He was secretly annoyed that she might prove that he was wrong about something.

"You said that frustration was a bad thing and that it was not healthy," said Heba. "That's not true, but perhaps you haven't realized it yet. Or maybe you haven't ever stopped to give your frustrations some real thought."

"Hey, I'm frustrated because I'm moving so slowly. I don't need to stop and give it a lot of thought. Besides, it's a feeling, not a thought. If I stopped the feeling would only get worse."

Jamil had a look of satisfaction, as though he had told her a great and irrefutable truth.

Heba smiled. She was pleased about where the conversation was taking them.

"And boredom too... that definitely has to be bad for you," said Jamil. He was pumped up by the belief that he was right, and it was going to be easy to defend his point of view.

"I'm curious," said Heba. Curious was one of the gentle challenge words that she used. "Are boredom and frustration related in your mind?"

"Of course, they are," said Jamil. There was a small whine in his voice. He realized that he had answered too fast; so fast he had barely given it any thought.

"How come?" asked Heba.

She waited for an answer. The silence was deafening.

Finally, he said, "Well, boredom is when you don't have anything to do that would be fun or exciting. Frustration is when you've been bored too long. So, I guess they are related."

"When you started running away from the Bedouin Bandits were you having fun?" she asked. It seemed like a harmless question. She was referring to an episode that happened with the caravan of Magi. Bandits isolated and attacked them. They chased Jamil, but he was much too fast for them.

"Sure."

"My question was about when you started to run away," she said, clarifying the idea. "I am deliberately trying to be specific."

"Okay, let me think about that. I guess when I started running, I was scared to death," said Jamil. He was quick to add, "But when I knew I was going to get away from them because I am so fast—then I wasn't afraid anymore."

"Were you bored when they started whipping you?" she asked.

"Bored! Hardly, I was terrified. I thought they were going to kill me. I was scared to death. You can't be bored and be scared to death at the same time."

"Precisely," said Heba.

"Yes, so?" asked Jamil defensively.

"Well, were you having fun?" asked Heba.

"No, I wasn't but I guess you could call it excited."

"Really. I thought you said you were terrified. There isn't a difference between excited and terrified?" asked Heba.

She watched the muscles of his powerful forequarters ripple with impatience.

"I hear you. Okay I wasn't having fun, I wasn't excited, and I wasn't bored."

"Were you bored in the desert during the long stretches where the landscape went on forever and nothing changed?" asked Heba.

"Certainly," he said looking up at a hawk in the sky. "I remember when I spotted an eagle overhead and how grateful I was that there was a change in scenery."

"That leads me to my definition of boredom," she said.

"So, what is it?" Jamil asked.

"It's when you think you know what is going to happen, you don't look forward to it, and you're convinced it will continue."

"Then what is your definition of frustration?" he asked.

"Frustration is when you have a goal to accomplish and for some reason you are unable to achieve it. That's a positive frustration. The other type—negative frustration—is when you keep achieving something that you don't want but are unwilling to change."

"Which leads us to the whole topic of how to get really good at something without being bored."

"What are you really good at Jamil?" she asked.

He knew the answer and immediately blurted it out. "I can run like the wind and not disturb the baby if I had to."

"Yes, and did learning that require any boredom?"

"Sometimes. It was more like overcoming my

unwillingness to concentrate and stay focused," said Jamil.

Suddenly a large serpent appeared in the road. Both animals reacted immediately and veered off the road. Jamil went to the right and Heba moved to the left. The snake leaped at Jamil but was too late. The camels moved over the soft earth on the side of the road with ease.

Joseph and Mary were startled but a few moments later the two camels were back in step on the road. If they had been horses, they would have sunk into the soft dirt and possibly twisted a leg. Instead, they continued marching toward Rhinocolura as though nothing had happened.

"Did you see how effortless that was?" asked Heba.

"What was?" Jamil was already thinking about something else.

"Avoiding the serpent."

"Oh, yes. It was easy."

"A few years ago, you couldn't have done that while carrying a load," said Heba.

"Especially with the child Jesus and Mary on board."

"The Magi taught you while they were on caravan. You went through curiosity and learning to a state of boredom, but you persisted to mastery. You can carry the child and run like the wind without even thinking about it."

"Is it really like that? Everything that we want to get good at requires that we tolerate periods of boredom or tediousness?" asked Jamil. He sounded disappointed.

"That's the way it is with most things. That's why it is so important to learn to master the things that God has created us for because they are fun."

"I think the problem is figuring out what God has created us for," said Jamil with a laugh.

"Well stated. That's half the battle. When you pursue a skill that God has designed you for, it's more interesting and more fun. The boredom is less and marveling is more."

"That's why a tortoise doesn't try to learn to run over the hot sands of the desert," said Jamil.

"And why a camel shouldn't try to learn to pull a plow," said Heba.

"Or learn to swim," Jamil added.

"It's a lot easier to work hard on the path the Sustainer has chosen for you than it is to be lazy on the wrong path."

Heba looked at Jamil to make sure he understood. She saw the look of comprehension on his face.

"I guess I was wrong about boredom being bad for me, wasn't I?" said Jamil.

"Once you thought about it, you realized the truth." She recognized that Jamil didn't like being told that he was wrong.

"I mean, I'm trying to admit to you that I was wrong."

"Thank you. I know it's hard for you to admit when you're wrong," she said.

"Hard? It's almost impossible. I hate to admit it. I would rather be right than happy."

"I know," she said with a smile. "Sometimes you are."

†

"What was that?" asked Mary.

She was alarmed but as soon as her camel came back to the road and she saw that Jesus was okay, she calmed down.

"There was a huge serpent in the road," said Joseph. He had held on for dear life when Heba swerved to the left and went off the road.

"I didn't see it until we were almost on top of it," said Mary.

"It was as though it had appeared out of thin air. Suddenly it was there in front of us," said Joseph.

They were both perplexed by the serpent but glad to have it behind them. It was very unusual for snakes to be out in the open. They preferred to slither around under the cover of tall grasses. Sometimes they would hide behind rocks, but they almost never directly exposed themselves to the sun's harsh rays.

Joseph sat quietly upon his camel. He wondered about it. In the distance he saw the walls of the city of Rhinocolura and breathed a sigh of relief. They would stop for lunch before taking on the second part of the day's journey.

Mary leaned over and stroked her child's head. He had been so patient on the first part of the day's journey. She knew that as soon as they sat down to eat and Jesus smelled food, he would start to clammer and clown around to let her know that he was hungry. He rarely whined.

Mary stroked Jesus' head. He had a small linen cover that served as a hood, but he kept knocking it away when he kicked his legs and raised his arms. She was delighted that her child enjoyed the camel ride so much, but she would be glad when their traveling was over.

✝

A shabbily dressed man stared at the two camels from about twenty paces away. The look made Jamil nervous.

"This time Joseph didn't even finish unloading your burden," said Jamil. He was irritable and trying not to stare back at the man.

"Yes, I know. He is probably in a rush to leave after they have their midday meal," said Heba.

"That's not fair to keep you loaded with cargo."

"Patience, young one. He did take the largest pack off and carry it with him to the tavern."

"It's been close to two hours so they must be getting ready," said Jamil. He was anxious to be back on the road in the open country.

"You're probably right. Some of the guests have come out already."

"Like that man over there. Did you notice how he staggered when he walked?" asked Jamil.

"You don't know what that is, do you?"

"No, but I get a bad feeling when he stares at me," said Jamil.

"He is suffering the effects of too much wine. He is a man who drinks his wine without water mixed in with it. Crassis is what the Romans call drinking undiluted wine. He's a crass individual."

"How do you know all this stuff?" Jamil asked in amazement.

"I listen to the conversations of these humans."

"Did you notice the stick he's carrying?" asked Jamil.

"Yes, and I don't like it either. It looks more like a riding stick than a walking stick. Men like that beat their donkeys to make them move faster.

"So why is he staring?" asked Jamil.

"Who knows. Humans are a very unpredictable lot. You never know what they are going to do, but when they are crassis drinkers they are very unpredictable.

†

Joseph came walking out with the pack. Mary followed behind holding Jesus' hand. They both headed straight for their camels.

Joseph patted Heba on the snout. He was very comfortable with his beast.

"Here you go, lady," he said to Heba as he hoisted his pack onto her side. He took the empty grain bag that was next to her and attached it to her saddle.

Mary stood back and watched as the muscles in his sinewy carpenter's arms strained to place the load in the proper spot. Joseph was a strong man who was used to working hard. She wondered about how he felt now that they were heading back to Israel.

The man down the street started walking toward them. His eyes were bloodshot but his gate was steadier now as he approached. He had a look of determination on his face. He walked right up to Joseph.

"That's a fine-looking saddle," said the man.

"Thank you," said Joseph, eyeing him suspiciously.

Joseph was aware that there were still a few jewels embedded in the wood inlay of the saddle. Only a discriminating eye would realize their value. It was more likely that the man had noticed the fabric on Heba's saddle. It was fine linen with patches of silk decorations.

The man walked around Jamil admiring the animal.

"Are you looking to sell this animal?" he asked Joseph.

"No, not until we finally get home," said Joseph. He motioned to Mary that he was ready. She approached Jamil with Jesus.

Joseph held the reins and steadied Jamil as Mary lifted Jesus up into his saddle.

The stranger stepped back closer to Heba.

Mary reached around to tuck Jesus in and make him more comfortable. She asked Joseph to steady the child's seat. The straps underneath the saddle needed to be cinched up a bit.

As Joseph stepped around to help Mary, the man suddenly grabbed Heba's reins. He pulled on her reins. He was trying to make off with the camel and all the parcels on her back. He gave a hard tug and Heba turned to look at him.

Two Roman legionnaires noticed the man's actions and started to walk over. They were not in much of a hurry though.

Heba balked. Jamil spun around and spit at the man.

The stranger gave up pulling on the camel's reigns and now tried to climb on Heba. He managed to get on board and then beat Heba with his stick. Heba just knelt down.

Joseph stood and watched in amazement. He couldn't believe the man would try to steal all their belongings. When he realized that the man was intoxicated and that the camel wouldn't leave, he started to laugh.

Jamil, however, was enraged. He moved around in a full circle, spinning quickly. Jesus had no sense of danger and squealed with delight.

Joseph grabbed Jamil's tether but was having trouble controlling him. The camel reared up, changed direction, and swung his back around toward the man.

Mary was terrified because Jesus was in the seat. She watched as Jamil moved until his rump was facing the back of the man who was still trying to get Heba to move.

"Easy boy," said Joseph, trying to calm the young camel down.

Mary stepped in to help Joseph. She tried to lift Jesus out of the seat, but Jamil kept moving back and forth. She reached out and touched his head. He started to settle down almost immediately.

Just when the camel seemed calm, Jamil let out a violent back kick that caught the crass man right in the buttocks. It sent him sailing through the air over the head of the kneeling Heba. He rolled toward the Roman legionnaires who were now running to investigate the problem.

The legionnaires helped the man to his feet and then held him by his arms. He was in much more serious trouble now that the Romans decided to step in. No one dare disturb the Pax Romana or the Roman Peace as it was called.

"Are you all right?" asked one of the soldiers to Joseph.

"Yes, we are fine," said Joseph.

"I don't know why he was trying to take your animals. They wouldn't go with someone they didn't know," said the legionnaire with a smile.

The man struggled for a moment and the guard tightened his grip.

"Be still you fool. If you think what the camel did to you was bad, you haven't seen anything yet."

"May we leave?" asked Joseph.

"Where are you headed?" the soldier asked.

"To Raphia, Gaza, and then on to Jerusalem."

"Of course. You are Jews heading to your homeland," said the soldier. He nodded his head and motioned for them to move along.

Joseph helped Mary onto Jamil's back and then climbed on top of Heba. As the camels passed in front of the intoxicated man who was now a prisoner, Jamil swung his head around

and spit right in his face. Mary was embarrassed by the spectacle. The camel startled the poor man, who was rubbing his sore backside. It took Mary a few more moments to calm Jamil down. A short time later they were on the road to Raphia.

✝

"Why did you just lay there and let him try to steal you from this kind family?" asked Jamil. He was seething with anger.

"I wasn't letting him steal me," said Heba calmly. "I laid down."

Jamil's hooves were slapping the road loudly. He was keeping a rather vigorous pace, unwilling to slow down. Heba considered it best to keep the two of them together so she matched his pace. Jamil had a smooth, even gate that didn't sway too much. Both Mary and Joseph were comfortable, and not concerned that they were traveling so quickly. They were glad to leave Rhinocolura.

"You didn't do a thing. That fool was pulling on your reins trying to get you to run off, and you didn't do a darn thing," said Jamil. As he spoke, he became more irritated and intolerant. His hooves sounded even louder.

"I passively resisted his futile attempt to commandeer this pack animal and her goods," said Heba. She was having fun with him, and she knew that it was annoying him.

"You laid down!"

"Yes, that's true."

"He…"

"He couldn't do a thing with me. He couldn't drag me away. He couldn't lift me, and I refused to move when he hit me with his stick."

"You even let him hit you," said Jamil. He was exasperated with how calm she was.

"Of course. We have been trained never to hurt a human being," she said.

"Then I suppose you were upset when I kicked him," said Jamil.

"Not really. He deserved it. It was as though you were pushing him into the hands of the authorities. You pushed him, let's say, a little too hard. But I understood."

"I clobbered him good. He's not going to sit down for a week," said Jamil. He was proud of the punishment he had inflicted.

"I was disappointed with you, though, when you spit at him," she said.

"What? He deserved at least that," said the indignant young camel. "I should have kicked him twice."

"No, you shouldn't have. The mother was embarrassed by your behavior too."

"She was not. The Roman soldiers thought it was funny. That was a man so low that he had to be disciplined by an animal."

"That's wrong, Jamil. It is not our place to discipline humans. They have been given dominion over the earth and all its creatures. You weren't supposed to do that. Humans discipline each other."

"I'm starting to get annoyed with you too," said Jamil. His temper was flaring and he was ready to spit a fit.

"You're suffering from a very common problem among camels," said Heba.

"Am I now? So why don't you go ahead and tell me what it is," said Jamil.

A small animal scurried across the road, and Jamil tried to adjust his pace to step on it. He missed.

"Are you disappointed that you didn't squash that innocent little creature?" asked Heba.

Jamil was embarrassed by the question because he was indeed disappointed.

"You're suffering from raging indignation. That's a common character flaw that we camels have. We have short fuses. When we get frustrated or don't get our way, we fly into a rage. Sometimes we even fly into a rage when it's not called for. We do it because we enjoy being upset."

"Now I know you're talking about me. I love to be upset."

Heba laughed at Jamil.

"What does upset mean to you?" she asked.

"Oh, that's simple. It means being angry."

Heba gave him a questioning look.

"Okay, it means something even more. It means when I get angry and lose control; but sometimes it means less than that, when I'm annoyed or irritated."

"And usually it means?" she asked.

"Usually, it means I'm out of control, spitting at someone."

They both laughed at his honesty.

"It's a character flaw, you know," said Heba.

"What is?"

"Raging indignation. It's one of the many that we camels have, although some of us have it more than others."

"What's a character flaw?" asked Jamil.

"It's the opposite of a virtue. It's a quality that is the opposite of the qualities of the Sustainer. If the Sustainer is truth, then the opposite is dishonesty. If you're dishonest most of the time and lie when you could just as easily tell the truth,

then you have the character flaw of chronic dishonesty."

"Are you saying that I have a flawed character?" asked Jamil.

"Yes, but I'm also saying everyone does. Every camel has certain flaws."

"That's news to me. I thought I was doing pretty well, and my character was okay."

"Your character is okay for where you're at in life," said Heba. "You just have a few flaws like everybody else, and you need to work on them," she said.

"Look Heba, with all due respect because you're old and more experienced than I am, don't you think carrying a burden is enough work for a camel? We shouldn't have to work on changing our character."

"There is no other work, young one."

"Huh?"

"There is no other work. Everything you do should have the outcome of polishing your character. Nothing is more important. Nothing is more crucial," she said. There was seriousness to her tone that made him take notice. He slowed his pace a bit.

"How does a camel polish his character?" asked Jamil.

"It takes time, but it is a most rewarding experience," she said.

"That tells me nothing. And besides I thought character was written in stone. We're camels. We get upset. We like to be right. We're stubborn. That's our character. It's programmed into us like the eyelids that protect us from the sand."

"Yes, it is." She paused and looked at him and said, "But then again it's not. We have the ability to let go of a flaw or two and change our character."

"Are you saying that I have to let go of my flaws to make my character better? That sounds like a really disgusting idea. I wouldn't be me without my temper. I wouldn't be me without raging indignation and my desire to be right all the time. I wouldn't be a camel if I wasn't stubborn." His voice rang with passion as he spoke. He was getting inflamed with his need to be right and enjoying it.

"You'd still be you if you were a little slower to anger and you'd still be a camel if you weren't quite as stubborn," she said with a smile. "You will always be a camel."

"That's for sure, and I'll always be quick to anger and stubborn."

"But if you were a little slower to anger and stubborn only when absolutely necessary, you would be a better servant to mankind," she said.

"So, what," said Jamil defensively.

"So… being a better servant to mankind makes you a better camel."

†

It was still afternoon when the two-camel caravan passed by the walls of Raphia. No one took notice of their arrival. The city was filled with Jews. The ancient city of Raphia was part of the Herodian kingdom. Once again, the Holy Family was in Judea. They were back home in Israel.

The city's gates were broad, as was the fashion. The main via or street ran to the center forum where the market was set up, as was the Roman custom. Upon entry, unlike some cities, Raphia had a large fountain and a deep well that was used by travelers to refresh themselves after being out in the hot countryside.

Joseph paused at the well near the main gates. Mary refreshed herself at the fountain and chatted with other ladies while Joseph steered the two beasts to the side trough. He let the camels quench their thirst in the small animal trough and talked to a few of the men.

"They are beautiful animals," said another traveler, an old man by the name of Shimon.

"Thank you, my name is Joseph," he said. "It's a fine day to be back in the land of our forefathers."

"Yes, perfect weather." The old man extended his hand and said, "I am Shimon. Where is your family from?"

"We are from Galilee," said Joseph. "We are on our way to Jerusalem."

"I am from Jerusalem. I am a jeweler traveling to Egypt to purchase stones," said the old man. "Are you staying here tonight?"

"No, we are heading to Gaza," said Joseph.

"From Gaza, you will be in Jerusalem by midday if you start early in the morning," said the old man.

"How is the shining city on the hill?" asked Joseph.

"It is a little better now that Herod is gone." The old man spat on the ground.

"I take it you didn't like him," said Joseph. He was amused by the man's open show of passionate distaste.

"He was evil. I lost a grandchild because of him. He would have been a little older than your baby," said Shimon. His eyes filled with tears as he spoke.

Joseph caught his breath.

"But Herod is dead now, thank God," Joseph said to the old man.

"Yes, may he rot in hell. His son Archelaus is now in

control of most of his kingdom. It was divided among three of his disgusting children, Philip and Antipas received smaller kingdoms as well."

"What kind of man is Archelaus?" asked Joseph.

"You can't trust anyone who has the blood of Herod in his veins. Do you know Herod had a half dozen wives and about thirty children? He had all those offspring and yet he hated children. He even put to death some of his own sons. How can you trust his offspring?"

"I heard that he had killed hundreds of babies," said Joseph softly. He wanted to find out more but didn't want Mary to hear him talking about the atrocity.

"Yes, that was three years ago. If your child were in Judea at the time he would have been killed too. The persecution only lasted a few days, but he was obsessed by it. He was a maniac."

"What about Archelaus?" asked Joseph.

"He is the most evil of the three. That's why he was bequeathed more of the kingdom. The more evil you were, the more you got. I don't trust Archelaus for a moment. You shouldn't either," Shimon said with certainty.

Joseph shuddered. Something inside him sensed that the man was right, but he and Mary longed to return to Bethlehem. That is where his family was from.

"Is it safe for male babies now?" asked Joseph.

"Who knows for certain," said the old man. "I can tell you what I would do if I were you. I would head to Ascalon rather than stay in Gaza tonight. It's safer and closer to Jerusalem."

Joseph didn't understand why. The old man read the confused look on his face and explained it to him.

"Gaza was ceded to the Province of Syria and is under direct Roman rule, but there are still a lot of people loyal to Archelaus. Ascalon is a town with its own territory. It has been so for a long time. It is not part of any of the three areas that have fallen into the hands of Herod's foul offspring. The Romans recognized the autonomy of Ascalon, so Archelaus can't put his hands into that territory. There are few people there who are loyal to Herod or Archelaus. You are in the Promised Land but out of the reach of Archelaus, Philip, or Antipas."

"How far is Gaza from here?" asked Joseph.

"About eight leagues and perhaps another four to Ascalon. That's a short ride with your animals. You should get there before nighttime."

"Thank you," said Joseph, who turned and walked over to Mary and some other women at the well.

"Let's push on a little further to Gaza," said Joseph with a smile.

Mary looked at him with a questioning face. She knew that they had plenty of time to get there and that they were not in a rush.

Joseph gave an almost imperceptible nod to her.

She excused herself from the ladies and placed Jesus back into the saddle.

They mounted their camels and started riding back through the gates.

"I saw you talking to that old man," said Mary when they were outside.

"It was an interesting conversation," said Joseph. He looked around to make sure that they were alone and not followed.

"Is that why we are heading to Gaza?"

"Yes, Mary, but we are not stopping in Gaza," he said.

"Where are we going?"

"Ascalon. It's a neutral territory. I am concerned that perhaps Archelaus in no better than his father. We are more likely to hear the truth about him in Ascalon than here."

They discussed what he had heard. Over the next few leagues, they made plans. Mary was silent and patient. Joseph grew silent and concerned. They both prayed. They prayed for guidance.

✝

"You know Heba, what you said about being a better camel touched me deeply," said Jamil.

She recognized that this was a rare moment of vulnerability for her younger friend. She waited patiently to see what he was going to say.

"I mean, I really do love being right. It feels so… so…" he hesitated and then simply said, "right. I guess."

"It's a wonderful feeling this 'being right', isn't it?"

"Yeah, it really is. It's hard to see how it could be wrong to be right if you know what I mean," he said. He smiled because for a moment he thought he might have stumped her.

"It's not being right that is wrong, it is being so stuck on being right that you would rather be right than happy. It is being miserable and fighting with other people over whether you are right or not and allowing it to destroy your friendships," she said.

"I think I get it," said Jamil.

"Remember the man who was drunk, the one you kicked so vigorously?" she asked.

"Of course," said Jamil.

"What was his problem?"

"He was an ebriatus as the Romans call it, an inebriate. He drank too much," said Jamil. "It made him crazy."

"That's what he did about his problem. His real problem was he was an ebriatus or addicted to the alcohol."

"What do you mean addicted to it?" asked Jamil.

"He couldn't stop drinking even when he wanted to. The crassis or pure wine was the answer to his problems. He probably drank when he was unhappy, and when he was glad. He probably drank when he was with people and when he was lonely. Ebriatus or addicted means he couldn't stop doing it even though he was miserable when he did it," she said.

"I know where you're going with this Heba. You're going to say that I'm an ebriatus too. I'm addicted to being right; that I like to be right even when it makes me miserable, and it would be better to admit I'm wrong."

"Exactly."

"Well, I hate to disappoint you but that's the way all camels are. We are addicted to being right, in case you haven't noticed."

"I've noticed," she said smiling.

They were both moving at a fairly brisk pace and would shortly pass by the city of Gaza.

"Have you noticed that even though we all have that character flaw, some of us have it less than others?" Heba asked.

"Yes, that's true. You definitely have it less than most. And…" Jamil paused to think.

Heba started to interrupt but he cut her off.

"Let me run with this idea, if I can reduce the amount of time that I am addicted to being right, I will become a better camel?" Jamil pondered.

"And isn't that what life is all about, being the best camel that you can be?" Heba asked.

"But what I don't get is what happens to you when you stop being right?"

"You don't have to stop being right. You don't think I've stopped, do you?" she asked.

"Heavens no, Heba. You're right more than any camel I have ever met."

"See what I mean. What you have to do is give up being addicted to being right. You have to give up making the key to your happiness whether or not other people think you're right."

"I might be willing to do that, but how would I be happy? What would replace the addiction to being right?"

"Dignified humility," she said calmly and waited for him to think about the words.

After a few moments he said, "I'm not really sure I know what dignified humility is."

"It's the opposite of the addiction to being right."

"Sure, I figured that, but I still don't know what it means," he said.

A gentle wind was blowing from the west and picking up as the evening sun set lower in the sky.

"It's being happy whether you are right or wrong because the goal is to be open-minded and willing to learn. It is being happy to find out what is right whether you are right or wrong. It is being humble enough to maintain your dignity even when you are proven wrong."

They both looked at the city of Gaza as they passed around its walls. Sometimes it was faster to skirt the city rather than pass through it. With horses and chariots, it was easier to drive through because the roads were hard. Camels could cross through the open fields or along the barren terrain as easily as the road when they passed by a city.

"Didn't you think we would take the road right through the city?" asked Jamil.

"Yes, that would have been my guess, but I was wrong."

"They must be in a rush to get to the next city before dark."

"You are probably right."

"But I'm not addicted to being right," he said with a laugh.

"When you are, you don't admit it. An addiction to being right is like trying to find self-respect or self-esteem through other people. You can't find your self-'anything' through other people. Dignified humility is having enough self-respect and self-esteem to hear the truth even if it means you were mistaken. Then everything becomes a learning opportunity."

"Everything?"

"Yes, Jamil. That's the power of using a virtue instead of a character flaw. You are always in a learning mode. You are always learning what the Sustainer wants from you."

"Okay, so what's the virtue that is the opposite of raging indignation?" he asked.

"I call it profound peacefulness. It is really powerful."

"There is power in peacefulness? I always feel more powerful when I am enraged. I'm showing my power, my anger, and my wrath," said Jamil.

"Sure you do. You feel like you have the power of the wrath of God when you do that," she said.

"So doesn't that contradict what you were saying?" asked Jamil.

"It would if you had God the Sustainer's power when you were angry, but you don't."

"I find that hard to believe," he said. His desire to be right was rising rapidly.

"Oh, really now? The last time you were enraged did you feel like you were in control or that you were losing control and had to fight."

"I see what you mean. When I kicked… no, when I spit at the man I was out of control and frustrated with him."

"Precisely, young one. When you are able to confront your anger, work with your frustration, and maintain your peacefulness you are using the Sustainer's power. It's the virtue called profound peacefulness."

Jamil was thinking about all the times that he had been in fights. There had been arguments, spitting duels with other camels, and an occasional kicking battle. He could have refused to fight but didn't see how there would have been much to gain from it except humiliation and frustration.

'There's a great payoff for practicing profound peacefulness," Heba continued, interrupting his thoughts.

"I can't for the life of me see what that could be," he said.

"Hope. Profound peacefulness nurtures your capacity for hope. It makes it possible for you to visualize a positive outcome in a situation where you are wrong or mistaken. It makes it feasible to hope even when you can't control a situation. It makes it possible to bring love into a situation

instead of rage. When you bring love to any situation you automatically bring hope."

†

There was a large, engraved stone on the side of the road. In Latin it said, "Entering the autonomous territory of Ascalon."

Mary and Joseph looked at each other. There was a shared feeling of relief to be out of Archelaus' reach.

"How much further until we reach the city of Ascalon?" asked Mary.

"One and a half leagues, but the road will take us closer to the Mediterranean. Ascalon is a small port city."

"I see my husband is well-informed," she said. The relief for both of them was obvious.

"I am now a world traveler. I have been abroad to strange lands, but it is comforting to be in the land of our forefathers." He played with her because he was happy to be in the autonomous territory of Ascalon.

As they came upon the top of the next hill, they could see the walls of the city and the top of what seemed to be a palace in the distance.

Joseph grew silent as the camels took them, one step at a time, toward the city.

The gates, which had at first seemed small in the distance, loomed above them as they marched into the city. A Roman legionnaire stepped forward and blocked their path.

"What is your business?" he asked sternly. He was part of Legio IX which maintained strict order in the Legate of Syria.

"We are Jews headed for Jerusalem, looking for lodging this night," said Joseph. He dismounted and then helped

his wife down. They quickly noted that the city was not predominantly Jewish, even though it had been part of the Holy Land for centuries. There were Jews, Assyrians, Greeks, and Romans.

"You'll need a decent stable for your animals too," said the Roman. "The Jewish area is in that direction. You will find what you need."

Mary picked Jesus up out of the seat and gave him a big kiss. He was sleepy but woke up completely when she set him on the ground. He was at full attention looking around at the people and buildings.

All the roads led to the central forum, a typical plan for Roman cities. Ascalon had been partially rebuilt by Herod with the Roman plan in mind. When the Holy Family arrived at the forum they asked about the Jewish quarter.

"Most of the city is Jewish, but for lodging you would do better looking in that quarter," said the man Joseph asked. They were pointed in the direction the legionnaire had shown them.

"I wonder what that palace is," said Joseph.

"It's huge," Mary said.

When they were in the midst of what was definitely a Jewish area, Joseph asked a young man where he could find lodging. They were referred to a small inn near the eastern gate of the city.

During their dinner the innkeeper, a man named David Menorahm, came to their table. He was a short round man with a long beard dressed in traditional Jewish garb. On the left side of his head his Hassidic curls had gray strands of hair running through them. He had large lips, larger teeth, and the biggest hazel eyes Joseph and Mary had ever seen.

"May I sit down. I assure you the food will not give you indigestion, nor will my talk," he said with a broad smile.

The innkeeper Menorahm wiped his hands on his apron and then sat down without waiting for them to nod. He offered a sweet cookie to Jesus and said, "May I?" to Mary.

David Menorahm didn't wait for permission but handed it to Jesus. "Mamma, may I, please?" The small hands quickly brought the sweet to his mouth.

Mary smiled and said, "Just a taste Jesus, you have to finish your dinner first."

"Please join us. You have a very nice inn," said Joseph.

"I'll stay only for a moment," he protested.

"It is very clean," said Mary.

"My wife. My wife, she beats me with the broom if I don't keep it clean. I am like an Egyptian slave," David said rocking back on the chair.

Mary and Joseph looked at each other and started to laugh.

"She works me to the bone," the innkeeper said rubbing his rotund abdomen. There was no bone to be felt anywhere on his body.

"Who does the cooking?" asked Mary.

"My wife… my wife, she does the cooking and forces me to eat it too," said David.

He abruptly stood up.

"Speaking of the little princess… my wife, Sharon!"

David Menorahm bowed to his chubby little wife as she approached with a bowl of fish stew and half of a large loaf of bread.

Sharon Menorahm was shorter than her husband with the same full lips and large teeth. Her hair was jet black, tied

in a long braid, and covered by her veil. She was naturally beautiful and had very white skin that contrasted with her dark hair.

"Fish stew, our specialty," she said. She set the bowl on the table in front of Joseph.

Mary reached over and served her husband and child the stew. They bowed their heads in prayer and said a traditional blessing over the food. Joseph then broke bread and handed it to his young bride and a smaller piece to Jesus.

"Did you notice, Menorahm? The little one stopped eating while they blessed the food and waited," said Sharon. Her husband sat down again and made himself comfortable at their table.

Mary simply smiled. She had noticed it too.

"It's good to see a child his age. There aren't too many that were spared by that swine of a being, Herod," said David. He reached over to the next table where olive oil and figs were and moved them to their table. He smiled and raised his eyebrows with each item as he set them down.

"We heard terrible stories," said Joseph. He looked at Mary and saw that she hoped he would change the subject.

"What you heard was true. It was horrible," said Sharon. She watched as Mary crumbled some bread into the broth of the stew for Jesus. She also crumbled the fish making sure there were no bones. He wanted to feed himself and Mary let him even though it made a little mess.

Joseph tried to change the subject.

"That's an awfully large palace you have here. I didn't know that the city had such buildings. It's beautiful," he said.

"Herod had it built. In order to construct it he had to tear down dwellings that belonged to families for centuries. The

whole city was up in arms. That man was hated here," said David.

Joseph saw that it was useless to change the subject and decided he would go after information directly.

"So, tell me about his son Archelaus. He lost control of this area somehow."

"He's as big a fool as his father. The Roman general of Legio IX hates him and saw to it that the emperor gave Ascalon to the Legate of Syria. It was a deliberate slap to his pride. Everybody hates him even his own brothers, especially Antipas up north in Galilee."

"We are heading to Jerusalem in the morning. We've been away for some time. Has it changed?" asked Mary.

"Jerusalem doesn't change. The players change but the theater is still the same," said David.

Sharon nodded in agreement.

"Is it safe?" asked Mary.

Sharon saw her look at Jesus and knew what she was asking.

"Probably, but Herod was obsessed about killing a future king. Archelaus may be just as crazy. If you have family there, you'll probably be safe."

"Of course, it's safe," said David with a big smile. "Everyone knows the slaughter only lasted a few days.

"They managed to kill a few more that they found hiding," said Sharon.

Mary shuddered at the thought.

"It's safe now. After Herod's death, the kingdom was divided, and the Romans increased their supervision of the area. They aren't going to allow the sons to be as brutal as the father."

"Is your family from Jerusalem?" Sharon asked Mary.

"We're from Nazareth, but my husband wants to sell the camels in Jerusalem before we return home."

David heard Mary's answer, interrupted the two women, and said, "Jerusalem is the best place to sell such animals, but you could also sell them in Gabae. There's a trade route to Persia and Assyria. It's closer to Nazareth."

Joseph heard him and grew pensive. He reached for his plate.

"How's the stew? Is it to your liking?" asked Sharon. She saw that Mary was uncomfortable and wanted to change the subject. She was still standing and motioned for her husband to get up.

"We should leave you to eat together as a family," said David. He turned to leave, taking his wife's arm as if it was his idea.

Joseph and Mary smiled at the couple.

"Are you sure it's safe in Jerusalem?" asked Mary softly.

"I'm not sure of anything, except that I am unwilling to go to Bethlehem again. The innkeeper who loaned us his stable will remember the Magi and us. That wouldn't be safe. I'm sorry too because my family is from those parts, and it would have made it easier."

David turned back and said, "Make sure you try the cookies with the pine nuts. They are a specialty of this region, and my wife makes them better than anyone."

He smiled at them and then patted his wife playfully.

"The shadow of Herod is long and dark," said Joseph. He was in a pensive mood and was tired from the day's travel.

"Let's finish our supper and get some rest. We have a

long road ahead of us. It will take us five hours to get to Jerusalem."

†

Joseph awakened with a start. He was filled with energy. He was excited and relieved. Resting on his arm he reached over Jesus who was sleeping between them and gently nudged Mary. He smiled broadly.

"Mary, we have had an answer to our prayers," said Joseph.

Mary blinked her eyes open and looked up at Joseph. She saw the peaceful easy look on his face. She then looked down at Jesus to make sure he was still sleeping.

"What is it, Joseph?" she asked softly.

"I was visited again by an angel. We have to head to Nazareth," he said. "We will set up our household there."

Mary had been hoping to return to her relatives in Nazareth and was quite relieved.

Actually, Joseph hoped to return to Jerusalem. He was definitely not planning on returning to Bethlehem, but to the Holy City of Jerusalem. He had his heart set on it until the dream.

"Nazareth it is," he said, "but the angel said to first travel to Gabae. We are to sell the animals there."

"Have you ever been to Gabae?" she whispered.

Little Jesus stirred so she sat up quietly and motioned for Joseph to follow her. They moved to two chairs near the window. Birds were chirping outside and sunlight was not yet visible on the horizon.

"Certainly. I passed through it on the road to Jerusalem. Gabae is near the plain of Esdralon. It's up north more than

thirty leagues. We should start early. We could be in Apollonia by midday and in Gabae by nightfall. It's an autonomous region like Ascalon, but it is not in Archelaus' territory." His voice had urgency to it.

She understood why he wanted to start moving. They would be traveling through the regions controlled by Archelaus all day. Even if someone were suspicious of them it would take more than a day for orders to detain them to come back from Jerusalem. They would spend one more long day on the road and then be safe.

Mary couldn't wait to return. She knew that it was best to live in Nazareth.

At the same time Joseph was relieved to avoid Jerusalem with the animals. He knew that they could safely travel back to Jerusalem during any number of religious festivals. The city would be full for both Yom Kippur and Rosh Hashanah. When the Passover Feast arrived no one could keep track of who entered the city, not even the Romans.

"I'll get Jesus ready, while you retrieve the animals."

Mary started gathering their belongings. She would have them ready to leave in a few minutes and hopefully get it all done before he awoke. Then she would attend to Jesus.

Mary softly hummed a hymn.

†

"We move quickly, young one," said Heba.

Jamil smiled back to her. It was a delight to be sauntering at nearly a run. He had plenty of reserve speed. He could feel the extra reach and the quicker step, but he held back. Still, this faster pace felt more at home for him than the gentle saunter that most humans wanted him to keep.

Jamil watched the couple smile as they passed the more crowded road from Ascalon toward Jamnia. There were a variety of people out moving merchandise. By the third hour though, the road would be deserted. The Romans preferred that their slaves moved merchandise during the night and commerce was set and ready in the marketplace by the third hour. They would have the road to themselves shortly. Only an occasional traveler would be their company. Since they were moving at a quicker pace, they would have very little company.

By the second hour, the little caravan was past the city of Jamnia and on the way to Joppa. Here the road swung closer to the sea. The water's fragrance drifted up to them long before they could see it. The view was spectacular. The calm sea had clear blue waters. Small waves lapped at the white beaches. The road was on an elevation that allowed them to see the waters out to a distance of a few leagues. It seemed to go on forever.

"This is really fun," said Jamil. He was elated to be moving quickly. Every muscle in his body was working. It was a nice easy rhythm for him. He felt fully alive.

Heba on the other hand was getting old. She was pacing herself to handle the work. When they first started their journeys, Jamil was young and smaller than he was now. He was always quick, but early on, he was not as powerful as he was right now. Now Jamil was both quicker and more powerful. He was capable of outrunning a swift horse and could carry more than a mule could on his back. Because of the training he had received at the hands of the Magi, his gate was as smooth as silk.

The contraption that used to fit so perfectly now

rode higher on his hump. Joseph had redistributed their belongings with more of the weight given to Jamil. Heba was grateful and capable of easily handling the pace they were traveling at.

The day wore on and by the fourth hour, they were at Joppa and stopped for water and a short rest.

Heba watched while Joseph talked to a few of the men near the well. He was getting better at handling us, she thought. The good husband was capable of tending his animals and maintaining conversation. Mary fed Jesus and gave him water.

"They intend to be in Apollonia by midday," said Heba.

Jamil agreed. He had no idea where or how far that was, but he could tell by how quickly they started back out on the road that they were in a rush.

"They didn't feed us," he said with a whine.

"You'll live. You have a hump filled with stored food for energy," she reminded him.

"Yeah, I know," he said. "Most humans think it's filled with water, so they figure we drink to fill it up."

"Yes, humans are strange. If your hump starts to shrink, however, I'll see if we can get more food."

They both laughed and kept sauntering. Slowly the city of Apollonia rose on the northern horizon. The sun shone high in the sky and it was midday.

†

"Mary, you go to the marketplace and get some bread and cheese. I'll take care of these blessed beasts," said Joseph.

They were off to the side of the gate at a fountain. A few fig trees grew in a courtyard next to the watering trough. The

trees were so big that the branches extended over a wall and into the street. The trees didn't provide much relief from the sun, but the top branches could be picked from the nearby window. The branches were obviously too high for a horse to reach, but a camel was much taller. Jamil was straining his neck to reach up and taste one.

"I don't think a camel should eat figs," said Joseph. He was filling his water skins and had stopped to pull at Jamil's tether. He was trying to be discrete. Meanwhile, the owner of the building in whose courtyard the trees grew was watching him closely from a balcony.

The man appeared to be Greek. The city, Apollonia, named after the Greek god Apollo, was originally a Greek settlement and even under Roman rule was largely inhabited by Greek sea traders. Inside the confines of the city was a fine institution of higher learning that many of the Romans in Israel sent their children to. The Romans cherished a Greek education.

The Greek man frowned, and Joseph smiled up at him while he tugged at the tether and pulled Jamil away.

"Hey, Jamil," said Joseph softly, "Don't attract attention now. We want to get out of this town as quickly as possible."

Mary came walking back. She was smiling with Jesus on her left shoulder and a few flat loaves of bread, some honey and yogurt, and cheese for Joseph in her sack. Apparently, she liked the quality of the food. They were much closer to what she was accustomed to in Nazareth.

"Joseph, you should see what I purchased," she said. Her delight was obvious.

He was looking out the gate and north toward a row of Mediterranean pines. Their broad flat branches would provide shelter under which they could eat.

"Let's head over there and have our meal. It would seem odd for us to leave too early, but if we were already outside the gates, no one would notice."

She nodded and slipped Jesus into the seat and then tied her sack over the other side of the saddle.

Joseph watched as she got on the camel. She did it so effortlessly now. His camel lifted off its knees and then stood up. No matter how often he mounted the beast he still couldn't get over how tall she was and how high up in the air he was. After years of only occasionally riding an ass, this was like being on a tower.

Jamil started reaching up for a fig again, and Joseph moved Heba between the tree and Jamil. Jamil swung his head sideways and pushed Heba out of the way. He grabbed a fig and a leaf.

Mary pulled on the reins and Jamil, out of habit, moved away. He would have loved to have a few more.

"I think he wants more figs," Mary said with a laugh.

"Yes, I've been trying to pull him away from the trees."

"I think he's angry too," she said.

"Let's get outside before the owner gets angry," said Joseph. He smiled again at the man, who nodded.

A few moments later they were outside the gates and under the shade of the flat-topped pines.

†

"They were trying to be discrete and not attract attention, and you head-butted me," said Heba. She sounded angry. Her head was still sore.

"Yeah, well, I was just about to get another one of those fruits when you pushed me out of the way, you old she-

camel," said Jamil. His anger was obvious. The fig was delicious.

Mary and Joseph had dismounted under the trees. Mary took Jesus from his seat and brought him under the large Mediterranean pines. He started to run around, happy to be out of the saddle.

A cool breeze was blowing, but it did nothing to cool Jamil's anger.

"I can't believe it. I finally figured out how to pull the branches down, and then you pushed me out of the way. You deserved the head butt. I hope it hurt."

Jamil was getting angrier as he talked.

"It did hurt, but I think I'll forget about it and get on with life," she said.

"It's your fault. You brought it on yourself," said Jamil.

"Oh really? And how did I do that?" she asked.

Heba was working on controlling her own resentments now and trying not to get angry with Jamil.

"You could have hesitated. You saw what I was doing. If you had given me a few seconds more I could have had a few more of those things."

"First of all, that would have been stealing. Second, 'one of those things' are called figs. And third, Joseph did not want you calling attention to his family. I could go on but you're addicted to being right again."

"Oh yeah, smart one, I could have eaten ten before the man could have come down to complain," he said.

"That many would cause an upset stomach. You would have had indigestion for the rest of the journey."

"I could have handled it. I've eaten them before, and I did not have indigestion just a little gas. They are so sweet."

"You were also putting the family's safety in jeopardy. Your purpose in life is to serve these people and to bring them safely to where they need to go. If they were detained because their camel had damaged someone's tree, God only knows what else would have happened."

"Like what?" asked Jamil. He was a little less angry and really did want to know.

"We are in Archelaus' territory. Someone might have noticed that they had a young child of Jesus' age. That's not too common around here. Also, they could have figured out that Joseph's family was from Bethlehem and then put two and two together. Archelaus' men would have taken the baby and maybe sent you off to slaughter for camel meat."

"That seems a little far-fetched to me." The thought of being camel meat didn't excite him at all.

"It's not that far-fetched. First, you think your right, then you get angry, and now you're into blame and resentment. It's a common progression."

"Oh yeah? What's that, another character flaw, Miss Perfect?"

Heba nodded yes.

✝

Joseph stepped in between the camels and pulled on Jamil's tether, just as he was about to head-butt her again. He tied the reins on a nearby tree, away from Heba.

"I don't know what's gotten into this camel," said Joseph. He looked back to Mary who was helping Jesus eat and watching Joseph.

"He's acting strangely. I wish we knew a camel driver we could talk to," he said. He petted Jamil's side and then

offered him a feed pack. Jamil took it hungrily. He ate with a vengeance.

"I think he was hungry," said Mary.

Joseph walked over to Heba and put a feed bag on her too.

"They better be ready to go soon. We are more than halfway to Gabae, but a good part of the next thirty-five leagues is uphill."

"Where does this road take us?" asked Mary.

"First through the plains of Sharon to Caesarea and then over the Samarian mountains. The road from Caesarea is uphill for nearly three leagues. The animals will be tired."

"The Lord of Israel will protect and provide," she said.

He simply nodded. Once they reached the top of the Samarian Mountains, they would have a quick journey down the northern side to the Plain of Esdraelon and into the Valley of Jezreel where Gabae was located. They had to make it over the top of the small mountains before nightfall. At the pace they had been traveling it would be easy until that stretch into the hills.

✝

Joseph reloaded the camels quickly and the Holy Family mounted. By now, Jamil was cooled off. Time was a balm that soothed his irritated soul. Though Heba suspected that it might also have had something to do with carrying the little child. Jamil always seemed calmer with the child on board. He was quiet for the first few leagues which placed them a couple leagues northeast of Caesarea at the foothills of what were really not mountains. The Roman road through these hills was well-maintained.

"I'm sorry Heba," he said as he moved a little closer.

"Apology accepted," she said softly back.

"It was a stupid thing to do."

"You were hungry. When one doesn't get to eat it is easier for a defect of character to show up. You know what they say."

"A hungry camel is only a friend to one who feeds it," said Jamil.

"That's right. When a camel is hungry, angry, lonely, or tired, he loses the polish on his character. It is easier for a flaw to surface."

"What was mine again? I know about being right and rage, but you said something else."

"It was blame and resentment, young one," she said.

"Sorry about calling you an old she-camel," he said.

"That's okay. It's the truth. One must never be offended by the truth."

The hill started to incline more steeply, and she slowed down a bit. This was going to be a long two hours for her.

"So, what's blame and resentment all about?" he asked.

"It's a flaw that we camels use when we want to shift the focus away from ourselves to others. When we fail at something—and we do hate to fail—we look to blame someone for the failure. We only like to take credit for what goes right."

"When I head-butted you?" asked Jamil.

"Well, partially. That was blame, but the resentment was the worst part. You didn't want to give it up. You didn't want to let go. You wanted to hold a grudge and keep fighting with me. That's the part that is dangerous."

"I could feel the resentment feeding the raging indignation."

"That's right, Jamil. One character flaw feeds another. They reinforce each other. Blame and resentment are really the same thing. One is a single event and the other is going back over the event and reliving it or going over a series of events and stacking the anger up."

"I felt so lonely when I was doing it," he said.

"Blame thrives on rejection. The more rejected you feel the greater the flaw grows. It's the opposite of forgiveness and tries to get you focused on vengeance."

"I'm sorry," he simply said.

"You need to work on the opposite," said Heba.

"Which is?" asked Jamil.

"Responsibility and discretion... when you are responsible and discrete, your soul nurtures others. Accepting responsibility is a big step towards maturity. Discretion is maturity."

They both grew quiet and continued walking up hill.

✝

As the road wound up the hills they looked back over the broad expanse and saw the sculptured land. Orchards and vineyards covered the Plain of Sharon like a quilt that had been carefully laid upon the earth by a higher intelligence. The endless leagues of cultivation seemed to make more sense the higher they traveled.

"It is really quite beautiful," said Jamil.

"Yes," said Heba. She was conserving her strength. The next couple of hours would tax her. She wanted to use her resources well. Speaking to Jamil about the beauty she saw wouldn't enhance the view. Certainly it would acknowledge

the beauty, but it was so gorgeous that even commenting on it was redundant.

"I don't know about climbing mountains like these," said Jamil.

Heba just looked at him. Complaining about the height of the mountain didn't make the steps to the top any easier. In fact, the more one focused on the difficulty the more difficult it seemed to be. She kept her mouth shut and worked on keeping the pace even. Steadiness and focus in a situation like this were more important than strength. When times were tough, the camels that survived the test weren't necessarily the ones with the most physical gifts, but the ones with the most focus and the most discipline.

"This road looks like it gets steeper by the minute. You know, Heba, we're camels. The Sustainer designed us for great distances over flat desert. I don't think going uphill—or rather up a mountain, to be precise—is good for our skeletal system. In fact, I am convinced that this is harmful. I can feel a little stiffness in my upper back already. This is much steeper than even the steepest sand dune."

Jamil looked over at his older friend and waited for a response. When there was none, he started talking again.

"I was never really trained to climb mountains. Sure, there's a road and it was built by brilliant Roman engineers, but when did I get trained to climb like this?"

He waited.

"Well, I can tell you when… never," he said. He was emphatic.

Heba just kept her mouth shut and marched on with that steady pace she always seemed to have. She could hear his complaints, but she made a conscious effort to ignore them

and focus on the task before her. She enjoyed the warmth of the sun and the cool mountain breeze.

"That's two major reasons why I don't think I can or should go on," said Jamil. His tone was adamant. He slowed the pace a bit.

Jamil waited. Heba didn't say a thing and she didn't alter her pace. In fact, he had to pick up his pace to catch her.

"Let me restate my case so I am perfectly clear. First of all, I am a camel. Camels were not designed to haul loads over mountains. The Sustainer gave us the ability to carry great burdens over flat land. This terrain is for asses, goats, and maybe even an elephant. Certainly, a horse could do this work if he was asked, but it's not right that they should demand of us—camels that we are—to lug all this stuff to the top of the world. And the altitude… it can't be good for you to breathe the air way up here. It's thin, cool air. We were designed for desert air, thick, hot, and refreshing."

There was still no reply from Heba, but he could see that she had heard him.

"Secondly, not only were we not designed by God Almighty for this task, but nothing—let me say that again— nothing, nothing in our training has prepared us for this task at hand."

For the next hour or so Jamil kept it up. He used the same two excuses, with minor variations on the two themes to complain and protest. He did change his approach for explaining the obvious to Heba, not so much for her understanding, but to keep from being bored by repeating himself. As he grew more tired his tone took on a decided whine.

When they finally reached the highest point on the road Joseph stopped for a moment to take in the panorama. It

was absolutely beautiful to behold. A huge valley lay before them. The lush green with vast areas under cultivation spread before them like a verdant ocean.

"Are you okay, Heba?" Jamil finally asked.

"I'm a little more tired than I would like, but it's all downhill from here," she said.

"I can explain that. You're tired because…"

"Turn it off. I don't want to hear about your inadequacy and self-pity," she interrupted.

"What inadequacy and self-pity? I was just about to explain why you are tired."

"No, you weren't. You were going to explain to me that as camels we don't have the ability to haul heavy loads over mountains."

"Yes, well, you have to agree with that don't you?"

"No. In fact, Jamil while you were bellyaching, we were carrying a heavy load up over the top of a mountain. So that disproves your first theory."

It was Jamil's turn to be quiet.

"We not only had the capabilities, but we proved it by doing the work. We are camels and we camels don't ever need to give in to self-pity. You just didn't want to do the work. Yet doing the work is the only way we have to discover if we have the abilities or not. We go out and get the job done and then we know we are capable."

"We weren't designed to do it or trained to do it," he said weakly.

"God designs raw materials. It's up to us to discover the uses. Furthermore, life is its own training."

"Yeah, well you look pretty tired. You have to admit that."

"Yes, Jamil, I am tired. But I am also very satisfied because I gave it all I could and made it to the top."

Joseph pulled on the reins and Heba started walking downhill. Jamil followed.

"It wasn't actually self-pity," said Jamil as a way of justifying his complaints.

"Regardless of what you call it, it wasn't resourceful sufficiency."

"Resourceful what?" asked Jamil.

"Sufficiency. Resourceful sufficiency is a virtue based on faith. The Sustainer gave it to you. It's a resource that you can use to face the challenges of life. Resourceful sufficiency is the faith-based belief that challenges come as a way for God to reveal to you your great strengths."

"Like when I closed my eyes in the desert storm and realized I had two pairs of eyelids; one for regular stuff and one for storms?" asked Jamil.

"Precisely. For a moment, you closed your eyes and hoped that you had what it took to make it through that storm. If you had closed your mouth on the way up and hoped that God had given you enough power to make it over the mountain, the whole uphill climb would have been easier."

"That's what you did, isn't it?" he asked.

"Yes, and I prayed. I'm too old to waste time worrying about the challenges that face me. I have to keep my mouth shut and get on with it."

†

"There in the valley is Gabae," said Joseph sitting tall in his saddle and pointing.

Little Jesus looked down the mountain and kicked his feet with joy. He was too young to fully understand, but he was delighted, nevertheless.

"Is that where you think we can sell these wonderful animals?" Mary asked.

"Yes, and after that, we will head to our hometown of Nazareth," Joseph reassured her.

"I wonder how far it is," she said.

"I don't know exactly, but it is off to the distance in that elevation there." He pointed to the other side of the valley that ran below them into the distance.

The valley was lush and verdant. Vineyards and wheat fields filled the view. Small gardens outside the city gave way to large areas of farmland. This was a land of milk and honey. It was the area of their home. The small village across the valley, visible from their lofty heights, was Nazareth.

"We have to sell the camels first," he said. "I think we should get a donkey and a small cart. That would be a useful investment for me."

Joseph was already thinking about his work as a carpenter. They would have enough money after the sale of the animals to be able to buy, new tools, carpentry supplies, and a small plot of land for a vegetable garden. Then he would be out to market with his skills as a carpenter. After three years, their house would need repairs, but their cousins would have kept an eye on things for them.

"We will need to repair our home, Joseph," she said. "I will take care of it first, and we should add a room for Jesus."

"I've been thinking about that. We should be able to get a good price for the saddles too."

"We have one little gift box from the Magi left too," she

added. They had used the gifts to survive on for the last three years.

"Depending on how much we get for the camels we might buy a small patch of land," said Joseph.

"My relatives will help you. They know many people and will help us make a wise decision," added Mary.

Mary was comforted by her belief in Joseph's ability to provide. The rest of the way down the mountain she thought of how lovely she would make their little home.

✝

"Did you hear what they said?" asked Jamil. There was panic in his voice.

"What part?" Heba asked calmly. She was carefree. She seemed to be enjoying the jaunt down the hill. The pace was more rapid than before, but it was easier.

"The part where they said that they would sell us?"

"Does that concern you?" she asked.

"Of course, it concerns me. I was getting used to them. They are such a nice family." Jamil spoke quickly letting his worries show.

"But after the journey is finished, they will have no need of our services," she said.

"They could put us in a stable again. That is until our services are needed again," said Jamil.

"He's a carpenter who is looking for a place to settle down and provide for his family. Why would they ever need us again?"

"I have a really bad feeling about this. I'm not too sure this is a good idea."

"We are camels. Unless our owner is going to travel in

caravan all the time, we will be sold. That is how it was for me. I was sold many times to people who only had one voyage to make. Rarely I was sold to someone who would make frequent trips. But in the end, I am not destined to live hidden away in a stable just in case someone has an emergency and needs a camel."

"I don't know. I've grown accustomed to this little family," Jamil said.

"I have too, but even so I am ready to be placed on the auction block. It's the door to adventure for a camel. It's part of the path to the next journey."

Jamil looked at her for a while. She seemed so content with what she had said. It irritated him. He was thinking about what would happen to them. It had happened to him once before at the oasis. He had heard from other camels that it had happened repeatedly to them too. He knew that he would be sold off to someone who had someplace to go. It would be the start of uncertainty and doubt. *Where would he be going? How long would it take? How could he be certain that his new owner would not take them into harm's way?*

Jamil looked over to Heba and said, "You know, you seem awfully calm about this whole thing. I have a lot of concerns about what is going to happen. Our future may not be very bright once we let go of this wonderful family."

"Jamil, you don't know that. You have no idea where we will wind up, and you're trying to figure it out before it happens," said Heba. "That's impossible to do."

"Well, it may be impossible to do, but I have some ideas of what could happen to us or me, and I am not really happy about what they are. I've heard stories in the past from other camels about how difficult life can get."

"It would be a lot easier if you just trusted the Sustainer and stayed positive. You'll probably go somewhere very nice and have a lot of wonderful journeys. Be confident. You'll find that you're more resourceful that way."

"God, Heba, you are so unrealistic."

"I am simply an optimist."

Jamil looked at Heba with disbelief. "Actually, that's not it at all. I am the realist, and you are not considering all the possibilities here, only those that are positive. That, old wise one, is unrealistic," said Jamil.

Heba laughed and then snorted.

"What? You don't agree?"

"No, I don't, young one," she said. "I operate from confident expectation, and you are a dread seeker."

"I'm a dread seeker? Out of what hat did you pull that idea from? I know what a dread seeker is. I used to listen to them at the oasis when I was younger. They were crybabies, always afraid of the next voyage. I'm not like that. I'm ready for the next journey to wherever, but I don't have a good feeling about it. That's all."

"And why is that?" she asked. She was trying fruitlessly to keep the amusement out of her voice as they moved further down the hill toward Gabae. She knew her tone would annoy him.

"I told you already. I'm the realist here. It's an intuitive thing. I have this sense of what is going to happen in the future, and I feel like something bad is going to happen," Jamil insisted.

"You can't believe that you will have as much fun on another journey to somewhere else?" Heba asked.

"Right, because like I said, I have an intuition something

bad will happen."

"You're a dread seeker, looking for doom and gloom. You'll get over it, I hope."

"Really? And what do I do when I get over it?" he asked.

"You learn to live with confident expectation, soaring on the wings of hope and faith, trusting God, and believing beyond your capacity to believe."

"Sure. It sounds just lovely."

Jamil was being sarcastic.

"No, really. You will learn to hope beyond your capacity to believe. It just takes a few more journeys to develop the confidence."

†

The walls of Gabae were open and welcoming to the Holy Family. Roman soldiers stood guard and took note of the camels but little else. As Joseph, Mary, and Jesus rode through the gates, they were immediately struck by the colorfulness of the marketplace. Vendors had set up permanent stalls where they could sell their goods. The sun was setting to the west, but it was not yet nighttime. The marketplace was still open and active.

People were arguing over prices and having a wonderful time doing it. The merchants and the shoppers both enjoyed the art of the bargain. It was an art form for the vendors. They appreciated their customer's attempts to get them to lower the price. It was great fun and a game; though some pretended to be insulted, others acted offended, and a few lost their tempers to stress a point about quality or cost.

Jesus was wide-awake with all the commotion. He stared in wonder at the colors of the merchant canopies. His legs

kicked joyfully in the saddle. He was pointing to the vendors and called out, "Mamma" and "Abba." Mary leaned down and stroked his head, talking softly to him. Jesus loved his mother's sweet voice. She had kept a light conversation up with him for most of the trip down the side of the mountain. Now she described what the merchants were doing and what they were selling. Jesus hung on her every word.

"Joseph, the food from the stands smells so good," said Mary.

"I think there must be a bakery with a well-used hearthstone nearby," he replied.

"Wherever it's from, it is going to make our little one very hungry soon. We should quickly find a place to stay," she said as they came to a stop near the corner of the forum.

Joseph got down from his camel first and then helped Mary. She lifted Jesus out of his riding seat and turned to look around. Gabae was a lovely city. Cloth canopies suspended by two poles hung over the doorways of a few of the buildings. The stones in the buildings were mostly white limestone that glistened with orange as the evening sun took on a golden hue.

While she turned and scanned the forum, Joseph asked a passerby for advice on lodging. The man looked at his camels and shook his head approvingly.

"There is an inn toward the east gate," he said, referring to the giant door to the city on the eastern side. "It is not exactly a caravansary but has huge stables. Its owner is a trader with Pella and beyond to Mesopotamia."

Joseph thanked him. He knew that if a man were trading with Mesopotamian merchants, he would have the necessary accommodations for their pack animals. Usually,

a caravansary had the stables attached so that the caravan could store all its goods and the camel drivers could keep watch over them. Sometimes an inn would keep its stable a little further on the edge of town, especially if it were close to the food market. The mixing of animal and food smells didn't help the market.

As they walked toward the northeast area of the walled city the sun dipped toward the sea. It was dark by the time they arrived at the inn.

Joseph knocked on the door with the large brass knocker that hung by a short chain. *This is an extravagance,* he thought as he waited for the door to be opened.

"May we help you?" asked a young man. He was polite and well-groomed.

"We need a place to stay for the night," replied Joseph who looked beyond the young man into the great room of the inn.

The young man looked behind Joseph. Mary and Jesus were standing at his side. He eyed the two camels.

"We heard that you would have accommodations for our pack animals too."

"Yes, of course," the young man said.

"Ben, who is that at our door?" asked an older voice from inside.

"A young couple with camels, my father," said Ben.

"And a child," said the older man as he walked up to greet them. "Please invite them in and hold their animals for them. I am Benjamin, obviously the elder."

The innkeeper held his hand out in greeting to Joseph. Mary entered with Jesus at her side holding her hand. Ben the elder nodded to Mary.

"Elli, come here. We have a mother and young child. And he is beautiful," the innkeeper added. He was good at making his guests feel at home.

Mary smiled with the delight of a proud mother.

"We need to take a few things from the camels and then come in," said Joseph.

"My son and I will unload your belongings and bring them to our storage area. It is locked and secure. Take what you need for the night," he answered. Obviously, the innkeeper was accustomed to storing valuables for his guests. He had eyed the saddles and realized that they were of great value.

In a few minutes, the beasts were unpacked. The young man moved them to the Gabae Stables, a caravansary just on the outside of the city with pasture and grazing. It too had a secure storage area for valuables. The saddles would be kept there.

"Make sure you tell them to keep the saddle and that contraption on the male beast in a secure place," said Ben the elder.

4

A NEW LIFE

New life often started without great fanfare. Sometimes it was noticed by the small stirring in a mother's womb. Other times it was a delicate shoot of green poking up from rich soil, giving the hint that new life was on the way.

This morning the air was filled with the sweet songs of birds that were familiar to the young couple. Familiarity with small things was the sign that they were finally starting their new life over. Soon they would settle into a life of familiarity and routine. They felt very much at home as they awoke to the soft stirrings of their young child. Jesus was awake, bouncing himself and climbing into the arms of his mother. They were happy to be close to their final destination, and Gabae was as safe as any small city they could travel to, if not safer.

"We have a lot to do today," said Joseph after finishing his morning prayer ritual.

"Ben the elder should know someone who would want to buy our camels," said Mary.

"I hope so," said Joseph.

"I've been thinking about the saddles," said Mary.

"I've also been thinking about them. We must sell them

with the beasts. They could be used by Herod's son to trace us if he cared to."

"I thought that too. What if someone doesn't want to buy the saddles?"

"We would have to take them with us. The leather on the child seat could be employed for something else," said Joseph.

"Like a carpenter's apron? We could utilize the silks as decorations for our house," said Mary. "They are lovely."

"The saddle doesn't fit the little one as well as it used to," said Joseph. "He has gotten bigger and stronger."

"Let's trust that God will take care of the details," she said.

†

"Joseph, good morning," said Ben the elder. "When will you be needing your animals?"

"I'm glad you asked. I am looking to sell them. I wish to buy a donkey and a wagon," said Joseph.

"The wagon and donkey are easy to come by, but selling the camels may be a little more difficult."

"Do you know who I can speak to?" Joseph asked.

"The stable manager will know where to get you a donkey and a wagon. Let me think about which of my guests I could ask. There are some that might want to purchase a couple of extra beasts to carry goods back to Mesopotamia. Especially this one fellow who is carrying a couple of small Roman statues."

"Thank you," said Joseph.

"Ask for a man named Ravi. He is the proprietor, a friend of mine, who will help you get a fair price for the animals.

He's an honest man. Tell him I told you that."

He nodded politely and then left for the stable, which was not more than a hundred meters away from the inn. It was just far enough to keep the animals' aromas from the inn, though the streets were filled with horses and other animals. The Romans had built grooves into the streets to serve as sewer drains. A fountain overflowed and washed into the street, carrying debris away. Joseph was careful not to get his sandals wet.

Gabae was a very prosperous little city. It handled Mesopotamian trade from the East as well as from the Roman Empire in the West. Many of the merchants from Mesopotamia preferred to stop in Pella and trade. From there, their intermediaries would carry goods to Gabae and on to Ptolemais, Dora, or Caesarea. Sometimes the goods that were traded were bulkier than that which they brought in, and they would need more pack animals. Joseph was hoping he would find someone who needed two more animals.

✝

"What are they doing?" Jamil asked as he was led out to a large, enclosed field.

"This is where they let us run a little," she said. Heba had seen a lot of caravansaries and stables in her time. This was not too different except that the area was not large enough to get up to full speed.

"How do I run in such a small place?" he asked.

Jamil loved to run and hadn't been doing enough of it in the past few months. The most fun he had in a long time was running away from the Bedouin bandits in Persia when the Magi were on their voyage to visit the newborn king. Even

though he had been frightened, it was fun to use his speed and energy.

"In some places, they tether the camels together and run you for exercise. That's a little more fun. In other places, they put a rider on you and exercise you. That's good too."

Jamil was already running around the enclosed area. He couldn't reach top speed, but he was moving pretty fast. That's when he noticed the latch on the gate as he went by.

†

An old man named Casimer, who had stiff white hair sticking sideways out from under a cap, watched in amusement.

"Can you saddle that animal and let my son take him for a ride?" Casimer asked.

"We usually like to ask the owner first, but my boss might allow it," said Malthace, a tall Samarian who managed the Gabae Stables.

"Will he be here soon?" Casimer wondered out loud.

"He was here earlier and should be back shortly," answered Malthace.

"I'm back already," said a voice from the front of the stables. It was Ravi, a Galilean who operated the stables. He was well-informed in the area of trade and commerce, but his real talents rested in the cure and husbandry of horses. He understood camels but was not a lover of the breed.

"I think this is a special camel," said Casimer, shaking hands with Ravi.

The men knew each other for many years. Casimer was a frequent patron of the Gabae Stables. He was an energetic old man with a passion for wagering at races. Though old, he

still dreamed of being able to see the chariot races at Rome's famous Circus Maximus. Most of the time he wagered on camels. It was a popular sport in Persia and Arabia. A few times there had been races in the Gabae area organized by Ravi. Casimer had attended and was delighted with the sport.

There was something special about camel racing that made it more fun than horse racing or even the chariots. Maybe it was the love of the animal and the fact that Casimer knew how difficult it was to ride them at full speed. Or perhaps it was the way they moved. Camels had an awkward movement that lent itself to mystery and created an air of struggle beyond that of the race. It was as though the camel had to fight with itself just to keep moving. They moved both legs almost together on the same side. It was like a human walking or running with four legs.

"So, tell me why this is a special camel. You're the expert on these beasts, not me," said Ravi.

"Many years ago, there was a legendary camel named Shooting Star. It was allegedly the fastest camel of its time. Someone had managed to tame it and race it."

"Was it good at the races? A fast animal isn't always as good when it is saddled and driven on a circuit," said Ravi. He had experienced that problem with horses before.

"It was a bit of a problem. It didn't like to be ridden and it hated running in circles, but it was fast. Eventually, it ran away into the desert. They couldn't catch it and bring it back. It ran wild for years around an oasis in Persia called Kashan.

"Is it the same beast?" asked Ravi.

"Impossible, it's too young. It could be the son of Shooting Star or even its grandson. See the blaze on his forehead?

That's what gave Shooting Star his name."

There was palpable excitement in the air as Casimer spoke. He watched Jamil run around the enclosure, frolicking with Heba.

†

"Heba, you slow old lady. When did you wear out? You used to run faster than that," said Jamil.

"I used to run almost as fast, but I was not as reckless as you," she said laughing.

Heba was sauntering slowly, going through the paces but paying attention to something else. She noticed the men talking and pointing to Jamil. She was watching them carefully, trying to understand what they were up to. Humans were hard to understand. Their motives were often incomprehensible.

Jamil was around to the other side of the corral looking at the gate.

"Hey, Heba, look over here. The gate is unlocked. I'll bet that if I hit it, I can get the thing to swing open," Jamil said.

Jamil gave the gate an enormous nudge with his nose and it popped open. He stopped and looked outside hesitating for a moment. Then he slipped through and took off on a mad dash toward the hill. He was flying now, running at full speed, and making bellowing noises as though he were king of the desert.

Heba stepped through slowly and then wandered a few meters off to taste some of the wildflowers that were growing in the field.

†

"Oh, God in heaven! He's out of the stable yard!" shouted Ravi.

"If this beast is as fast as I suspect, you won't ever get him back either," said Casimer. Suddenly his dreams of having found a great racing camel were fading.

Malthace went running for his horse. It was going to be his job to corral the camel.

When Joseph arrived at the stables, the workmen were standing together having a heated discussion.

"I'll wager that this is him now," said Ravi.

"I hope so," said Casimer. "I also hope his camel likes him."

"Good morning gentlemen," said Joseph politely. He spotted Jamil outside on the hilltop and Heba in the stable yard.

"Sir, I am Ravi the owner of Gabae Stables. He extended his hand to Joseph who took it but was watching Jamil run along the crest of the hill.

"That's odd. These two camels never seem to be apart," said Joseph.

"I am sorry to say your younger beast has gotten out of our yard quite by accident," he said.

"So why don't you just call him back?" asked Joseph. He watched as Malthace rode in a large circle trying to get around Jamil. The camel quickly outran the horse. It was obvious to Joseph that Jamil was having the time of his life.

"I sent my stable man out to capture him, but your beast is too fast and doesn't seem to want to come back," said Ravi.

"It shouldn't be a problem. The little one loves being around the older one. They're inseparable," said Joseph. He walked out to the corral and grabbed Heba's tether. Joseph walked her out to the open field.

Heba followed dutifully and the men stood and watched.

Ravi doubted if Jamil would come back while Casimer hoped and prayed that he would.

"Come on in, Jamil," Joseph shouted. He turned to the men behind him. "His name is Jamil and this one is Heba. Come on boy. We don't have a lot of time for foolishness."

Jamil came running right back down to Joseph and bayed loudly.

Joseph laughed and took his tether in hand.

"I will never understand these animals," Joseph said. "I much prefer a donkey."

The other men laughed. Malthace rode up and quickly closed the stable yard gate behind Joseph and his two animals.

"Where do you travel to from here," asked Casimer politely.

"We are looking to settle down in Nazareth. I have just started a family," answered Joseph.

"Would you be interested in selling the younger beast," asked Casimer. He was convinced that this was the fastest camel that he had ever seen.

"Actually, I am, but I would prefer to sell them both together. I also intend to sell their saddles with them."

Casimer nodded to Ravi, who understood that they would bargain for a while. It was not just good business to bargain, but it was a social custom. To refuse to bargain was to be rude. To bargain was to develop a friendship, a relationship, and an opening for business in the future.

"I don't know much about these animals, but I would like to get a fair price. The innkeeper told me you were an honest man who be able to help me find a buyer," Joseph said to Ravi.

"If I'm not mistaken, Casimer is your buyer," said Ravi.

"Yes, and I definitely want the animal with the shooting star shaped blaze. The older one I don't need," said Casimer.

"I am selling them together," said Joseph. He was being firm to test the man's resolve.

"I don't want them both," said the Persian with a smile.

"You probably do want that, but you just don't know it yet," said Joseph with an even bigger smile.

"Why is that?" asked the Persian merchant. His curiosity was teased.

"Because if the young one gets away, you will never catch him. As long as you have Heba, Jamil will return."

"That's interesting. Are you certain?" he asked Joseph.

"They are inseparable. The man who cared for them in Egypt told us he had never seen two camels so attached. I also want to sell their saddles. They are very fine pieces that were gifts to my family," said Joseph.

"Malthace, go bring those unusual saddles in," said Ravi.

Malthace returned and set the saddles on the ground between the two men.

Casimer gasped. He realized that the saddles were extremely valuable. He recognized the workmanship as unmistakably Persian, but of the finest quality.

"I didn't know you were royalty," he said politely.

"We are not royalty," said Joseph with a smile. "They are beautiful pieces, aren't they? Both were gifts to my family."

"I can't afford to buy the camels and the saddles and give you what they are worth," said Casimer. He was up examining the two saddles. The one with the contraption was obviously even more splendid than the other saddle. Casimer knew Persian craftsmanship, but the silks in the

contraption weren't Persian. They were perhaps from the Indus Valley or beyond.

For a few moments they bargained on the price. Finally, Casimer made a firm offer and Joseph looked to Ravi for guidance.

"Should I accept?" asked Joseph.

Ravi said, "No, the little animal is racing stock, and the saddles are more valuable than what he is offering you."

Casimer was disappointed. He looked at Ravi, slightly annoyed and puzzled by his friend's comment.

"I can't help it. It's the honest thing to say. I know you're going to tell me that if he wants to accept, that's his business. I shouldn't interfere," said Ravi, "but the truth must be told."

"I can't afford to pay him what they're worth. The saddles are out of my reach," said Casimer. "Let me have the camels without the saddles?"

"I would prefer not to," said Joseph.

"I have an idea," said Ravi. "Look, you could use the contraption to carry that ugly statue you bought for your granddaughter."

"Don't start in on me again. She wanted the statue. It's not ugly to her. I'll make it part of her dowry and never have to look at it."

Joseph watched the two men closely.

"You have to give him a fair price," said Ravi.

"Impossible to do. If I was back in Pella, I would get a few friends to invest with me."

"Can you tolerate a partner like me in your camel racing business?" asked Ravi.

"It would be an honor to be in business with you," said Casimer with a laugh. "This little camel will make us rich."

Joseph watched the two of them talk for a few more minutes. When they finally came back to him, they had a simple plan.

"We don't really want the silks. You could give those to your wife. We can pay you fair market value for the animals and the saddles," said Casimer.

"The price will be more than enough to purchase a donkey and cart. You will have enough left over to set up your home in Nazareth," said Ravi.

Joseph looked at them both. He was amazed that it was so simple.

"Is that not enough?" asked Ravi. "We are giving you a very fair deal."

"It's enough," said Joseph. He extended his hand to confirm the deal.

"When do you need the donkey and cart?" asked Ravi.

"As soon as possible. We wanted to get to Nazareth by this afternoon," said Joseph.

"That's only a short journey and the road to Sepphoris is quite good. You have to leave the road about three-quarters of the way there and head to the northeast."

"I know the road," said Joseph. "How long will it take?"

"In a donkey cart... a few hours at most," said Ravi.

"I will leave the choice of donkey and cart up to you?" asked Joseph.

"On the contrary. You can come with me on your way back to the inn and I will introduce you to a man who makes carts. He might have a sturdy used one that you could purchase. I will take care of that. As for the donkey, I have a wonderful beast. Gentle, a little too smart and stubborn, but well behaved for the most part."

Ravi escorted Joseph out of the Gabae Stables and headed toward the cart maker.

"My wife will want to say goodbye to the camels," Joseph said to Ravi as they walked down the street to the cart maker's shop. "She's a good woman, gentle, and kind. The animals, especially Jamil, really like her."

Ravi nodded. He understood.

†

The cart maker was a Roman named Lignus. The name meant wood. No one believed that it was his real name. He was a good carpenter and wagon builder, but his true talent was wheel making. This was an art that the Romans had perfected.

Joseph was glad for that. He could modify and repair the wagon itself, but the wheels were a problem. He was a trained carpenter who had apprenticed at the feet of a master carpenter in Jerusalem and Bethlehem. Wheel making, however, was never a part of his training.

The cart had to be as sturdy as possible. It was to be a tool that he would use to make a living. Carrying lumber day in and day out required a well-built gurney. The wheels needed to be very strong too.

"What type of bevel did you use to cut this edge?" asked Joseph.

Lignus raised his eyebrows a bit.

"You should be more concerned about the joints than the artwork," he said to Joseph.

"I can see that you do fine doweling, and you've made the corners out of dove joints. I was just curious because the cut is so unusual," said Joseph.

"You must be a carpenter then," said Lignus.

"That I am," said Joseph.

The two men immediately started to discuss building techniques. Ravi stood back and watched them discuss the various carts.

"Do you have a lot of things to carry with you?" asked Ravi.

"No, not really," said Joseph.

"What do you need then?" asked Ravi.

"The man needs a cart to carry the wood that he has hewn. He's not buying a cart to go shopping with or to take his wife to market with. He needs to carry the tools of the trade and his lumber," said Lignus. "It has to be something study and large."

"I see," said Ravi, who was starting to worry that the cart was going to cost too much. He thought about it for a moment and decided that perhaps he shouldn't worry.

Joseph examined the last wagon and noticed the iron clasps on the back of the cart. They were particularly sturdy. It was a little larger than some of the other gurneys and the wood was very fine.

"I built this one for a wealthy stone merchant. He didn't like the iron and wanted it done in brass. We got into an argument because he refused to believe that the iron was more useful than the brass. The man insulted my side panels which are removable for easy loading. That's when I refused to sell it to him," said Lignus. "I'll let you have this one for much less than it's worth because it will aggravate him to know that it sold."

Ravi laughed and said, "You Romans are all the same. Let a man insult you and you look for every opportunity to pay him back."

"And you get a great cart in the bargain," said Lignus. He ignored Ravi's remarks.

Joseph nodded. It was more than adequate. He would get many years of good work out of it.

"Is the donkey up to pulling such a large cart?" asked Joseph.

"If you were moving stone then perhaps a horse would be better, but a donkey will have no trouble. It's larger than the others and the wood is heavy enough to handle a large pile of beams."

"Good. It is settled then?" asked Ravi.

"Yes," said Joseph.

Lignus extended his hand and Joseph took it.

Ravi paid and said to Lignus, "Have the cart delivered to my stables immediately."

Then he turned to Joseph and said, "We will hitch the donkey and deliver it immediately to you at the inn."

†

"Hey, Heba, here comes the family," said Jamil taking another mouthful of food. He was eating a strange mixture of grain with some fruit. It was delicious. He could hear them in the front of the stables talking to Ravi and Casimer.

"That's racing fuel," she said with a matter-of-fact tone.

"Is that so? It's delicious, kind of sweet and tart at the same time. I like it."

"That's odd, Jamil. I can't see why the family would want to race you."

"It's because I'm fast, Heba. I'm really fast. Did you see me outrun that horse? I could see it in the horse's eyes. He thinks camels are ugly. Well, I think horses are slow."

Heba laughed.

"You think I'm kidding?" he asked.

"No, not at all. Horses think they are beautiful, extremely strong, and smarter than anyone else. I never really had a problem with them because I spent so much time in the desert."

"What's that got to do with it?"

"Jamil, did you ever think about what it's like racing a horse over sand? We make them look like they're lame. We fly over the sand, barely sinking in. Their small hard hoofs push right through the sand. We drive them crazy in the desert."

"Plus, they need to drink too much water and they sweat so much," said Jamil. He had a dried fig hanging from the side of his mouth. "Figs, can you believe it? They're dried, right? So, I can eat them?"

Jamil snapped his jaws around a fig before Heba could even comment.

"Horses. They are so arrogant," said Jamil.

"And they smell funny, not sweet like us, right?" said Heba.

"Right." He inhaled another fig and ground it between his right molars.

"Did you know that horses smell great to other horses?" asked Heba.

"No? Do they really?" asked Jamil, he was amazed. He was listening attentively but shoved his face back into the feedbag.

"They think we stink," said Heba with a laugh.

"Aww, come on," said Jamil pulling his head out again. "What are these purple things?"

Heba slipped her head into the bag and took a mouthful.

"They're grapes. Don't eat too many, they will give you bad wind."

Jamil raised his eyes at that comment.

"There are so few in the bag," he complained. He was trying to eat and talk at the same time, hurrying the last few mouthfuls before Joseph, Mary, and Jesus came over.

"I still can't believe that horse. He was so pompous. I would have loved to run against him in the sand."

"They have a character flaw that isn't one of yours," said Heba.

Jamil stopped chewing.

"Really? There's one that I don't have?"

"Yes, extreme self-regard," she said.

"What's that about?"

"It's about animals who think they are so wonderful that it's a pleasure to be around them. It causes horses to think that they are so beautiful that you are fortunate to get to look at them. They know that they are sleek and that it's your honor to rub them down. And of course, they believe they are so fast that it's your opportunity to ride them."

"Not very modest," said Jamil.

He dug his face back down into the feed bag and pushed to get something that smelled unusually good.

"But it sounds like horses to me," he said with a full mouth.

"Racehorses are the worst. They really think they have it all; thinness, beauty, speed, and grace."

"Immodest arrogance or extreme self-regard. So, what do they need to do about it?" asked Jamil.

"Demure marveling. Be so modest about yourself that

you can marvel at all the richness and diversity in other beings and in the world."

"I do that all the time," said Jamil.

"Is that true? Can you give me an example?" asked Heba. She was curious.

"Food. I never prejudge food and think I'm better than what people are serving me. I'll try anything, and I don't eat like a horse. They're so temperamental... and they eat all the time, though I tend to do that too."

Heba laughed. "Also, you never put on airs when you meet people, whether it's a stable hand or one of the Magi. They're all just people to you."

"Is there a difference? They all seem similar," said Jamil.

"That's what most people think about camels. We're all basically the same. Some people can't tell one camel from another," said Heba.

"They must be blind." Jamil said as he played with a grape.

"Many animals think their own breed is the best there is. If you simply love others as yourself then you treat everyone the same. That puts an end to extreme self-regard," said Heba.

"That's hard to do for some breeds," said Jamil. "I have trouble with wolves and those big cats."

"The Sustainer has created every manner of animal and each one has a purpose," she hesitated and raised her head. "Here they come."

✝

"Jamil," Mary called out as she entered the stable area.

She walked over to the stable, holding Jesus by his hand.

"Jesus, here's your friend Jamil. It's time to say goodbye."

Jesus put his little hand out and Jamil nudged it with his nose. The child giggled and pulled his little hand away. "I love you, Jamil," Jesus said.

Heba walked over and stood next to Jamil. Both camels' heads were over the half door looking at Mary, little Jesus, and Joseph.

"Say shalom, Jesus," Mary said, waving her hand. Jesus waved goodbye too.

"They're going back to Persia where their home is and we're going to where our home is. Jamil is going to become a racing camel and run like the wind. Heba is going to stay with him because she's his best friend," Mary said to Jesus.

Mary reached her hand out and petted both snouts. Jamil nudged her affectionately. A few years ago, she didn't want to have anything to do with these two beasts. They were the last gift of the Magi, refused. They were the final gift that the wise men from the East wanted to give her. She had rejected them, but the Magi had wisely left them in the desert where Joseph and Mary found them as they fled Herod. Now, she was grateful. They had carried her family out of harm's way and brought them back to the Holy Land. Part of her was sad to see them go, but she realized that a better life awaited them.

"Jamil, you promise that you will run like the wind. Make us proud of your strength. Do the best you can every time. You're going to a place that's better for camels than here in Galilee," she said, stroking his shooting star-shaped blaze.

"And Heba, you take care of this guy. He's a little impetuous at times and needs your wisdom and counsel." She stroked Heba's face and ears and then said, "Goodbye."

Joseph watched and then took Jamil's head in his hands.

"Thanks, Jamil. You're a terrific camel."

He reached over to Heba. "Thank you too. You are a marvelous lady camel. I wish you all the best."

They turned and left.

Outside the Gabae Stables, their new cart and donkey awaited them. Their possessions were not many, and there was a lot of room for everybody. Ravi and Casimer were standing with them and said their goodbyes.

"Remember Joseph, about three leagues ahead you will be able to see Sepphoris to the left. There will be a sign marking the road to Nazareth, but you'll already be able to see it off to the right."

"I will know where I am going by then," said Joseph with a smile. They were almost home.

†

"Casimer, look what I found on the contraption," said Ravi excitedly.

He showed his partner two beautiful tiny star sapphires.

"Where did you find them?" asked Casimer.

"They were embedded in the wood, and when we were taking the saddle apart the stableboy saw them. I am going to get the jeweler to appraise them and then send payment to the family."

"They could be worth a month's wages easily," said Casimer.

"We shall make a ring for each of us as a symbol of our partnership," said Ravi.

5

A PROMISE REMEMBERED

Thirty-Two Years Later

The Euphrates River ran silently in the distance. Its waters washed the banks at the turn near Babylon just as they had since time immemorial. The river had seen the coming of the Tower of Babel and the birth of many languages. For the river, one morning was not unlike another. It streamed on relentlessly like the passage of time. Today the river was swollen from the effects of a late-night storm. It would continue to rise for the next few hours and then gradually ebb.

It was early morning, birds were chirping, and the wind barely rustled the leaves in the trees. Abdul was already awake. He looked out the back door to his property at a nest of birds in a tall tree. The birds had finished raising their young and were now rarely in it. The little ones were off discovering the talents that God had placed inside them. Eventually, they too would build their own nests. He popped a freshly picked fig into his mouth and marveled at its rich sweetness.

With that thought, Abdul's attention drifted to his right. The small stone dwelling of his son Jordan's family was

attached to his own as was the custom in their small town. He could hear the stirring of grandchildren next door. Soon they would be eating bread and yogurt and then run next door to their grandparents.

His house was quiet for the moment. Soon his wife, Zaffira, and youngest child, Soraya, would be awake and the noise would begin. Women talk too much, he thought with a smile. His daughter was at the age where she had become a woman but was not yet ready to marry. She was a tough tomboy who dreamed of adventure and didn't want to settle down to marriage. He laughed at how unlike a boy she really was. It was becoming more evident every day.

Abdul and his family lived on the very edge of the ancient village that had existed along the banks of the tranquil river since before recorded history. Families kept their dwellings close together in this village.

Each family had a plot of land that they tilled for vegetables. The Euphrates was a very fertile plain and the land managed to support a thriving population.

After many years of travel throughout the region, he was finally settling down to a slower pace; watching the vegetables grow in the garden and the vast rows of wheat blow in the field. Abdul had spent the previous evening picking figs from his trees. He and his son would bring them to the market today. Their sweet golden insides were a treat to the palate, but there was not much money to be made because everyone's figs came in at the same time of the year. And while farming was a mostly rewarding endeavor, Abdul remained a camel driver in his soul.

Abdul's love for the adventure of the caravan had diminished as he grew older. He had two daughters who

were living in a nearby village, a son who lived next door, and a daughter who should have been born a boy. She would have been off on a caravan as soon as she was old enough. She had inherited his love for adventure, more than his son Jordan had. She was also the best rider Abdul had ever seen. Since she was old enough to climb on board a camel she was obsessed with speed. Every time Abdul turned his back, Soraya was on a camel dashing off, riding faster than most men. She was a natural. He hoped that she would settle down and raise a family one day.

Abdul was now a grandfather too and enjoyed the presence of his grandchildren more than the starlight filled skies of the vast deserts of Arabia and Persia. He had traveled to distant lands many times in his lifetime. He had visited the courts of kings, wandered through the bazaars of rich merchants, and traveled the trade routes to India. None of the voyages were more memorable than the one he had made nearly thirty years ago to Judea in the Roman Empire. That had been a trip that he recalled with fondness even to this day. Last night the storm woke him up, and he thought about that night after he and Nemir had left the two camels in the basin.

In the past, Abdul had wondered about what had happened to the bolt of fine linen fabric that he returned from the two camels given to the Holy Family. For a long time, he had forgotten it completely. Last night's howling winds and strong rains made the memory linger. It was not a night to be out in the desert wilderness.

Abdul heard the knock on the door.

"Papa," said Jordan walking in right after the knock.

Abdul smiled at his son. Jordan was a well-muscled

young man, almost thirty-two years old, and fully matured. He was taller than his father.

"We're lucky we picked the figs yesterday, before the storm hit," said Jordan. "We'll get a better price because the supply will be less."

"Don't rejoice in the misfortunes of others," said Soraya. She entered with a flourish, her smile lighting up the whole room.

"Aww, come on, I rejoice in our fortune, not in others' misfortune," said Jordan with a smile.

Abdul raised his eyebrow. Part of him loved to watch the children bicker as long as it was well intended.

"We pray that all the people of the world may be prosperous," said Abdul. He meant it too.

"And may they spend their money on our figs," Soraya said with a laugh.

"I have children to support," he said defensively. "Your nephew and niece to be precise. When you have your own, you'll understand."

"He's right," Zaffira, Abdul's wife said. She entered the room and took a pan and motioned for Soraya to fill it with water.

"Tea for the men," Zaffira said.

Soraya bristled.

"My brother can get his own tea," she said to her mother.

"But Papa can't," Zaffira said shaking her head.

Abdul watched the whole scene and wondered when it would end. Would his daughter ever find a suitable man and settle down? *She's too headstrong I fear*, he thought to himself.

"Let's get the figs," Abdul said to his son.

They had eight bushels of figs ready to go to the

marketplace. Jordan quickly started moving the bushels out to the front of the building where their camels were tethered. It was only a short distance to the marketplace but eight bushels were more than they could carry without their beasts. Jordan would go into the marketplace, help unload the beasts, and then bring the animals back to their confines. He smiled as he hoisted the first bushel. The huge camel was very still. It was a patient beast and had carried many large burdens in the past. The four bushels of figs were not much of a load.

"Abdul," called Zaffira. She had rare deep blue eyes and her name meant Sapphire in Persian. "Bring some fresh bread back from the marketplace."

"Can I go too?" Soraya asked.

Zaffira handed Abdul a crust of bread that he popped into his mouth along with another piece of fig.

"My father tries desperately to eat all the produce before we get it to market," said Jordan.

"I woke up hungry," said Abdul. It was a weak apology.

"Can I go, Papa?" Soraya asked again.

"You always wake up hungry father," Jordan said. He popped two figs into his mouth and picked up three more as he walked back into the house.

Zaffira raised an eyebrow and handed him some bread.

"I take after Papa," he said by way of explanation.

"Is somebody going to answer me?" Soraya asked. There was irritation in her tone.

"Come right back," said Zaffira. "Sell the figs, get some bread, and then I will leave for the center. I have a lot of small things to buy."

"Does your wife Jasmine have you so well trained

yet, son?" Abdul asked. It was more of a complaint than a question.

"She's working on it, Papa. Mother is a wonderful teacher."

Both men laughed.

"Please can I go too?" Soraya asked one more time.

The men stopped ignoring her. Abdul looked at his wife with a question in his eyes. She nodded.

"Okay, come along, but behave. No arguing with the merchants," Abdul warned his daughter.

"Let her ride your camel," said Abdul.

She was already climbing on board.

†

When the father, son, and daughter reached the marketplace it was already bustling with activity. Everywhere they looked there was a frenzy of movement signaling the sale or trade of merchandise.

"Let us go to Rheza, the baker, first and exchange some of the figs for bread. We'll get a better deal for the bread if we barter," said Abdul.

His son nodded. They had often made a straight exchange of merchandise with the baker. It was always better for them because the exchange was made at wholesale.

"Abdul, Jordan, and lovely Soraya," said Rheza brightly. He was a merchant who remembered the name of every customer, and every baked good that they bought. He could remember a wife's preference for specific breads, grains, and pastries. Rheza had a knack for making shopping effortless. He also gave children a lot of free samples. Jordan, who had his own son and daughter now, still expected a free sample.

"Hey Rheza," said Soraya brightly. "Here, try this!" She handed a fig to Rheza.

Rheza took the offering and nodded approvingly. He then broke the fig in his hand and held the fig further out, away from himself. He was trying to focus his vision on the inside of the fig. His eyes were losing their strength.

"Here," said Soraya, taking another fig and holding it far away. "How does this one look?"

"Don't mock me. When I was your age, I could see as good as you, but I couldn't taste as well as I do now."

"Why was that?" asked the now curious Soraya.

"Because I was always in such a rush that I swallowed my food before I could taste it."

"These figs are so sweet that even my son can taste them. And you know how fast he eats," said Abdul.

"Okay, I can make fine pastries with them, but let me pick the ones I want. Soraya, I have a nephew who will be by soon. I think you should meet him. He is handsome and very shrewd. He will make a fine husband.

"When I'm ready I'll let you know," she said with a laugh.

Abdul and Jordan stepped aside and let the old man select the ripest figs. Soraya helped him sort them quickly. When they were done, he handed them four loaves of bread. He knew exactly which ones they would have selected and took the liberty of giving them to Abdul and his son. To Soraya, he handed a baklava dripping in syrup.

"I hope it is sweet enough for you," said Rheza. "If you stay awhile, remember, my nephew."

"No thanks. The baklava is enough sweetness for one day," said Soraya.

"Don't go offering my daughter to your riffraff nephew," said Abdul.

"Riffraff! Abdul, he's a good boy, even docile enough to put up with your daughter," said Rheza.

"She's far too headstrong for him," said Abdul. He was serious this time.

The trio left the baker and entered the bazaar. They were looking for a fruit vendor, Aleppo, who was their distant cousin. His stand was piled high with fruits and vegetables. The fruits were set up to form pyramids on the outside of the stand. Aleppo was a loud and boisterous man. Selling fruit was not really about selling fruit but about giving recognition to people. He loved to yell out a person's name as they approached his stand. Aleppo was skinny and fidgeted quite a bit. He always had a knife ready to cut open an apple or an orange.

"Hey, look who's here!" Aleppo shouted when he saw his cousins. "The beautiful and exotic Soraya, her strong and handsome brother Jordan, and..."

Aleppo hesitated for a moment. He wiped his hands on his apron and greeted them warmly. He excused himself from his customers and started over to the two men.

Aleppo's wife was with him. She took Soraya aside.

"Help me with my customers for a few minutes. A young woman is good for sales," said his wife.

Abdul watched as she took the customers so that Aleppo presumably could busy himself with Abdul's figs.

"Abdul," he whispered, "come back here."

There was urgency in his voice. Aleppo motioned for Abdul to move toward the back of the stand.

"Take the bushels to my wife and help her set up the

display," Aleppo said to Jordan. He pointed to where he wanted Jordan to start setting up the produce.

"Come back behind my tent, Abdul," urged Aleppo. He looked around the town square at the bazaar. His face scanned the throng of shoppers.

Abdul walked back wondering what the intrigue was about.

"The bazaar was visited very early this morning by an emissary of a prince from Babylonia."

His cousin pulled out a handkerchief and nervously wiped his brow.

"Aleppo, there are many princes from Babylonia. What's one more," said Abdul.

"Yes, but he was looking for you."

Aleppo's face had *see what I mean* written all over it.

"What on earth for? What did he say he wanted?"

"He wouldn't tell me," said Aleppo. "I made the mistake of telling him that you were my cousin. When he refused to tell me his business, I got worried. He was accompanied by another man whom he consulted before he addressed me."

Abdul thought about it for a moment.

"I no longer journey. Did you tell them that?" Abdul asked.

"I did. The man simply smiled and went to wait for you. He is at the tea shop eating a pastry. He is armed, Abdul," said Aleppo.

"That doesn't mean he has bad intentions, Aleppo. Point him out to me and I will go speak with him," said Abdul. He was calm, almost pensive.

"Father," called Soraya. "There are two men out front who would like a word with you."

She was chatting amiably with them.

"Oh God, they're back. Tell me what you have done. We'll think of something quickly," said Aleppo.

"I haven't done anything. Stop worrying," said Abdul and then turned to his son. "Tell the gentlemen that I will be right there."

Abdul looked at his cousin for a moment and then laughed.

"When the conscience is clear of evil deeds, the heart is clear of fear," said Abdul.

The cousins walked out to the front of the fruit stand. Two men were waiting for them. They were obviously emissaries of a very powerful man, though one man, the older of the two was not dressed in traditional Persian garb. Abdul recognized it immediately as Arabian. Abdul studied them closely.

The first man, the Arabian, stepped aside as Abdul approached.

The second man, the elder, a Persian, stepped forward. He smiled warmly.

"I am Akreb. We are looking for a man called Abdul, a camel driver of some renown. This young girl proudly pointed you out as her father," said the Persian.

Jordan looked at his father and shrugged. He had tried to get her to stop talking but she wouldn't listen to her brother.

Abdul looked at his son and reassured him that it was okay.

"I am Abdul, formerly a camel driver, but as far as my renown, I am generally unknown outside of my town," said Abdul. He bowed politely, never taking his eyes off the two men.

"I am looking for an Abdul whose deeds were known as far as India in the court of Gaspar. I have been sent by my liege, the Magus Balthasar."

Abdul smiled broadly, but before he could say anything the younger man, the Arabian, stepped forward. He said, "I too look for this camel driver, Abdul. My name is Merak. I am from the court of Melchior. Our masters have need of your services."

Merak's voice was loud and clear. His posture was extremely straight, almost rigid, like a soldier's. He was handsome with chiseled features. His dark hair was pulled back, and his beard was trimmed short, Arabian military style.

Soraya was impressed by his rigid posture and yet graceful stiffness. She wasn't sure if it was because he was a warrior or because he was so strong but at the same time nervous.

"I am an old man and don't lead caravans anymore," said Abdul with a twinkle in his eye. A part of him started to hope and then grew excited. He noted with great curiosity the names of the Magi. His thrill was barely contained.

"Master Balthasar said that you were a man of your word, and you would remember that you made a promise which you have sworn to keep," said Merak. He looked Abdul directly in the eye as he spoke.

Abdul remembered his promise quite well.

"The time has finally come for the return of the cloth?" he asked, unable to contain his excitement.

"Of the task required from you, I have no word. I do know that Master Melchior has sent envoys to find a certain Nemir and asked that you assist us in finding him too," said Akreb the elder.

"Nemir! Yes of course, I can find Nemir for you," said Abdul.

Jordan and Soraya were studying their father's enthusiasm.

"Children, we need to return home and tell your mother that I must leave," said Abdul.

"Where will you be going?" asked Jordan.

"Can I come with you, Papa?" Soraya asked.

"To bring a final gift to a great king. It is a small token, I am sure, but on my honor, I have promised to one day deliver it," said Abdul.

The two men mounted Arabian stallions and followed Abdul and his children home. After Abdul made quick introductions, they stepped back and allowed the couple to talk privately. The intermediaries of the Magi waited patiently as Abdul explained to his wife that he had to leave.

"But how long will you be?" she asked.

"It couldn't possibly take more than six months," said Abdul.

"I will head to Judea, deliver my package, rest for a few days, and then return home," he said.

"It's just like you to take off and leave me with all the affairs of the house while you go entertain yourself in the court of a king."

Zaffira frowned at him. She was not angry that he was leaving but was concerned that it might be dangerous for an older man to be traveling such long distances.

"Will you at least bring our son with you?" she asked.

"No, he must stay here and manage our affairs," Abdul said to Zaffira.

Jordan nodded.

"You watch over the lands and take care of your mother, your wife, and the children," said Abdul.

"Can I go with you father?" Soraya asked.

"A girl can't go on a trip like this," said Abdul.

"I'll keep an eye on her for you father," said Jordan.

Soraya moaned, "Papa, please! I can cook, help you with the animals, and I could do your laundry too. You wouldn't smell so bad when you came back."

She was not one to mince words.

"I don't know," he said.

"You said that if you ever went on a caravan that was fairly safe you would one day bring me along," she continued to protest.

"I didn't think I would ever go on another one."

"Please?" she asked with a sad look in her eyes.

"I don't know." He looked at the two emissaries with a question in his eyes.

"You may bring your daughter with you to the court of Balthasar and make the request yourself. I do not answer for Master Balthasar," said Merak. He looked to his side to see if his colleague agreed. It would be an unusual request.

Abdul was struck by Merak's formality and Akreb's relaxed attitude. The older emissary was at ease and probably used to representing authority while Merak was young and less sure of himself.

"Well then," said Abdul, "make yourself ready, Soraya. We shall leave as soon as your items are packed."

Zaffira looked at her husband and her daughter. She loved them both deeply and was worried that the journey would be very difficult, but Zaffira knew that her husband

was capable of taking good care of their child. If Nemir was with them, she would be even safer.

The two travelers, with the help of Zaffira and Jordan's wife, quickly packed their baggage. They brought with them the traditional bedrolls that would fit over the camel's hump. It had been quite some time since Abdul had traveled to distant lands, but this would be the first long journey that Soraya had taken. Zaffira was used to having Abdul out of the house and on the road, but not having her daughter around would be very different. The families of camel drivers often tolerated separation. This was a familiar way of living for them. It was a normal part of the camel driver's life.

†

Abdul was excited. There was an energy and an enthusiasm that he had not felt in many years. Abdul thought about being present in the court of a king. He relished the idea of being treated as a royal emissary, not about the hard times on the road, nor about the dangers that such travel would entail. Years had gone by and expectations of this call had been gradually placed in the back of his mind with the fond memories of that first trip.

Soraya didn't really need her father's protection for a trip like this. They were probably going to travel through Roman territory. The Pax Romana had provided great protection for traveling merchants. She was young, headstrong, and courageous. She would relish her father's wisdom and experience but already concluded that when he traveled, he needed someone around to keep him organized. She saw herself as an extra hand, one of the guys, a camel driver.

Soraya didn't see herself as a girl. She was tough and

could ride a camel with the best of them. She was experienced in the care of the animals and had made a few very short trips with her father. She was allowed to accompany him more to appease her than anything else.

Zaffira and Abdul had hoped that the taste of the desert sand would leave an unladylike grit in her mouth, and she would soon forget her desire to go on adventures like her father did. It just wasn't done in their culture. It was dangerous. Instead of quenching her desire to travel, the few trips she did take had inflamed her passion for the caravan.

On one trip Abdul and Soraya had met a wealthy merchant and his wife who traveled together. She was in heaven.

"I am so excited!" said Soraya. She grabbed her bedroll and bound it to the camel's saddle.

Abdul smiled weakly.

"I won't let you down, Father... and I promise to obey," she said throwing more of her belongings onto her animal.

Soraya was concerned about her father. She knew that as a man aged, these journeys became more rigorous and more difficult to complete. She also knew that her father was impulsive and when together with Nemir, almost anything could happen. After a moment of thinking about her father and Nemir together, Soraya decided that if she did get to go it was going to be a lot of fun. In the long run, it was a caravan to the west, not too difficult and certainly easier than some of the caravans her father had been on to the Far East.

From Abdul's perspective, however, this journey was more than a simple caravan of traders traveling to the west to carry a piece of fabric to a king. It was the fulfillment of

an oath. This was the journey that Abdul had dreamt about for years. He had not just put it in the back of his mind with other memories of the newborn king but had sadly given up on it years ago. He remembered the time when after about seven years had passed, and Nemir had been by for a visit. They had concluded that the return trip would never be made. Abdul had been reluctant to let go of the dream of seeing the young king and secretly held out hope until about two decades had passed. Letting go of the goal somehow bothered him on a visceral level. He let go anyhow and had decided to get on with life. It was at that time that he retired from the caravan trade.

Now Abdul was ready to undertake the return. This was the journey to fulfill a promise made three decades ago. This was the journey to see the newborn king, now risen to his throne. The desire to go and the passion to keep his promise flooded through him like a river running rapidly in the spring. The intensity of the feeling startled him.

"How long do you think this journey will last?" asked Zaffira.

"That depends upon where the king is to be found. I will have to see what Master Balthasar and Master Melchior want us to do. I presume that the good Magi already know the whereabouts of the young king. Don't worry, I will send word as soon as I know where we will be traveling. I'll be able to give you a realistic estimate then," said Abdul.

Zaffira walked to the front of the house with her husband and her daughter. Jordan, his wife, and his two children met them.

Throughout the preparation process, the two emissaries of Balthasar and Melchior waited patiently. These gentlemen

were accustomed to serving others and thus graciously stood by while the family members said their goodbyes. They both knew that the journey contained uncertainties that no one could predict. They also knew that Zaffira had dealt with these uncertainties before.

Zaffira however, realized that Jordan's children had not had to deal with their grandpa being away for a long period of time. Jordan and his wife would have to get used to the children complaining about missing their grandfather just as Jordan used to miss his father. The fig didn't fall far from the tree. Zaffira was glad that Jordan had not develop his father's passion for traveling to faraway places. If he developed the 'taste for the unusual' as she called it, he would be certain to leave on many caravans.

Soraya on the other hand was another problem. She not only had the taste; she hungered for adventure. She was out of place on a caravan, but Zaffira knew that Abdul would protect her.

A strong sense of anticipation filled the air. This was a trip that Zaffira always knew her husband would eventually take. She hadn't given up on the idea. She remembered when he finally relinquished the dream and how his soul had ached. She sensed it and felt badly about his pain. She knew that this was more than just a trip. In part, it was a fulfillment of Abdul's destiny. It was the culmination of a previous journey that had been a pivotal experience in Abdul's life. Ever since Abdul had returned from that first caravan journey to visit the newborn king, he had been different, as though touched by a divine hand. He had been made gentler and more compassionate. She knew that a man could only live so long with an unfulfilled destiny. Abdul had been living with his

unfulfilled destiny for thirty years.

Zaffira hoped that this journey would bring Abdul a sense of completion to a task left uncompleted. She recognized that Abdul harbored a secret desire to see what had become of the young babe. If this journey allowed Abdul to finally discover what had happened to the child, then she was all for his traveling, even if it meant leaving the family for more than a year. She hoped it would only be six months at most.

Abdul's family moved outside the home. They were now ready for the short journey to Babylon. The goodbyes were brief but emotional.

"You be careful now," Zaffira told her husband. "And you, young lady, take care of your father and don't let him get into too much trouble. He's an old man now, and God knows that he should not be traveling all over the world."

"Yes, Mother, but you know how difficult it is to keep Papa out of trouble," said Soraya. She smiled as she kissed her mother goodbye. She then turned to Jordan, his wife, and two children.

"You be good for your parents," Soraya said to Jordan's children. She kissed them each. "I won't be there to watch you for your parents." Jordan pulled Soraya close to him and gave her a big hug.

"Soraya, be safe, and make sure you help our father," said her brother. He knew that his sister was the camel driver in the family. He knew that she was tougher than some men who went on journeys like this and that he shouldn't worry, but she was still his baby sister.

They each mounted their animals and started toward the city of Babylon. It would not be a long journey; just a quick trip along the pleasant banks of the Euphrates River.

The small winding road led to the area of the Euphrates River where they were going to have to cross in order to enter the main road that led to the city of Babylon. At this point in the river there was a wonderful bridge that was constructed of white limestone. Soraya's camel decided to stick his head over the side of the bridge to a look at the water. The men had made the mistake of not allowing the camels to drink when they approached the river system. Camels became preoccupied with the water when they cross a bridge. Abdul pointed that out to his daughter and smiled as he moved his mount between his daughter's camel and the river, blocking the view of the water.

"So how it is Master Balthasar these days?" asked Abdul. "I should think that the Magus is very old by now."

"Indeed, he is, sir. In fact, you will find that Master Balthasar is on his sickbed even as we journey. That is why we make haste to arrive in Babylon, so that you will be able to speak with him before it is too late," said Akreb, the older of the other two emissaries.

The news put a damper on Abdul's feelings and added an urgency to their trip.

Akreb, who was riding next to Abdul, dropped back. Merak, the younger, pulled up alongside him.

Abdul turned to Merak and said, "And Master Melchior, how is he?"

Merak straightened himself and rode at attention when he was addressed.

Soraya watched Merak's nervous energy and rigid posture with amusement. If she hadn't promised to be on good behavior, she would be teasing him. *He looks like there is*

a flagpole running up his spine, she thought to herself.

"My master is quite well indeed. You will soon see that for yourself because he is at Master Balthasar's bedside," said Merak.

"Soraya, my daughter, you will meet two of the wisest men in the world," said Abdul. He was excited about making the journey, but he was even more delighted at the realization that Balthasar and Melchior would be together.

"And where shall we find your friend, Nemir?" asked Merak. He was sitting erect in his saddle as if he was readying himself to look off in the distance.

"My friend Nemir lives nearby in a small village called Bahardea along the Euphrates on the other side of the river. We shall arrive there shortly," said Abdul.

†

"Soraya, legend has it that the village of Bahardea is so sleepy that the wolves can't stay awake long enough to catch the chickens. The chickens are so sleepy that they don't cluck with pride when they lay eggs. They actually yawn," said Abdul as they approached Nemir's town.

"Sure, Father. And Nemir sits on a rocking chair sleeping all day long because he's so tired," said Soraya.

"That's a fact. You're Uncle Nemir has gotten so lazy since we stopped traveling that he no longer gets out of bed to eat. He has gotten skinny. He's wasting away to nothing," said Abdul.

Soraya looked at her father and raised her eyebrows. She often referred to Nemir as Uncle out of respect. When her brother Jordan was born Nemir was present with Abdul. It was Nemir that had suggested the name Jordan, after the

river. As Abdul's family grew, his friendship with Nemir had grown too.

"You may find that hard to believe but wait until you see him," said Abdul.

The two emissaries kept a respectful distance and didn't intrude on the conversation. Finally, as they approached a small village, Merak pulled alongside Abdul.

"Is this the sleepy village of Bahardea?" he asked Abdul with a smile.

"Yes, it is," said Abdul. "Nemir runs a livery service on the outside of town. We should take the outer path and head directly there."

Abdul pointed to the fork in the road. He was thinking about how loud Merak's voice was when he spoke. He laughed to himself when he thought about how it would wake up the sleepy village.

A few minutes later, they approached the stables called the Hoof and Hump. It was a small stable that practiced husbandry, the art of breeding livestock. As its name indicated it specialized in both horses and camels.

"You didn't tell me that he bred horses," said the younger emissary.

"Camels too, but his horses aren't as good as your fine Arabian stallions."

There was a stable hand who had worked for Nemir for years standing outside. He was examining a fence that needed mending. When he saw Abdul, he smiled and motioned to go around the side. The men heard shouting from the side of the stables and looked off into the rolling green fields behind the stable. Nemir was sitting on top of a tall galloping camel yelling at the top of his lungs.

"Faster, you double-humped dromedary. You can do better than that. Come on, you're an embarrassment even for the town of Bahardea. How could you be so lazy? You're better than that. You were bred for speed," yelled Nemir.

The animal was flying down the hill at a pretty good pace. "Go, go, the race is almost over and you're about to win. Can't you feel it? It's the thrill you've been waiting for all your life. You were bred for this moment," said Nemir. The camel couldn't understand the words Nemir was speaking. He was motivating the camel with his riding techniques but kept himself pumped up by yelling.

The animal picked up even more speed, just as Nemir suddenly noticed the four men watching him. As soon as he realized that Abdul was among the men, he veered the animal toward them.

The sudden turn by the animal almost threw Nemir off, but he was strong, muscular, and had an amazing sense of balance for a man his weight.

"I thought you said he was thin," said Soraya.

"He must have gained some weight," said Abdul with a laugh.

"Papa, I think you were just telling me stories," said Soraya.

"It is the duty of a camel driver to tell stories," said the older emissary. "A good camel driver makes the time pass quickly on a long voyage with tales of misfortune that make us grateful for our own good fortune, tales of love that make us long for those left behind, and tall tales of…"

"Fat old friends who have grown so lazy that they nearly starve to death," said Abdul with a smile.

"Uncle Nemir!" called Soraya. She watched Nemir

skillfully bring the camel down the hill.

Soraya dismounted from her camel and joined her father who was already standing beside his own. Merak quickly alighted and stood calmly, waiting while Akreb slowly dismounted his horse. They both waited for Nemir to come to them.

"Is that you Soraya? You've grown so tall and pretty. You must take after your mother," Nemir yelled back.

As Nemir came closer he was able to evaluate the men with Abdul and Soraya. He saw their fine stallions and elegant saddles and realized that they were men of status and high rank. He hoped that Abdul had found some wealthy customers and was bringing them to him. He stopped his camel and dismounted. When he came close enough to Soraya, he took her hand and gave her huge dancing hug.

"Abdul, my old friend, who have you brought to visit me?" said Nemir politely letting go of Soraya.

"They are emissaries of the Magi. They have been sent by Balthasar and Melchior, who await us in Babylon," said Abdul.

The introductions were made quickly.

"Praise God, we finally go?" asked Nemir who immediately understood what the task at hand was.

"Yes, finally," said Abdul.

"I had never given up on the idea," said Nemir. "It always seemed a remote possibility... that was getting more remote."

"It was a remote possibility that was getting closer all the time, if you had never given up on it," said the older emissary.

Nemir nodded his agreement and headed toward the

small house next to the stable yard where he lived. He paused before he entered his home and bowed his head. The moment was not lost on the two men from the Magi's court.

"Is there something wrong?" asked Akreb.

"Nemir recently lost his wife. This will be the first time that he is traveling without his beloved to say goodbye to or to return to," said Abdul.

"He must miss her a lot, Papa," said Soraya. She saw the pain in Nemir's stride as he entered the house.

Nemir had a few words with his trustworthy hired help and then turned to his friends.

"Shall we ride camels or horses?" asked Nemir.

"As you wish," said Merak. "I prefer the horse, but it will depend on the route we eventually take. I presume that this time of year camels would be best."

"Camels it is then. We shall cut a dramatic figure in Jerusalem," said Nemir raising his right arm in the air and pointing to the west.

It had been many years since their first trip to Judea, but Nemir still remembered how everyone stopped to look at the Magi and the camels. He selected his favorite beast from the stable, and in a matter of minutes he was ready to travel.

6

THE COURT OF BALTHASAR

S trange smells filled the air as the five travelers approached the ancient city of Babylon. This was the last great city on the spice route from India. The cuisine was similar to that of the village of Bahardea, but the spices used here were varied. Merchants sold items that could be found nowhere else in the Western world. Though the great open bazaar was a short distance away, the rich aromas lingered in the air as though they were immersed in an exotic cloud. It was not too far past midday, and the men had not stopped to eat. Soraya was getting hungrier by the moment.

"Papa, will they have food for us when we arrive at the Magi's residence?" asked Soraya.

Abdul looked at the two men.

"The girl will not be disappointed," said the Akreb. "When I was your age I could consume great quantities of food, but you're only a girl so there will be more than enough."

"I ride like a boy, I can work hard, and I like to eat, but alas I don't eat like a boy."

"Oh," said Nemir, "Too bad."

"Uncle, boys eat like pigs," she said defensively.

"Are you implying that I eat like a pig?" Nemir asked.

He feigned hurt feelings.

"Uncle, have you ever raised a pig that ate as much as you?" she asked.

He loved to be teased.

"Only once, but it was a very big pig," Nemir said.

"Make sure you use your manners too," said Abdul.

"He's one to talk," said Nemir with a sheepish grin.

"Does my father sometimes forget to use his manners?" Soraya asked Nemir.

"Forget? No, I don't think so. I think he deliberately acts like he has none. It's so hard to take him to the courts of princes and kings.

"You're one to talk," said Abdul.

"It wasn't me who insulted that maharaja in the Indus Valley," said Nemir.

"How was I to know that you weren't supposed to pick up food with your left hand?" asked Abdul.

"You're left hand? I don't get it," said Soraya.

"Not only that, but you served one of the ladies of his harem with your left hand!" said Nemir.

"I didn't know," protested Abdul.

"Served ladies? That's very interesting. What was it you didn't know when you served them, Father?" asked Soraya. She was being coy, fishing for information.

Soraya was beginning to think that this trip would be a lot more fun than she could have imagined. Daughters have from time immemorial loved to discover the secrets of their fathers. Sometimes it was a good thing, often simply an embarrassment. She knew that her Uncle Nemir loved to embarrass her father.

"I didn't know that in India they never touched their food

with the left hand. They ate with the right and only used the left for other, less pleasant things," said her father.

"But you should have known. The merchant we were traveling with talked about their customs, and you fell asleep," said Nemir.

"I was lucky to make it home alive," said Abdul.

"Will there be strange customs in Jerusalem?" asked Soraya.

"One never knows. They are Jewish by race and religion but controlled by Rome politically. The customs change depending upon whose court you wind up in."

They were passing within a block of the great bazaar. The noise of shoppers and merchants arguing had grown from a soft din to a loud roar. People everywhere were carrying their wares in sacks or pouches. They were traveling along the side of the bazaar where merchants traded cloth. The bolts of fine silks and linens hung on great wooden spools outside of shops. Some temporary merchants had tents. A little further on there were permanent shops that sold silver and gold. They had massive doors that spoke ill to anyone trying to break in.

"What is that smell?" asked Soraya who lifted her nose higher and inhaled as they approached the meat market area.

"Roasted fowl… chicken, and pheasants I presume," said Akreb the elder emissary.

"I smell lamb," said Nemir.

"Goat," said Abdul. "That's goat, not lamb."

"You couldn't tell the difference if it was on your plate," said Nemir.

"Papa can tell the difference. It's goat," said Soraya.

It was becoming obvious that everyone was very hungry.

Soraya prayed that it was not much longer until they reached the dwelling place of the Magi. Her stomach rumbled almost as loudly as the bargaining shoppers.

A few minutes later, they found themselves before massive gates with ornamental iron on the sides and top. The gates opened to a palatial estate with rose gardens on the outside. Some of the roses climbed the walls and ran along the top, forming a protective barrier of thorns as well as a blanket of exquisite color. They were in full bloom with pinks, reds, and yellows bursting through the green of the climbing rose vine. Babylon had at least four full blossoms a year from their roses. The climate was ideal for many other flowers too.

"This is the palace of Balthasar," said the younger emissary. A guard opened the gate to let them in.

The palace was enormous. Turrets of stone stood high in the sky where men could watch over the city of Babylon.

Nemir looked up at the towers and smiled. Both Soraya and her father noticed Nemir's sly smile. He had a love for mountains and for climbing. Even though he was stocky he possessed tremendous upper body strength and loved to climb.

"Don't go climbing to the top unless you get permission. Besides, dragging a large object up that high into the sky has to be dangerous," said Abdul.

"You will be treated to a view of the city of Babylon from the tower, gentlemen," said Akreb. "It is one of the highlights of a visit to Master Balthasar's palace."

"I was thinking about climbing on the outside. I always wanted to be a mountain climber."

Abdul shook his head in disbelief.

Nemir suddenly stopped talking as the door made of

polished stone with a pink hue slowly opened to a wide foyer. A huge man dressed in black pants with a purple top and silver sash stood towering over him.

The enormous servant bowed to Merak and Akreb as they entered.

Spread out on the glistening stone was a colorful Persian rug, the likes of which they had never seen. On the walls were tapestries that were actual maps of routes to India, Arabia, and directly north to Mount Ararat.

"Do you remember the story of Noah's ark landing on top of that mountain?" whispered Abdul. He was in awe of the grand foyer.

"How could I forget such a story?" said Nemir. He looked up and back at the huge servant. "Did you ever see anyone that tall?"

"Don't go trying to see what it takes to get him irritated. He's twice your height and at least twice your weight," said Abdul.

They were led to a double doorway at the end of the foyer. The two emissaries waited while another servant opened both doors inward for the men.

"Master Balthasar, Akreb has returned with some gentlemen," announced the servant.

Balthasar was inside the room, resting on a couch. He looked very old, white-haired, and obviously in a weakened condition. Next to him stood Melchior, who was no longer a young man as the camel drivers remembered him, but a middle-aged man. His handsome features hadn't changed that much, but the gray at his temples stood out from the polished black skin of his face making him look even more distinguished.

"Ah, splendid. Gentlemen, please come in," said Melchior. He turned to the man on the couch and gently said, "Master Balthasar, they have arrived."

"It is good that you have come," said Balthasar. His voice was barely a whisper. "It shows that you are men of your word. I can also see that we have all grown older." There was a twinkle in his eyes as he said it.

Melchior motioned for them to each take a seat.

Balthasar motioned for Melchior to move closer.

"Who is the young girl with them?" asked Balthasar.

"I was just about to ask," said Melchior. He raised his eyebrows and smiled.

"Master Balthasar, this is my daughter, Soraya," said Abdul proudly. "I have a son who was born shortly after we returned home from our journey to the newborn king. She is my youngest."

"She is a fine-looking young lady," said Balthasar to Melchior. He looked up at Abdul and said, "Have you brought her along to accompany you on your journey?"

"If that would be permissible, sir," said Abdul.

"Permissible perhaps. The voyage will be difficult. What do you think Melchior?" Balthasar asked.

"I would normally not suggest that a mere girl travel across the desert," said Melchior.

Soraya bristled. She was not a mere girl and could ride a camel better than most boys.

"This is a very unusual journey, however," said Balthasar.

"Indeed, it is, sir," said Melchior.

"It is not often that a daughter gets to accompany her father on a voyage of spiritual significance," said Balthasar.

"There are dangers," said Melchior.

"Her father would permit it," Balthasar responded.

"Because the voyage is special to him, and he wishes to share it with his daughter," Melchior observed. He straightened his back and nodded; it was obvious that he would agree.

"This is as much a pilgrimage as it is a voyage of homage. We have been informed that the king is rising in power spiritually. From my dreams as well as Master Balthasar's, we have inferred that the newborn babe from many years ago is now a young man who has assumed enormous spiritual powers," said Melchior.

"He should be just about my son Jordan's age," said Abdul with a smile. Zaffira had been expecting during their first visit to Bethlehem.

The Magi nodded. Balthasar leaned forward and whispered to Melchior.

"Of course," said Melchior to Balthasar. He nodded to another servant who came to his side. The servant listened politely and then left. Melchior turned to the men and said, "We must offer you some refreshments. Master Balthasar wishes to know if you have eaten."

From the desperate smile on Soraya's face, he knew that they had not.

"I will attend to it my lord," said Akreb. Merak stood stiffly with him and exited to instruct the cooks.

Soraya's stomach rumbled loudly, but only Nemir and Melchior seemed to notice. Melchior smiled at the young girl. In some ways, she was like a boy. He wondered how much longer it would take before she outgrew her tomboy stage.

"Has your father told you about our visit to Bethlehem?" Melchior asked Soraya.

"Yes sir, he has many times," said Soraya.

"And has he told you that he and Nemir have given their word that they would return the cloth when required?" Melchior asked.

"Of course," said Soraya.

The door to the right of the Magi opened, and the servant who had whispered to Melchior reappeared with a bolt of linen in his arms.

"Ah, the famous cloth," said Melchior.

Balthasar nodded with a smile. He said, "We have kept it locked up and away from the moths all these years. Recently, we have had it laundered."

The servant laid the cloth at the feet of Abdul and Nemir. It was a beautiful piece of linen woven with a three-to-one herringbone twill with a Z-twist. It was obviously a very expensive piece of linen whose borders were sewn with linen thread.

"It was periodically washed with a soapweed solution to keep it from mildew," said Balthasar. "The Romans refer to it as a struthium wash. It's very effective."

"It looks as beautiful now as it did on our first journey," said Nemir.

"Can you be ready to leave at once?" asked Melchior.

Abdul and Nemir looked up and nodded.

Soraya reached over to touch the cloth. It was of excellent quality and finely made, but to her it seemed only a bolt of linen. It couldn't have been more than fifteen or twenty feet of cloth at most. She couldn't understand the fuss.

"We will cover your expenses because you are serving as our emissaries," said Balthasar. He was whispering in his weakened state. Yet he made the effort to be gracious.

Soraya strained to hear what he was saying while still rubbing the cloth between her thumb and first two fingers.

"It's just linen, Papa," she said softly to her father.

"Yes, fit for a king. It also represents my word and the word of your Uncle Nemir. What is a man if his word has no value? We made this promise years ago. We must make certain that as long as we still have the strength to keep our promises that we do."

Soraya looked at her father with admiration. It was a good thing to be raised by a man of honor and integrity. Her father was faithful to his word, even though at times he would lose his temper and huff and puff at everybody. What he thought was what he said, and what he said was what he did. Soraya was proud of her father's dependability. As a young lady, she was learning how difficult it was to be that consistent. She was learning that many men didn't keep their word.

"Soraya," interrupted Melchior, "Your father's word was his bond, a vow of sorts. We knew he would return the cloth. We never doubted that. What we have not ever been able to understand is why it didn't get taken by the young family. Gaspar, Balthasar, and I each had prophetic dreams that told us to purchase the cloth to begin with, and then we wound up returning with it. I personally was perplexed by it for years."

Balthasar leaned forward and spoke softly to Melchior, who nodded his head.

"Let me give you some history. The evening after we had performed the last ceremony at the Mount of Hystapes we each dreamt that we must bring frankincense, gold, and myrrh to the newborn king. We also dreamt of a contraption

to carry the baby on the side of the camel. Each of us, mind you, had the same dream. In it, one of the gifts we were supposed to deliver was the bolt of linen with a camel, a special camel with a blaze on its forehead. The linen was to be offered to the newborn king attached to that camel and not as a separate gift as the others were.

"We delivered the gold, frankincense, and myrrh, but the young mother, a woman named Mary, didn't want a camel. The little beast spit and had a temper tantrum as camels are wont to do. This frightened her and she politely refused. The night before we left, we had a dream in which we left the camels in a great basin. We decided to have your father and uncle deliver the camels to Mahktesh Ramon in the desert of Southern Israel. Mahktesh Ramon was a great chalk basin that sank deep into the earth on the side of the route that we took as we returned back home. Your uncle, I believe, decided the baby and linen both wouldn't fit in the carry seat and put his cap in instead," Melchior paused and looked up at Nemir.

"I prefer to blame Abdul," said Nemir with a broad grin.

Balthasar nodded his head at the comment as if he expected Nemir to deny it. It was obvious to the two Magi that even after three decades Nemir and Abdul had not changed much. Their friendship and their personalities had remained essentially the same. Nemir was still the clown. Abdul was still the worrier.

"We accepted the fate of the cloth and brought it back with us, but we considered that it always belonged to the child. It was his fabric to do what he wanted with it. Recently we both had a dream that the young man has ascended to his full powers. Though it was a strange dream indeed."

Balthasar nodded his head in agreement.

"What was the dream?" asked the ever-curious Nemir.

"We dreamt that he had been anointed with water and oil and was standing on a great lake looking to the shoreline where his subjects were. He was glistening white and shining with God's spirit."

The dream didn't make much sense to Nemir, but he was confident that the Magi would understand it. Magi had been using dreams to help them understand God's will for countless generations.

"May I ask a question?" said Abdul. "Did Gaspar send word that he had the same dream?"

"It's very perceptive of you to ask that question. Gaspar sent word to Master Balthasar just prior to my arrival. I was coming to see my friend and mentor after I had the dream," said Melchior.

"Do we know if the young man is the ruler of Judea yet?" asked Nemir. It was an unusually practical question for Nemir.

"Unfortunately, we have not received any word of his ascension to the throne. The land of Israel is still under Roman rule. We have questioned merchants who returned from Jerusalem in the last few years and heard nothing."

"Will we be bringing any other gifts to pay homage to the king?" asked Abdul.

Melchior hesitated and looked to Balthasar.

"We have weighed this question for a long time," said Balthasar softly. "We think that our only mission is to bring the cloth, to finish the first journey's task."

Nemir was a little disappointed because he had envisioned traveling with a large entourage and bringing

very expensive gifts. If the new king were vain or arrogant, a simple bolt of linen would have little value.

"We understand that the lack of proper tribute may compromise your status, but after careful consideration, we believe it would be in your best interest," said Melchior.

Balthasar sat back and nodded.

"Papa, am I missing something? Do we even know where the king is?" Soraya asked.

After a moment of pondering the question Abdul looked at Nemir, and then both men looked at Melchior.

"We do know where we are going, don't we? Nemir asked.

"Not exactly," said Melchior. "We presume that the young man, named Jesus, is in Judea."

"Do we know his last name?" asked Abdul.

"No, we simply know that he belongs to the House of David. That would be the royal family that he is descended from," said Melchior.

"I thought we would have more information. This could make it exceedingly difficult," said Abdul. There was worry in his voice.

"Well, we have a first name. That's a start," said Nemir. He was trying to be optimistic.

"We also have the name of the royal family," said Soraya, trying to be positive too.

"How many descendants could the House of David have?" asked Nemir.

"That's a problem. It's tens of thousands," said Melchior. "Apparently, there are a great many scattered through the territories of Judea and Samaria. It is even more complicated. The land that was under the rule of Herod has been divided

into three sections, but I still think the best bet will be to go directly to Jerusalem and make queries."

"Master Melchior there is a problem with this," said Abdul. He was being respectful, but his doubts were beginning to plague him.

"There are many problems," said Balthasar quietly.

"What if he hasn't ascended to temporal power? You have said that your dreams told you that he has spiritual power. What if no one has recognized his kingship yet? Or worse yet, suppose he is a rogue, a renegade, or an outlaw king? The Romans don't allow kings in their empire. My understanding is that theirs is a republic with Caesar as the imperial ruler of the whole empire."

"You know your politics well. We have thought about that at great length, which is why we believe it might be safer for you to carry just the linen. It would be less likely for you to run into trouble if the man is a rogue or rebel. Who would begrudge a simple piece of cloth to a man?" said Melchior.

"No gold, frankincense, or myrrh this time," said Nemir.

Balthasar leaned forward as said something that none of them could hear.

"Yes, of course," said Melchior to the older Magus.

The others waited for a moment while Melchior thought.

"It is difficult for me to send you on a journey such as this. When we first went, we followed a new star blazing brilliantly in the night. It led us to Bethlehem. At first, we lamented that we don't have that star to follow, but yesterday we dreamt of that little camel again. Nemir and Abdul, you remember him. His name was Jamil. He had a blazing star on his forehead. I think that he might be the key to finding Jesus the King."

"The camel? You mean to tell us that a camel could somehow lead us to find him?" asked Abdul.

"How is a dumb beast going to help us find him? Do you have the camel here?" asked Nemir. "He was a good little fellow—fast as the wind, strong, and temperamental—but I don't know how we're supposed to use the animal to find the king."

"Again, we must point out that we dreamt of the camel, not that we have the camel," said Melchior.

"This doesn't sound possible, Father," said Soraya softly. She knew that she was out of place to speak. Her father shot her a glance that said to hold her tongue.

"We believe the key to finding Jesus somehow remains with little Jamil. Our dreams showed us the camel's blaze, which looked like the star that we followed. In it we followed the camel's star back to Judea to find the king," said Melchior.

They were interrupted by Akreb and a host of servants bringing in plates of food.

"Pardon us gentlemen," said Akreb, but sometimes it is wise for men to hold a discussion for nourishment. The empty stomach is not always a cauldron for wisdom."

"How true, and the young lady seems to be quite hungry," said Melchior with a big smile.

"The empty stomach is often a stimulus to work," said Balthasar softly.

Bowls of food and plates were placed before them. Before they passed the food around Melchior looked to Balthasar who nodded and bowed his head.

"May the eternal light of the heavens who illuminates the world so that this food might be produced, bless those who grew, gathered, and prepared this feast. Bless us who

consume it, and may we use the strength it provides to fulfill your will and bring peace, love, and joy to all mankind," Melchior prayed.

There was roasted chicken on a platter and two large bowls of stew. One was colored orange and very fragrant and the other was brown, but its aroma was equally delightful. A large bowl of rice flavored with honey, milk, and almonds stood in the center of the men. Yogurt bowls were placed next to each plate. Servants stood at attention with gourds of wine and nectar of fruit.

Merak watched as Abdul and Nemir took rice pilaf and piled it on their plates. Then they took the stew from each bowl and placed it over separate portions of the rice. Each man was careful not to mix the two dishes. Soraya, on the other hand, was less careful because she was more concerned about eating rather than tasting the food. Nemir and his niece piled their plates high. Abdul wasn't that hungry and knew he could take seconds if it wasn't enough. Soraya was hungry and planned on taking seconds.

"Gentlemen," said Merak. He looked at Nemir and Abdul and then gave a wink to Soraya. "Could you take a moment and taste the orange stew and tell me if it is goat or lamb."

Abdul looked at Nemir and smiled. "Go ahead. You were the one who said you could smell the difference. You even get to taste it."

Nemir took a piece of meat on his fork and lifted it into the air with a flourish. He then sniffed it and then let his head drop back with his eyes closed as though he had just taken a whiff of paradise.

"Stop clowning around," said Abdul who reached over,

took a piece of meat, and unceremoniously popped it into his mouth.

"It's lamb," said Nemir with a smile.

"All that sniffing and swooning and you still can't tell the difference," said Abdul. He reached out, took a piece of carrot, dipped it into the orange gravy, and smelled it for a moment. "It is certainly goat, and I think it is cooked with carrots and saffron."

"Very good Abdul," said Akreb. "Nemir, your belly belies your culinary expertise. Taste the brown one and tell me if it is beef or lamb."

"What happens if I don't get it right?" he asked nervously.

"You can't have seconds," said Merak with a laugh.

"Why are you testing him Akreb?" asked Melchior.

"There was quiet a discussion about gustatory prowess on the way here," said Akreb.

"Lamb," said Nemir. "Pass the bowl. I get to have seconds."

They all laughed.

†

After dinner Balthasar excused himself.

The men stood as the Magus rose from his couch.

He moved off with assistance to another area of the palace for post-prandial rest. Melchior lovingly watched his ancient mentor move slowly across the stone floor. Each step was measured. The old magus practiced a patience with his weary bones that was born from years of wisdom.

"God bless you all. Have a wonderful evening. My home is yours," said Balthasar as he turned back at the doorway to address them all.

Melchior waited until Balthasar was gone. He smiled at them and said, "Is there anything else that you would like? I am prepared to take you on a tour of our city, if that would please you?"

Nemir, Abdul, and Soraya nodded in agreement.

"Good, then we shall start with a climb to the top of Balthasar's tower," said Melchior.

Merak and Akreb quickly moved to the doorway that they had entered. The men walked through the corridor and then made a turn to their right. A long hallway led to a small door at the foot of a winding stairway.

"This is the famous tower of Balthasar. It was built nearly three centuries ago by Balthasar's ancestors. The top has a bright gold canopy that has been called the tip of the candle by the inhabitants of Babylon."

"I'll bet the view is terrific," said Soraya.

"You can see ten leagues into the distance. The last time an army marched on Babylon, the Babylonians were able to predict their enemy's movements because of the tower," said Melchior. "The citizens proclaimed the tower was worth its weight in gold. Master Balthasar had the canopy put on in response to their gratitude."

"I love high places," said Nemir.

"Not me," said Abdul. "I prefer to have my feet on the ground."

"The best times of my life were on the mountain passes into India. They were magnificent," said Nemir. He pushed his way to the front of the line and then looked at Soraya. "You go first. You're younger and quicker."

They climbed the circular stairway quickly, pausing to

look out the square observation windows that were simply holes in the walls large enough to shoot an arrow out. As they reached the top, the stairway suddenly got much steeper, perhaps to limit the size of the opening so that more of the top of the tower was usable. There was a wooden platform that sat over the opening to the top.

"Just push up on the wood and then slide it to the side," said Melchior.

Soraya did as she was instructed. The wooden cover was much lighter than she expected. She slid it toward the center of the tower and then quickly pulled herself up through the opening.

Nemir was the next to come through the opening. "Ah," he sighed. He was thankful that the walls of the tower were not so tall that he couldn't look over them.

Next came Abdul followed by Melchior. Akreb and Merak waited politely.

"This is magnificent," said Nemir. He pulled himself up to the top of the wall and was sitting on the edge with his legs dangling inside.

Melchior looked at him and then back to Abdul.

"Don't worry about him, Master Melchior. He could climb up the outside of the building like a lizard. What a beautiful city," Abdul said with awe. "You can see the mountains off to the west."

"Papa, look over there, boats are on the river."

"What's that over there? The Dromidrome?" asked Nemir. He was looking north to a large structure with a track for racing camels in it.

"Yes," said Merak. "Have you raced your animals there?"

"Of course," said Nemir.

"There is a race this evening at sunset. Shall we go?" asked Melchior.

Nemir jumped down from the wall.

"Of course!" he said. He was excited.

"Then it is done. Do we need to spend more time up on the tower?" Melchior asked.

Merak held the trap door and motioned for them to descend. First Soraya and then the men climbed down. Merak closed the tower trapdoor. He was watching the young girl with fascination. She was a few years younger than he and was losing her tomboy appearance by the moment.

†

Brightly colored pennants flapped loudly in the evening breeze. The wind which had been calm earlier was picking up, cooling off the crowded open theater. The Babylonian Dromidrome was a long oval track with narrow turns at either end. Limestone stands sat on one side of the straightaway where the wealthier people watched the race. Opposite the stands was a slight incline covered with short grass. The general public watched the races from this area. There was a huge crowd already in attendance, and people were still streaming in.

At the north end was the entrance. At the south was the stable area. Many of the jockeys who would be riding tonight gathered in this area to watch their friends ride. This was the venue for some of the greatest camel races of all time.

"Papa, what are those men screaming about?" asked Soraya as they entered.

"They are wagering with each other. One is calling the

other a coward for not giving him better odds," said Abdul.

"The other is telling him that he's being played for a fool," said Nemir. He was smiling broadly. He hadn't been to the Dromidrome in a few years and wanted to see how fast the camels were compared to the animal he had been training. He hoped that he had a fast one at home, but there was really no way to tell except to enter him into the races and see what happens.

"Are you a gambling man?" asked Melchior, who was accompanied by both Merak and Akreb.

Nemir looked his way and nodded. "Only when I am fairly certain of the race. Here I would be out of my league."

Abdul shook his head no. "I have children to feed, and I can't afford such luxuries."

"The man didn't bet when he was single either," said Nemir referring to Abdul.

"You are a prudent man. Gambling is a vice that can grab a man's soul and twist it until he gives up on life," said Melchior.

"If you ever gamble," said Nemir, "only do it with money that you are willing to throw away. If you can toss the money into a fire without being concerned about it, you may be able to gamble with it."

They were walking up the steep limestone steps leading to where they wanted to sit.

"But you gamble, Uncle," said Soraya. "So, what's that about? I didn't know that you had so much money that you could throw it into a fire."

"It's money that I would be willing to live without. I place wagers on the horses and camels that I run. It looks very bad if you are unwilling to bet on your own beast."

"They pay you to bring a camel to the races. Isn't that so, Nemir?" asked Merak.

"Yes, precisely. They want fast animals, only the best. I raise the animal and bring it to the races. They let me bet on it, and then I sell it," said Nemir. "I never bet more than they pay me to run the animal. I make money when I sell it."

"There are some men, Soraya, who sell their souls to gamble. They wager on a camel and then scream and yell as though it were the end of the world when the race is on. When it's over all that they think of is the next race. I could never do that," said Abdul.

"And Mother would hit you in the head with her broom if you did," said Soraya.

All the men laughed.

This evening there would be four races followed by a final of the four camels that had run those races. Each circuit took about two and a half minutes to run. There would be a rest period of approximately one hour during which dancers were brought out on a platform in front of the crowd.

"Are you going to bet on any of the camels, Uncle Nemir?"

"Only the last race. I want to watch how the animals run to see which one I think will win," said Nemir.

Uncle Nemir explained the racing saddle and the techniques for making the animal move faster. Soraya was fascinated but was more interested in the bright colors that the jockeys and animals were wearing.

"It's mostly good breeding," said Melchior calmly. "The best animals come from the fastest ancestors. All the techniques make little difference."

"I disagree," said Nemir.

"Really?" asked Melchior.

"Really good nutrition and training are what brings the best out in an animal. Nowadays the camels are all fast, faster than they were when I was Soraya's age. The challenge is preparing them to run two races one hour apart."

A stranger moved closer and listened to the conversation. It was obvious from the way he dressed that he was a wealthy merchant.

"I would take good breeding over training, but you may have a point. Nowadays they look for both," said Melchior.

"If breeding is so important, how can you bet on the race without knowing what it is?" Soraya asked.

"You mean who the camel's ancestors were?" Nemir asked.

Soraya nodded.

The stranger stood even closer and listened. Nemir smiled when he noticed that the man was listening. The stranger smiled back. It was a warm sincere smile born of confidence.

"Do you mind if I listen?" asked the stranger.

"Be our guest," said Melchior.

"Good question, Soraya," said Nemir. "You need to talk to the owners. Most of the fans in the Dromidrome don't have any idea what the breeding is."

"I thought age was important too," said Abdul.

"Sure it is, but most of the animals are in their prime. They rarely race after a certain age."

"There was one animal called Blaze that raced well beyond its prime age," said the stranger.

"That's very unusual," said Nemir.

"It was the sire of an animal in the fourth race. I own a

great animal named Hot Wind. He will race in the second race."

"My name is Nemir," he said introducing himself and then presenting the others.

"I am Gilead. I am a fabric merchant from Pella. My animal will win its first race, but I am not sure that it will win the second," Gilead said.

"You're very confident about that first race," said Nemir.

Melchior and the others moved back as the merchant and Nemir started talking about camels.

"The Magus here is very perceptive. My animal is of the finest breeding, but in the last race is Candle Light, daughter of perhaps the greatest racing camel ever."

"What camel was that?" asked Nemir.

"Blaze. He was a jewel. For years I tried to buy him from a friend in Pella. I wanted to use him to breed. He beat the sire of my camel Hot Wind even though he was years beyond his prime."

"I have heard tales of Blaze. They say he ran faster than the wind and could race without rest," said Nemir.

"Did you ever see him, Uncle Nemir?" asked Soraya.

"No, but I wish I had. I didn't' get involved in racing until a few years ago. I never attended the races just to gamble. I had a fast camel and was encouraged to enter him by some of my friends. That's when I heard the tales of this Blaze," said Nemir.

"He was a great animal. Strong, patient, and had a cadence that barely caused the rider to move. He was as smooth silk and slipped around the turns like a river in bend."

"So, can I ask you something?" Soraya asked.

"Certainly, young lady," said Gilead.

"How will you know if you should bet against the offspring of Blaze?"

"I have to see how my animal runs. Then I will watch how Candle Light does."

The first race was about to start, and everyone turned to the circuit. A horn was blown, and the camels started racing down the track. At first, they looked like they would have trouble getting to top speed. They were accelerating slowly. They built up to top speed by the time they hit the first turn, and then they had to slow down. They reached top speed about halfway down the straightaway and then slowed down again at the other end.

The standard race was two complete circuits. When the camels thundered by the starting line a gentleman with a large pennant walked out to what was now the finish line. He stood on a high platform so that everyone could see him. Two spotters stood on opposite sides of the finish line. They would judge the winners.

Soraya couldn't believe the excitement. She had chosen a camel as her secret favorite and then cheered for it. It was running in third place and didn't look like it would win, but she could see herself on top of a camel riding to victory. Her blood was coursing through her veins with excitement. She wanted to be out on the track riding one of the beasts.

The camels thundered around the first turn and flew down the back straightaway. One of the riders fell off on the last turn, and a groan went up from some of the crowd.

Soraya's camel came in third. She was glad that she wasn't a betting girl.

An hour later it was starting all over again.

"Which camel is yours," asked Melchior.

"The one with the royal blue colors," said Gilead.

The camels had colored blankets under the saddles. The riders wore clothing that included a cloth hat that was tied with a strip of the same color. It was easy to tell which one was Gilead's.

"Merak, you may place a wager on my behalf for the fabric merchant's camel. The winnings will be given to the poor," said Melchior.

Nemir stopped speaking when he heard the Magus's words.

The animals lined up on the starting line. For a moment there was confusion, and then suddenly all the animals stood still. An instant later, the horn sounded and the beasts slowly accelerated down the track. That is all but one. There was an explosive acceleration by one animal. It was Gilead's Hot Wind, and it was in the lead.

On the first turn, the rider leaned inward to his left, almost laying down. The animal barely slowed down.

The lead grew by the time it reached the second turn and again the animal barely slowed.

Soraya was yelling for Hot Wind to win. She could see that the jockey was doing a terrific job and riding the animal exactly like she would have.

Nemir was jumping up and down with excitement. Melchior watched the chaos with his calm. Merak was stiffly waiting, ready to collect the wager and have money to distribute to the poor.

When the race ended, Hot Wind was six or seven lengths ahead of the rest of the pack.

"What a magnificent animal!" said Nemir. He was ecstatic.

"Father, did you see that?! What a beast. He's like the wind," said Soraya. Her soul was screaming at her, *You could do that if they let you!*

The third race started and went much the same way as the first, but the men weren't paying attention. A friend of Gilead, a man named Japor, walked up the steps to where they were standing to say hello.

"Gilead, you old fool. Would you like to bet against the daughter of Blaze?" the man asked.

"I'm not that much of a fool," said Gilead.

"Yes, but you are curious to see if your Hot Wind can blow out Candle Light's flame," said Japor.

An announcer called for the fourth race. There was a flurry of activity at the stables as the camels, with the jockeys on top, were led down the track. The men leading the camels brought them right up to marks on the track. Each one was numbered with a Roman numeral on a small slab of stone. As each camel arrived to their mark, the men quickly retreated away from the activity. It was not safe to stand on the track when a race began.

The camels lined up and were almost ready. A massive beast on the end kept moving forward nervously. It kept the starter from blowing his horn. It was a good sign that the animal wanted to run. Perhaps he was young and not yet accustomed to the start. On the other end draped in deep red with a silver studded bit and reins stood Candle Light. Her muscles quivered with expectation, but she was perfectly still. She was like an arrow pulled taunt in a bow. She was ready to fly, but perfectly motionless, patiently waiting for the right signal. On her forehead was a white blaze that was shaped light the flame of a candle.

"Would you like me to wager on Candle Light?" asked Merak.

"Don't bother, sir," said Gilead. "No one will cover your bet. No one bets against any of Blaze's offspring until they have been well-tested.

Nemir and Abdul were standing close together, pointing at Candle Light.

"Who does that camel remind you of Nemir?" asked Abdul.

"The blaze is a little different, but the white in the center of the forehead brings back memories. It's like Jamil," said Nemir.

Melchior was listening to the two of them and took a closer look at Candle Light. "You're right, gentlemen. The animal bears a resemblance."

"What are you talking about, Father?" Soraya asked.

"See the marking on the forehead of Candle Light?"

"Sure," said Soraya.

"Well, Jamil had a mark that looked like the star that the Magi followed to Bethlehem," said Abdul.

"It was more like a shooting star or comet," said Melchior. "It's an auspicious sign that this animal should remind us of Jamil."

"Who is this animal Jamil?" asked Gilead.

"He was a beast that the Magi gave as a gift a long time ago," said Nemir.

"And he had a shooting star blaze on his forehead?" asked Gilead.

"Yes," said Nemir.

"How long ago?" asked Gilead.

"Thirty years ago. He would be a pretty old beast at this time."

"He was fast?" Gilead asked.

"Like lighting," said Nemir.

The horn blew and the race started. Candle Light burst forward ahead of the pack by at least two lengths.

"Jamil could have held his own against any of these animals," said Nemir. His attention was focused on the race as was Gilead's.

On the first turn, the jockey leaned in, but was obviously not as skilled as Gilead's young man. Candle Light was still ahead but had lost a few paces. Down the next straightaway her speed picked up, and she separated herself further from the rest of the camels. She slowed on the turn just a bit. It was obvious that the jockey was taking it easy and looking to preserve an easy win.

Soraya watched the jockey closely and became more irritated with each turn.

Into the long straightaway that passed in front of the stands, the animal seemed to push herself. As they hit the turn, the jockey had to hold on for dear life. Candle Light didn't want an easy victory. She wanted to run full out, not just win the race. Soraya could see it, and so could most of the crowd. She wished she was on top of the animal. She would have ridden it to an even greater victory.

The jockey had no other recourse but to let her run her race. When she crossed the finish line, she was ten lengths in front of the second-place camel.

"Wow. She is awesome," said Soraya.

"Runs like Jamil too. She has that easy gate that doesn't rock the rider much at all," said Nemir.

"I can almost picture the special saddle on him now," said Abdul nostalgically.

"Me too," said Abdul.

"Remember the time he ran from the wolves in the desert?"

"Faster than what we just saw," said Abdul in matter-of-fact way.

Melchior smiled. He remembered too. He also remembered his dream. His reverie was interrupted by the music and dancers. The entertainment portion of the evening had started.

Gilead was off making bets for the final race with the four winners. He was confident because his jockey was much better than Candle Light's rider. He knew that the race would be close, but often the margin of winning was the strength and experience of the rider, not the speed of the animal.

Gilead was walking up the steps toward his group so that he could watch the final race. There was a small group of men on the periphery of the group who had made wagers with Gilead. They were there to enjoy the race with him and perhaps to taunt him. It was all in fun though.

"Won't Candle Light be more tired than the rest of the camels, uncle?" asked Soraya. She had decided that Candle Light was who she was going to cheer for.

"It's all a matter of training. That's one of the reasons the merchant Gilead is willing to bet against her," said Nemir.

Gilead reached the group and turned around to watch the race. The final preparations were being made. The four animals were led out from the stables and walked down the track. They were paraded in front of the stands so that everyone could see them.

"Master Melchior, might I ask you a question about that

animal you had given as a gift to someone many years ago?" said Gilead.

"Certainly," said the Magus.

"Did you give him to a merchant from Pella?"

"No, a carpenter and his wife," said Melchior. "They were from Bethlehem I presume."

"Oh, that's too bad, because I thought for a moment your Jamil was the famous racing camel known as Blaze," said Gilead.

"Really?" asked Nemir.

"Blaze had the famous comet on his forehead, but the owner was from Persia, a small city by the name of Pella."

"What did the comet look like?" asked the Magus.

Gilead motioned with his hands and drew the comet in the air.

"I only saw the animal about ten years ago. He was at the end of his illustrious career, but he was still a wonderful animal all the same," said Gilead.

"He had an easy gate that hardly moved the rider?"

"That's exactly what he was like, Nemir," said the merchant.

The race was almost ready to begin.

"Who was the merchant from Pella?" asked Melchior.

"His name escapes me for the moment," said Gilead. "I do remember he owned the camel in partnership, and the two men became wealthy racing him."

"Do you remember anything else?"

"Yes, there was one other thing I remember about the merchant. The gentleman always brought an older camel along to accompany Blaze. It was always there with Blaze. He was a bolt of lightning and it just sauntered around slowly.

They were inseparable except during the race."

"It was a female camel, right?"

"Yes, Nemir. How could you have known that?"

The horn blew and the crowd roared. Candle light and Hot Wind shot out of the starting area like arrows out of a hunter's bow. People were cheering wildly. Gilead was perfectly calm and watched. He had placed a lot of money on his camel and rider and wanted to watch what happened like an impartial observer. He stood quietly and waited for the first turn.

Hot Wind took to the inside on the first turn. He was as fast as Candle Light, and they arrived at the turn neck and neck. Hot Wind's jockey leaned in and whipped the hind quarters of the animal. The camels swung around the turn at an unbelievable speed.

Candle Light's jockey pulled up a little and entered the turn to the side of Hot Wind. Then she slipped behind Hot Wind and followed through the turn. When they hit the straightaway, Candle Light's head was next to Hot Wind's jockey.

Gilead nodded. He wasn't displeased, but it wasn't as much of a lead as he had hoped for.

"Go! Run!" yelled Soraya. She jumped up and down with the crowd.

"Who are you cheering for daughter?" asked Abdul. He was yelling to be heard over the roar of the crowd.

"Candle Light, Papa. I want them both to go as fast as they can, but I hope Candle Light wins," said Soraya.

In the straightaway, Candle Light quickly pulled even and when they entered the turn she was ahead by the length of her neck. She was on the outside again and fell back a little

into the turn. As they entered the straightaway, Candle Light poured on the speed and was ahead by a neck coming to the next turn.

Again, her jockey slowed her down just enough to leave Hot Wind in the lead. This time he was ahead by almost a full body. Candle Light picked up speed on the straightaway and almost caught up with Hot Wind coming into the last turn.

The crowd was roaring mightily as the camels pounded into the turn. It was no longer a four-camel race. The race was between two great animals and would be decided in the last stretch. Each time they moved into the straightaway, Candle Light had been able to catch Hot Wind by the time they got to the next turn. This time she would only have half the straightaway until she reached the finish line.

The referee with the pendant suddenly realized that he was engrossed in the race. He needed to be on the platform to monitor the finish. The two spotters were already in place as he scurried up the steps to the platform.

Gilead was feeling confident. All Hot Wind needed was a small lead coming out of the turn to be able to beat Candle Light. It would be only a few more seconds. He smiled and stood calmly watching as they moved around the turn.

†

Candle Light was a natural race animal. She loved to win and hated to lose. She hated to be held back by her jockey and wanted to run full open. In the turn she felt the slight tug on her reigns but refused to slow down. The two camels came out of the turn neck and neck.

Now it was hers to win. Her jockey let her go. He had no

choice. She was going to run with reckless abandon until she passed the finish line.

Hot Wind's jockey started to whip the hind quarters of his animal in a fruitless attempt to get him to run faster. Candle Light heard the whip crack and picked up her pace. She was pulling ahead.

The crowd roared as she passed the finish line. The pennant waved.

✝

"Shall we walk down to the stables?" Gilead asked. He had just finished paying off the last of his wagers. He was good natured about it. He laughed and shook hands with everyone as they said goodbye. Most of them enjoyed teasing him more than winning the wager.

"I would be interested in meeting the owner of Candle Light," said Melchior.

"You have a hunch about who Blaze really was?" Nemir asked.

Melchior nodded.

"What's going on, Father?" asked Soraya.

"We will find out in a few moments," said Abdul as the group walked down the stairs and then headed for the stables.

"Gilead, I have waited ten years to beat you!" a voice yelled from the distance. It was Chad, a merchant from Basra who owned Candle Light.

"Chad, you scoundrel. If I didn't know better, I would say that you cheated," said Gilead.

The Magus waited patiently to be introduced.

"Cheated? That's nonsense. I had the faster camel," said Chad with a huge grin that told everyone he was extremely pleased.

"Excuse me, I'm sorry," said Gilead to Melchior. "I would like to present the Magus Melchior. He is a good friend of this city's famous Balthasar. He was telling me an interesting story of an animal he gave as a present many years ago to a carpenter."

Chad looked at him with a question in his eyes.

"This camel is not from a carpenter. She was sired by a camel owned by a man from Pella. She was born in Basra from my best racing she-camel."

"I know that, but Master Melchior would like to ask a few questions," said Gilead.

Melchior stepped closer to Chad and smiled.

"I really would like to know about her father, Blaze," said Melchior. "Are you certain that this animal was sired by that animal?"

"Absolutely. I provided the female and had to bring her all the way to Pella to get her husbanded by Blaze. It is a long trip from Basra to Pella."

"Yes, I know. How many years ago did you go there?" Melchior asked.

"It was about seven years ago," said the merchant from Basra.

"Do you have the name of the man who owns this camel Blaze?"

"Yes, sir, he is called Casimer. He is well known in the city of Pella," said Chad.

Melchior looked at Nemir who was standing next to him trying to contain his excitement.

"Nemir, do you wish to ask a question?" Melchior said graciously.

"If I may sire. This camel Blaze, did he have a mark on

his forehead that looked like this?"

Nemir bent down and drew a comet in the dirt.

"Yes, precisely," said Chad. "You have seen him race before then?"

"Not race, but I did see him a long time ago, I think," said Nemir.

"Was there another camel with him, an old female?" asked Abdul. He couldn't contain his excitement either.

"Yes. There was always this companion camel. They say she traveled with Blaze even when he raced," said Chad.

"See, just like I told you," said Gilead.

"Did this Casimer ever mention where he got his camel from? Did he tell you who sold him Blaze?" the Magus asked.

"I never asked, and he never mentioned it. We talked mostly about the races that the animal had run. He had a partner there visiting him from somewhere in the West. I forget where," said Chad.

Melchior looked around to see if there were any more questions.

"I guess we're going to Pella," said Soraya excitedly.

"Yes, and we will start first thing in the morning," said Abdul. There was a hint of worry in his voice. He tried to hide it.

"We'll have a grand time, Father," said Soraya.

Abdul admired his daughter's enthusiasm but wasn't sure what they would find in Pella.

Melchior and his group bid the camel owners goodnight and started back toward Balthasar's palace.

"How long will it take to get there, Father?" asked Soraya.

"I am not sure. There are two routes. One is north through Palmyra. The roads are better, but it will take us a few weeks

longer than the southern route," said Abdul.

They all could hear the worry in his voice.

"We should take the old trade route through Aram toward Palmyra. We can head north to the Decapolis region. It is held by the Romans and is fairly peaceful," said Nemir.

"What's Aram?" Soraya asked.

"Syria, girl. Didn't you study your history?" asked Nemir.

"The route will take you through the desert of the Nabateans. It would be much faster. That's how we came back if you remember. You should then head to the Roman held Amman and over to Filadelphi and north to Pella," said Melchior.

Abdul hung his head.

"What's the matter my friend?" asked Nemir.

"That would mean crossing the Arabian desert."

"So, you've done that before," said Nemir.

"Not at this time of the year," Abdul said.

"What are you worrying about?"

"I'm not sure this is the best time of the year for the oasis," said Abdul.

"It would save us at least a month," said Nemir.

"He has a point. It would be quicker to travel through the Arabian desert. It might only take a month, while the northern route could take two or more," said Melchior. "I think we best speak of this to Balthasar and ask his wise counsel."

7

THE DRY ROAD TO PELLA

They were awakened early to the sounds of servants scurrying around talking. Men were rushing to pack provisions for weeks of travel in the desert.

Abdul woke Soraya with a fatherly shoulder shake.

"Get ready quickly. We depart early," he said to his daughter. "I have already sent word to your mother that we are leaving."

They dressed quickly and walked into the great room. Nemir was already awake. He had just started discussing the route with Melchior.

A few minutes later, Master Balthasar entered with the assistance of two servants. One carried a parchment with a short message of greeting for the king. Balthasar had agreed that the southerly route was best.

"The important issue is to gauge your provisions correctly so that you make it to the next oasis. There you can replenish your supplies and head out to the next. You must be especially careful of the water you carry. The distance before Filadelphi is long, and it will be extremely important to manage properly."

"We might need an extra camel as a pack animal at this time of the year," said Abdul.

The other men nodded in agreement. The extra camel could carry water for the others.

Melchior motioned to Merak to make a note of it.

"Stable the pack animal in Filadelphi and then proceed north to Pella. You'll make better time if you travel lightly from that point on," said Melchior.

Abdul and Nemir both nodded in agreement.

"When you get to Pella, I want you to purchase Jamil and Heba back from this man Casimer. Explain to him that you are going to travel to Judea to visit the original owners. I have a feeling that after all these years he might be persuaded to let go of the animals." Melchior handed Nemir a small bag with gold coins.

"Yes, Master Melchior," said Abdul.

"Excuse me," said Balthasar.

"Yes, sir?" Melchior looked at Balthasar.

"Take them to my armory," said Balthasar.

"To the armory?" Melchior asked.

"Yes, you know that this is not a good time to pass through the Arabian desert. I had a strange image in my dream last night. I saw a wolf chasing Nemir. It was amazing how fast that short round body moved," said Balthasar with a smile.

The others smiled too. It was an image that was not too difficult to conjure up.

But Abdul was worried about his daughter.

"If there is the possibility of danger, then I will have Merak escort them," said Melchior.

"Yes, my liege," said Merak, standing at attention.

"An armory, Papa?" Soraya asked her father.

"A man of Master Balthasar's status would have to have a small armory. It is responsible to protect your home," said

Abdul to his daughter. He was worrying more now.

"If I am going to be chased by wolves, then I would like a sword and a good knife," said Nemir. He was looking at the crossed swords that hung on the wall.

"A broad sword is not as effective as a spear against a wolf," said Merak. He had risen from his seat and walked over to the door. "It is this way, gentlemen."

"At least they won't need hoods to protect them from sandstorms this time of the year," said Melchior.

"Pack hoods for them," Master Balthasar said to one of his servants.

"Why, Master Balthasar?" Melchior asked.

The servant paused waiting for a response. Balthasar simply nodded to him to get the headgear and didn't respond to the question.

Melchior shrugged his shoulders as if to say, Balthasar knows best. They got up and headed to the armory. The entire group, except Balthasar, proceeded down the hallway and into a short stairwell. At the end of the stairwell was a doorway that led to the armory.

"This is amazing," said Soraya as she entered the room and saw the cache of arms.

There was an unspoken problem that was not being discussed directly. This was the time of the year that caravans stopped taking the southern route. It was harder because of the climate. There would be rain and mud. The temperatures would be colder, especially in the evening. They had discussed these problems. What no one was talking about was that the reduced traffic on the southern route meant that the bandits who patrolled certain areas were more daring and more dangerous. Men were expected

to be able to defend themselves, but increased numbers of caravans meant security. It was a security that they would not have this time.

Nemir thought about the possibility of a wolf chasing him and decided that a spear looked fine. He picked one up that was leaning against the wall.

"It's all in the balance. You need to be able to move it quickly and yet keep the attacker at a far enough distance," said Merak. He picked up a broad sword and a lance. As soon as Merak's hands touched a weapon he was transformed. It was immediately evident that his rigid posture was really the fine-tuning of a warrior.

Full armor, which included a helmet and shield, would be out of the question and only slow them down. They were after speed and efficiency. Chances were good that if they were attacked showing a willingness to fight would go a long way to protecting them.

Melchior was not convinced that there would be a problem, but he was a practical man. He knew that Merak was a highly skilled warrior and could defend them. If anyone was foolish enough to attack them, Merak would be very intimidating. Often a man's will to fight was determined by the fear in his opponent's eye. Thieves were more likely to press an attack on individuals who were afraid or unwilling to protect themselves.

"Is it really so dangerous, Father?" asked Soraya.

Abdul looked at his daughter. She was the love of his life.

"The Pax Romana doesn't extend into a small portion of the trade route. We must be willing to defend ourselves," said Abdul.

"The more willingness you have to defend yourself, the

less dangerous it is," said Nemir. "Just don't cut yourself with that sword and you'll be okay."

Soraya had a beautiful short sword in her hands. It was longer than a dagger but smaller than a full sword. It was lightweight. She was opting for speed.

"Are you going to allow the girl to carry a weapon?" Melchior asked.

"It shouldn't be necessary," said Merak. "I will be there to defend them."

"It is up to the father," said Melchior.

"Abdul, should the little rowdy be given a deadly weapon?" asked Nemir.

Soraya shot him a dirty look.

"Everyone should be armed, Uncle. It's a person's duty to defend oneself," she said.

"Give her something light and easy to use," said Abdul.

"And very sharp," she added.

Merak looked at the small sword she was holding and shook his head.

"Here try this one. The balance will be better for you and it's very sharp," said Merak.

He took a small knife with a delicate blade and an ivory inlaid handle and said, "This is a lady of the royal court's weapon. I will show you how to hide it and retrieve it quickly."

The soldier then picked out a pair of throwing knives and put them in a special sheath. "Would you mind showing me how to throw those knives?" asked Nemir. He was holding his spear in his right hand. Merak nodded to Nemir and looked around to make sure everyone had a proper weapon.

As they walked out of the armory, Merak motioned

for one of the servants to bundle a net. It was his favorite weapon. He preferred a net to a shield and could gracefully flick it into the air over his opponent in an instant.

Merak smiled to himself as the net was rolled and tied with slip knots. Within the hour they were ready to leave.

"May the Eternal Creator of the universe bless you and keep you in the palm of his hand as you make your journey westward," said Melchior.

"My blessings for a safe journey," said Balthasar, and they were off.

†

The first few days of the southerly route took the small caravan through verdant fields. As they proceeded westward, the route was marked by small villages that grew less frequent the further from Baghdad they traveled. Between the villages rolling sheep pastures were dotted with animals and their shepherds. The pastures were shorn short by the grazing animals, which made them look barren. The further west they proceeded the fewer villages and houses, until it was obvious that they were in the desert.

Nemir was humming a soft tune to himself. Off in the distance was a rumble of thunder.

"You seem glad to be in the desert, Uncle," said Soraya.

"It is where I am most peaceful," said Nemir. He looked up at the sky and noticed the thin clouds that were slowly obliterating the stars. In a few minutes, only the hazy outline of the moon would be visible. They were followed by even darker clouds which were off in the distant west.

"A man should learn to find peace wherever he finds himself," said Merak. He too noticed the sky but was looking

over the hillside, his eyes searching for something.

"This is true, sir. I first found that I was capable of peace in the desert. It grounds me to the experience of trusting God. Gradually it has spread to other places and other times in my life, but the peace of the desert is unlike any other."

"Father, was Uncle Nemir always such a philosopher?" asked Soraya.

"No, he wasn't," said Abdul.

"What changed you?" Soraya asked her uncle.

"Old age," said Abdul. He was answering for his friend. Abdul looked into the sky and then back to Nemir.

"Are you saying that your friend has grown older and become wiser?" Merak asked.

"No, I think it's because he has grown older and doesn't have the energy to act as unwisely as we did when we were younger," said Abdul with a laugh.

Nemir gave his friend a look that said, *Don't put words in my mouth.*

"Oh, I'm sorry. Was I answering for you?" Abdul asked with a sly smile.

Merak shook his head. The two friends had been bantering nonstop for hours. He seemed to have spotted something that interested him.

"I've become wiser, calmer, and more serene as the years go by," said Nemir. He too spotted something.

Everyone kept a straight face, but Soraya couldn't hold it back and started to laugh. The rest did too.

"We should stop for the night and set up camp. Right, Papa?"

"Soraya, my daughter. Do you see the clouds off in the distance?" Abdul said. He was looking at Nemir again.

"Yes, Father. It's a storm that is coming," Soraya said. She was unconcerned.

"Do you see streaks of rain falling from the clouds?" asked Abdul.

"No, just the fog underneath."

"That's right, no rain streaks, but it's not fog, Soraya," said Nemir.

"No, it's not," said Merak. "What about that small cluster of shrubs and rock?"

"Looks good to me," said Abdul.

Soraya was more confused than ever about the conversation.

"It looks like fog," said Soraya.

The men turned their camels toward the shrubs. Everyone was calm but their speed picked up.

"Is it a sandstorm, Father?" asked Soraya. Now she started to worry.

"Yes, but it's a long way off. We're on a higher plane here and we can see about ten leagues. If we were in the full desert, it would come on with maybe two minutes warning."

I've heard they're very dangerous," said Soraya. She looked at her father and then to her uncle.

She was looking for clues to how worried she should be. If they were worried; they weren't showing it.

"If they catch you by surprise they are. Your father and I have been in many of them," said Nemir.

The men dismounted and calmly positioned their camels in a partial circle around the bushes.

"What do we do when it hits, Uncle? Is there something special I need to know?"

There was a hint of fear in her voice.

"Don't breathe the sand," said Nemir. He was standing inside the circle tethering camels together.

Abdul laughed at his friend and shook his head. Don't scare my daughter. Remember she's tougher than most boys.

The animals went down on their knees, and one by one their burdens were unloaded.

"It's strange don't you think?" Abdul asked Nemir.

"Yes, we are too far east for this to occur," said Nemir.

"Could it be that some evil force doesn't want us to visit the king?" Merak asked with a raised eyebrow.

"I hope not," said Abdul.

"Strange though, it seems to be taking it's time reaching us," said Merak. "It almost has me lulled into complacency."

"Well, don't get too complacent. They move faster as they get closer."

The older men knew that a sandstorm could move very rapidly before it blew out. A caravan could be in the desert at the base of a sand dune, and when they reached the top, they would suddenly run into a storm. It was dangerous to be at the base of a dune when one struck. The side of a large sand dune could collapse and bury a traveler before he even knew what hit him. Often the camels knew where the best site to hide was. When a camel driver tried to get the camel to go down and wait out the storm, the animal would refuse until he picked a better spot. It was instinctive for the camel. It was learned by the camel driver.

What made it more dangerous was when the rains came right after a sandstorm. That meant that the caravan would be covered with wet sand and mud. The wet sand wasn't dangerous in and of itself, but it slowed everyone down. In an environment where a day's delay in getting to

the next oasis could mean death, extra weight was a major problem.

"Make certain all the packs are sealed tight," said Merak.

"The water jugs are fine, as are the yogurt pots," said Nemir. It was a custom to carry yogurt in clay pots in the desert. For untold centuries desert nomads had been carrying their boiled milk, transformed into yogurt. It would last for weeks if it was covered properly.

"Cover the yogurt well," Abdul shouted. "You're the only man alive I know who can eat yogurt with sand in it. The rest of us like it plain."

"You just have to learn to keep the sand from the teeth," said Nemir with a laugh. He finished lashing the packs and was getting ready to sit down.

Abdul and Merak were putting on their face veils. This was a hood with a veil in front that covered their head, ears, and nose. The veil was then pull tight over the eyes to keep the sand out. They would sit patiently with the storm battering them until the winds died down. Then they would come out of their face veils.

Merak finished first and then tucked each arm into his sleeves and waited. He sat erect. A sandstorm was hardly reason enough to have bad posture.

"Here, niece, let me help you tighten the veil," said Nemir. He motioned for his niece to sit down next to her father and then adjusted the way the cloth was positioned.

Soraya felt the first stinging sensation of sand on her hand and then remembered how Merak was sitting. She tucked her hands into her sleeves and relaxed. She felt a hand checking her sleeves.

"Be patient child," Abdul said. "Even Uncle Nemir

doesn't do much talking during a sandstorm."

They sat back and waited. The wind changed its sound to a strange hum. It was deep and soft. It got louder as the storm came closer.

With the fabric pulled tightly over her nose and mouth, Soraya started to worry that she wouldn't be able to breathe. She had to keep reminding herself that her uncle and father didn't seem nervous, so she probably didn't have too much to be concerned about. But she worried in spite of herself.

The air felt heavy. It was almost a weight pressing against her. It was as though there was not enough room in her skin to fit her body. Soraya started to sweat. She was taking deeper breaths trying to calm herself down. She tilted her head back to get more air into her chest and her veil loosened slightly. She could feel the wind-blown sand stinging her closed eyes. The sound was louder now, more like a buzz than a hum. It was as though she was sitting inside the stomach of a huge evil insect, and it was buzzing as its stomach tried to crush her. She pushed aside the ridiculous thought. It was too bizarre to contemplate. *I'm in a sandstorm with Papa and Uncle Nemir. I'll be all right,* she forced the thought to stay in her mind.

Soraya reached up to reattach her veil and make it tighter. The sand stung her hands. She realized that if her skin was unprotected for even a few minutes the sand would grind the skin right off of her. She had heard tales of men running blind in a sandstorm and dying from the sand burn.

Was the veil tight enough? she wondered. She forced herself to sit still. She still felt like her skin was too tight and that the world was closing in around her. Her breathing continued to bother her. If she could only get a little more air, she would

feel better. She moved her legs and realized that the sand was covering her feet. *What if we are buried alive in the sand?* she thought. She had heard of men getting covered with sand while they waited out a storm. The buzz increased. It became a roar.

Suddenly the impulse to jump up and free herself from the sand gripped her. She couldn't shake it. She wanted to stand up and run until she was free... until she was away from the sand and away from the sound.

"Now is the time to practice patience," yelled Merak over the roar of the wind and sand. "Patience is the key!"

It struck Soraya as funny that Merak had to scream to be heard and funnier yet that he was screaming to remain patient. He didn't sound patient. Patience seemed like an impossibility. The wind was buzzing. The sand was burying them, and she had that almost uncontrollable urge to jump up and run. Only now it was stronger.

Soraya felt her father's hand on her knee. Then she felt her father's shoulder against hers.

"When this is over daughter, ask Uncle Nemir about the time in Western Egypt. It will make you laugh until you cry," her father yelled into her ear.

Feeling her father's hand on her knee and hearing him speak had a calming effect. She took a deep breath.

"How long will this last, Papa?"

She was trying to be brave. She was trying to get rid of the feeling that everything was closing in.

"Not too long. Do you hear how the sound of the wind and sand has changed?"

"No," said Soraya. She was straining her ears with every ounce of concentration she could muster.

"Yes, Soraya, the wind has changed. It no longer has that deep rumble to it, just the buzzing noise. It's getting lighter by the minute," said her father.

"You're nuts," shouted Nemir. "I don't hear it getting any less noisy."

"Come on Nemir, listen to it," Abdul shouted back.

"That's what you said that time in Egypt. You claimed you could hear the winds change. Do you know the problems that caused me?" yelled Nemir.

"How did I know you had to go to the bathroom?"

"I got my backside sanded and couldn't sit down properly for a week," Nemir said. He wasn't shouting as loud anymore, and the winds were dying down.

"How long do we have to wait until we take these stupid hoods off?" Soraya asked.

"The camels will stand up when it's time. They don't want to kneel down too long," said Nemir.

Soraya took her hand out of her sleeve and reached over to touch her animal. The beast was breathing easily and seemed calm. Suddenly it stood up. The other animals did too.

"I guess the camels think it's over," said Abdul.

"I hope so because I'd hate to get a sand burn again," Nemir said laughing.

Soraya felt hands on her veil. When she pulled the face cloth off, she saw that her father had his hood off and was helping her untie her own.

Merak was beaming. "Very good, men," he said, "and lady."

"This was a small one," said Nemir.

"It bothers me," said Merak.

"Why?" Soraya asked.

"Because this is not the season for sandstorms. It is most unusual for us to have this kind of storm at this time of year," said Merak. He was fingering his hood.

"Good thing Master Balthasar asked us to bring the hoods," said Nemir.

"Strange actually," said Merak. "Remember how Master Melchior questioned him about them and he just nodded to his servant to get them? No discussion or anything."

"I thought that was strange too," said Abdul.

Nemir gripped his spear and worried.

†

The next morning brought a cool breeze and a magnificent sunrise. Sleep had washed away the remnants of any anxieties and refreshed the memories of the storm— rewriting it as a brave battle they had fought, overcoming and rather bravely withstanding nature in her glorious fury.

"Soraya, did you know that many people, especially those who live in cities, don't often see the sunrise?" asked Nemir. The deep red that was emerging from the royal purple made him feel passionate about life.

"Why is that? We see it all the time at home," said Soraya. She was barely paying attention to its breathtaking beauty.

"That's because I taught you to get out of bed in the morning when it is still dark, before the sun rises to greet mother earth," said Abdul.

"Thanks Papa, but I think you taught me to rise early to milk the cow, make sure the fire didn't go out, and to get you your tea."

"A man who rises early is wiser than the fool who takes extra rest," said Merak.

"Did Master Melchior teach you that?" asked Soraya.

"No. I had a good father too," said Merak with a smile and a wink to Abdul.

"I used to try to convince my father that if I rested a little longer in bed, I would have more energy to get my chores done," said Nemir.

"What did your father say to that?" Soraya asked.

"He said that he could better motivate me with the cat-o'-nine-tails."

Everyone laughed.

"Laziness is a great sin. You should work until you can't do it anymore. Then you can say that the day hasn't been wasted," said Merak.

"My father—your grandfather, Soraya—used to tell me that those who worked hard were privileged to eat well," said Abdul.

"My father said the same thing," said Nemir. He rubbed his belly and continued, "I really took that advice to heart."

The men bantered for a while, but there was something on Soraya's mind. She didn't want to ask and seem impolite, but after thinking about it there was no way for her to solve the dilemma. She had to ask.

"Merak, would you mind a little question?" she asked softly.

"Certainly Soraya. Just ask," said Merak.

"Why did you think it was so important to yell patience during the storm?"

"Did I yell?" he asked calmly.

"You screamed," said Nemir. "Scared the living daylights out of me. I thought I was going to drop dead with fright."

Abdul looked at Nemir and then both men started to laugh.

"I didn't mean to frighten you. I was recalling a lesson from Master Melchior, and it seemed important to communicate it to you all during the storm. I was afraid that I wouldn't be heard over the sound of the wind," said Merak.

"He taught you how to be patient in a sandstorm?" Nemir asked. He was still laughing about it.

"Not exactly. He taught what he calls passionate nonchalance," said Merak.

The two older men looked at each other as if to say, *What is that supposed to mean?*

Soraya, however, thought out loud. She said, "I don't get it. What is passionate nonchalance supposed to mean, and how is it related to a sandstorm?"

"Being nonchalant to Master Melchior is to have poise and spontaneity and yet be calm and unaffected by the trials and tribulations of life. For Master Melchior, it is facing life with composure and ease, never giving in to the impulse to be embarrassed or feel awkward."

"Aplomb," said Abdul.

"A what, Father?" asked Soraya.

"It means coolness," said Nemir. "Melchior was always a cool one. Nothing seemed to bother him. Do you remember when we visited the court of Herod? He marched in there and was at home. The Roman Emperor himself wouldn't have been so calm."

"Master Melchior is a genius, but part of his genius comes from trusting the Creator. That's what makes him unflappable. We've seen it in action," said Abdul.

Nemir nodded.

"It's more than that. I've watched him for a decade now, and I've listened to him talk about how patience is the greatest virtue. He claims that patience is the foundation for real charity and tolerance. Without patience, you have no hope. I can hear his words in my mind. Hope is founded on patience."

"Okay, so why were you screaming then?" asked Nemir. He had a big smile on his face that told Merak that he was being teased.

"Sometimes, I'm not too relaxed," he admitted.

"I wasn't too relaxed during the storm either," said Soraya. She was defending Merak.

They were becoming fast friends. The two younger travelers were bonding because of the adversity. Nemir and Abdul were aware of it and approved, but Abdul was wondering if there was more than friendship. Was his little girl finally attracted to a man? Was his little girl growing up and becoming a woman before his very eyes?

Abdul looked over to Nemir. He was certain that Nemir had noticed it too. He would keep a closer eye on them.

"Your father and I never had much patience for this sort of conversation," said Nemir. He never knew when to stop teasing.

"Uncle Nemir was never much of a philosopher," said Abdul.

Merak looked at both of them. He was shocked, and then it dawned on him that they were both teasing him.

"To tell you the truth, Merak," said Soraya. "I'm glad you yelled. I was starting to panic. What you said really helped."

"Thank you," said Merak with a nod.

Soraya was telling him in a subtle way that he had come to her rescue. Something inside him was delighted.

†

A large cliff stood off in the distance. It had what looked like the face of an elderly man with a big nose protruding awkwardly from it.

"We are approaching Filadelphi," said Nemir. "See the old man in the mountain. The Romans call it Proboscis Mount. It means we are about a day's journey away."

"What man?" asked Soraya.

"Right there, Daughter," said Abdul. He was pointing to the cliffs.

"I don't see him either," said Merak.

"It's a rock formation. See where the trees stop and there is bare rock? Look a little higher and you will see a profile," said Abdul.

"Actually, you'll see an ugly profile. That nose is big enough to hit with a stick without hurting his face. I once knew a guy that looked just like that," said Nemir who was suddenly very animated.

Everyone else turned to watch him speak. A story was coming.

"Do you remember, Abdul?" said Nemir graciously. It was evident that he was in the mood to clown around.

"When?"

"It was about thirty years ago. I remember because the entire trip you told us stories about how brilliant Jordan was. I think he had just started talking. We were in Damascus delivering spices for that Persian gold merchant," said Nemir.

Soraya was annoyed that the subject of Jordan's brilliance had come up. He was the one that everyone thought was so smart and she was just a girl.

Abdul hesitated for a moment. He noticed Soraya wasn't listening.

"Sure, I remember. The gold merchant had a lady friend who owned an inn and he wanted to send her some spices and perfumes," said Abdul.

"That's right. Do you remember her husband?"

"The drunkard?" Abdul started to laugh.

Nemir nodded.

Soraya was paying attention again.

"You're right! God was he ugly," said Abdul.

"That's him. Can't you see him. Remember when he suspected the gold merchant and his wife?"

"Yes, his nose turned purple with rage," said Abdul.

"He drank so much that his nose was always red," said Nemir. He laughed and rubbed his own nose.

"But he suspected everyone. He didn't trust his wife. I think the alcohol made him crazy."

"Do you remember when I put the piece of hay in his nose while he was sleeping," said Nemir.

"Yes, and then you yelled snake!" Abdul said.

"He jumped up and thought that a snake had crawled into his nose."

Nemir was laughing and pointing at the cliff.

"He thought his nose was big enough for a snake to hide in," said Abdul looking at Soraya and then back to Nemir.

Soraya watched the two men laugh hysterically. She had never seen her father have so much fun over something so stupid.

"What was it you said to him when," Abdul paused to chuckle, "when he jumped up with the straw in his hand?"

"Yes. He was screaming," said Nemir. "I said be quiet or

you'll wake up that snake. Then you pointed to the floor next to him and he jumped out of his skin," Nemir said.

"Yes, and those rocks look more like him with every step we take," said Abdul.

"I always wondered why she stayed with him," said Nemir.

"Understanding women is a mystery that men will contemplate but never comprehend," said Merak solemnly.

Soraya gave him a look.

"The young man speaks with the voice of such experience," said Nemir playfully.

"No, I am just repeating what I heard my father say," said Merak.

"He was a wise man then," said Abdul.

"Men," Soraya said grumbling.

The sun was slowly sinking behind the small mountains to the west. It was almost time for them to set camp for the evening, but the days were longer now, so they could cover more distance before sunset. Proboscis Mount was just above them now.

"I'm glad that the nose doesn't fall off the cliff," said Soraya. She was turned sideways in her saddle and straining to look up.

"It doesn't look like much of a nose now," said Merak, who was also looking up at the cliff.

"It will when you get to the fork up ahead," her father said.

"I'll race you to the fork," Soraya said to Merak.

"A girl could hardly beat me on a camel," said Merak with a smile.

Soraya took off.

"He's in for a surprise," said Nemir who watched Merak race after her on his magnificent beast.

"That's the truth. Can you imagine what she would do on an animal like Candle Light?" asked her father.

Soraya reached the fork in the road just ahead of Merak who was laughing.

"Beaten by a girl?" Soraya asked.

"You started before me," said Merak. "Nevertheless, I am deeply impressed."

Merak and Soraya turned to look at the older men.

"We take the north fork, Daughter," said Abdul. He answered her questioning look.

"Where does the other road lead to?" Merak asked when the two caught up with them.

"That's the road to Esbus. The Esbus-Filadelphi fork comes just after Proboscis Mount. Everyone knows that," said Nemir.

Off in the distance they heard a lone wolf howl.

Nemir reached down and touched his spear.

Abdul shuddered. "I think it's time to make our evening camp. We will be in Filadelphi tomorrow and staying at an inn."

Abdul's feigned cheerfulness didn't calm Nemir but alerted him to the fact that his friend had heard the wolf too.

"Where shall we make our camp?" Merak asked.

"I would prefer the other side of that grassy field near the rock," said Abdul.

Nemir was looking at it too. It provided protection on one side and made the camp easier to defend. It was only a short distance through tall grass to get there.

"The camels could graze, but I like that spot over near

the stream," said Soraya. "I hate when you make me the water girl."

But Nemir had already pulled his camel's reins and was heading toward what looked like the safest location.

Soraya shrugged her shoulders and said, "I guess we're not going to discuss it tonight. The old man must be tired."

Suddenly Soraya's camel froze. The animal tensed and its muscles twitched. Soraya could feel its fear. The camel spit and moved its front legs back, throwing Soraya off and to the ground.

Soraya sat up, and then she froze too. Now she understood the animal's fear. Directly in front of her in the grass was a huge snake coiled and ready to strike. Soraya didn't know what to do. The slightest movement would cause the animal to launch its body toward her. She knew that she was in range and in danger. She didn't move a muscle, just prayed.

"Hold still," whispered Merak, who was ten feet away trying to keep his animal from bolting. He had a throwing knife in his hand and was slowly raising it.

Abdul and Nemir's animals had been spooked and were further away. They dismounted carefully. Nemir grasped his spear with both hands, while Abdul looked in the grass for more snakes.

Suddenly, with a flick of his wrist the knife flew out of Merak's hand and impaled the snake. It twisted in agony for a couple of seconds until Merak's sword ended its misery.

"God help us," said Nemir whose spear just impaled another. He decapitated it to make sure it was dead.

Abdul's camel bolted for the road and was followed by Nemir's. Merak held the reins of Soraya's animal and handed them to her.

"Be careful. There is a nest of snakes here. This is a very poisonous type," said Merak.

His sword flashed, and a moment later another snake was dead.

Nemir was jumping up and down and stamping his feet. He looked like a man gone crazy. There was fear written on his face.

"Make vibrations. It will scare them away and then head to the road," said Nemir. He decapitated another and picked up the carcasses of four snakes.

When they got to the road Nemir had four headless snakes hanging over his shoulder.

"What in God's name are you doing, Uncle," said Soraya who was still shaken by the incident. Snakes made her skin crawl.

"They are venomous, dangerous, and disgusting to look at, but tasty. I am going to cook them."

"You're nuts. I'm not going to eat a poisonous animal," said Soraya.

Merak looked at Soraya and Nemir, wondering who was right.

"I mean what Nemir said is right. They're delicious, just hard to catch," added Abdul.

"Let's set up camp near the stream," said Soraya. She was in no mood to eat snake. Some dried grains and a little yogurt from the pot would suit her just fine.

✝

When the aroma of the roasted snakes filled the air, Soraya's stomach started to growl. She had made a promise to herself that she wouldn't eat the things, no matter how

good Uncle Nemir insisted they were. She was starting to wonder though if she had made a hasty decision.

The fire was roaring, and the welcome heat made the atmosphere seem alive and happy. Nemir was telling stories that Abdul had heard a thousand times before, but he was telling them for Soraya and Merak's sake.

Abdul was egging him on. The provocation was unnecessary, but welcome. They were a team. One clowned around and the other applauded. Soraya was starting to see why her father and Uncle Nemir had gone on so many journeys together. The friendship was deep. The respect was broad and the tolerance for each other's goofiness was immense.

The aroma of the roast tantalized Soraya's senses.

"Smells good, doesn't it?" Nemir asked Abdul as he slid some of the meat off the spit.

"Wonderful," said Abdul, trying to take a taste. He burnt his fingers, so he blew on his piece.

"There's enough here to feed four more men," said Abdul as he handed an entire spit to Merak.

The young man smiled gratefully. Merak's appetite matched his energy. He ate even more than Nemir but burned it off with an unceasing tenseness. He was a young man who fidgeted and never seemed to relax. He spent an enormous amount of energy on vigilance and ate an equivalent amount of food.

"Come on Soraya. Take a taste with me," said Merak. He already had a piece in his mouth and was making faces like he had died and gone to heaven.

Nemir went right up to Soraya's face.

"I saved the best one for you," he said.

"You know, it does smell wonderful," Soraya said, "but I promised not to eat any."

"You don't have to keep that promise," said her father. "It was made in haste and in a moment of fear."

"Yes, niece, a moment of fear. Or do you still fear the snake. It's probably because she's just a girl and won't eat it," said her uncle.

The taunt worked. Soraya grabbed the cool end of the spit and slid the meat off into her dish. She looked at the rest of them.

They each stopped what they were doing and waited.

She looked at it for a long moment struggling to convince herself that it was okay. Then she took a bite. It was just a tiny, dainty little bite.

"She eats like a girl," said Nemir.

Soraya took a big bite.

They all laughed.

"Hey, this is good. I mean, this is better than I thought, much better," admitted Soraya.

"Yes, we all knew that. They're just too difficult to catch and not worthwhile to raise," said Nemir. "If not, I would have started a snake farm."

A wolf howled off in the distance.

"Who will keep first watch?" asked Nemir. He was suddenly on edge. He remembered the words of Master Balthasar and had no intention of trying to run away from a wolf.

"I will, Uncle," said Soraya. She had heard the wolf this time. "If I can eat snake with you men, I can fight a wolf."

They laughed.

Nemir looked at his spear. It would be close to him tonight.

"Save the layer of fat from the snake. I need it," said Nemir.

Abdul nodded like he understood, but Merak and Soraya didn't have the faintest idea why. She wasn't eating the fat anyway.

"Now, tell me, what does it taste like?" Soraya's father said with a broad smile.

"I was going to say chicken, but it's sweeter," said Soraya.

"It tastes like snake," said Merak. He was matter of fact about it. "Nothing tastes like snake. I hate when people say it tastes like chicken. Nothing tastes like chicken except chicken."

"Well, there is this fish from the Mediterranean, a kind of pufferfish that blows up when you scratch it. It tastes like chicken," said Nemir. He was pretending to be serious.

"See that's what I mean," said Merak seriously. "I've had pufferfish stew, pufferfish grilled and roasted. It tastes like pufferfish, not chicken."

Soraya was smiling. "Tastes like chicken to me. I would never have known that I was eating serpent."

"How do you know you're not eating pufferfish, niece?" Nemir asked.

"I don't, Uncle. This may be some other food too," said Soraya.

She was watching Merak's response to her teasing. She didn't notice that her father and uncle were watching too.

"And why do you say that?" asked Abdul.

"Well father, it's simple," said Soraya. She looked to her Uncle Nemir for the answer.

"Because it tastes like chicken!" said Nemir playfully.

Merak shook his head. "Tastes like snake, marvelously

prepared mind you, but snake nevertheless."

Merak was dead serious but playing. They had never seen him play before. He was only just a little less rigid.

When they finished the meal Nemir prepared bastones or fire clubs. He took pieces of dried wood and shaped a handle out of the bottom and then placed them in the fire. He continued to turn each one until it had a layer of charcoal all around it. When the bastone was pulled from the fire it burned brightly. Nemir then put the bastone out with a little dirt and brushed them off carefully. Then he took the left-over fat from the serpents and rubbed it into the wood.

"How do your bastones work, Uncle?" asked Soraya.

"You stick them into the fire and a few moments later they ignite. Fire will keep wolves at bay. They don't like it a bit," said Nemir.

†

Merak didn't want third watch. He wanted last, but Nemir had insisted. A wolf waited to kill toward the end of the night when its prey was sleepiest. Both men knew that the wolf had the instinct to tell if its prey were asleep, so it was essential to keep awake.

But Merak was tired. He had eaten too much, and the heavy meal left him feeling sluggish. *A little more time,* he told himself, *and he would wake Nemir.*

Merak was an early riser. If he could keep himself awake a little longer, he would be wide awake and vigilant. Once he was awake the two hours earlier than usual that came with fourth watch, he could stay up the rest of the day. After he was up, he was fine. He should have insisted on the last watch. Third watch was the one he had the most trouble with.

The smell of fragrant tea made him feel warm inside. He knew the blend but couldn't quite remember what it was. *Where did the tea come from?* he wondered, and then it hit him with a jolt. He was dreaming!

A hand on Merak's shoulder was shaking him gently. His head came upright with a jerk. His eyes opened wide. Nemir's square face with a finger over his lips warned him to keep silent.

Merak understood immediately. He reached to his right for his sword and then laid his left hand on his net. He picked them up slowly. He was ready for battle. Every muscle was tense. Energy coursed through his body and up his spine.

The men knew that wolves didn't hunt alone. They came in a pack. Merak knew that they would attack suddenly and try to separate their victims. Worse yet they might go after the camels and scatter them. Without the camels the men would be lost.

Soraya was up now. She heard the noise in the distance. She turned her head to look at Merak and then back to her father. She watched for a signal from her father who was silently moving toward the camels. They were tethered together and starting to get nervous.

Merak moved slowly.

"The bastones," whispered Nemir.

Soraya picked up two and brought them to the fire. Abdul had already thrown more kindling and more wood on it to make it burn brighter.

Merak and Nemir stood on one side of the crackling fire waiting. Merak's usual tension was intensified. Every fiber in every muscle of his sinewy body was tense. He felt most alive just before a battle.

"Take two bastones each and stand to the sides of the camels," said Nemir.

Abdul and Soraya followed his orders. They held the bastones out from their sides creating a protective barrier of fire.

Merak smiled tensely. He was nervous but now it was turning into excitement. He knew his net and sword could handle at least one of the wolves, but no one knew how many there were.

There was a loud snarl from the side with the camels.

"It's a feint. Wolves are smart. They are going to attack on this side," yelled Merak.

Suddenly a wolf leapt out of the cover and made a lunge toward the camels.

Soraya was startled. She instinctively shoved the flaming wood right at the wolf's face but missed. The wolf backed away and snarled viciously.

She was suddenly more angry than scared.

"Don't go after it, Soraya. They want one of us to separate away," said Abdul, who was fighting the impulse to attack the wolf that just attacked his daughter. He knew his girl was tough, but a father wants to protect a child no matter what.

"Stand closer to the fire," Merak shouted.

Nemir turned to look.

"Don't turn, Nemir," screamed Merak. "It's a diversion. The pack is going to attack on our side."

Then it came, three wolves at once. One headed directly at Merak and two at Nemir.

Merak was ready. The net flared suddenly and a moment later the wolf was tangled, struggling viciously to get free.

Nemir's spear caught the shoulder of the closer wolf and

mortally wounded it before it knew what happened.

Soraya's wolf moved at the same time and bolted toward Nemir from the side away from Merak.

Nemir struggled to keep the three animals at bay and lunged with the spear. The first animal moved back and Nemir lunged again. They played cat and mouse for a few moments and then Nemir suddenly realized that he was in the open away from the fire.

Watch your back," screamed Merak who had managed to kill his wolf and was yanking at the net. He gave up in frustration and ran at the wolf in front of Nemir.

Merak was graceful and precise. He nicked one wolf and with a fluid motion brought the blade behind him to ward off another.

Suddenly Nemir stumbled and lost his spear. He scrambled to get up and started to run. A wolf was on him immediately trying to get to his neck.

Nemir felt the fangs searching for flesh under the fabric of his garment.

Merak dove for the spear, grabbed it, and rolled back to his feet.

Nemir was desperately trying to keep fabric between his neck and the wolf's fangs. There was a thump and the wolf let go. He turned to see Merak holding the end of the spear which was embedded deeply into the wolf's body.

The other two wolves ran off to fight another day.

"Are you all right Uncle!" yelled Soraya. She came running over with the wood still burning brightly.

"Your bleeding sir," said Merak.

Nemir had a small flesh wound on his shoulder.

"It's nothing. I'm alive and well... thanks to you," he said.

"The wolves never had a chance," said Soraya. She was looking at Merak with admiration. Nemir was thinking about what Balthasar had said.

"Did I look funny running away from the wolf?"

"No, just scared to death," said Abdul.

"You think you can chase me without suffering the consequences?" Nemir asked the wolf that had bitten him. He kicked the carcass to emphasize his point.

"Aren't you going to cook them, Uncle?" asked Soraya teasingly.

"No."

"At least save the pelts?" Soraya persisted.

"No, they're too rough."

"But a hermit could use them for a cloak," Abdul joined in.

"Well, perhaps if we bring the three pelts to Filadelphi today we can procure a bottle or two of wine and a good meal."

†

Merak made arrangements with the innkeeper. As the Magi's delegate he handled the expenses and the travel arrangements. Up until their arrival in Filadelphi he had had little to do. Now, however, he wanted to make certain that their accommodations were adequate. He also wanted to make up for the harshness of the first part of the journey.

"There will be four of you then?" the innkeeper asked, looking around for the other two.

"Yes, we have two others," said Merak.

"Not wives or consorts?" he asked looking at Merak and then to Abdul.

"No, only this gentleman's daughter and the girl's uncle."

"They will be back presently," said Abdul.

Merak had taken off his cloak. Underneath he wore fabrics that were obviously of a higher class than Abdul. This confused the merchant who had already presumed that Merak was the servant.

The door behind them swung open.

"Papa, look at what Uncle Nemir just bought," said Soraya as the door swung open.

Nemir held a small statue of a wolf suckling two young babies.

"What did you get?" Abdul asked.

"It's a Romulus and Remus. See the twins," said Soraya.

He was referring to the famed twin brothers who founded the city of Rome many centuries earlier. For its first five hundred years it was the Roman Republic. Since the time of Julius Caesar, it had become the Roman Empire.

"I hope you didn't pay a lot for that statue," said the innkeeper. "They have gone out of favor in Tiberius' reign."

It didn't matter to Soraya. She was thrilled to have a statue small enough to take back with her.

"Did you make them drop the statue into some boiling water?" asked the innkeeper.

"No. He offered and that was enough," said Nemir, who understood what the innkeeper was referring to.

It was a common practice to take cera or wax and fill the mistakes in a statue's surface. *Sine-cera* or without wax was the term used to mean someone was honest or sincere. If the statue was dipped into boiling water, the wax would melt off and the defects would be visible. Nemir knew that merchants cheated by filling the dings or holes in a statue.

When the merchant offered to, it was enough for him. He believed the man was sincere.

They moved into the dining area of the inn and sat down to a warm dinner.

"Tonight we sleep in beds, a comfort that I have become accustomed to in my old age," said Nemir. He raised a goblet of wine mixed with a little water as was the Greek tradition.

"To the wolves who provided us with the drink," said Abdul. He raised his goblet back.

"In gratitude that we don't have to keep watch at the campsite tonight," said Merak.

"I'm just glad we get to sleep in beds like Uncle Nemir said," added Soraya.

"And that we have a hot meal that isn't grilled snake meat," said Nemir.

"Uncle Nemir, do you have to bring that up again?" she scolded.

The waitress brought them roast chicken. It was nice to eat something normal for a change. It was accompanied with a bowl of vegetables, olives, and lemons.

"It tastes like chicken!" Soraya exclaimed.

†

Merak sat high in his saddle. His perfect posture stood out among the four travelers. He was enjoying the warmth of the sun's rays as they soaked into his being. It was the type of glorious day that follows a peaceful sleep. None of them had realized just how tired they were from the struggles of the night before until they had retired for the night. Then it hit them. They were exhausted, both physically and emotionally. It was then that Merak suggested a few extra

days in Filadelphi to recuperate. They had welcomed the rest and were ready to go.

Staying the extra days also gave Merak more time to stable the water carrying camel. It wasn't needed from this point forward. They would pick it up on the return trip and take it back with them. Now they were in the Provincia Arabia and wanted to move quickly. The territory was controlled by the Romans, but the Nabateans had the power of taxation. Every city that they stopped in left them open for questioning. Merak had taken care of the caravan tax, but the bureaucrat had irritated the young man. Abdul was already explaining why the return trip should take the northern route, but they would worry about that later.

Right now, they were in the easternmost reach of the Roman Empire so the roads were in better repair. The distances were easier to cover, and the towns were much closer together.

The group was moving faster now. Soraya rode next to her uncle and behind Merak. She found herself enjoying looking at him. His strong shoulders and broad back sloped down to a narrow V at his waist. She realized that she had been staring and then guiltily looked over to her uncle to see if he had noticed.

He leaned over to her and whispered, "He is handsome, isn't he?"

She blushed.

Merak continued to talk to Abdul about the road ahead. It was nearly forty leagues to Pella. They would be able to cover the distance in three days with no trouble. Abdul thought that they could do it in two days. Merak hoped that the stopover in Gerasa for their midday dinner would not be a problem.

It wasn't that Merak didn't know how to talk to bureaucrats or taxmen. He had years of experience. The problem was explaining the purpose of the journey. He was concerned that he shouldn't talk to any government officials about the "new king" for fear that they would be seen as enemies of the state. They would have to be very discreet when they arrived in Judea. The Romans could become very nasty, very quickly. Merak wasn't usually so cautious when representing Magus Melchior. He normally entered a new kingdom and presented his document of passage and paid his respect to the crown.

The Roman Empire, or at least the arrogant Romans presented two problems to him. First, they believed that they controlled the whole world or specifically the part of the world worth controlling. They had complete control of the Mediterranean region, the most fertile area in the known world. They also believed that their form of government was the most enlightened way of governing ever created by man. They were a republic while most other areas around the Roman Empire were kingdoms or patriarchies of one sort or another.

Merak was concerned about presenting their mission to the caravan taxmen in a way that wouldn't invite too much curiosity. He had finally resolved to explain that the family they were visiting were personal friends of Magus Melchior and that the two camel drivers had been ordered to deliver the bolt of linen because they had failed to do so previously.

Keeping the truth simple, made life simpler.

Merak discussed his concerns with Abdul but not with Nemir. Abdul was serious and easy for Merak to speak with. Nemir drove him to distraction with his constant antics.

Soraya couldn't help noticing the similarity in style

between Merak and her father. Both were serious, reliable, and tended to worry. Merak described his reasons for each of the explanations he would give, while Abdul listened patiently.

They discussed the finer points about court etiquette and reasons why they should reveal as little as possible to the caravan taxmen.

"Think of the political intrigue we could be involved in," said Merak.

"It's true, Merak," said Abdul seriously. "We could be walking into a hostile environment when we get to Jerusalem. Who knows what the young king has done."

"We don't want word to proceed us to the Roman procurator. We should try to find the young man before we speak to them."

"Absolutely. That's a good point," said Abdul.

Soraya thought it was cute that they spent so much time talking.

When the cloth bearing quartet arrived in Gerasa, Merak was calm about his presentation for their journey.

He had spent hours discussing what the politically correct way of presenting themselves to the officials that interviewed caravans on entry to the cities. Now he looked for the ever-present bureaucrat at the porta or door of the city.

A pair of Roman legionnaires stood guard to one side of the gate. As they passed through the gate, one of the Roman soldiers looked up for a moment. He took notice of Soraya and then returned to his conversation with his colleague.

Merak and Abdul looked around. There was no bureaucrat, and the soldiers didn't ask either.

"So Merak, we entered and you didn't get a chance to explain our purpose, mission, and calling," said Nemir. He was laughing as he spoke.

"They didn't even ask," said Merak. There was genuine relief in his voice.

Soraya giggled.

Merak turned to look at her. They made eye contact for a moment and then she averted her eyes.

Why did I look away? Soraya asked herself. She suddenly felt flushed and warm.

Merak turned back toward the front and leaned over to Abdul. "Those two behind us are teasing me," he said.

"I can't help you. Once they get started it's already too late," said Abdul. "They are merciless."

"I think we should discuss the reason for the cloth and not the gifts of gold and frankincense," said Nemir.

"Oh, Heavens no, Uncle," said Soraya.

"No? How about myrrh?" asked Nemir with feigned incredulity.

"No, I think we should discuss the reason we don't know the name of the royalty we are going to visit," she said with honey-like sweetness.

Merak turned to give her a look, but all he could muster was a smile.

"My, how those two worry," she said to her uncle.

Her father turned to look at them.

"We worry because it is the right thing to do," said Abdul.

"Come off your high camel, Abdul. You worry because you both enjoy it," said Nemir. He pulled his camel to the right.

"Where are you going?" asked Merak as the group split in two.

"I smell a roast house," said Nemir.

Merak sniffed the air and caught the aroma floating on the breeze. They followed their noses until they found an inn with a series of spits filled with fowl, game, and lamb.

"I am so hungry," said Merak. He dismounted quickly and tethered his camel to a granite post with an iron ring on it. It was a place to tether horses.

"You're always hungry," said Nemir.

"Yes, I amaze myself," said Merak politely. He smiled broadly as they walked to the entrance of the roast house.

The owner rushed to the door and brought them to a table. He was tall and very thin. He was so emaciated that Nemir started to stare.

"I guess you don't eat your own cooking," said Nemir.

Soraya rolled her eyes in embarrassment.

"Can you get a boy to water and feed our animals?" asked Merak.

"Immediately sir," said the thin man.

The inn owner clapped his hands and a servant appeared.

"There are some animals for you to groom while these people enjoy a repast," said the innkeeper. He patted his own slender stomach for emphasis when he said the word repast.

Abdul smiled.

Nemir looked at Abdul, "A repast? I just want a meal."

"Uncle, leave the gentleman alone," Soraya said. She felt sorry for anyone who was that thin.

"Okay. I will, just for you, though," said Nemir, but he was in a mood to clown around. Once he started it was difficult for him to turn it off.

The innkeeper was used to being teased about his weight. He could eat anything and still remain skinny.

"Are you the cook?" asked Nemir.

"No, I just eat the food," said the slender innkeeper. He was smiling and didn't mind Nemir's teasing.

'Not too much though," said Nemir.

"Oh, no. I only eat the smallest amount. It cuts into profits when you eat your own food."

"I guess you are a very rich man then," said Nemir.

"Practically a king," said the innkeeper. "May I suggest the capon that has just come off the spit? Or the wild boar with mushrooms?"

They all nodded hungrily.

"Bread, pilaf, and bamni?" The innkeeper rattled off a series of items that were cooked. Bamni was a vegetable that was a cousin to okra.

Merak kept nodding his head yes to every item.

"Youth," said Abdul.

"Yes, I wish I could eat as much as I wanted and not gain weight like Merak does."

"You eat as much as you want, Uncle. I've watched you," said Soraya.

"No, Niece, I don't. I always eat just a little... *more,*" he said. He laughed because he had caught her off guard.

✝

It was the custom in this part of the world to offer a place to rest after a large meal. Merak never needed to rest after he had eaten. When the offer came, Abdul and Nemir both took a post-prandial nap in the upper floor of the small inn.

"I'll take care of the camels," Soraya offered. She was acting tough like a tomboy again.

Merak wanted to tend to the camels himself and make certain everything was in order. He was glad the older men were going to rest. He wanted to push the trip and ride hard all the way to Pella. They would be more willing companions if they were rested.

"You don't have to groom the beast, Soraya," Merak said.

"I can take care of my own camel," she said a little too defensively.

"I paid the young boy to groom them. Would you take his livelihood away?" Merak asked.

She saw that he was teasing her now. She wondered if he didn't want to clean animals with her, but just be alone with her. The idea thrilled her softly.

"Let's take a walk around the town," said Soraya. She couldn't go walking around by herself because she was a girl. She was excited to explore the town, but she was uneasy about being alone with Merak. Being alone with the guys had never been a problem for her. She was tough and could handle herself. Now she felt a funny kind of jitter, but only for a moment.

"There is not much to see in Gerasa," said Merak. He looked around him as if to emphasize his point and then looked at the saddles and cinches on each of the camels.

"There's more here than we have in my hometown," said Soraya.

"That's not too hard," he said. "Your town is really just a village."

She was proud of her little village, but he made it sound so insignificant. She felt a slight wound to her pride.

"I know it's a quiet, little—or should I say—a sleepy, little village. But it's home." Soraya replied coldly.

"I didn't mean that as an insult," he said softly. "I just meant…" he trailed off.

Soraya softened. She could see that Merak was being sincere. "It's okay," she whispered.

Merak smiled while he finished what he was doing and gave instructions to the young boy who was watching the animals.

"Wait until we get to Jerusalem. It's a jewel of a city. It's a shining beacon upon a hill. Jerusalem is dazzling white, and when the sun sets, it lights the palaces up with a fire that warms your soul."

She was enthralled.

Merak stopped and listened to what he just said. It was so unlike him to be poetic.

"Shall we walk together?"

Merak extended his arm and she took it. He suddenly noticed how she felt much more like a young lady rather than a little girl. Her hand felt warm on his arm.

She smiled at him. The glow of her smile and the joy in her eyes made him feel alive. It was a glorious day, with the sun shining brightly. The whole world was inside resting, trying to keep out of the sun. The two young traveling companions had the entire city to themselves.

Merak wished he could tell her about his land, Arabia, and his city, Riyadh. It was so much larger and more magnificent than this little village on the trade route.

"I know so little about you Merak," she said.

"I know."

He was always so uncomfortable during conversations with the opposite sex.

"Are you deliberately trying to be mysterious?"

"No," he said. A moment later he realized that he should say something.

She waited patiently.

"I am Arabian," he said.

He thought it was a dull thing to say.

"That's very intriguing. Is Arabia very big?" she asked.

"It is at least twice as big as Persia," he said proudly.

"Really? What is the name of your city?"

"It's Riyadh. It's twice as far away from Babylon as Babylon is from Jerusalem," he blurted out.

She stopped and looked at him. For her, it was an enormous journey to distant lands. It had never occurred to her that this journey was only the smaller part of a much longer one for him.

"Is Riyadh large?"

"It's like Babylon, a city."

"As big as Babylon?" She couldn't contain her surprise.

"Smaller, but it has its own magnificence. Master Melchior is from the royal family. Their palaces are not unlike Magus Balthasar's," he said proudly.

"And what is your opinion of this little place?"

Merak looked around and thought for a moment. He wanted to say the right thing. "It's a cute little town and a perfect place for a walk with such a lovely young lady."

The warmth of her smile told him that it was just the right thing to say.

They turned a corner and started down the street that led to the forum or town square. She stepped over the well-

worn chariot and carriage groove in the road and squeezed his arm tightly to keep her balance. He was solid like a pillar of marble. She had never really gone for a walk with any man other than her father and brother.

I'm in a foreign land with a handsome young soldier to protect me, she thought. The idea sounded nice to her.

A few young children who were playing with sticks stopped to look at the two of them. Soraya wished she was dressed differently. Merak was in very colorful robes that were native to the Arabian Peninsula. His fabrics were very expensive and very bright.

Her clothes were typical of a village girl's clothing from Persia, bright and yet modest, but not of the same elegance as his.

"The children are looking at the handsome prince from a faraway land," she said. She looked up at his dark brown eyes and noticed how perfectly formed his eyebrows were. She thought, *they must have been painted on by angels. His eyelashes are very long too.* She was surprised at her thoughts.

"They are looking at the beautiful young princess who is being escorted through a foreign land," said Merak. He made the words sound majestic.

She was suddenly curious to know what it was like being the emissary of Melchior. After all, she thought, *he is a powerful Magus, and Merak is his delegate.*

"Do you live near Master Melchior's palace?" she asked. They were in the center of the forum looking around at the low structures. It was a very small town.

"I am part of the royal guard and live right on the grounds of the palace," he said.

She noticed that his tone became formal when he spoke about his duties.

"How did you become his emissary?"

"I inherited the position. My father was his emissary for many years. I took over the responsibilities from him just a short time ago," said Merak.

"And before that, Merak?" Soraya asked. Saying his name felt delightful. She suddenly found that his life seemed wonderfully interesting too.

"Before that, Soraya, I was in training to become Magus Melchior's personal assistant."

When he said her name, she felt a tingle. She was aglow with joy. It was a delight to have him pay attention to her. She felt the feelings and then realized that she was acting like the silly girls that she had criticized for so many years.

"Take me back to the inn, Merak," she said. Her change in tone was too abrupt for him not to notice.

"Is there something wrong?" he asked politely.

"No," she said.

Nothing was wrong, and that's what she was afraid of.

✝

A cool breeze blew softly from the west as they took to the road refreshed by either their after-dinner nap or their walk. Merak and Soraya rode together while Abdul and Nemir talked incessantly about the proper age to train a camel to carry goods. They argued about the age to teach a camel to let a rider onboard. Nemir gave Abdul his opinion about feed, training schedules, and the latest techniques in stabling racing camels.

"When did you become world's greatest expert on racing camels?" Abdul asked.

"I have always been the world's greatest expert about everything," said Nemir. He looked at his friend and chuckled.

"Some of the things you're saying go against common sense," said Abdul.

He disagreed strongly with certain points, but he was arguing because it was always fun to argue with Nemir. Abdul loved to see Nemir get excited. His friend was passionate about everything.

"You just don't want to admit that while you were off raising figs and milking cows that I've learned a few things," said Nemir.

"Some of these new ideas don't match my personal experience. That's all I meant," said Abdul.

"Your personal experience doesn't encompass thoroughbred camel racing, my good friend."

"No, you're right. I'm used to driving animals that were bred for carrying large quantities of goods, not a short jockey and a light saddle," replied Abdul.

"See, there is the possibility that I might be right," said Nemir.

They continued the discussion league after league over the now more frequent hills on the road to Pella.

Merak and Soraya just watched. They were grateful that the two elder men were so engrossed in their conversation. It gave them a few hours to be together and just talk. Neither Merak or Soraya were aware that Abdul and Nemir were watching them closely.

"Have you made many journeys as long as this one,

Merak?" Soraya asked. He had become much more of an adventurer after this afternoon's walk.

"Master Melchior rarely travels. This is the longest thus far," said Merak.

The conversation faded into the background as the lead camels moved further out in front.

"You have to be careful with breeding," said Abdul to Nemir. He was smiling broadly.

"Yes, when you find a champion, it is important to recognize it," said Nemir.

"The offspring could make a grandfather proud," whispered Abdul.

Nemir knew he was talking about Merak.

"I suggest you give him a hard time," said Nemir.

"Why is that?" Abdul asked. He looked back to make sure that they were far enough ahead of the two young people that they wouldn't be heard.

"Because he's military and would love to be tested to prove himself worthy, and your little tomboy back there is such a rebel. As soon as she suspects you like him, she'll pull away."

They both laughed. It was true. She had entered the age where Abdul could reasonably offer her in marriage as was their custom, but he knew she wasn't ready. At least until this trip he thought she wasn't ready. They both knew that she was stubborn and thick headed and couldn't be forced into a relationship she didn't want. Abdul didn't mind keeping his youngest girl around a few extra years, however, because she had become his favorite. She was the baby of the family, only he could never say that in front of her.

"You know the only thing I regret with my wife was that

we never had children," said Nemir. He still mourned her death deeper than he realized.

"I can understand that," his friend said.

"She was so disappointed about that, but we married a little late. She was so much fun. She would have been a terrific mother," said Nemir.

"You would have made a wonderful father. Children are a great blessing. I didn't understand it fully even when I had them. It's only now that I have some grandchildren that I finally understand how much a child is truly a gift from God," said Abdul.

They were far enough in front of the young couple to risk talking more freely.

"She is taken by him, isn't she?" asked Nemir.

"Nemir, I never thought I would see the day. She only came on this journey to prove to her brother that she could travel further than him," said Abdul.

"She is so competitive and so tough," said Nemir.

"She's tough, but I think she has the biggest heart of all the children. She became a tomboy so she could hang out with me," said Abdul. Memories fondly drifted through his mind as the world rocked gently around him from the motion of the camel.

Soraya was his youngest child. She was always his baby, and he knew that she loved being special. She didn't like being treated like a baby though and had compensated by becoming tough. She was the first one to fight with her brother and sisters if she were teased. She was easy to manipulate, however. All her brother and sisters had to do was accuse her of being afraid. A dare worked like magic to motivate her.

"How is she around the house?" asked Nemir. He was Persian and practical. A young woman was expected to know how to keep a household and how to cook.

"I think she'll do all right. I wonder what it's like in Arabia?"

Abdul was thinking aloud about the Magus Melchior and how his mansion was set up. He really had no idea whatsoever, but as long as they were far enough away, they could talk to each other about these things without alarming Merak or irritating Soraya.

"What would your wife think?" asked Nemir.

"You mean about Arabia?"

"Yes."

"It's a long distance away from the rest of the family," said Abdul.

They were climbing toward the pass that led through the last small range of mountains before the road descended to the valley where the city of Pella was located. There were small caves and crevices in this part of the hill and small streams that ran down the hillside from higher above. Because of the steepness of the short hill that they were on and the hour of the day, they were engulfed in shadows. When they reached the top, a magnificent sunset awaited them.

Nemir and Abdul crested the hill about a half league ahead of the younger pair. They paused for a second and admired the sunset and the valley that unrolled before them. Within the hour they would be in Pella. Abdul turned to look at his daughter and Merak and then followed Nemir down the other side of the hill.

Suddenly two horses burst forth from a cave hidden in the shadows. Their riders, dressed in black with their

scraggly beards and pocked faces covered, charged down the hill toward Abdul and Nemir.

"Oh my God! Bandits!" screamed Soraya. She started to chase after them.

"Stay back, Soraya," yelled Merak. His sword was in his left hand and his net was unfurled in his right.

Merak whipped his camel with his net and crouched in the saddle, holding his balance perfectly in the stirrups. His mount charged up the hill distancing itself from Soraya's.

Merak looked back pleading with his eyes to Soraya. He prayed that she kept back. There were only two bandits, and he was a trained military officer, proud, courageous, and battle tested. He could handle the situation, but the distraction of someone you love in danger could cause a warrior to make mistakes. Mistakes in battle were deadly.

As Merak crested the hill, he saw the two camels running as fast as Abdul and Nemir could get them to go, but they were together.

"Turn, split up," Merak said out loud to himself. His camel was faster than theirs and faster than the horses. If they split up, chances were that the bandits would only follow one. Before they figured out what happened, Merak would be on them.

He turned to look, and Soraya was charging down the hill. Her light sword was out, she was screaming, and tears were streaming down her angry face. His worst fear was coming true.

"Papa!" her voice rang out clear with terror. She was flying down the hill now.

"No, stay back, Soraya," yelled Merak.

She was going to catch him in a few moments. He was

afraid that the bandits would go after her.

"Papa!" she yelled again.

As only a father could, Abdul heard his daughter's screams. He wheeled around to look for her and pulled his camel into a sharp turn. The two bandits let him go and maintained their pursuit of Nemir.

Merak came thundering by, hurling a booming Arabian battle cry to the Heavens. His camel charged by Abdul who was racing to intercept Soraya.

Nemir was no fool. He had his spear out and was standing in his saddle holding the sharp end behind him to the right so that only the man to his left with the slower horse could get near him.

"Allelale," yelled Merak as he let his net fly. For a long moment, he watched as the web unfurled and created a huge umbrella over the slower bandit. As soon as the man reached up to untangle himself, Merak gave a violent tug and slowed his camel. The bandit was hurled to the ground and landed with a loud thump. Merak left him to Abdul and continued after Nemir and the other bandit.

Abdul was on top of him in a moment. He clocked him in the skull with the base of his sword and then started binding his hands and feet.

The bandit on the faster horse drew his sword, turned his mount, and charged at Merak. He was betting that the horse could quickly outmaneuver a camel on the battlefield.

"Your net?" yelled Abdul.

"I don't need it," said Merak.

Merak was standing erect in his saddle, sword in his left hand. He reached down to his boot, and with a flick of his wrist, a throwing knife hurtled at the man's throat.

The bandit was quick and covered his throat with his left arm taking the blade deep into the flesh of his forearm. He wasn't ready for Merak's attack but managed to raise his arm just before Merak slashed the bandit's hand causing him to drop the sword.

The bandit tried to turn his horse to escape, but without the use of his arms he quickly fell off the galloping horse.

"Merak! Are you all right?" Soraya dropped her sword and was running toward him.

"Stay back until the man is subdued," Merak said as though barking an order.

She froze and watched.

The man with the wounded arms tried to run away. Merak quickly caught him and hobbled him.

"Don't move or you are a dead man," Merak said calmly.

"I am a dead man already," said the bandit. He was looking down the valley toward Pella. A small platoon of Roman soldiers was riding up the hill. The punishment for road bandits was swift and severe.

Merak turned to look for Soraya. She ran right into his arms. They embraced each other for a long moment, and then Merak realized that Abdul and Nemir were watching.

"Your father," said Merak.

"I don't care," said Soraya. "You could have been killed." She held him tighter before she let go.

Abdul and Nemir were both smiling.

✝

The Roman legionnaires brought the two bandits before the magistrate of Pella. The trial was quick, efficient, and just. The brutal punishment was typical for a Roman magistrate.

He could either have the bandits crucified or scourged. He wouldn't do both because that was unheard of.

The magistrate considered scourging for the men, but there were two practical problems with that. First, the men would still be alive, and one of them would probably go back to robbing traders along the trade route. If both men had wounded arms as the one bandit had, he might have offered them scourging. The one man would never hold a sword properly and might be less of a threat to the community.

Secondly, they had been terrorizing the route for some months now and had embarrassed the Romans by disturbing the famous Pax Romana. Lack of respect for the Roman Empire was a worse crime than robbery. It earned severe punishment. When all the factors were weighed, the magistrate leaned toward crucifixion. It was the most common form of punishment for capital offenses such as treason and murder. It was a brutal form of punishment reserved for non-citizens and thus was appropriate in this case. Roman citizens were never crucified.

The problem was that this was technically not a capital case. The magistrate needed more evidence to raise the level of offense to capital.

Nemir, Abdul, and his daughter were questioned by the centurion in charge of the men who arrested the prisoners. It was all very simple. When Merak was interviewed, the politically astute centurion saw what he considered some fascinating extenuating circumstances.

The magistrate finished listening to the counsel for the bandits. He was not really concerned with their guilt. He was looking for a way to increase the penalty to rid the empire of the riffraff.

"Would Merak, the emissary of Magus Melchior of Arabia, please step forward," the magistrate said loudly.

"Yes sir," Merak said while standing rigidly at attention.

Abdul, Soraya, and Nemir sat by him, and for once, Nemir thought it wise to hold his tongue.

"Come forward young man," said the magistrate.

Merak approached and stood before him.

"As you might have figured out, these two men are not Roman citizens but are uncivilized bandits on the fringe of our civilization who have terrorized this area for more than a year," said the magistrate.

Merak noted that the man seemed to be thinking out loud as if to present an argument to himself for analysis.

"You represent a Magus; I presume a potentate of the Arabian lands?" said the magistrate.

"Yes, sir. My liege is a lord of many lands, possibly equivalent to a Roman senator," said Merak.

He did not presume to equate Melchior with the Emperor. That would be in bad taste and insulting to the imperial ego.

"I would venture to say possibly as high as king in some lands or a procurator for the empire," said the magistrate.

"Yes, sir, you could say that, but I am not an expert on these matters," said Merak.

"What business do you have in the Roman Empire? Is it commercial?"

"No, sir. It is personal. I am escorting these two men and their daughter to a family that is friends with Magus Melchior. They have a small gift to bring that was inadvertently not delivered on their previous visit," said Merak.

Soraya watched proudly.

"He finally got to try his explanation," whispered Nemir. He smiled broadly at the thought.

"It sounds good to me," said Abdul. He was being careful to use a soft voice.

The magistrate looked their way and gave them a look that said, *Is there something else I should know?*

Nemir nodded and was quiet.

"You have done the Roman Empire a great service, and we extend our gratitude to Magus Melchior for this service. You may be seated," said the magistrate.

The Roman judge then looked at the two bandits.

"Because this man was the emissary of a foreign leader, a diplomat, the crimes you have committed are crimes against the Roman Empire and are a serious embarrassment to Tiberius Caesar. Therefore, they rise to the level of capital offense. Stand for your sentence."

The bandits stood. Their worst fears were about to be realized.

"Crucifixion beyond the west gate and outside the city limits."

The executioner frowned.

"What's the problem?" The magistrate was annoyed.

"If we don't do it in the regular crucifixion site, we have to use an X cross. There are no stipes out there," said the executioner.

Usually, the executions were done in a place where people could see them as warning to those who would break the law. There typically was a stipes or an upright piece of wood in the ground. The condemned man carried the cross piece, the patibulum, on his shoulders, and it was hung on the stipes. The magistrate was trying use poetic justice and

crucify the men on the road that they had terrorized. It was extra work for the executioner.

"Use an X instead of the usual cross then. What's the problem with that?" asked the magistrate. The irritation in his voice was obvious.

"What about crucifragium?" asked the executioner. This was the custom of breaking a man's legs while crucified so that they would die more quickly. It was a brutal act of mercy in a gruesome execution process.

"Yes, show them some mercy."

"Crucifragium is an act of mercy?" Abdul whispered.

"Yes, they die quicker, and the executioner can get home to his wife and children and a hot meal," said Nemir. He was being sarcastic about the gruesome practices of the Roman Empire.

✝

A pair of Roman legionnaires walked in front of the four foreigners. The crowd near the market made room when they saw the staff with the banner SPQR on it. The escort was a courtesy.

Soraya was glad to leave the magistratum or court house and be out in the city. The thought of the two men trying to kill her father haunted her even more than the thought of them being crucified. She walked next to her father and held tightly onto his arm.

"Merak, I am really grateful to you," said Nemir.

"It goes without saying. I have a duty to protect you. Magus Melchior assigned me as your escort."

"I know all that. I'm grateful just the same," said Nemir.

"I am honored," said Merak.

"Papa, I am so glad nothing happened," said Soraya.

"Merak is a very brave man," said Abdul.

"Yes, and if you weren't in danger, I would have thought the whole episode exciting," she said.

It was exciting for her. She watched in fascination at Merak fought with the two men. He was methodical, precise, and calculating. She knew that it was his training that had kicked into motion as soon as there was a threat.

"He is a kind man too, I think," said Abdul.

Soraya looked at him and gave his arm a squeeze. She knew what her father was doing. He was signaling her that he liked him and would not mind if she liked him too.

"Brave and kind, Father, that's how I always see you."

"I am flattered by my daughter's assessment. You see me as a warrior like him?" he asked. It was said in a very formal tone as a joke.

"And a worrier like you too," she teased back.

They were walking back to the caravansary where they would be staying for a few days. The camels had been stabled earlier, and the four of them had been escorted across the city to the magistratum. As was usual for Romans, when a crime was committed and the evidence was overwhelming, justice was done swiftly before the criminal had too much time to think about and justify their actions.

They were anxious to get back to the caravansary to talk to its owner. It was probable that he would know Casimer and the whereabouts of Jamil, or Blaze as the famed camel was called now.

They turned a corner and saw that they had arrived. The two escorts saluted them with the classic Roman military salute. Merak saluted back with an Arabian salute. The Romans were intrigued by it.

Nemir walked into the caravansary first, not out of rudeness, but in his excitement over finding Jamil. Soraya frowned at him and then smiled broadly at Merak who was holding the door for her.

"Thank you, Merak," said Abdul who was watching them with more curiosity now.

When they got inside the steward of the establishment greeted them. He was a rather thin, yet handsome man whose brow was perpetually furrowed. He had a tendency to look down his long aquiline nose toward people when he spoke. He was looking down at the very short Nemir but didn't seem interested in listening. Word had already gotten out that Merak had captured the two bandits. He was treated as the hero of the day. He wanted to speak with Merak to hear about the battle on the west road, but Nemir had him cornered and was peppering him with questions.

"His name is Casimer," said Nemir.

"But there are a lot of men named Casimer," said the steward. He looked to Merak and said, "Congratulations sir. Your bravery is already legend in our city, and it is an honor to have you as a guest."

Merak was surprised to hear that.

"But this Casimer had a camel," said Nemir.

"I see sir. You are looking for a camel owner named Casimer," said the steward. He was looking at Merak and smiling. "There are a lot of men who come to Pella and stay with us named Casimer."

"I am looking for a..." Nemir stopped and composed himself. "Listen to me young man. When I speak to you, you look at me."

"Papa, Uncle sounds like you when you talk to us kids,"

said Soraya. She was watching the steward and Nemir with amusement.

Merak moved next to Nemir and looked at the young man severely.

"Would you please pay attention to Nemir. We have important business to conduct, and your inattention bespeaks a lack of education and etiquette."

The owner of the caravansary hurried into the room when he heard Merak's tone. He had been having trouble with his steward for a while now. The young man didn't enjoy working with him. He was from a fairly wealthy family who had fallen on hard times. He did them a favor by taking their son in and training him to be an innkeeper. He didn't have the pleasant personality that was needed. In fact, he tended to be rude, snobbish, and stuck up. He saw the caravan traders as wandering nomads rather than well-to-do merchants who traveled at great risk to bring exotic goods to the Roman Empire.

"May I be of service, sirs," said Ahmed the owner of the caravansary.

He dismissed the steward with a stern look.

"We are looking for a man named Casimer," said Nemir. He was frustrated to start all over again, but hoped that the owner would be of assistance.

Soraya enjoyed the scene. The little episode highlighted the contrast between Merak and the steward. She was pleased to see how obvious Merak's fine character and training set him above the average. And Papa likes him, she thought to herself. Her reverie was interrupted by Nemir's excitement.

"Yes, he raced camels."

"Was perhaps this camel named Blaze?" asked Ahmed.

"Yes, it was a great racing camel, a legend, and he had a shooting star mark on his forehead," said Nemir.

"But of course," said Ahmed, "Everyone in Pella knows this camel."

"And Casimer, can you tell us where he can be found?" Nemir asked expectantly.

"Casimer passed on a few months ago. It was a sad time for all his friends. He was an enormously popular man who liked to celebrate and share his success," said Ahmed.

"Passed on," said Abdul and Nemir at the same time.

Soraya looked at Merak. The dust storm, the bandits, and now this worried her. Were they ever going to get a break? She thought it would be simple. The idea that the Magi had dreamed of Jamil seemed to indicate that their trip was divinely ordained. She believed it would be guided by an unseen hand whose benevolence her father and uncle trusted completely. She also naively believed it would be effortless.

"Yes, sorry to say, passed on. I am friends with his family. Did you have business to conduct with them?"

Nemir nodded.

"If you would like, I could perhaps introduce you, however, they are still in mourning," said Ahmed.

"See what you can do," said Merak.

†

The following morning, they mounted Ahmed's chariot and started off for the estate of Casimer. Ahmed was delighted to be of service. The merchant's family was more than willing to see the visitors from Persia and Arabia. Casimer's family was well known in Pella. Since the time of Blaze's racing victories, Casimer's wealth had become famous. He was a

celebrity in racing circles in the major cities of Persia, such as Baghdad, but in Pella, he was simply its most famous citizen.

Every small city in Persia and Arabia had camel racing as a popular diversion, but the deeper one went into the Roman Empire, the less likely one would find it. Pella was essentially Persian in its roots but was on the fringes of the camel racing culture. Casimer's famous animal Blaze and the animals that had followed it, had brought fame to the city. What made that so important was that it brought cultural pride that connected it to its pre-Roman roots.

The general population was thrilled with the idea that the most famous camel in Persia came from their land. The heart of the common man of Pella was more aligned with the peoples of Assyria and the fertile triangle of the Tigris and Euphrates. The Roman Empire was a relatively recent political alignment for the people of Pella. Though the Legate of the Provincia Arabia was an eminently just and fair man, these people were not used to a republic form of government. They didn't trust it and didn't fully see themselves as Roman.

Casimer became a local hero because he connected them to their past glories. He did this with a camel that spent most of its time racing in other parts of the world. Casimer was the recipient of lavish gifts by those seeking to breed their racing stock with his animal. Even though a caravan's final destination was only a short distance away in Jericho, caravans would stop in Pella so that people could say that they saw Blaze.

The lavish victory parties that Casimer threw were an excuse for doing what his wife Mica loved the most, entertaining. The villa that they lived in was palatial, replete with furnishings from various cities in Assyria, Persia, and

Arabia. When they traveled, they were the welcome guests at the houses of other camel breeders. Mica didn't like to travel with Casimer but preferred to stay home and manage the estate.

Casimer's family assumed that the travelers from Baghdad were friends of his who had only recently heard of his death. When they found out that the travelers were heading to Judea, they welcomed them graciously, but there was a favor they wanted to ask.

†

Sadness filled the stable, like an emotional fog on a dark day of the soul. The younger camels knew something was up but as usual they weren't paying much attention to anything but their own needs. Youth avoided darkness principally because seeking light and joy were natural to a young soul. More importantly, it took a mature soul to grasp the great lessons that come from darkness, struggle, and desperation.

Jamil kept to himself. He was luxuriating in the bittersweet joy of fond remembrance. When most of one's life was behind him, joy could be culled from the past with the same degree as with hope from the future. Jamil allowed himself the luxury of a flood of memories. He watched silently as his mind took its own tortuous path, discerning events out of order, but with an ever-increasing emotional impact. When the stable hand came in to feed him, the now old camel just looked at the feed and knelt down. He needed to reminisce not eat. He didn't need to be in the now moment. He needed to review his lifetime with this man Casimer who had treated him so well for so long. This kind human, Casimer, who was no more.

Jamil had been around long enough to know that when humans wailed something serious had happened. He had heard the wailing before sunrise a few days ago. Shortly afterward, his fears had been confirmed. He had told himself to expect that Casimer would soon die. The death, however, had taken him by surprise.

Heba used to say that, he thought. She used to say that death came as a surprise to most people. It was an ambush, a startling event that shattered the way humans lived. That seemed strange to Jamil, whose fur around his mouth and nostrils had turned gray. His teeth were worn down from years of eating grains, and he could no longer run like the wind. He was aware that his death was approaching. It was a date with destiny that couldn't be avoided. The Sustainer had given him so many signals that he was aging.

But for humans the signals were even more obvious. Jamil mused about human aging for a moment while fondly remembering Casimer. The merchant's hair had turned white, and he had lost quite a few teeth. The last few years he walked with a stick and seemed to lean forward more. Surely, Casimer had realized that death was approaching, though he never seemed to let on. The old man's gate had changed too. *It was more obvious with humans,* thought Jamil. Their steps get tighter just like old Casimer who had started to shuffle. Their hair fell out too, which amused Jamil. He was glad that camels didn't lose their fur. Humans always seemed surprised when death came knocking at their door, yet they watched it slowly approach for years.

"What was it that Heba said about human aging?" he asked himself out loud. "She used to say that the human spirit doesn't age as fast as the human body."

"Hey, Blaze, you old dromedary... who are you talking to?" asked a young camel named Delia. She laughed at him and caught the glare of a few of the older beasts.

"Why, Delia, I am a senile old fool talking to myself out loud so that you wouldn't have to strain yourself trying to figure out what I was thinking," said Jamil.

Delia had been on Jamil's case since she arrived. She was swift—gifted in fact—but more temperamental than any camel he had ever met. She had the mark of the guiding star on her forehead. Casimer had said that she was probably his granddaughter, but camels didn't keep track of such things.

Jamil looked at her and shook his head. *Heba would have been able to deal with this one*, he thought. She would have known what stories to tell her, but Jamil was at a loss. Perhaps it was because he was tired. Or maybe because he was sad. He always wanted to argue back with her when she was sarcastic with him. Perhaps there was another reason that he avoided taking a look at. Conceivably he was jealous. He dismissed the thought as quickly as it entered his mind. He was excited about her potential and irritated by her flaws. That mix of feelings was common among camels.

Casimer had been excited about her too. She was beautiful, headstrong, and graceful. It was a terribly complex combination of flaws and virtues. Speed of hoof and speed of tongue was a brutal combination in any animal. Yes, Delia was a wonderfully complex beast, graceful and tactless. One day she would be a great racing camel if she could be taught.

He let the thought slide to the back of his mind. He missed Casimer and didn't feel like teaching anyone today, let alone this impetuous beast whose mind was as fluid as her body and just as quick. The stable boy interrupted his thoughts by

holding the feed bag out and shaking it. He missed Casimer and didn't feel like eating. Casimer, Heba, and Jamil. Now there was only Jamil left. How sad and how strange.

The stable boy let Jamil out to graze. The boy meant well, and Jamil walked out to the large area that was used for pasture. Jamil's eyes wandered across the property. There was the house off in the distance and part of the town up on a hill. The camels were never allowed up to the streets of the city anymore because they were racing stock. He watched as the back gate to the courtyard opened. Mica, the mistress of the estate, was out walking again. She was wearing black, grieving the loss of the man she had been wed to for more than fifty years. Jamil knew that she must have expected his death, but just like Heba said, humans rarely seemed prepared. Death was an ambush that trapped a weary body, but the soul, young forever, escaped to celestial abodes.

Jamil watched her on her lonely walk. She reached over and picked up a flower and looked up to the sky. It was clear blue, not a cloud anywhere, an empty blue sky. Jamil watched with fascination as Mica turned back toward the house and her posture changed. He noticed the young grandchild running toward her.

"Life goes on," he said. He afforded himself the pleasure of talking to himself without the critical eyes of the younger camels. Not that he minded the criticism. He used it to train their minds. Invariably the ones who criticized the most were hiding something deep that they needed to develop. Their fears kept it hidden underneath a blanket of sarcasm, so that the pain and frustration of giving birth to something so noble that others might criticize was avoided.

Sometimes the young camels poked fun simply because it

was easier than paying a compliment. The sarcasm, so quick to flow, was a sign of laziness. It had to be harnessed and gently transformed from sarcasm to critique, from critique to analysis, and from analysis to praise for what worked. Cynicism and sarcasm were the games of weak intellect and lazy thinking. He had learned from Heba that training a camel's mind was a far greater task than training its body. If he could get them to discipline their minds, he could get them to train their bodies for racing. The stable hands and the race trainer had no idea how it worked. They simply thought that some camels instinctively took to their workouts with more passion. It wasn't instinctual, it was instructional. He had been doing it for years. He learned how at the hooves of the great master Heba. She was wonderful. She was gone, but her life's philosophy lived on in Jamil's teachings.

A few of the younger ones were getting it. He could tell. None of them were the great racer that Casimer had been looking for. It didn't matter. Jamil taught for the sake of spreading the word that life was to be lived with the expressed purpose of refining one's character. At first, Jamil kept pinning his hopes on another marvelous animal who would race in Persia, Arabia, Syria, and Egypt. That would be the special animal who would spread Heba's message to the world. Now he knew that the message would go out in a different way. He heard the stable hands talking. In a few weeks, most of the camels would be sold off to other racing stables. That meant those who understood his message would spread it to distant lands. Heba would have been delighted.

✝

"We wish to offer our condolences to your family," said Merak as he entered. He gave the formal salute of the Arabians and then introduced each of the other travelers.

"Please come in and sit with me," Mica said. She turned to a servant and gave precise instructions for refreshments.

Mica's granddaughter ran into the room and stopped. She looked at all the people. Mica smiled and then let her little granddaughter climb into her lap for a few moments.

"I asked the servant to bring something sweet for you," she said to the little girl. She received a big hug in return.

The little girl then jumped down. She raced off to the kitchen to see what they were preparing.

"Now tell me, how did you know my husband?" asked Mica after each of them had taken a goblet.

"Actually, we only knew of his reputation," said Merak politely.

Mica looked at Ahmed who squirmed. He had partially misled her. The story had better be good because it was not right to bring strangers into a house of those in mourning.

"We were sent by the Magi Balthasar and Melchior to find your husband," said Merak.

"They owned a camel named Jamil, many years ago when it was very young," said Nemir, who had been fighting to keep quiet.

Mica looked at him.

"We've never had a camel named Jamil," she said.

"We think your husband renamed him Blaze," said Abdul. He was excited about telling the story but was trying to remain respectful of Mica's grief.

"Blaze?" she asked smiling. "I know the story of Blaze. I was never told that a pair of Magi owned him."

"Three Magi, to be precise," said Merak. "But would you be so kind to tell us the story?"

"I would be delighted," she said. Her eyes suddenly misted. "My husband, Casimer, would have loved telling you. He loved that animal almost as much as the children. He used to tell the story all the time. I know it well. He didn't get the camel from any Magi, though."

"The Magi didn't sell it to him," said Nemir.

"If you're referring to Ravi then you are still mistaken," said Casimer's wife.

"Who's Ravi?" Merak asked.

"The co-owner. My husband's business partner."

When they didn't seem to understand, she explained. "Casimer had a good friend by the name of Ravi who ran Gabae Stables in Gabae. They bought the camel together."

"Do you remember who they purchased Jamil from?" asked Nemir.

"They purchased Blaze or Jamil if you insist, from someone who was boarding him at the stable. My husband—he told the story many times—saw the animal running in the pastures. It had gotten loose and even the horses couldn't catch it. They brought the other camel out and it came running back."

"The other camel was a female?" Abdul asked.

"Yes, and her name was..."

"Heba," Nemir blurted out before she could say it.

"Yes, how could you have known? She's been dead quite a long time now," said Mica.

"They were brought together by the Magi and given to a young family. Jamil and Heba were unusually close," said Abdul.

"Perhaps they were the same animals. My husband said that he bought them from a family and that the mother was young."

"She had a young boy?" Abdul asked.

"I think so," said Mica.

"Where was this family from?" asked Abdul.

"It is important for us to find the family. We are bringing a gift and greetings from the Magi to them," said Merak.

Mica thought about where the family might have been from and shook her head while trying to remember the stories she had heard from Casimer.

Soraya was growing impatient. Fortunately, the pastries were delivered, and she helped herself. They were very sweet. She and Mica's grandchild examined them closely and didn't reject a single one. Abdul didn't pay attention to the little girl or his daughter. Nemir was anxious too. He watched them take the pastries and started helping himself. He ate a couple more pastries and waited for an answer.

Mica finally said, "I couldn't begin to tell you."

"Would your late husband's business partner know?" Merak asked. It sounded more like a suggestion than a question.

"Ravi? Perhaps. He's old, but the man's mind is as sharp as ever. You know..."

She paused.

"We still don't know if it was the same camel. Would you know him if you saw the beast?" Mica asked.

"I would recognize him for certain," said Nemir.

"How is that? One camel is much like any other," she said.

"The shooting star on his forehead," said Abdul.

She nodded. "Very good, but someone could have told you of the mark. It's quite famous. There was something else," she said softly.

"Another mark? I don't remember one," said Abdul. "And we groomed that animal every night for months."

"Something else," said Mica. She was fingering a ring that her husband had made for her after a very important victory with a very large purse for the winner. The star sapphire on the ring was a gift from Ravi to Casimer. He had the ring made at the same time as Ravi had a similar one fashioned for his wife.

Nemir eyed the ring as she touched it. It reminded him of something and then it came to him, the contraption.

"Many years ago, when we crossed the desert to bring the gifts to the family with the Magi, there was something else that distinguished Jamil from the other camels," said Nemir.

Mica suspected he was stalling, but she played along.

"Was it another mark on the camel that you now remember?" she asked.

"No, but it was something so obvious that you could pick out the little fellow from a half a league away. He stood out from the crowd."

Now Nemir was stalling. He wanted to see if Abdul could guess it too.

"Uncle, are you going to tell us or keep it a secret?" Soraya asked. She licked the sweet sticky syrup that had covered a baklava from her fingers.

"Yes, how could you pick Jamil out of all the camels from a distance?" Abdul was curious too.

"Abdul, don't you remember standing above the basin

watching the two camels. Even from far away you could tell which one was Jamil and which one was Heba," said Nemir.

"Of course, one was old and the other was young. One had a plane saddle and the other..."

"Yes?" Said Nemir.

"The contraption!"

"Exactly. One had a contraption on it for carrying the baby," said Abdul. He looked at Mica to see if he had guessed right.

"Ah, you even know about the contraption?"

"It was a baby seat," said Abdul.

"When Casimer came back with that animal with that funny-looking saddle, I thought he had lost his mind. I thought that he had it made to carry this ugly statue that our daughter wanted." Mica smiled at the memory.

"And the ring is made from one of the stones on the saddle. If I remember correctly, they were near the clasps on the side that held the baby in. Those star sapphires were gorgeous and that's one of them." Nemir nodded his head toward the ring.

"Correct," said Mica. She whispered something to a servant, and he left the room.

A few minutes later he brought in the old saddle.

"Ah," said Abdul. The look of recognition was written on his face.

"You couldn't have known about the saddle. No one but my daughter and I know of it."

"Who would know the whereabouts of the family that sold your husband the camel?" Merak asked.

"Perhaps Ravi would remember," she said. "I believe that they lived in a town north of Gabae in what is now called Galilee," she said.

"That doesn't make any sense. We found them in Bethlehem," said Nemir.

"Where did you give them the camels?" Mica asked.

"South of Beersheba," said Abdul. "I remember the town. It had a special well in the center dedicated to some Jewish ancestor. I remember it like it was yesterday."

"That's what they call Idumaea now," she said. "It's a long way off. You would have done better to travel south through Moab to get there."

"The Magi told us to find the camel first," said Merak. "It's a waste of time coming this far north. We're not near Bethlehem or Beersheba, and we have to go south to get to Jerusalem," said Abdul.

"Yes, but the camel was purchased from them in the North," said Nemir.

"The family was from the South. Remember it was at the time of the census," said Abdul.

"Maybe they moved," Nemir said back.

"Families don't move that often. We've been in our house for five generations," said Abdul.

"They were in a stable," said Nemir. "That certainly couldn't have been their house."

The two men started to argue with each other The rest of them waited patiently.

"Master Balthasar suggested that we offer to purchase Jamil," said Merak. He was trying to be tactful, but somehow the offer seemed a little abrupt. Everyone was quiet for a while.

Mica was lost in thought.

Finally, she said, "I can't sell you the whole camel."

"I don't think we should buy just one end," mumbled Nemir.

"Uncle, that's rude," Soraya said softly.

"I wasn't suggesting you buy an end. My husband Casimer would have liked him," she said pointing to Nemir and smiling.

"What are you suggesting?" Merak asked.

"I own half the animal along with Ravi. I would be willing to sell you my half interest with a stipulation. If Ravi wanted to sell you the other half, then you could have it. Otherwise, if Ravi wants to buy out your interest, you must sell it to him because he should be offered the first option to buy."

"How would we know if he wanted to sell the animal to us?" asked Merak.

"You could accompany the animal back to Ravi and ask him yourselves. I would have one favor to ask though," she said. She had been waiting to ask this favor since the group had arrived.

"Ask anything. It would be my honor," said Merak.

"I am going to close our racing stables. I don't want to take over the business affairs. The animals we have we will sell. There is one animal that my husband was enamored with that he wanted to give to Ravi."

Merak listened attentively.

"Would you deliver the animal to him as a gift from me?"

"Certainly," said Merak.

"Then we could ask Ravi where the family is," said Soraya who had put it all together.

"First, we must decide on a fair price for your animal," said Merak. "I presume he is still valuable breeding stock?"

"Not really. He is far too old," said Mica. "At least I think he's too old, but I don't know much about these things."

"I could examine him and tell you," said Nemir. "I have

bred camels for years. They rarely get too old."

Nemir reached over and took a few dried figs and put them in his pouch for later.

Mica's granddaughter came running over to show her the sweet that she found. Mica lifted her up and gave her a hug. She let the little girl feed her.

"Grandma, I miss grandpa," she said softly.

The little girl's eyes looked deeply into her grandmother's, trying to discern if the deep level of hurt that she had seen all this week was still there. She knew something was wrong but couldn't quite figure it out.

The room grew silent.

"We all miss him," said Mica.

"Even these new people?" said the child.

"Even these new people."

Mica paused and looked at the group.

"Perhaps it would be best if you went down to the stables to view the livestock. You could tell me if it was really your Jamil."

†

Jamil waited to see if Mica would come out again and finally gave up. He sauntered over to the stable and nudged the door. He had learned how to let himself in years ago. The stable boy treated it as though it were a trick that he had taught him.

"Hey old one, did you get your exercise?" Delia said.

"Yes, I exercised my mind," he said back.

"What did you do, think about running?"

"Precisely. Can't you tell how out of wind I am?"

"Was it fast? Were you as swift as the wind?"

He didn't answer. She didn't know when to stop, so he usually just got to the point where he simply stopped talking to her.

"Are we finished? Is that the end of the conversation?"

"Give it up Delia. It wasn't a conversation. We never really have conversations. You insult me, and I joke back with you."

"So why stop now?"

"Because I'm tired and sad. I don't feel like getting into a long discussion with you today," said Jamil. He looked at her hoping that she would understand. He didn't see anything that gave him hope.

"We never discuss anything. We argue. You said so yourself," Delia said. She waited for a response.

Jamil knew she was right, but he had nothing to say. He preferred to let his mind linger on Casimer and Heba. It restored a sense of gratitude when he thought about them.

Delia waited quietly. That in and of itself was unusual.

"I once lost someone I was very close to," said Delia in a soft voice.

"Then perhaps you understand," said Jamil.

"My first owner was a boy. I was supposed to be his camel. I was only a few months old, just barely weaned. It was when love still existed and…" She stopped talking.

Jamil looked at her with wonder. There was no toughness in her voice now, just pain.

"What happened?" Jamil asked cautiously.

"He died. I was sold like a thing. End of story."

"You're young. It's never the end of the story."

"It was for the little boy. We were a team. We were going to race together, young David and I, flying around the

Dromidromes, ahead of all the others. He had a fever, and a few days later he was gone. Just like that." She tapped her front hoof on the ground for emphasis.

"And then you were sad for a long time," added Jamil.

"No, I never got a chance to be sad. I was herded off to an auction. I went to the highest bidder, a bizarre old Arab who hated camels but loved gambling. I was sold three times in a row by speculators. I was a thing that could possibly make them wealthy. All they ever cared about was how fast I could run."

"So, tell me how you came to be purchased by Casimer," said Jamil.

"I deliberately ran slowly. Each time I was sold the owners lost money. They bought me because of this star on my forehead. That same stupid star that you have," she said. She was bitter.

"It's not a stupid star, it's just a star," said Jamil. He hesitated and then added, "It's a birthmark, a family inheritance. You are part of the clan even though you deny it."

"Everyone comes up and touches this stupid thing, and they say, 'Oh she has the star. Must be a descendant of Blaze.'"

"What's wrong with them touching it?"

"David used to touch it and called it a beauty mark. He touched it with love. They touch it and feel greed. Then they want to pick the perfect name for me. He called me Delia. When I was sold everyone had a different name for me. I was Star, and then Comet, and then Shooting Star. They were really original," she said.

"They hoped that changing your name would bring out your great speed," said Jamil.

"Yes, and then they expected me to run like the great Blaze of yesteryear because they had changed my name," she said angrily.

"And you refused," he said.

"Of course, I refused."

"And then they sold you off?" asked Jamil.

"No. First they beat me. That seemed like it was the logical thing to do for them. They were angry and blamed me for getting them angry. Thus, they beat me."

"They said it was your fault because you didn't run as fast as they wanted."

"That's right. It was always about what they wanted. The only thing I ever wanted was to be David's Delia. I could tell he loved me. He was kind and gentle and always had a treat. Here, just like everywhere else, they weigh the amount of feed, count the dried figs and the special treats. David never counted. He gave them to me out of love."

"Didn't I see the old man Casimer slip you fruit now and then?" asked Jamil.

"Yes, but that's different. He was trying to be my friend so he could use me."

"I knew Casimer for many years. A lot of the camels that he kept weren't great racers. They were okay, but not great. He treated them nicely just the same."

"Sure, and you raced because you wanted to."

He let the sarcasm pass and then said, "Yes, because I wanted to race. It was my way of having fun," Jamil said.

"I can't believe it," she said.

"Sure, you can. If David were still alive, wouldn't it be fun?" he asked.

She nodded.

"Casimer never beat me. I knew he loved me. We had fun together. We traveled the world together," said Jamil. He waited and then added, "He never let the riders beat me either."

"And now he's gone. It's the same thing either way. Humans abandon us. We're just dumb camels to them."

"To some of them perhaps, but to others we are beautiful, fun friends and bringers of great joy," said Jamil.

"Sure, but after they are done using you, they don't remember you. They are through with you and have no use for you. You're not a friend. They're not your friend. We are beasts of burden and racing stock. So, because of this star—which means I can run fast—I'm racing stock."

"That's probably true, but it doesn't mean you can't have fun," said Jamil.

"Yes, it does. I can't have fun. I have to run. 'You run, she-camel. This is no game.' That's all they kept saying to me," said Delia.

She glared at him and then finally averted her eyes.

"I wish I could bring them back," Jamil said softly.

She looked up at him and said, "Who?"

"Your David, my Heba, and Casimer. But I can't and I miss them. When I reminisce, I think that perhaps life was better when they were around."

"Perhaps better? Of course, it was. Sometimes I think you say the dumbest things. Of course, it was better," said Delia.

"No, it wasn't better. As long as I love now, this is as good as it gets. Life with or without the ones I care for always holds the opportunity for me to love. When I love, that's when it is as good as it can be. Sure, it was easier to love when Casimer was grooming me after a race and singing, or when

Heba was teaching me one of her timeless lessons. But you know what, half the time she was teaching me I was upset and angry with her because she didn't see life my way. I was miserable. Back even when I was carrying the newborn king and his mother, when life was perfect, I was complaining. Now I look back fondly at those times. I love those times, and that's what makes them so good."

Jamil looked at her to see if she was getting it.

"What's the bottom line here?" she asked.

"The bottom line is that when you love others, life is as good as it gets."

"I think the bottom line—*O Wise One*—is that when you love others, they leave, and you get hurt."

"Such a cynical way to live," said Jamil softly.

"I've heard you talk about the people you have met in your lifetime, but it seems to me that you've only had a few owners," she said. Delia made it sound like it was bad that he did not have many owners, and it was somehow his fault.

"Actually, I had four. The people who sold me to the Magi, the Magi, the family, and Casimer. Of course, he co-owned me with Mr. Ravi, but I hardly ever saw him."

"That's not the point Jamil," she said angrily.

"What's your point?" he said calmly.

"The point is that none of your previous owners care about you or wonder where you are or what has become of you. Little David really cared about me. That's unusual."

"It's not really. Humans are better than you make them out to be. They generally do care. We camels don't care as much as they do."

"That's ridiculous."

"Oh, really. Who was your father? Can you remember?" Jamil asked.

"Not really, but that's not important to camels," she said defensively.

"Oh, really now. Who was your mother?"

"She was Tara of the Little Zhab River."

"Do you remember her?"

"Not really, but I'm a camel," she said.

Jamil could see that she was getting very angry.

"Your father was one of my sons and you don't remember because camels don't remember who they are related to. We do remember our human masters," he said.

"I don't believe you said that. You make it sound like we are so low."

"Delia, in the cosmic order of things human beings come first. We are put on the earth to be of service to them. It's an honor whenever an animal gets to serve a human. That's the way the Sustainer envisioned it. The world was set up that way. Don't you find it strange that the only one you really remember, not your camel mother or father, is your first owner, a little boy overflowing with love? That's the secret. Humans are so filled with love that we animals are blessed when we get to serve them."

"Come off it, Jamil. You've placed them too high on a pedestal."

"No, I haven't. They are loved by the Sustainer even more than angels. That's because they have God's ability to love. That's a sacred thing, to love deeply."

"Yeah, well this young she-camel has met a lot of humans who didn't know how to love," she said.

Jamil knew that she was annoyed with him, but he

figured he should end the argument with something she couldn't disagree with.

"A lot of humans don't seem to know how to love, but that doesn't prove a thing. You know one human who was able to love you. It touched you so deeply that your life will never be the same."

"What's the use arguing with you," she said. She knew he was right, but she absolutely hated losing an argument.

"Once you have a true human friend, you have a friend for life. It's about time you started making some friends," he said.

✝

"Wallah!" shouted Nemir as he entered the stable. He saw Jamil's head sticking out near the end of the stalls.

"There he is and just as handsome as ever," said Abdul, right behind Nemir.

It was obvious to everyone but most importantly to Mica that the men knew who Blaze was. They recognized the camel instantly.

The two men ran to Jamil and started stroking his head. The camel immediately started making playful noises and nudged his nose right into Nemir's neck.

"He recognizes you," said Abdul.

"Of course, he recognizes me. I treated him like a king. I gave him lots of extra food," said Nemir.

Jamil swung his head over and nuzzled Abdul.

"Hi, my friend. You're an old camel now, but I can't believe how good you look," said Abdul. He was stroking Jamil's head and rubbing behind his ears.

Mica came up behind them and smiled. She was convinced of their story.

"Soraya, this is Jamil. Jamil, this is my youngest daughter Soraya," said Abdul.

"And this is Merak, an escort from the house of Magus Melchior," said Nemir.

He pulled Merak up to the camel.

Merak reached out and touched the mark on Jamil's crown.

"We have heard such wonderful stories about your racing," said Merak.

Jamil honked a couple times and then nudged Nemir who was looking at Delia. The she-camel was standing at the back of the stall away from all the activity. Nemir almost tumbled into Delia.

She spit at him.

"What, Nemir! Have you found a camel than likes you? Just like Jamil all those years ago," said Abdul.

He turned to his daughter and explained, "When we first picked up Jamil, he repeatedly spit at Uncle Nemir."

"That's Delia, the one I was telling you about," said Mica.

"She's a temperamental one, isn't she?" asked Nemir.

"Yes, Nemir. Be careful. She has a bad temper," Mica warned.

Delia backed away from Nemir, but Jamil pushed him toward her again.

"Hey Jamil, she doesn't want to meet me right now," said Nemir. He reached into his pocket and pulled out a piece of dried fig that he had taken from the house and put it near her mouth.

"Are you feeding her already?" asked Abdul.

"She's going to go on a little journey with us to Gabae, so I want to make friends fast," said Nemir.

Delia took the fruit and backed away.

Nemir moved back to Jamil.

"You look marvelous," Nemir said. He couldn't get over how good Jamil looked. He gave Jamil a fig too. He sneaked a peak at Delia and saw that she liked the fig too. *She must be his progeny,* he thought.

"So, do you think that you would be able to bring the animals to Ravi?" Mica asked.

Abdul looked at Nemir who nodded.

"Yes, it would be our honor," said Abdul.

"Could we discuss the price for Jamil," Merak said. He wanted to get on the road as soon as possible.

The entourage walked out of the stable into the back area. Jamil and Delia were let out into a large corral while Nemir watched them run.

†

"Who are these people?" asked Delia. She looked around the corral and decided not to run.

"They were my second owners. See how they remember. The little one is great for giving treats. When I was young, though, I tortured him."

"Why did you torture him? What did he do to you?" asked Delia.

"Nothing really. I was young and foolish. I didn't think he cared for me, and I was scared of where we were going."

Jamil started running slowly and then took a victory lap around the corral. Delia stayed with him, breathing easily and not breaking out in a sweat. He knew that she had the same makeup as he had. When another camel ran, he felt an irresistible urge to run too.

"Go ahead and show them what you can do," said Jamil. He picked up his speed and she had to go faster to keep up with him.

"I will not. I am not going to race for anyone. They will want to use me," said Delia defiantly.

He ran a little harder and she laughed.

"Hey old man, don't strain yourself," she said. She had no trouble keeping up with him. The urge to run welled up in her. It was so normal that she didn't even notice.

"I thought you were fast, he said. Maybe everyone was wrong."

Jamil ran harder and pulled away from her. He was straining now.

Delia was irritated with him, but she caught him and he pushed harder.

"Damn, you old fool, slow down," she said. Now she was starting to understand just how fast he was. She struggled to catch him.

"You're actually a lot slower than I thought," said Jamil. He pushed as hard as he could.

Delia was really angry now and blew past him out of spite.

She stopped when she saw him slow down.

"You're pretty fast, but I would have taken you in my heyday," said Jamil.

"Are you satisfied?" Delia asked.

"No, but they are," he said motioning for her to look at the crowd that had gathered around.

"Fools, I won't run for them," she said.

"Not if you run that slowly," said Jamil, still egging her on.

"Yeah, you want to see how fast I can run?"

She took off like a camel possessed. She flew around the corral, pushing herself to her limits. Jamil watched closely and realized with certainty that they were kin. They had the same gait, the same fluid movements. Now if he could only get her to run for the joy of it.

†

"That's an unbelievably fast animal," said Nemir in a whisper to Abdul. When he looked to see his reaction, he saw that only Soraya heard him.

"Unbelievable," Soraya whispered back. "She's like the wind."

"She's very small though. She'll need a tiny jockey," said Nemir.

"Someone very small," said Soraya. Her whole body tingled with excitement.

"Yes, a girl perhaps," whispered Nemir.

Mica moved closer to the fence near Nemir.

"What do you think of those two?" Mica asked.

"First, Jamil is still breeding stock, so you should ask a reasonable price. Second, the little camel is as fast as Jamil was."

"There is a problem with her though. She won't let anyone ride her. When someone does try to ride her, she won't race. Casimer was convinced that she would eventually compete, but it would take a lot of training to have her ready for a Dromidrome," said Mica.

†

The young camels gathered around Jamil to listen to his last story before his journey. Jamil watched a couple of

young ones on the periphery out of the corner of his eye and wondered whether they were getting it. He hoped so. Camels were difficult, especially the young ones. These were camels who were gifted athletes—champions who would race in the great Dromidromes of the world. Most of them were spoiled. Jamil knew it, but they had no idea. They thought that their training was near torture.

"Excuse me, *O Wise One*," said Delia, her voice dripping with sarcasm, "But how can you tell us that we have to think *outside the corral?*"

"I'm asking to use creative analysis, to think beyond the little picture here in the stable. I'm asking you to look at every problem as solvable. There are no unsolvable problems. If there is no solution, then it's an enigma not a problem. If there are solutions, but no good ones, then it's a dilemma. The difference between a dilemma and a problem is the creativity of the individual stuck with the problem."

Jamil looked at Delia. She frowned.

"You can't change a dilemma or an enigma into a problem simply because you refuse to accept the fact that there is no solution. That's unrealistic," said Delia.

She was being bold in her arguments. Jamil liked that.

"She's right. You're asking us to use creative analysis to solve problems that seem unsolvable," said another young but rather outspoken camel, named Nabob after an Indian king that Casimer had met years ago. Nabob was thin and wiry and liked to natter while running. He was great running extra-long distances but didn't have the heart or physique for a sprint.

"You're avoiding the real issue here. Our little team is being broken up and shipped off to everywhere. You heard

Mica. She said she was going to sell each of us off to different stables. Nabob is going to Egypt. You're being sold to Merak and will probably wind up in Arabia," said Delia.

She stopped talking because she was frustrated and angry with the unforeseen change in her life.

"Things have changed here, Delia," said Jamil softly. He looked at the others. They understood.

"Yeah, old man Casimer died," said one of the other camels who hung his head down. "I liked him."

"He's only one man. There are thousands of people in this city. Their clan is huge. Why should this make such a difference? His kids could run the stable or something..." Delia was stumbling to find the right words.

"One man can make a tremendous difference. You should remember that. Just like one of you could make an enormous difference. Never underestimate the power of one. One good man can make the world a better place and impact the lives of many more. One good camel can save a whole caravan," said Jamil.

"Not in our case. It's just the opposite. The life of one man is having a disastrous effect on all of us," said Delia.

The other camels nodded in agreement.

"Sloppy thinking again," said Jamil.

They all waited. They knew he loved to pick apart sloppy thinking.

"The life of a good man makes a big difference. The death of a good man also can make a great difference to the world. He comes to us and brings the good works of his spirit and changes things for the better. When he dies, he seems to leave us with a gap, but his character and his work live on and continue to bring good to the world. A man's body is

temporary, but his character is forever. Casimer was a good man. Here is your sloppy thinking, 'The life of one man is having a disastrous effect on all of us.' What you should have said was the *death* of a good man only *seems* to be having a disastrous effect on us."

"You mean that it's not having a disastrous effect on us? You can't be serious," said Bolcrest, a huge sprinter who had a rather abrupt manner. He towered over the other camels and was obviously from transporting stock.

"This is where you need to respond with creative analysis rather than react with hypercriticism. You're all running around here depressed and forlorn. 'It's going to be terrible. It won't work out where they send me. This is a stupid plan. We can't be split up.' And yet I'm telling you that each of you will wind up where you're supposed to be and with whom you need to be with. You'll all race and have a wonderful time. Bolcrest, you'll wind up doing sprints at the Dromidrome in Alexandria. They have specialty races for sprinters. You may even be entered in a power carry."

He was referring to a special race with the camels loaded with huge packs. He was perfect for this type of racing.

"Nabob, you'll wind up in the longer circuits or distance runs between cities in the scorching Arabian heat, where the races are long and challenging. You'll be able to natter and chatter to your heart's content because you have great endurance. You each have to learn to be creative with your talents. The Sustainer has given you each special gifts. It's your decision how and when to use them."

"Excuse me," said Delia. She sounded rude to everyone but Jamil who understood that she was afraid.

"How can you say we each have talents that make us

special. I get so sick of listening to this stuff. Some camels are just losers."

Jamil smiled.

"The only loser is the one who has not tried, who has not gotten into the arena and run the race with the other camels. The loser is the one on the sidelines thinking that he shouldn't try because he might fail. You each have special talents. Make no mistakes here. Casimer didn't select you because he wanted extra camels around filling up the empty stalls of his stable. He saw something in each and every one of you. There is some God-given talent that he was going to help you discover, to draw forth, *educare* as the Romans say. Yes, he was going to educate you."

"And now he is gone," said Lasha, a rather pretty, petite young camel.

"And you don't know why he wanted you here," said Jamil.

"Yes, I don't get it. I never did," said Lasha.

"So now you are forced to discover your talents on your own. Some of you understand them already and are using them. Some of you know your talents and refuse to use them. And a couple of you haven't got the foggiest idea. That's where I started. I had no idea why I was here or what my talents were."

Delia was annoyed that he had singled her out as having talent and refusing to use it. She couldn't complain because he hadn't actually used her name.

"You each will carry a special gift to wherever you go," said Jamil. He waited to see if they understood what he meant. He caught a glimmer of understanding from Delia but could tell she rejected the idea.

"It has to do with Heba and her philosophy?" Delia asked.

"Yes, it does. You each can carry the word to every other camel you come in contact with. You can teach them the lessons of character development and have a tremendous impact on the well-being of camels all over the world."

The camels nodded their heads. Only Delia seemed annoyed with the idea.

"We have to believe it first," she said.

"More than that. You have to live it. Anyone can see the truth in letting go of raging indignation for profound peacefulness but putting it into practice is so much more difficult. Anyone can see that victim syndrome will ruin your life, but service to the least of my brothers will give you an unconquerable spirit."

"I understand addicted to being right, but I find it so difficult to practice dignified humility," said nattering Nabob.

They all laughed. His character flaw was the easiest to understand.

"You bring the possibility for a better style of living for other camels. Heba was wise beyond what you can imagine. Her lessons are yours for the giving, but you have to be willing to give them away to understand them. You each know what I am talking about intellectually. But once you are on your own, listening to the complainers, the whiners, and the poor unfortunates who don't understand how life is lived, you will see the wisdom in her ideas. Teach it. That's all I'm suggesting. If you want to learn it and make it yours on a gut level, all you have to do is teach it."

"I'm not sure I'm capable of teaching it," said Bolcrest.

"Of course, you are, just don't go into raging indignation when someone disagrees," said Jamil.

The others chuckled, imagining Bolcrest reading the riot act to anyone who differed with him.

"Remember, when you're stuck somewhere in a foreign land thinking, 'How can I get them to understand?' your duty is to explain and clarify it in your own mind. They may or may not get it, but in the process of teaching it the knowledge becomes yours."

"I don't think I'll ever want to teach this stuff," said Delia.

"It's a good thing that Jamil is going to Gabae with you," said Nabob. "At least he'll be teaching it there."

"Yeah, sure," said Delia. She slipped off to another area of the stable.

✝

Heat lightning illuminated the vast horizon to the west. Traces of the mountains lingered for a moment and then faded into a dim memory. There was no rumble of thunder, just flashes indicating that the heavens were uncertain.

Delia was on her knees but couldn't get to sleep. The gnawing emptiness in her heart mixed with a dread of the future left her awake. She longed for the oblivion that sleep could provide, but no matter what she did she stayed awake. Her mind rambled from one disconnected thought to another along bridges of fear. "I must be losing what little of my mind I have left," she said out loud.

Her self-talk was as cynical and sarcastic as her conversations were with the others. This came as no surprise. It felt natural. Even though it was uncomfortable it was natural because her sarcasm was a familiar friend.

The heat lightning flashed again. No thunder rumbled, but a shiver went through her. The unseasonably warm spring air didn't comfort her. *Maybe I'm getting sick*, she thought.

She was sick of life. It seemed absurd to her that she was so fed up with everything that all she experienced was a sense of disgust—no joy, no hope, no happiness.

"I'm sick of life," Delia said out loud. She didn't expect anyone to hear her, but her own voice was comforting and left her feeling less alone. The dread was larger than she had feared. It filled her chest and belly with a feeling of being too large almost as if the emotion was looking for a place to overflow. It intensified in her heart. The emotion was so large that she felt like her chest was going to burst.

"Maybe the next stable will be nicer," she said, trying to comfort herself. It didn't work. Casimer's stable was the finest there was. She knew that. Gabae couldn't be better and probably would be a lot worse.

As soon as she drifted off to sleep, she was startled awake. The presence of danger was in the stall where she was kept. She could sense it. She moved her head slowly as she looked around. Whatever it was, she didn't like it. She didn't want to stay in the stable. She wanted to be out running. *I am faster than any other animal, and I can outrun anything. I could outrun the danger. The key was to run. I need to run. Then I would be happy.*

"My thoughts are driving me crazy," she said.

She listened awhile longer. There was nothing in the stable with her but her own dark fantasies of what the future held. *You dread the future*, her thoughts said in an ominous tone.

"And what if the future holds a purpose that will be revealed to you by the Sustainer," Jamil's voice said in her memory.

That small voice of hope wanted to comfort her. She pushed it away. She didn't trust hope. She had no faith. She wanted reality to be clear so that she could deal with her misery head on.

Yet, she didn't really deal with misery well. She tried to identify it so that she could hide from it. It made her shaky to hide from it, but she hid nevertheless.

"Damn," she said out loud in frustration.

"Awake, are you?" Jamil asked in the distance. His voice was soft, smooth, and kind.

She thought about not answering, but said, "Can't sleep."

"Oh?"

When she didn't say anything, Jamil said, "Concerned about the trip to Gabae in the morning."

Delia refused to answer. She preferred to feel the loneliness and the sorrow that filled her soul. She missed the fun. It had been so long since she had done anything for fun. She missed David. She loved David deeply. He was the only one she had fun with.

Is it possible that I will never have fun again and just be miserable for the rest of my life? Delia asked herself. She yawned and shivered at the same time. It came out like a shaky sigh.

"Delia, I'm here if you need me," Jamil said softly.

Jamil's voice was a distraction that she was not going to answer. She was exploring the self-pity. It seemed deep, almost bottomless. She had this strange need to feel sorry for herself, to grieve her own loneliness. *What would David say now if he found me awake like this?*

"He would comfort me," she mumbled. She realized he would promise her that she would run. He always promised to take her to the hills and ride like the wind. Her eyes filled with tears at the realization that running was her comfort. David had known it. Using her great gift was the solution to her fears. Using her talents broke the cycle of self-pity and ridded her of the feelings of despair.

Running wouldn't work anymore. She remembered the night they came by and told her that David was gone. She had vowed not to run again until he came back. When she realized that they meant he was never coming back, she promised never to run again, at least not with joy for the thrill of it.

Her eyes filled with tears. When David left, he had taken their dreams with him. When he left, she buried the part of her that cared, felt joy, relished life, and avidly sought to discover the talents that the Sustainer had given her.

She heard a voice laugh deep inside her. It was a part of her mocking herself, criticizing the path she had taken. She felt colder now. She knew that she had to move around to keep warm. She needed action to change her feelings, but the dark night would keep her in the stable, confined and unable to run.

†

Dawn broke with the sweet singing of birds as the stirring of life once again made the presence of God evident to all who had eyes to see. Delia turned a blind eye to the brilliant colors on the eastern horizon. She wanted to stay asleep.

It took me hours to fall asleep and now these damn birds wake me up. Is there no justice? she asked herself.

The stable hand came in and walked by her stall. He looked in and then walked down to the end of the stable and looked at Jamil.

"Well, Blaze, you are off to another adventure. I don't think there was ever a camel who traveled more than you," said the hand. "Be careful. Nasty is going with you."

He was referring to Delia who was known for kicking people she didn't like.

"Hey, *Nasty*, I mean Delia," said the stable hand as he opened the top door to the stable.

She stuck her head out through the door to look around. He had to step back to keep from being butted by her. She smelled his hand. It had the aroma of dates. She nuzzled it until she found one, then the hand put a bit into her mouth. The stable hand tethered her so he could put a harness on her. He thought about it for a moment and then remembered that the two animals would need saddles. They were going to be tethered together and tag along for the trip.

When Nemir, Abdul, Merak, and Soraya arrived, Mica was already waiting. Her stable hands had the two camels ready. She had a parchment document with a wax seal in place, ready for Merak to present to Ravi when they arrived in Gabae later that evening.

Nemir and Abdul went up to Jamil and stroked his side and caressed his long forehead and nose. While they made a big deal about Jamil, Merak took Delia and tethered her to his camel.

Soraya walked up to Delia and stroked her thin back. She noticed how much smaller Delia was than her own camel. She checked the bit to make sure it fit properly. The camel's muscles twitched.

"Here you go, girl," she said affectionately and adjusted the bit slightly and then gave her a date. She was told by the stable hand that both animals had a fondness for them.

"Trying to make her comfortable?" Merak asked.

"Yes, she seems uncomfortable, doesn't she?" asked Soraya.

"Don't kid yourself. Camels are smart. She knows she's being given away," said Merak.

"You're right. I'll bet she doesn't like changing owners so frequently," said Soraya.

"She doesn't like owners," said the stable hand. He threw a small harness over the camel's hump and secured a couple packages.

"What are those?" asked Soraya.

"Gifts for Ravi," said Mica who was still standing next to Nemir and Abdul.

Delia shook her head from side to side, pulling on the tether and causing the bit to irritate her mouth. She moved a little closer and spit. It looked like she was deliberately spitting at Merak's beast. The well-trained animal turned his head back and looked at the smaller animal. He was much larger than Delia and it seemed like he was giving her a look that told her to behave.

"I think she's testing your animal's patience," said Soraya.

"He can handle her," said Merak with a laugh.

"She's very temperamental," said Mica.

"We will be careful," said Merak. He tested the tether to make certain it would hold. The last thing he wanted was for this little one to get away. They would never catch her.

"You'll be just fine," said Soraya. She petted Delia again.

"You're a beautiful animal. You just need someone who understands you."

The small caravan left the stable and slowly headed west on the road to Gabae.

Soraya looked back at Mica who was standing watching them as they marched in a procession up the hill leading out of town. She saw Mica's hand move up to her eye and wipe away a tear. It was the end of an era.

†

"And now we are on the road to a new adventure," said Jamil.

Delia didn't answer.

"Did you hear the young girl? She said you just needed someone who understands you," said Jamil.

He was in a more talkative mood than usual. Delia didn't like that. She didn't understand that there was a part of him that was more than excited, it was nervous too.

Delia tugged a bit at the tether. She could tell it was strong. Merak turned to look at her. He checked the tether to make sure it was secure. She looked him right in the eye. This was a self-assured man, but not a mean one. She could tell that.

"What do you make of them?" Jamil asked.

"Who knows," she said with a dismissive tone.

"One never knows, but sometimes you get a feel for people," said Jamil.

"They seem nice, all right? They always seem nice at first. It takes a while to get to know humans. I've found you can never really tell. They seem okay one minute, but you should never let your guard down. They have their own needs and

their own private agendas. As long as you serve their needs, you're okay."

"Camels were placed on earth to be of service to man," said Jamil.

"Sure, and they beat you and mistreat you when your service isn't up to their expectations."

"Talk about being bitter," he said.

"I'm practical. I've got my own experiences that tell me to watch out. You can never tell what they're up to. You never know, so you have to be very careful," said Delia.

"I respect your right to your opinion…"

"I have a personal past that forms that opinion," she said cutting him off.

"You have a right to form your opinion based on your personal experiences, but don't go thinking that your experience is the whole thing. Every camel has his own experiences with humans. For the most part they are good. They feed us, groom us, and care about what happens to us."

"Yeah, right, whatever."

"These are good people. I can tell, especially the girl," said Jamil softly.

She ignored him. His reassurances fell on deaf ears. It wasn't that she didn't think these were good people. She had an inkling that they were. But her hopes ended where her fears began. They were moving on to a new stable and a new owner. She had been down that road before and she knew it was better not to go into the new situation with her hopes too high. Even if these were good people, she was going to be turned over to the man in Gabae named Ravi.

†

They were in the open country again. In a short while they would cross the River Jordan.

"Is this countryside starting to look familiar?" Nemir asked.

"You mean the river?" Abdul said back to him. He stood high in his saddle. He could see it off in the distance.

"Yes, the Jordan River," said Nemir. He reached back and checked the tether to Jamil. He wanted to make certain it was tight.

"Remember how skittish he got when we crossed it the first time?"

"How can I forget, Abdul? The little guy was jumping out of his skin. All that water was making him crazy."

"What happened, Papa?" Soraya asked. She moved her camel closer to her father's.

"We had finally reached Judea with all three caravans of the Magi joined in one huge and colorful caravan. All we had to do was cross the river at a point where it was shallow and make sure the animals didn't panic," said Abdul.

"Sounds easy, doesn't it?" Nemir asked.

"Yes, very," said Soraya. She knew that camels could handle shallow water fairly well as long as there were strong hands managing them.

Merak pulled up closer to listen to the story. They were in a line; four across with the two camels trailing behind.

"We didn't figure that it was the first river Jamil had ever crossed. It was mind boggling for the little fellow. He got to the middle of the river and just about laid down," said Abdul.

"He was in camel heaven, Soraya. He was ready to drop to his knees and thank the Creator that he had been brought

to paradise. Every muscle in his body twitched," added Nemir. He laughed at the recollection.

"Do you think we'll have trouble with him now?" Merak asked.

"Probably not," said Nemir. "He's older and has traveled far and wide."

Delia tugged at the reins and lifted her head to smell.

"I think you're going to have trouble with her though," said Nemir.

"I can handle it," said Merak confidently.

†

"You smell that don't you?" asked Jamil.

"It's marvelous, fresh, invigorating…"

Jamil waited for her to stop talking. She was sniffing the air forcefully, trying to get as much of the aroma in as she could.

"I can't believe it. It's like a pond, only more full-bodied and fresher."

Jamil smiled at the excitement in her voice.

"It's a river. Perhaps the biggest you've ever seen," said Jamil.

"I crossed the Euphrates when I was very young. We were kneeling on barges though," she said.

"Water isn't always a friend to a camel. You have to be careful when you cross a river. There's an unbelievable urge to let yourself go. To get into it with your whole body," said Jamil. He could remember his first crossing like it was yesterday.

"Sounds good to me," she said.

"If you lay down in the water, it will carry you

downstream quickly. You're not designed for water. Camels can't swim," he said.

"Yeah, so what do camels do when they get carried downstream?" She was being sarcastic.

"They get completely covered with water and drown," he said.

"That doesn't sound too bad."

"Except it's horrible and you can't enjoy it. At that point you're dead."

"Oh, I see," she said.

Jamil wasn't sure that she got it.

They came to the top of a slight rise in the road and could see all the way down into the valley. Before them, winding silently through green fields, was a body of water that seemed to flow forever.

"We're going to walk right across that river," said Jamil.

He was watching Nemir pointing to the wide part of the river and talking to Merak. The conversation was animated. Every now and then, the two men looked back at their two camels and checked their bindings.

"They're concerned that we won't make the crossing without giving them trouble," said Jamil.

"How do you know that?"

"Listen to them and watch how they keep checking the bindings. By the way, follow the animal in front of you. If you swing too wide and the river deepens you could slip into a hole. That's not a lot of fun," said Jamil.

She looked at him suspiciously.

†

"The road leads right to where we need to cross," said Nemir.

"How can you be so sure?" Abdul asked.

"These Romans probably have the river marked where it's safe to cross," said Merak. He had forded a lot of streams and small rivers. This was not a real problem for him or his camel.

Merak smiled at Soraya.

"Do we stop and let them drink when we reach the banks?" asked Soraya.

"It's probably best," said Abdul. He would be cautious, especially with the younger one.

"Come Abdul, you old worry wart. Jamil will be fine and Merak can handle the little one."

"Uncle Nemir, you're always so confident," said Soraya. She was glad that he was positive about life and didn't worry like her father.

"But we should take special precautions just the same," said Merak.

He sounded like her father again. It annoyed her but also touched her heart because she understood him so well.

"The young man sees my point. A river is always a problem for camels. The younger they are the worse it is," said Abdul. He was feeling justified.

"And Soraya, the little camel is too fast to chase after if she gets away," said Merak.

"More importantly, if she gets caught in the flow of the river she could drown," said Abdul.

"Oh, stop worrying. The crossing was at a point in the river that was smooth as silk, a sandy bottom, no rapids, no holes. It was as simple as walk in town," said Nemir.

Delia lifted her head, sniffed hard, and made a honking sound.

"Nevertheless, we'll be careful," said Merak.

Soraya dropped back and leaned over to stroke Delia's side.

"Easy girl. Everything will be fine, and yes, we've been talking about you."

Merak smiled at her. "You like this little camel, don't you?"

It was more of a statement than a question.

"She's not only beautiful, but she runs like the wind," said Soraya. She gave Delia an extra pat.

"Do you think you could ride her?" he asked.

"Of course, and better than you could," she said. There was a playful challenge in her voice.

"Perhaps, you are smaller, and she is not a large animal."

"It's because I'm a better rider than you," she blurted out and then regretted it.

"Oh, really? What do you base that on?" Merak asked. Normally he was fiercely competitive, but now he felt playful. It was like he was getting ready to dance rather than compete.

"Hey Uncle Nemir, tell Merak what kind of a camel rider I am," said Soraya.

"Watch out, Merak. She's the best. I've never met a man who could beat her time on an animal," said Nemir.

"She rides first perhaps and then the heavier man tries to beat her time on the same animal?" Merak suggested.

"First or second, Merak," Nemir yelled.

"Feeding a little fire, are you?" Abdul asked softly.

"It'll be fun to see them fight a little, so they know how

they handle themselves," Nemir said back.

"I heard that Uncle Nemir," Soraya chided.

She smiled at Merak.

"If we race, my brave soldier, I will not spare you but test your mettle," she said with a polite nod.

Merak bowed toward her, "And I will make you proud."

"Don't cut her any slack," said Nemir. "If you're a good man, you'll beat her. He can probably take you Soraya."

"Nemir, don't egg her on. She's going to embarrass him if she beats him," said Abdul.

"I don't think so," said Nemir.

"You know how she rides."

"I mean I don't think he'll be embarrassed. This is a man who is self-confident and doesn't need to win everything to feel good about himself," said Nemir.

"I hope you're right," said Abdul.

†

Merak and Soraya brought the little camel to the water. They wanted to let her drink. It would be easier if she were satiated before attempting the crossing. She would be less tempted if she went across without dipping her muzzle into the water.

When Delia was finished, they brought her out. Soraya stayed with her.

"Here you are girl. Take a date. Its sweetness will linger in your mouth after the water," Soraya said. She lifted her hand to the animal's mouth. She could tell the animal wasn't hungry, but the date was too much for her to resist.

Merak and Nemir brought Jamil to the water. He was no problem for them. One by one the men watered each of the animals.

All the bindings were checked and secured to make sure nothing would fall into the water as they walked across. The occasional pocket or hole in the riverbed sometimes made an animal stumble causing goods that weren't secured properly to fall.

Merak walked out into the river and inspected the bed. It was smooth all the way across. There were some holes and it got deeper a few yards further downstream, but for the most part this was a perfect place to ford the river. The Romans had chosen wisely.

They tethered all the animals together in a line. Abdul would go first followed by Nemir with Jamil next. Merak was behind Jamil and Delia came next between Merak and Soraya. As they entered the water it occurred to Nemir that they should have switched Jamil and Delia so that she was between the two best handlers, Merak and Nemir.

Abdul was already moving across the river.

✝

"So did you ever try to lay down in a river?" Delia asked.

Merak's camel looked back at her like she was crazy. Jamil, however, knew what was going on. He started talking to keep her attention away from the water.

"I never did, but I did see an animal drown once. They used it for food that same day. It was disgusting," said Jamil.

"You're just trying to scare me," said Delia.

"That's true. It's so you'll respect the river. Water is the friend to most animals, but water can be treacherous. As much as it gives us pleasure and relieves our thirst, too much of a good thing isn't wonderful. It's dangerous," said Jamil.

"You never just laid down and let the water flow all around, and under your body?"

The thought was tantalizing. She couldn't help feeling a little shiver of pleasure rush up her spine.

"Look at the vegetation on the other side of the river," said Jamil. He was trying to get her to concentrate on the goal.

"Yeah, so?"

She looked at it for a moment and then looked down at the water.

"Focus your attention on the other side," said Jamil.

"Hey, the water swirls around my legs. That's so fun. It really feels good when it does that," she said. It seemed harmless enough to her.

Jamil was alarmed. He knew that she shouldn't be looking at the water. All the other camels held their heads high watching the other shore.

"Don't look down at it. It will fascinate and capture you," said Jamil.

"Oh, come off it, you old buzzard. You don't know how to have fun."

They were approaching the deepest part of the water. It wasn't so deep that it was a problem for a normal camel, but Delia was a little smaller. The water rose almost to her belly. It was swirling around her thighs, cooling them in a way that she had never experienced in the desert.

"Wow. Is this wonderful or what?" she said. Her tone was a little too loud and alarmed Jamil. He turned to look, but Nemir kept pulling his tether to keep his head up and looking forward.

Merak was trying to do the same with Delia.

Another inch or two deeper and I could feel the water on my belly, she thought. She let her legs bend and felt the water rushing under and around her.

The sudden surge of pleasure was too much to resist. She gave in to her impulse to taste the forbidden fruit. *Just for a moment, let me feel the full pleasure of it,* she thought and let her knees bend. She was going in now. There was no turning back, no matter how much she had been warned.

The water enveloped her. The delight was unlike anything she had ever known. At once it was more incredible than she could have hoped for, yet at the same time it wasn't enough. It could never be enough. She let herself submerge completely, hoping desperately that she could somehow get enough to last a lifetime.

†

Merak felt the tug and then the sudden pull that yanked his camel to a halt. He looked back and saw the little camel go under.

"Oh, God!" he shouted. The strain nearly toppled his camel. Merak's hand went into the water as he tried to reach back.

Merak's camel saw what was happening and bolted forward suddenly, straining the tether.

"Merak, watch out!" yelled Soraya.

Merak grabbed the tether, but when his wet hand touched the leather, it slipped off and Delia was free.

Soraya's camel was tethered to the Delia and started being pulled into the water as Delia was washed sideways by the current.

Merak's camel bolted causing the others to rush toward the bank.

Soraya could feel her camel being pulled deeper and reached for her knife. She jumped off the beast and cut the

line to Delia. Her camel charged forward toward the shore.

"Soraya!" called her father. He watched in horror as the little camel choked and struggled to get up. Soraya was running at full speed splashing through the water to get to her.

Merak was running back into the river to help.

"Let her go Soraya!" Nemir yelled. He was terrified that she would be pulled downstream with the beast.

But Soraya had the tether and was holding onto the camel for dear life. Delia's body was still sideways, but floating downstream. If she could just hold on until the animal reached a shallow enough area, she knew that Delia could stand.

Just as she was pulled into a deep pocket in the river, Merak got to her.

"Let go," he begged as he jumped in to help.

Soraya and Merak were both pulled into the deeper area and swept along. Soraya was unwilling to let go. Her head was under water as she was straining to hold on and hold her breath.

Suddenly Delia hit a shallow portion. With Merak and Soraya holding on she was slowed down enough. Delia stood up.

Merak and Soraya struggled to the shallow area and grabbed Delia.

"You poor thing," Soraya said, stroking her head and checking to see if the bit had hurt her.

Her father and uncle came charging into the water to get them.

"She's shaking," said Merak moving the camel toward the shore. He walked cautiously forward and kept checking

to make sure there were no more deep pockets, but Delia surged ahead of him to get out of the water.

"You'll be okay, baby," said Soraya, her face close to the camel's.

✝

Delia was still coughing up water when she reached the shore. Soraya was running alongside of her, talking to her in soothing terms. Merak's animal backed away, and Delia charged right up to Jamil. She was shuddering uncontrollably.

"I didn't know it would be like this. I thought I was going to die," said Delia. She moved close to Jamil, almost leaning against him.

"I tried to warn you," said Jamil.

"I didn't believe you. I didn't want to believe you. It felt so good, so delicious."

"Pleasure is its own reward but often brings its own punishments. Water was given us by the Sustainer to be used in moderation," said Jamil.

"I was choking. It wasn't pleasurable. It was painful, terrifying, and horrid," said Delia. She shuddered again.

"You'll be okay. Perhaps the value of the lesson will serve you well."

She felt the hands of Soraya stroking her side, gently soothing her. He continued to talk, but her attention faded away.

✝

"I'm okay, Papa," she insisted.

Abdul was still shaken. He had seen his daughter almost taken away from him. A parent should never see a child die,

he decided firmly. It was not God's way. He made it so that parents pass first to save them the unbearable pain of losing a child.

Merak and Uncle Nemir stood back and let her father have a moment with her.

"I thought I was going to lose you," Abdul whispered softly. His eyes were filled with tears.

"I wouldn't let that happen, Papa," she said.

"Merak had a hold of Soraya, and from the looks of things, I don't think he was going to let her go," said Nemir.

Merak gave him a look. He didn't want to be embarrassed by Nemir, but enjoyed it nevertheless.

"She's so stubborn and headstrong, just like her mother," said Abdul, who was getting over his trauma of almost losing her.

"You mean, sir, that she's determined and spirited," said Merak defending her.

Soraya smiled. It was good to have a man who defended her.

8

IN SEARCH OF THE
NAZARENE

"Well, this is Gabae Stables," said Nemir. He was looking up at a hand painted sign that hung over the door to a rather large building. They had found Ravi's establishment easily. Over the years it had grown larger and was now a full-fledged caravansary with lodging for the camel drivers and not just their camels.

Merak had dismounted and handed the reins to his camel to Nemir. Abdul did the same and then Soraya shrugged her shoulders.

"Here Uncle. I guess you're stuck with the beasts until we find their stable hand," she said.

"Hey, what is this. I want to come in too," said Nemir. He looked around at the hitches and then decided not to tie them up until someone came out to watch them.

Two boys came running out and took the reins from Nemir. They started marching the camels through the gate that was at the center of the building. It served as the main entrance to the caravansary and allowed the caravan to enter and be fully contained while the travelers negotiated for rooms.

"How many are you?" asked the clerk, Josephus. He

was a solicitous dark-haired young man whose brown eyes revealed an alert and cunning mind.

"We would like three rooms," said Merak. "One for the two gentlemen, one for the young lady and one for myself."

The clerk eyed them carefully and then nodded. "Would there be anything else?

"Yes, we need to speak with the proprietor, if it is still Ravi," said Merak.

"It is, and what shall I tell him is the nature of your business?" The clerk was already putting the ledger away and getting ready to call the owner.

"We have just come from Casimer's widow, and we bring him news and a gift," said Nemir. He moved his hands to signal 'get going' and then looked around.

Josephus was insulted to be dismissed.

"I could have handled that better, Nemir," said Merak.

"Nice place," said Nemir. "This guy must be loaded. Racing's quite a business. If you win, you live like a king. If you lose, you're a pauper."

"Uncle, do you have visions of living like a king?" Soraya asked. She moved her hands to each side of his head and pretended to straighten his crown.

"He's too short to be a king," said Abdul.

"Gentleman and young lady," a voice boomed.

Though Ravi was an old man, he came rushing down the stairs with his arms out like they were long lost friends. Josephus was right behind him.

"Ravi?" Merak asked.

"I have recently heard of the death of my great friend. I am greatly grieved by his passing. Have you brought news from his family?"

The introductions were quickly made, and immediately Ravi barked orders to his clerk and a cook to bring refreshments. The entourage went into the main parlor of the caravansary.

Merak politely handed the sealed letter to Ravi. He opened it and sat down. The weight of the death of his friend Casimer was too much for him to bear standing. The old man's eyes glistened as he read.

"How does she seem to be dealing with the loss of her husband?" Ravi asked. His voice was soft now and cracked under the strain of his grief.

"The family is doing well as far as I could determine," said Merak.

"She's selling the stable," said Nemir. "I think that tells the story."

"In her letter, Mica says that you wish to purchase Blaze from me and take him back to Babylon. She also said that once I hear the story, I will want to let you have the camel too," said Ravi.

"I hope so," said Nemir.

"You haven't said much," Ravi said to Abdul, who was sitting quietly.

"I was thinking about the real purpose of our journey," said Abdul. "This talk of buying camels and bringing them back is a nice distraction from a more important task."

"What could be more important than racing camels?" Ravi asked.

Josephus had entered with a few more sweets and pretended not to listen. That triggered an alarm in Merak who noticed the young man even more now.

"Keeping one's word," said Abdul seriously.

"Mica did say I would enjoy the story," said Ravi.

"They have a special gift from three Magi from the kingdoms of Arabia, Persia, and India," said Merak. "But they can tell the story best."

When Abdul and Nemir finally finished, Ravi sat back and wondered out loud, "So the stories we have been hearing of Jesus of Nazareth are probably true. I had dismissed them as the hysterical rantings of the Zealots wishing to overthrow the Romans."

The Zealots were a political group in Israel who wanted to free the Promised Land from the control of the Romans. They were constantly at odds with the Pharisees for control of the temple and the heart and soul of the Jewish state.

"You know the man?" asked Abdul.

Everyone was on the edge of their seats waiting to hear.

"I don't know him personally, and I only met the family about thirty years ago. They were a couple with a little child about three years old. She was very young, and her name was Mary. The father was a bit older and named Joseph. I helped them purchase a cart. Joseph was a carpenter, and they were heading to Nazareth."

"Yes, we met the family years ago too," said Abdul. "What do you know about the child, the man, I mean?"

"He's from Nazareth, and for the past year or so I've been hearing amazing stories about him," said Ravi.

Everyone waited for him to continue, but he was thinking about what Abdul and Nemir had told him.

"These wise men from the East knew he was destined to become the King of the Jews?" said Ravi. He noticed the clerk listening to their conversation in the hallway.

"Is Nazareth far from here?" asked Soraya.

"No, it's a couple hours' journey north," replied Ravi.

"Then we shall go there tomorrow," said Merak.

"It's the Sabbath, so you'll have to wait a day. People won't like it if you are traveling on the Sabbath, and the family might not receive you either," said Ravi.

"We'll go in a couple of days," said Abdul. He had decided that they could best use the extra day, making themselves presentable, and learning what they could about the young, soon-to-be king.

"Tell us what you have heard," said Merak.

"I've heard wonderful things, but I haven't heard that he had any pretenses to be the king," said Ravi.

Ravi looked at their faces and could tell that they wanted to hear everything he had heard.

"He performs miracles," Ravi said.

"Miracles?" Nemir asked suddenly confused.

They looked at each other and then Ravi continued.

"He heals the sick—you know, the blind, the deaf, the lame, lepers. Large crowds gather to hear him speak. They say that he is quite a sight to behold. I had dismissed it all."

"That sounds marvelous, why would you dismiss it?" Soraya asked.

"Because the coming King of the Jews, the Messiah who will liberate Israel, is not supposed to be a faith healer, doctor, or miracle worker. He's not supposed to be giving lectures on the scriptures. He's supposed to lead us to victory over our oppressors and set Israel up as the jewel of all nations," Ravi said.

He looked around at them and realized that they were not Jewish and didn't understand. He again noticed the clerk who pretended to be busy in the foyer of the establishment.

"If this Jesus of Nazareth is the Messiah, then we are in for a war of liberation, and I am not looking forward to fighting the Romans or anyone for that matter. I prefer peace. It's safer to make profits in peace," said Ravi.

Merak seemed to understand the significance immediately.

"Is this possibility well-known among your people?" Merak asked.

"It's being talked about more and more by the average Jew," said Ravi.

"Then why haven't the Romans arrested him?" Merak asked.

"The Romans may be cruel with their punishment, but they are just with their laws. If he has broken no law, he won't be touched. If he breaks the law, he will be dealt with swiftly. That's why there is relative peace throughout the empire. People like fairness, and they appreciate swift punishment of the guilty," said Ravi.

"Okay, we head to Nazareth in a couple days, and it's settled," said Nemir.

"It's good that you go to Nazareth, because bringing gifts to a man who would be king is best done outside of Jerusalem. That might cause trouble for the young man," said Ravi.

"Nazareth is easier," said Nemir. He wanted to change subjects and get on with the discussion of the camels.

"The high holy days are coming next week and there is a good chance that Jesus will be in Jerusalem."

"In Jerusalem, we would be obliged by protocol to visit the Roman prelate," said Merak. The idea seemed more of a problem now that ever.

"There's not a thing we can do at this point. Let's check on the animals and then retire for the night," said Abdul.

"Yes, and I want you to stay in Casimer's suite. He would have preferred that," Ravi said.

The clerk who had been listening near the top of the stairs quickly exited. He needed to tell someone what he had heard this evening.

†

"Papa, this is a palace," Soraya exclaimed as she entered the suite where they would be staying.

Ravi smiled, tilted his head, and with an elegant nod let them know that they were his personal guests.

"Let me show you the view from your balcony," Ravi said, opening doors that led to what was really the roof over a portion of the stable. It looked out onto a track that was built to train the animals that Ravi bought. He had become a merchant of racing camels and bought and sold with Egyptian breeders.

"We are honored by the accommodations," said Merak. He was standing next to Ravi but watching Soraya as she took a tour of their accommodations. Her expression was pure delight.

"The apartment belonged to my dear friend Casimer," said Ravi.

The men watched Soraya as she examined the furnishings and even looked at the window coverings. She dropped herself on a large couch with a plop. She was grinning from ear to ear. This was a palace.

"There are fresh clothes in the trunks that Casimer left behind. His daughter's trunk is at your disposal, Soraya,"

said Ravi. He pointed to a small room off to his left and smiled.

She popped off the couch and rushed in. Ravi followed her into the room.

Soraya hesitated.

"Aren't you going to open it up?" said Ravi. "She would wear these things when she was in Judea so that she fit in. Go ahead, she's much older now, and they would no longer suit her."

Abdul gave her permission with a nod.

"You will each have separate rooms and can have your meals down in the main dining area or brought up. Whatever you prefer," said Ravi.

"What would you prefer?" asked Abdul.

"Come downstairs. The dining area will be empty. Most of the caravans left before the Sabbath and outside traders know that next week is not a good week for merchants who aren't Jewish since it's the high holy days."

†

"I see that they put a racing saddle on you," said Jamil.

Ravi had just left the two camels. He had a lot to say to his Blaze, but mostly thanked him for being such a Godsend and boon to his family. The former stableman was now wealthy. Caravans stayed at his caravansary just for the sake of saying that they know the co-owner of the greatest racing camel ever.

"Yeah, and he sure had a lot to say to you," said Delia.

"A good human is a grateful human," said Jamil.

"Sure."

Jamil looked at her for a moment.

"An attitude of gratitude heals the wounded heart and lets one see that the present moment is a gift from God," said Jamil.

'Right, whatever," she said curtly.

"That man was always good to me and fair with Casimer. His gratitude says something about him," said Jamil.

"Oh yeah? What does gratitude say?" she said. It was not so much a question as another attempt to shut Jamil up with sarcasm.

"Gratitude says that he is smart enough to know that all good things come from God. The Sustainer provides us with what we need as we need it. That's a tough lesson to understand. Gratitude is the reflection of that understanding," said Jamil.

"Sure, the Sustainer provides what we need, just like I needed little David to die when he did," she said.

"You're not grateful for his life, just bitter about his death?" Jamil asked.

"Yup, you've figured it out."

"That's so sad. His life's mission was to love you completely and then he was called back to his Creator because his job was done, and you're not grateful," said Jamil.

Her breathing caught a hitch when he said that. Jamil could sense the pain but walked away from her. He wanted it to sink in.

She choked back her sadness, found her anger, and then went after him.

"You are so self-righteous. I can't stand it. Don't ever accuse me of not being grateful for little David. He was the most precious part of my life," she said.

Delia couldn't hold back the tears, so she left. She went

into the large corral and out to the track. She jogged around for a couple turns. The tiny racing saddle reminded her of David. She kept moving. She needed to move fast enough to keep the memories from catching up with her, but not too fast or she would catch up to the memories. They would rush in and envelop her.

Jamil watched from the stable entrance. He didn't want to interrupt her. She was a magnificent animal, with a grace unrivaled by any other. She loped around making it look like she wasn't even trying. She finally came to a stop and looked at him.

"What? Go ahead say it. I can see it in your eyes," said Delia.

"What?" asked Jamil.

"You want to criticize something," she said. "I can read your face Jamil. You've got that look."

"I wasn't going to criticize. You're over-sensitive."

"You were going to say something about my running," she said.

"Okay, I was going to tell you to relax your shoulders and let your head float a little higher. That's all," said Jamil.

"See, it's a criticism."

"No, it's not. You're running sad. You're running without your heart in it. You're thinking about David and it's making you tense. You need…"

They were interrupted by the sound of laughter.

"God, here they come," she said with dread.

"Ravi wants to see you run," said Jamil.

"Fat chance."

"See the little human with the thick arms walking next to Nemir? He's going to ride you."

"Marius is Roman," said Ravi, patting the young man on the shoulder. "He can ride, even though it's dusk on Shabbat. I had a saddle put on her. If what you say is true Nemir, this is the next great racing camel."

"You'll see, Ravi," said Nemir loudly. The wine had made him a little more jocular.

Soraya was walking to the side of the group. She had secretly hoped to ride the animal, but now there was a 'professional' rider. She was disappointed.

"I am the best Roman camel jockey in the empire," said Marius. His arrogance had a flair to it and made Nemir want to tease him.

"Is that because you're the only Roman camel jockey?" Nemir asked. He laughed at his own joke.

Soraya rolled her eyes. The wine had loosened his tongue.

"The greatest racers in the world are Persians," said Nemir.

"There are some good jockeys who are citizens of the Roman Empire, like the Egyptians and Syrians," said Abdul. He was trying to defuse the tension that suddenly showed itself.

"I am a Roman citizen from Maleventum, south of Rome. We have no camels there. I learned when I was almost an adult and in the last three years have won almost every race that I have been in. I have the ability to get speed out of any animal. Romans are better than Persians. You shall see."

"Oh brother, what an ego," Soraya whispered to Merak. Her father gave her a look.

The stable hand brought the animal over to Marius. He looked at her and slowly walked around examining her bone structure.

"She's a little small, but I like the blaze on her forehead. It speaks of a good heritage," Marius said.

When he reached out to touch the white mark, she spit at him.

Soraya giggled. She thought it was delightful that the animal could tell that Marius was a cad.

Marius grabbed the reins from the stable boy's hands and leaned forward toward Delia's face. "You may have a temper, you nasty little she-camel, but I will show you who is boss here."

Marius gave the reins a sharp tug to make sure he got her attention. His other hand reached behind his back to feel for the riding crop he was carrying.

"Do you understand me, Delia," he hissed.

The camel shuddered. She understood him.

"Marius, take her for a couple turns around the track. We'll watch from the balcony, and be careful because it is getting dark," said Ravi.

"No problem," said Marius. He mounted Delia in one smooth movement and then headed toward the gate. He hitched himself up in the saddle a couple of times making sure that he was comfortable.

Soraya was the first one up the steps to the rooftop. She watched the jockey take Delia around the track. He was good, she saw that. In a few minutes, he had her moving smoothly around the oval.

Soraya was disappointed to see him handle the camel so well. He hadn't gotten Delia to open up, but she assumed that would take time. She was horrified when she saw his hand go to his back and pull out the riding crop.

"That creep," she said out loud. "I have a good mind to go tell him off."

"Easy, Daughter," said Abdul.

"Don't worry, I'm sure Marius knows what he's doing," said Ravi who had heard her remark.

Marius urged Delia on. He hit her side a couple of times, and nothing happened. He was being gentle still and wanted to get a feel for how much pain she needed to be urged on. When she didn't respond, his blows got harder.

Soraya imagined that she could hear the thumping noise from where she was.

Delia, however, had other ideas. The harder the blow fell the slower she went, until she simply stopped, and headed in toward the gate. She'd had enough for this evening.

Marius was furious. He pulled on the reins to turn her back to the track, but the animal refused. He used his leather heels to dig into her side and she still refused to turn around. The man's fuse had burnt, and now he was exploding. He dismounted in the corral and held her reins while striking her on the side. Jamil had to move out of the way to avoid the melee.

"Do you think you can embarrass me? You worthless bag of camel meat!"

He hit her hard and shook her head with the reins held up close.

"Do you know what happens to camels when they refuse to run?"

Soraya was running down the steps directly at Marius with Merak and Nemir chasing her trying to keep her out of trouble.

"Stop, you pig," she screamed.

"Do you know what we do?" shouted Marius. "We use the carcass for food. We eat..."

The thud of Soraya's hands ramming him in the face interrupted his words. Marius ducked away from the hands and stumbled backward to the ground.

"You swine. You leave her alone," said Soraya. She had never hit a man before, just her brother when he teased her.

"What?" Marius said brushing himself off and getting up.

"You hurt her. Look at the welts, the bruises. She's cut!"

"You little Persian dog!" Marius was furious and raised his hand to slap her.

Before he could reach her Merak stepped between them and grabbed his hand. His short sword was drawn.

"I should cut your hand off for even threatening her with it," said Merak. He was furious too. He took the point of his sword and pushed it lightly against Marius' neck.

"Tempt me. You called her a dog. It's time to apologize or bleed," said Merak.

Abdul and Ravi arrived at the same time.

"I... I apologize," said the terrified jockey.

Merak let him go.

"My apologies," said Ravi.

"Accepted," said Abdul. He wanted to see the tempers settle down.

"You're fired. Don't let your shadow fall on my doorstep," Ravi said to the young man. He pointed to the door.

"Daughter, you need to control your temper," said Abdul.

"She was right," said Ravi. "You are my guests. My servants cannot be allowed such impertinence. Thank you

Merak. If you had removed that offensive hand, I would have been grateful."

"Look at the marks," she said to Nemir. "He was hurting her."

Soraya leaned her head against the animal's side and stroked her gently.

"I won't let anything happen to you, Delia," she said.

†

Waves of memories washed over Delia. She could feel the love from this one, this girl.

"She loves you," said Jamil.

Delia fought against the feelings. It was so familiar, the little head on her shoulder and the stroking motion. She could feel the love but didn't want to. She hated to trust more than anything.

"You owe her a ride," said Jamil. He knew that Delia was aching to run. He knew it better than anyone. They were alike. When he was her age, he lived to run.

"She did fight for me and wasn't trying to ride me or use me," said Delia.

"Oh, go ahead. Let her get on and take her for a ride. It will be the thrill of her life. You know it. You know how fast you can go," said Jamil.

"Maybe, if she wants to."

"And let your head float up. Keep your attention on the heavens. That's where love comes from and where David is."

"Jamil, if I didn't know better, I would say you're criticizing me," Delia said. But she was smiling, thinking about racing like the wind.

"Critique, not criticism. Critique points you to improv-

ing, to recreating yourself. When it's done with love it's wonderful. You loved David, and you can feel that this human loves you too. Run, fly like the wind, float on love, and enjoy running again. It's who you are."

†

At first when Jamil bumped her in the back, Soraya didn't know what he wanted. Jamil kept pushing and making noises to Delia and Soraya.

Finally, Nemir said, "He wants you to get on Delia, Niece."

"Yes, I think he does," she said. She looked at her father, who frowned and then to Ravi.

"Can you ride, young lady?" Ravi asked politely. He didn't want to contradict her father or see her get hurt.

"Can she ride? She rides better than me," said Merak proudly. "Let her have a go at it, Abdul. Maybe the animal will open up."

"I don't know," said Abdul.

"Please, Papa!"

"Come on, you old fool. Let your daughter do it," said Nemir. He reached over to lift Soraya up but wasn't tall enough.

She looked at Merak, and he gallantly picked her up. With a sweeping motion, he deposited her in Delia's saddle.

Jamil came up next to them and started nudging her toward the gate.

"I can't believe it, but Blaze wants her to run. He's smarter than I remember," laughed Ravi.

They all climbed the stairs to the balcony with the exception of Merak who stood at the gate with Jamil.

"I hope you're right old boy," Merak said softly to Jamil.

Delia started around the track with an easy saunter.

"Okay girl, if you want to run, you go ahead," said Soraya softly. She leaned forward in the saddle and stroked the camel's long neck.

"Go ahead," she said again.

Delia picked up the pace.

Soraya held on to the reins a little too tightly, and the animal held back waiting for permission.

"That's it, girl, just let yourself go and feel the wind in your face."

Delia raised her head a bit and the tension from the reins eased up. When she didn't feel the reins being pulled back, she let it rip. Her attention was on the heavens now, head held high, looking at the magnificent sunset whose colors spoke of a deeper more eternal love. She ran for Soraya, to thank her. She ran for love. She ran for David.

It was unbelievable. Delia was flying now.

Soraya held on for dear life, wondering how anything could move this swiftly.

"Go, run, race," screamed Nemir from the balcony. He was witnessing the fastest camel on earth, and he knew it.

"My God," said Ravi. "She can ride, and I think the animal likes her."

Jamil gave Merak a nudge.

"I know, old one. That's what you were like when you were young."

Merak waited until she slowed down and then walked out toward the track to greet Soraya.

"You were marvelous!" He yelled with pride.

"She's unbelievable, like the very wind itself," said Soraya.

She was beaming, and her face was flushed with excitement. She dismounted right into Merak's strong arms and gave him a huge hug. Soraya was so excited that she jumped up and down. She let go when her father came down the stairs. He had seen the emotions and realized it was a little more than just delight with the beast.

"My little girl rides and makes me proud," said Abdul.

"Wonderful, young lady," shouted Ravi as he came down the steps. He was having an intense discussion with Nemir. They were working through a discussion of some of the points of a deal that had been hatched while standing on the roof.

"I told you I could ride," she said.

"I always believed you," said Merak.

"Abdul, I have a proposition for you," said Ravi. His tone was that of a man looking to speak directly to another man.

Nemir was about to speak but then thought better of it. He held his tongue because it was better for the offer to come directly from Ravi.

"You and Nemir own one half interest in Jamil and were going to pay me for the other half, correct?"

"That is correct, if you wish to," said Abdul.

"I wish to sell you half interest in a camel, but I would prefer it to be Delia."

Merak and Soraya were listening intently now. Nemir nodded his head yes and looked at his friend. He was signaling him to agree.

"You want Nemir and I to own half of Delia?"

"Correct," said Ravi.

"Do we still own half of Jamil?" asked Abdul.

"Yes, but I will keep my half too," said Ravi.

"What would you have us do for our half?" asked Abdul.

"Race the camel of course, but there is one stipulation," said Ravi.

"Yes?" asked Abdul.

"I want you to let your daughter race her in the major Dromidromes in Persia," said Ravi.

Abdul was incredulous.

Soraya leaped with joy.

"She's a girl," said Abdul.

"Please Papa. I can do it. I know I can," she said.

Soraya turned to Delia and gave her a hug.

"You and me girl. We could race like the wind and win. We could beat anyone, and I could always be there to take care of you," she said.

Delia gave her a nudge back.

"She's a girl. She can't race. The men would abuse her. It's a rough life. They whip each other and fight while they race. She could get hurt," said Abdul. He was looking at Soraya and shaking his head as he talked.

"Soraya would always be in front of the pack. No one would catch her," said Nemir. He was convinced that she could do it.

"She's supposed to get married and have grandchildren for me not race beasts with crude men who like to gamble," said Abdul.

"Are you betrothed?" asked Ravi.

"No one has asked for my hand and my father has not found a suitable suitor for me," said Soraya.

She gave Merak a kick in the side of his leg. It didn't go unnoticed by the men. Nemir could barely contain himself.

"Abdul sir," said Merak cautiously. "I was waiting for a

suitable time, perhaps when we had returned to your village and in the presence of you wife," he paused to look at Soraya, "to ask for your daughter's hand."

Soraya melted into Merak's big brown eyes and was swept away by the feelings of love that engulfed her. She reached up and threw her arms around him.

"Daughter, I haven't given my consent, yet," Abdul said. He couldn't fake being stern to save his life.

"Oh Papa, this is wonderful," she said.

"Merak, you have my permission. The engagement will become formal when we are with your mother," he added.

"See, and he could protect her and see to it that the other men leave her alone," said Ravi.

"That's another story, Ravi. They would never let her race," said Abdul.

"If Magi Melchior or Balthasar ordered it, they would," said Merak.

"We could limit our racing to Babylon and the area near home," said Soraya.

"And when you started producing offspring?" Abdul asked with a smile. "It's a nice idea, but it won't work."

"Merak could ride when I couldn't. She's so fast that she could carry the extra weight and still win," said Soraya.

"No, that's not going to work." Her father was becoming more adamant.

"Actually, the real money will come when she retires after a season or two and we use the two camels for breeding," said Ravi.

"And that's where I come in," said Nemir. "I could breed the camels."

"Let's think about it before you make a final decision," said Ravi. "It's late and you're all tired."

✝

Josephus closed the door silently behind him. The Pharisee nodded for him to take a seat. He did as he was told.

There were two men sitting behind the Pharisee. Josephus strained to see their faces but the candlelight was too soft to allow him to make out the details.

"Josephus has a story to tell us," said the Pharisee. He was a bearded man who wore a silk shawl embroidered with stars of David.

When Josephus didn't say anything, the man said, "Go ahead. Repeat your story."

"These three men from Persia arrived with a young lady too. She's the daughter of the oldest of three men."

He was rambling and knew it, but he couldn't calm his nerves.

"Tell us why they are here," said the Pharisee.

"They came to bring gifts from the Magi of Persia, Arabia, and India," said Josephus. He deliberately said 'gifts' even though he had heard that it was just a cloth of some sort. He wanted to embellish it a little so that perhaps they would pay him a larger amount for the information.

"Go on, get to the point. And the gifts are for…" The Pharisee was getting annoyed.

"They're for the soon-to-be crowned King of the Jews. At least that's what they said."

"Did they name who the new king would be?" asked the elderly man to the Pharisee's right.

"A certain Jesus, a Nazarene. You know, the one everyone is talking about."

"Did they say if they were going to help him become king?" asked the Pharisee.

"No, they only talked about the fact that they had already brought gifts to him—big gifts like gold—and they had forgotten this one thing," said Josephus. He was immediately angry that he had slipped and said it was only one gift. Anger and greed were his only two feelings, not remorse or guilt for a betrayal. He was incapable of feeling guilt. Some men were like that. Guilt was as foreign to them as another world, another world where their guilt would be revealed for eternity to judge.

"Where are they staying, this party?" asked the Pharisee.

"They are at Master Ravi's caravansary."

"Thank you. That will be all," said the Pharisee.

Josephus stood up and waited.

"Yes, you want a reward," the man said sarcastically. He reached into his coin purse and gave him a small coin.

Josephus was irritated. It was much less than his information was worth. He should have asked for the payment beforehand. He faked a smile and left.

The man who had been silent throughout finally spoke.

"No gift shall be delivered. It would be tantamount to a foreign dignitary recognizing this rebel. We can't let him be acknowledged in any way whatsoever. Am I perfectly clear on this point?"

The other two men nodded their heads.

"It will be taken care of," said the man next to the Pharisee. "Do what we discussed."

"But it's the Sabbath," said the Pharisee.

"Then make it tomorrow night, but do it."

†

Merak and Nemir were downstairs early. Neither of them could sleep.

"So young man, you mean to marry my niece?" Nemir was more serious than usual.

"I want to take her for my wife, but I am afraid it is I who is taken by her," said Merak.

He had never felt this way about a woman before.

"It's the women who choose us and then make it seem like it was our idea all along," said Nemir.

"I never knew that. I thought we went out and chose the woman that would be a good wife, bear us children, and be a good mother."

"Merak, you're young yet. You'll see that it's the woman who chooses a good father, husband, and man. They know it's important for you to think it was your idea. This girl is a special one though. Of all of Abdul's children, she has always been my favorite."

"I will be good to her, Nemir. I will love her and cherish her," said Merak.

"Yes, you're quite smitten," said Nemir with a nod.

"Was it like that for you too, Uncle?"

"It's like that for most of us. We operated with our heads. We're logical, precise, disciplined men, and then suddenly our hearts get in the way."

"When I think of your niece my heart feels more powerful than my head. It's as though something has opened up in my chest," said Merak.

"Don't ever let it close—no matter how moody or difficult

she becomes. Women do that sometimes, and a mature man just weathers the storm," said Nemir.

"Weathers the storm?" Merak asked.

"You'll see. Marriage brings good and bad. The good is the love, the children, the family. The bad is that you have to look at your own faults and admit them in order to stay married, and sometimes women can be very difficult."

"I see," said the befuddled Merak.

"No, you don't. You couldn't possibly see all that yet. And make certain that you respect and love her parents. She loves them both deeply."

"Does her father like me?" asked Merak.

"Heavens yes! He thinks you're wonderful," said Nemir. He slapped him on the back.

"The men are up early," said a voice from the stairs.

Ravi and Abdul were walking down together.

"Let's see what the kitchen has to offer this morning. I wake with a small appetite, but I imagine the young man has the appetite of a horse," said Ravi.

"Yes, he does," said Abdul.

"Good morning, Father-to-be," said Merak. He was nervous and standing at attention.

Abdul smiled.

"You're going to make a welcome addition to the family, Merak. My wife will be pleased," said Abdul.

"Thank you, sir," said Merak.

"You can drop the *sir*. I am still very concerned, though, about the camel racing," said Abdul.

"Let it be. We eat now. He marries my niece later," said Nemir.

Nemir grabbed Abdul's arm and ushered him into the

dining area. There was an assortment of sweet, piping hot breads and some specialty pastries that Ravi had ordered on their arrival.

Merak was starving and was glad that the conversation was turning toward food. He grabbed a bowl of thick rich yogurt and a plate of pastries.

The older men jealously watched Merak eat with a passion until Soraya came down the stairs. She was wearing typical clothing of the region. Merak stopped chewing and swallowed. She was beautiful.

"Good morning," she said beaming.

"Good morning, Soraya," said Abdul.

"Good morning, Niece," said Nemir.

"Wonderful," said Merak. "I mean good morning."

The men smiled knowingly.

"I was thinking about doing a little riding on Delia today," said Soraya, "but the handmade told me it would insult the community to do it on the Sabbath."

"True," said Ravi. "It would be better if you took a walk around the center of our fair city and just relaxed most of the day. We spend the day in prayer and thanksgiving for our many blessings."

For the rest of the day the four guests toured the little city of Gabae. By the time evening had arrived, they were all tired. It was a day well spent however, as Ravi served as their tour guide and explained many of the customs. He explained how important the upcoming Feast of the Passover was and the history behind it.

Before they retired Merak and Soraya went down to the stables to check on their animals. The stable hand had everything under control, but Soraya wanted to see her new

racing animal just one more time before retiring.

"Hi, Delia," said Soraya. She held a fig in her hand and pushed it toward Delia's muzzle. The camel ate hungrily.

†

Merak and Soraya stood on the balcony and watched the pale moon, hidden by a thin veil of clouds. They were arm-in-arm, standing still. As was the custom of the times, a relative watched over the young lady's virtue. Nemir, however, had turned his chair toward the racetrack and away from them. The soft snoring noises that he made, indicated to the two young lovers that they were on their honor.

Soraya giggled.

"Your uncle is a great watchman," said Merak.

"It his way of telling you…" Soraya hesitated nervously.

"That he trusts me?"

"No, Merak. It's his way to tell you that it's okay to steal a kiss."

She trembled as he turned his face to hers, his lips just a breath away.

His lips brushed hers lightly and then they parted for a moment. He reached up and cradled her face in his strong hands. She trembled expectantly for a moment more, and then they kissed, fully, completely. They surrendered to the inevitable, letting their love flow into the togetherness that they formed like two rivers returning home to the same ocean after an eternity apart.

A dog barked down near the stables.

Merak tensed.

"It's only a dog, my love," said Soraya. She reached her right hand into the silky hair behind his head and pressed

herself against him. He relaxed into the wonder of the moment as their lips explored what they both new to be their future.

The dog bark viciously now and then with a short cry he stopped.

"Damn," yelled Merak as he separated himself from Soraya. He knew the sound. He ran for his sword and slapped Nemir's sleeping head as he went by.

"We have trouble, Uncle!"

Soraya suddenly got a whiff of an odor in the air. It was hay burning. She started running to the stables.

When she looked up at the balcony her father, her uncle, and Merak were running after her.

"Wait Soraya, don't go in alone!" her father yelled.

"I've got to get the animals out," she yelled back and kept on running.

"She's stubborn just like her mother." Abdul was grateful that Merak was young and fast and would catch right up to her.

In a moment she was in the stables. It was filled with smoke, and the hay filled area near the rear was a roaring blaze.

This area of the stables was separate from the living quarters precisely to avoid the tragedy of losing human life if the hay caught fire. Ravi arrived and hoped that the rest of the caravansary would be spared.

Everyone was there all at once—servants, friends, and neighbors. The noise was horrible. The animals were terrified.

Delia was toward the back with Jamil. Soraya headed directly for them. The heat was intense, and the smoke was quickly filling the enclosure. It was the smoke that was the

enemy, not the heat or the fire. They had to pull the camels out and keep their heads as low as possible, if not, the animals would inhale the fumes. If they passed out from smoke inhalation, they would die in the fire. If they didn't pass out, their lungs could be damaged, and especially Delia would never run again.

"I've got her. You get Jamil," Soraya yelled.

She struggled with the latch and forced it open.

"Come girl, you've got to get out of there," Soraya yelled. She could see that Delia was terrified and refused to move forward. She grabbed her neck and pulled her toward safety. As soon as the animal saw a way out, she would bolt. Soraya stepped back.

Delia burst through the door and was in the clear in a moment. Jamil was right behind her.

They managed to save the animals, but the stable was a disaster. A crowd of people stood and watched as the fire blazed brilliantly. Merak brought out the carcass of the dog. Its throat had been slashed.

"Someone set this fire deliberately," Ravi said when Merak showed him the dog. "I'm sorry. I hope your animals are safe."

"They're all okay," said Merak.

"Let's go see if we can secure the beasts," Soraya said. She was looking at Jamil and Delia who were grazing on the area in the center of the racetrack.

Merak nodded. "Come on Uncle, we'll need your help."

Nemir and Merak noticed the movement in the window of their apartment at the same time.

"Isn't father here with us?" asked Soraya.

"I'm right here," said Abdul.

Merak motioned for them to be quiet. He drew his sword and wrapped his cloak around his left arm for protection.

Nemir grabbed a pitchfork and followed him.

"Merak! Uncle!" Soraya yelled.

They motioned for her to be silent. Abdul held her and put a finger over her mouth as the two men silently crept up the stairs. The door to the apartment, which was left open when they ran to the fire, was now closed.

"Be ready to block the door and the window when I charge," Merak whispered. He motioned for Nemir to go to the other side of the door close to the window.

They could hear someone in the room looking through their belongings.

Merak charged through the door. As the wood slammed into the stone it made an enormous bang. That was nothing compared to the Arabian war cry that Merak let loose. He exploded into the room positioning himself against the wall near the door to the hallway. He stood in a fighting stance, looking to see how many men there were.

Merak was confronted by a strange sight. Before him stood a young man, about his age, holding the cloth and looking for a means of escape.

"Drop the cloth and put your hands on top of your head," said Merak.

"How many are there?" asked Nemir who was blocking the door. He looked ominous with the three-pronged fork in his hands.

"I think just one, but he's not following my directions," replied Merak.

Abdul was up the stairs, carrying a piece of wood that he could use as a club. Soraya stayed downstairs and waited.

Suddenly the man threw the bolt of linen at Merak and dove for the window. Nemir lunged for him but only managed to catch a part of his heal. They young man rolled through the window and was met by Abdul, who fiercely clubbed him on the shoulder. He yelled in pain but still jumped off the balcony, hit the ground, rolled, and then ran off. He was limping. Merak wanted to chase him.

"He was after the cloth?" Nemir asked. He was incredulous.

"Nothing else seems to be touched," said Merak.

Soraya burst through the door.

"You're all right?" Soraya asked.

She threw her arms over him Merak, rested her head on his shoulder for a moment, and then looked at his face to be sure.

"Yes, of course," said Merak. He was embarrassed by the look her father was giving him.

"He was after the cloth," said Nemir. He said it to Ravi who was breathing heavily after running up the steps.

"That's odd. There is so much more that he could have taken," said Ravi. He looked around carefully to see if anything was missing. When he satisfied himself that nothing else was taken, he walked over and fingered the cloth for a moment.

"It's strange, isn't it?" Abdul said.

"Why would anyone want to steal the cloth? It's not that valuable," said Nemir.

"It's a symbol. It's more valuable for what it says than what it's worth," said Merak.

"He only wanted the cloth because that was the gift for the king. You must be very careful," said Ravi.

They looked at each other and realized the truth. There were some who would go to great lengths to make certain that this Nazarene was not recognized as the King of the Jews.

†

It was a balmy spring day, but the aroma of flowers was hidden behind the stench of the fire.

"Our clothes smell," said Soraya. She was almost in tears. She had picked out her favorite of the beautiful robes in the trunk and hung it up the day before. Now it smelled like a fireplace.

"Maybe you could wear it and it would air out by the time we got to Nazareth," said Abdul.

"Papa, it would make me smell."

She had washed her hair and oiled it with perfumes, and still she wasn't satisfied.

Uncle Nemir walked over to console her.

"The smell is in your nostrils and in your lungs. Your hair is fine. Stop worrying. I've got lots of hair in my nose and the smoke is still stuck to it. Everything smells smoky, even the perfume for your hair."

Uncle Nemir stopped talking when he saw that there were large tears in her eyes.

"I'm sorry. I was only trying to help," Nemir said.

"Help? You're driving me crazy, Uncle. I don't care about your gross nose hairs. We are going to see a queen, the mother of a future king. I don't want to smell badly."

"The animals smell of smoke too," said Merak. He walked in with some bread and some sweets. He had been up for hours and had eaten twice already.

Soraya looked at him and then stormed out of the room.

"What did I do?" he asked the men.

"Nothing," said Abdul, "She's a woman."

"You said the camels smell of smoke," said Nemir.

"But it's true. Ravi is having them bathed with perfumed soaps to see if the aroma can be hidden."

"It's a stench not an aroma," said Soraya, who had peeked back into the room.

"Are you mad at me?" asked Merak.

"No, Merak. I'm sorry. I'm upset because I wanted to look pretty when we meet the mother," said Soraya.

He shrugged his shoulders and said, "You're always pretty. What's the problem?"

"You don't understand either," Soraya complained and went back into the room.

"What did I do?"

"Nothing," said Abdul. "She's…"

"I know. A woman," said Merak.

"Right," said Nemir and Abdul together.

"Get used to it kid," said Nemir.

When Soraya finally emerged from her room, she looked radiant. She had found a beautiful powder blue and white robe with a blue veil. The veil was decorated with small pink roses, hand embroidered along the border.

"What do you think?"

"You look perfect," said Abdul.

"You want me to smell it to make sure?" asked Uncle Nemir. He couldn't resist being a tease with her.

"You didn't say anything, Merak," she pouted.

"I'm… I'm… speechless," he finally managed to say.

That was enough for her to feel delight. She could go

now. She was dressing for Merak as much as for Mary. She wanted him to see how she would dress for the mother of a king.

There was a polite knock on the door.

Ravi stepped in and smiled.

"Your animals are ready. They are bathed and perfumed. I expect that you should be able to return for the evening.

A short while later they were on their camels' backs and heading up the winding road toward Sepphoris.

When they were at a fairly high elevation they turned and to see the beautiful valley with Gabae in it. The road to Nazareth was a small extension to the left while the main road continued on to Sepphoris.

✝

"I can't believe that we are almost there," said Soraya. She had settled down and now was excited about the short trip to visit the woman known as Mary.

"You know what I don't understand?" Merak asked. "Do we give the cloth to the mother or to the son?"

"Were the gifts for the king or for the mother when you first brought them, Papa?"

"I think for the king," said Abdul.

"Then why did we leave the camels for the family?" Nemir asked.

"I don't know," said Abdul.

"It was the mother who rejected the idea of camels to begin with," said Nemir.

"Yes, but he was a baby, and she was acting on his behalf," said Abdul.

The two older men argued about it all the way into town.

Nazareth was a small community, not a city by any means. They headed toward the biggest building and asked the first person, an old man walking by, if he knew of a man named Jesus.

"Yes," said the old man. He didn't stop walking but nodded and kept going.

"Do you know where we might find him?" Merak asked. He was being gracious, but the man was still walking away.

Soraya smiled at his plight and walked up to a woman and asked the same question.

"Son of Mary and Joseph, the deceased carpenter?"

"Yes," said Soraya.

"They live in that area, everyone knows them," said the woman.

After thanking the woman, they started toward where she pointed.

"No one is there," said the woman.

"What do you mean?" asked Abdul.

"Jesus is always off somewhere, and his mother is visiting family in Jerusalem. She left a few days ago. She'll be there for the entire Feast of the Passover."

They looked at each other in disbelief.

"Let's head over to where she lives anyway," said Nemir.

"What good will it do us, Uncle?" asked Soraya.

"Maybe we can get the name of a relative in Jerusalem," said Nemir.

"That would help," said Merak.

"Yes, Jerusalem is a huge city. It might be better to talk to a few people here before we go rushing around Jerusalem asking everyone we meet 'Do you know Jesus of Nazareth?'" said Abdul.

"Yes, that would be a real problem, and I'll bet it would make the men who wanted to steal the cloth really happy," said Merak.

"I guess we're going to ask first and then travel later," said Soraya.

"And we're going to be really careful not to tell anyone anything, just ask for Mary," said Abdul.

"What do you mean, sir?" Merak asked.

"I mean it's safer if we're looking for his mother than if we're looking for him. They have a feast coming up. Chances are the mother will know where the son is for the celebration. A woman likes to keep track of her offspring," said Abdul.

Merak and Nemir liked the idea.

They lost Soraya because she had drifted off on a fantasy about what it would be like to be a mother and watch over her children. She pondered what it must be like to bear the child of the man you love and carry on his family's legacy.

The men were talking among themselves, but her mind wandered back to something she had heard her mother say about her birth many years before. Soraya's mother had said, *"It was a cool rainy night before you were born. I was exhausted from the labor; the birds were singing, and the clouds were just parting to let the early morning sun shine in. That was when I first saw your face. I knew from that moment that I would love you forever."*

"God, that must be the most fantastic thing that could happen to a woman," she whispered out loud.

The men didn't hear her.

They were speaking to a neighbor who didn't know the names of Mary's relatives. She was an elderly woman who knew who Jesus was, but she did not know where he was

located at the present.

"Who would believe what we have heard?" said the elderly woman.

Another neighbor walked over. "I knew him when he was a boy. He grew up like a sapling before us, like a shoot from the parched earth."

"Yes, but there was in him no stately bearing to make us look at him differently," said the first woman.

"No, I dare say, there was no appearance that would attract us to him. He was Mary and Joseph's son," said the second. "We held him in no particular esteem."

"But do you have any idea who he might be visiting for the Passover Feast this week?" asked Merak. He was losing his patience as the neighbor women looked back and forth at each other and shrugged their shoulders.

"We've heard such wonderful things," the first woman said.

"He cured a blind man in Jericho," said the second.

After a few minutes they decided that this was a fruitless search. They turned their camels around and started heading slowly towards the road to Gabae.

"This is a blind chase," said Merak. "It could take us weeks or even months to track Jesus of Nazareth down."

"Do we even know what he looks like?" asked Soraya.

"Maybe the blind man could tell us," said Nemir sarcastically. "The elderly woman could tell us nothing."

"Be a little kinder. They were doing the best that they could. It might be better to track the mother Mary down first," said Abdul.

"Why is that?" Nemir asked.

"She could tell us if she was the same one that we met all

those years ago in Bethlehem."

It dawned on them that they hadn't really confirmed that they were searching for the right person yet.

✝

"Please stay with us, for the Holy Days. You would be our guests for the Passover," said Ravi.

"We've discussed this among ourselves, and though we do appreciate your hospitality, I don't think that we want to delay our primary mission," said Merak.

"We'll be back to pick up the camels on our way home," said Nemir.

Ravi was quiet for a moment.

"But Jerusalem will be so crowded for the holidays. Where will you stay?" Ravi finally asked.

"We can camp out on the hillside near the city. A place to stay for us is not that important," said Nemir. He looked around at the others who were nodding in agreement.

"We are camel drivers. It's not a problem," said Abdul.

"I'm warning you ahead of time. Every inn and every caravansary will be filled. People will be visiting their families. Everyone wishes to be in Jerusalem for the Passover," said Ravi.

"We were thinking about detouring to Jericho first to see if we could talk to some people there," said Merak.

"Jericho?" asked Ravi.

"Is there a problem with that?" asked Merak.

"It would be a detour of a half day," said Ravi.

"We were told that if we headed toward the Jordan River we could head directly to Jericho and then head east to Jerusalem.

"I suppose that might be just the same as heading directly through Samaria to Arimathea, but it still will be two days to get to Jerusalem. It would be better to get there early in the morning," said Ravi.

"What would Master Melchior do?" Merak asked himself aloud.

Magus Melchior would pray. Merak knew that. He told everyone that he was going to retire for the night. He was going to pray.

9

THIS YEAR IN JERUSALEM

As the sun rose over the East in Gabae, Merak checked the last cinch on the camels. All was ready. They had decided that they could ride hard during the early part of the morning and make it all the way to Emmaus by night fall. They wanted to enter the city of Jerusalem first thing on Wednesday morning. It would give them the whole day to find the man known as Jesus.

"Up you go," said Merak, as he lifted Soraya onto her camel.

Abdul watched in disbelief. She had never allowed herself to be lifted onto a camel, once she had gotten big enough to get on by herself.

Nemir lifted an eyebrow and smiled at his old friend.

"She's suddenly become a woman," said Nemir.

"Much more so than I would have guessed. Her mother used to tell me not to worry when she was going through her tomboy stage. Now I have something else to worry about," said Abdul.

Ravi walked over and embraced the men and bowed graciously to Soraya. "Godspeed, gentlemen."

"We ride hard this morning, old men," Merak said to Abdul and Nemir. He was feeling playful and bold. He had

become much less rigid than when they first started out.

"Don't push us too much, Merak," said Nemir.

"Pity on us, please," pleaded Abdul. He swung his camel around and headed out at a fairly good pace, not waiting for the rest, who scampered to catch up.

Ravi waved and watched them fade from sight.

†

The road to Arimathea was filled with pilgrims. They walked in clusters formed by extended families. At some parts of the road, they left little room for the Roman chariots and horse-drawn carriages. They were awed by the size of the camels, however, and quickly made room for them. The pilgrims did slow down their progress somewhat, but the distance was not too great. By midday they were in Arimathea and would be in Jerusalem by Tuesday afternoon.

"We made much better time than we anticipated," said Merak.

"It's because the flow of people was mostly in one direction. It made it easier," said Abdul.

"The ride has given me an appetite," said Merak.

Abdul laughed. "What's the ride got to do with it?"

"It's bigger than usual," said Merak.

"We should eat at that tavern here in Arimathea and then head to Jerusalem this afternoon," said Nemir. He was pointing to a tavern and inn just inside the walls.

"Do you think we'll find a place to stay?" Abdul asked.

"With the number of pilgrims that we passed, I doubt it," said Merak.

Soraya had tethered her animal and was looking at the fabrics in the front of a merchant's shop. The colors were

brilliant, and the materials were soft and luxurious. She was fingering the fabrics in her hand. One particular bolt of linen was deep purple. She touched the material to her cheek to feel its delicate texture.

"That's the royal color, young lady," said the shopkeeper. "Roman citizens, the important ones, can use that. I can't sell it to you unless you're related to a senator."

"You must not get a lot of requests for it," Soraya said.

"Not really, but with your skin and hair color this would be beautiful on you."

"If I was going to wear it outside the empire would that be possible?" Soraya asked.

"Yes," said the shopkeeper.

"But I'm more interested in white," said Soraya. She let her hands run over a gorgeous white fabric with an intricate design woven into it.

"That's wedding material," said the shopkeeper.

"Daughter, come away from that shop. We're going to eat."

"Yes, Father," she said. She smiled at the merchant and then turned to join the others.

It was barely time for the midday meal, but Merak was ravenously hungry from the ride. He went bounding in through the door and ordered a table for four, wine, roast meats, yogurt, grilled vegetables, and some bread. He barked orders for food all the way to the table without consulting anyone else.

"I can't wait to eat," said the young warrior.

"Did you order enough for everyone?" Soraya asked. Everything he did now seemed to delight her.

"I think he ordered enough for six people. Three meals for himself and one for each of us," said Nemir.

"I ordered two for you," Merak shot back. He slapped Nemir a little too hard on the shoulders and then dropped into his chair after holding still a moment to wait for Soraya to sit first.

"We have Roman-style couches for your dining pleasure," said the waiter, "If you don't prefer the board here."

He was referring to the board that was set up as a carving table for them.

Merak and Soraya looked at one another for a moment obviously confused by the request.

"Romans eat their main meal reclined on their left side," said Abdul.

"Really?" asked Merak.

"Merak, it's a custom that allows them the freedom to eat for three hours and engage in lively discourse. If one of them gets tired, he can sleep. I rather like the idea. Eating wears me out now," said Abdul.

"Oh Father, it does not," said Soraya with a laugh.

"Well, I like lying down to dine, so that I don't choke on my food while I snore," said Nemir.

"We're fine here," said Merak. "I could eat a horse," he added under his breath. The servant seemed a bit flustered by Merak's insistence.

"This is not our dining area," said the servant, and then directed them to the dining room.

Couches were set in small clusters with serving tables in front of them.

Nemir made himself comfortable on the couch and one of the staff adjusted the small table so that it was within arm's reach when he was on his side.

"This is perfect," said Nemir.

"We have roast horse, goat, and fatted calf," said the servant.

He waited to see if Merak would change his order.

Merak looked at Nemir for a moment then said to the servant, "Do you have a mixed roast so that we can taste different things?"

"Certainly," he nodded and then sped off to the kitchen.

Another servant brought bowls of water for them to wash their hands with. As soon as they had finished the food started coming out and kept pace with Merak's impatient appetite.

About midway through the meal, the innkeeper walked out from the kitchen and introduced himself. He was a short rotund man in his early forties, named Aaron. He had huge hands and bulging forearms, a clear sign that the man had been kneading bread dough for decades. He wiped his hands on his apron as he approached the table.

"Good day to you," said Aaron.

Merak was the first to reach out and shake the man's hand.

"Good day to you, sir," Merak said with a young man's enthusiasm.

"You are getting your fill?"

"The calf and lamb are wonderful, and the vegetables are delicious," said Merak. He had picked up a piece of grilled eggplant to emphasize his point.

"Try sprinkling a little lemon over that sir," said the innkeeper with a laugh. He loved to see people eat with a passion.

Soraya had the lemon in hand and gave it to Merak as soon as he turned to look for it.

"Thanks," he said. His mouth was still full with the first piece. He looked around for more.

"I overheard you speaking about going to Jerusalem tonight. You are obviously not Jewish, so..." the innkeeper hesitated as he looked at the three men, trying to decide who was the decision maker.

"We're not Jewish. That's right," said Nemir. He was watching the man intently. He knew he was going to be sold on something and liked to dance with merchants, as he called it.

"Well, this is not a particularly good time to visit Jerusalem," said Aaron the innkeeper.

"I thought this was a terrific time to visit Jerusalem," said Nemir.

"Yes, we passed thousands of people who are making a pilgrimage to your Holy City during our travels today," added Abdul. He could see Nemir wanted to have fun.

"Were they all mistaken?" asked Nemir.

"No, they were all Jewish," said Aaron.

"And?" Nemir asked.

"And it is an auspicious time for an Israelite to come to Jerusalem, but..."

"But not for a Persian or an Arabian?" asked Nemir.

"Precisely. You won't find a place sleep unless you have family there. I can tell, however, that you probably don't," said Aaron.

Nemir and Abdul laughed.

"That's true. We have no family in Jerusalem, we're not Jewish, and we are not going to be celebrating the holiday. So, what do you suggest?" Nemir smiled and waited. He had

already formed an opinion of the man but now needed to see if his presumptions were right.

"You should stay here until the holiday is over and then do your business in Jerusalem. We have comfortable accommodations at my inn, and you are within a two-to-three-hour journey to the city. You may not find any more accommodations closer to Jerusalem. You will save money and perhaps you could even do some business here," said Aaron.

Nemir was impressed. His presumptions were right. The man was selling his services as an innkeeper, offering them a place to stay and a base from which to do business. He didn't even know what their business was.

"Emmaus is closer, and we were planning on spending the night there. Besides, I'm not sure that staying here is suited to our business," said Nemir.

"Perhaps, perhaps not," said the man. "What is your business in Jerusalem?"

"We are making a simple delivery," said Nemir.

"A simple delivery?"

"That's right, a delivery," said Nemir. "A simple delivery of some linen."

Merak watched them both intently. He wanted to start asking people if they had heard of Jesus of Nazareth as soon as his hunger had been assuaged. This seemed as good a time as any.

"It's a rather large party for the delivery of linen. Is it a large quantity of linen?" the innkeeper asked.

Nemir knew the man had probably looked at their beasts of burden, so he knew the answer already.

"No, not very," said Nemir. He was deliberately short spoken and abrupt.

"Well, no matter how big or small your goods are, the closer you get to Jerusalem, the harder it will be to find a place to stay," said the innkeeper.

"I can't believe there were so many people," said Soraya.

"We say a prayer at the end of our Seder, our Passover supper. It goes like this, 'Next year in Jerusalem.' It is considered a blessing to be able to spend your Passover with family in Jerusalem," said Aaron.

"Thus, it's not likely that we'll find any room at an inn in Jerusalem," said Abdul.

"No, nor would you find it in Emmaus. Some people will stay there and go into Jerusalem by foot to be with their families. The walk from Emmaus is only an hour or so."

"We planned on pitching our tents in the valley outside of the city," said Nemir.

"Many pilgrims do that," the innkeeper said.

"We are used to spending the night out of doors and under the stars of heaven," added Merak.

"Do you plan on staying with the people that you deliver your goods to?" Aaron asked.

"We don't know," said Merak.

"It would be customary to offer you a place, but at this time of the year it would be an inconvenience, even might I dare say, an imposition, to expect accommodations. You would be able to ease your host's burden by reassuring him that you had a place to stay," said Aaron.

Nemir really liked the guy now. He was thinking about renting a room just because of his persistence.

"Is the person you make your delivery to a Jew or a Gentile?"

"He's a Jew from Nazareth who we believe will be staying in Jerusalem for the holiday," said Merak. He wanted to ask the man if he had heard of Jesus and was getting impatient. Thank God he was still eating, or he would have interrupted already.

"Then he will be staying with family or friends. It might be best to wait a day or two because some people don't like to do business during the Passover."

"It's not business. It's a social call. We're bringing a gift that was meant to be given to this gentleman a long time ago," said Abdul.

"Is he a prominent businessman in Jerusalem?" asked the curious innkeeper.

"No, he's from Nazareth. Jesus of Nazareth. Have you heard of him?" Merak asked.

"The prophet? Of course. Who hasn't heard of him? He's probably already in Jerusalem for the Passover, but who would know?"

Aaron looked down at the tables and ordered some of the things removed and more wine brought in. It was obvious that he was thinking about something.

"There is a man, a rather wealthy man, in Jerusalem. His name is Joseph. He grew up in our little town of Arimathea, but now is a prominent member of the Jewish council. I have heard tell that he has been enamored with this prophet. He might know where you could find Jesus."

"How would we find him?" asked Merak.

"You would go to the temple and asked for Joseph," said Aaron.

"Just go to the front door and knock?" asked Nemir.

"No, of course not. First of all, you are not Jews so you would only be allowed inside the Court of the Gentiles. It is an enclosed outer court. Second, there is not a front door per se. You would have to ask to speak to a rabbi and ask if the council were in session. Then ask for Joseph of Arimathea."

"What if it's not in session?" Abdul asked.

"They won't give your message to Joseph."

"Then do we just ask anyone if they know where Jesus is?" asked Nemir.

"No, that's not wise," said Aaron. He lowered his voice as he spoke because one of the servants had come back in. He continued, "I would be careful about what you say. I wouldn't trust everyone to be delighted with the fame of this man from Nazareth. Just ask for Joseph. He's a good man and an old friend. Tell him Aaron the innkeeper from Arimathea sent you."

Abdul and Nemir looked at Merak. This was a real lead. It was as good a suggestion as they could have hoped for.

†

The sun hung low in the western sky casting a golden glow upon the city on a hill. Jerusalem's white limestone shimmered in the waning light. From a distance the golden hues made the limestone look like it was gold not stone.

"My God, it's beautiful. It's like a giant golden city," said Soraya.

They were quiet as they drew closer to the city. The road from Emmaus ran up the hill toward the Essenes gate on the northern end of the east wall. In the background of the city at the easternmost point was a huge temple; unlike anything

they had seen before. It was large enough to fit a few thousand houses inside. The walls were smooth at the base, but toward the top of its walls stood beautiful columns. Toward the center of the great temple rose a series of square towers. To the west of the six towers was a huge T-shaped tower, from the top of which one could see the Mediterranean Sea.

"That must be the temple, gentlemen," said Merak somberly. The grandeur of the edifice subdued his tone, making it more solemn than usual.

When they got to the Essenes gate, Roman legionnaires of the Syrian Legate under the Roman governor, Pontius Pilate, stopped them.

A young soldier stood directly in front of them and blocked their path.

"What seems to be the problem?" Merak asked.

"The animals sir," said the legionnaire.

"We can't bring the animals in?" asked Merak.

"You can't ride them from this point on," said the legionnaire. "It's crowded this week and we're asking that you walk your animals on tethers. You may want to hire someone to board your animals once you get to your destination."

"Thank you, we're heading toward the temple area. Which road should we take?" asked Merak as he dismounted.

About a hundred yards ahead the road forked. The others were off their animals and starting to enter.

"Both are good, but if I needed to get there quickly, I would ride my horse around the outside of the walls and then head toward the Damascus gate or the Genneth gate. They would be faster. Take the Genneth gate it's the next one you'll come to."

Abdul, Soraya, and Nemir stopped and waited to see what Merak wanted to do.

"We would save time," Merak said.

"Yes, but walking through the city would be more fun," said Soraya. She was looking up the main street to what looked like the confusion of a marketplace.

"You could still see the city but get to the temple area quicker if you went over to the Genneth gate and went in through that door," said the legionnaire.

"Merak, please let's go right through the city," said Soraya.

"You'll be right in the center of the city at the Hasmonaean Palace," said the guard. He expected them to understand what that meant. They didn't.

Abdul nodded and turned his camel around. Nemir followed. Soraya pouted for a moment and then mounted her beast. There was a road running around the outside walls of the city from the Essenes gate to the Genneth gate. Soraya was on her way up the road before the rest of them mounted.

"She's a little headstrong," said Abdul.

"Yes, so I've noticed," said Merak.

"You should have told her the market was at that gate," Nemir said to the Roman legionnaire. "Persian women prefer to enter a city through its bazaar."

"But sirs, the main marketplace is near the temple's southern wall. She'll be pleased by that," he said as Merak mounted and hurried after Soraya.

"Wait, slow down a bit," said Merak.

She smiled because he was following her.

"Don't you want to hear what the legionnaire told us as you left?"

"No. Why should I?"

"He told us that it is better to enter near this other gate because the main market is in front of the temple," said Merak.

"That's nice."

"What are you so upset about?" asked Merak.

"I wanted to… I don't really know. I just thought that you would stand up for me and go with me."

"I was trying to figure out what was best for you so I could go with you. Don't you trust me?" he asked.

She was silent, looking at his eyes.

He was frustrated and wondering if women were always so difficult.

"I'm sorry, Merak."

"Okay, let's go find that gate."

They slowed down so that the elders could catch up.

As they moved around the curve in the road, they came to a pool where women were washing clothing. Just beyond the pool was a large quarry. At the easternmost portion of the quarry, men were cutting stone, but there were no horses pulling huge carts with blocks on them. They were leaving the rubble in neat piles further out in the quarry.

"They are preparing burial caves," said Nemir. "The Jews either bury in the ground or in caves."

"It must be an exhausted quarry," said Abdul. "Didn't we hear that they used to mine travertine marble. It was good for floors and tabletops, but not for statues."

"What's that, Father?" Soraya was pointing to an outcropping on the side of the quarry that was closest to the walls of the city of Jerusalem. It had an unappealing aura.

The face of the rock leading up to the outcropping looked like a skull.

"That's Golgotha, the skull, if I remember correctly. We weren't given a tour of the city last time we were here, but we were told about their justice system by some of the soldiers that accompanied us to Bethlehem," said Abdul.

There were stanchions on it for crucifixions. Three of them stood together straight up. No men on cross pieces hung on them for now. They served as a gruesome reminder that Roman justice was swift, painful, and final.

Soraya looked at Golgotha and shuddered. It was a place where men died. Beyond it however, was a series of green hillsides running up toward the Mount of Olives. The hills were filled with wildflowers, the lightest colored of which shimmered brilliantly in the setting sun.

"We could make our camp tonight in that valley there," said Merak. He was pointing toward the foothills at the base of the Mount of Olives.

"For now, let's concentrate on getting some information on the whereabouts of Jesus without letting too many people know that we bring a tribute from the Magi," said Abdul. He was worried about the politics in the city. The message from Aaron of Arimathea was clear—watch what you say and to whom you say it.

They came to the Genneth gate. Here the wall of Jerusalem turned on itself, forcing whoever was planning on entering to walk by the Hippicus tower and into a large fortress-like tower. The fortress was a part of the wall and was dwarfed by Hippicus tower. The door itself was a passage through the fortress.

"You will dismount," said a guard as they entered.

They smiled and got off their beasts. The guard wasn't too interested in them beyond their compliance with his command.

The small group had to make a sharp right turn under the fortress, which left them in a large open square next to the Hasmonaean Palace.

"This is beautiful," said Soraya looking at the palace.

"This is not the palace that I remember, Abdul," said Nemir.

"Me neither. It was larger and there was the short wall with all the trees behind it," said Abdul.

Merak stopped a passerby and asked where Herod's Palace was. The passerby pointed toward the direction to their right.

"And the temple?" Merak asked.

The man pointed to their left and looked at them with curiosity. They certainly weren't Jews and had no business at the temple.

Merak smiled at the man and headed in the direction he had indicated. It took them right by the front of the Hasmonaean Palace, whose guards were at attention, watching the crowds of people in the streets.

"It sure is crowded," said Merak.

"It looks about the same as I remember," said Nemir.

The temple loomed in the distance above the rest of the city. When they turned the corner of the palace the road narrowed for a bit and then opened again to a triangular plaza. There were vendors everywhere and the noise was unbelievable.

"It reminds me of the market at home," said Soraya. "Only louder and more chaotic."

She was excited about purchasing gifts for her mother and her brother's family. She especially wanted to bring something for her niece and nephew.

A wide via led up a hill toward the temple. They continued to walk, now single file with Merak in front, Abdul next, his daughter following him, and Nemir bringing up the rear. People stopped what they were doing to look at them for a moment. When they could see that they were not bearing goods for the market their attention went back to what they were doing.

Merak wondered what he would say and who he would talk to at the temple. For now, however, he walked slowly and took in the colorful sights.

"Merak, what do you think that is up ahead?" Abdul asked.

He sounded worried to Merak. He could see why when a young woman with a basket on her head moved a little to the right. Further up the via, the road ran onto a pontine-like structure and right into the temple.

"It's a bridge," said Merak.

"The road runs right into the temple," said Nemir from behind. "That's amazing. I've never seen anything so large."

"There are columns right in the middle of the road though," said Merak.

"Yes, but you could bring a cart through there, it's so wide," said Abdul.

In a couple of minutes, they were at the base of the bridge. A young rabbi walked over to them and stopped them before they could walk up the structure to the temple.

"You can't bring a camel up there," said the rabbi.

The bridge was about one hundred and fifty yards long

and steeply inclined near the halfway point but leveled off three-quarters of the way to the top and ran level to the temple.

"Are any of you Jews?" asked the rabbi.

"No, young man. What do you suggest?" It seemed odd for Merak to use the term young man, because they were so close in age, but it was clear to the others that Merak was now back into his role as an emissary of the Magus Melchior.

"You could proceed by foot, and the rest could wait at the xystus," he said pointing toward the garden walk to the right of the bridge. It connected to a terrace which was flawlessly landscaped.

"I'll wait with the camels. Abdul, Soraya, you two go up onto the terrace and look around. Merak see what you can find out," said Nemir.

Merak nodded in agreement and started walking up the bridge. He turned and looked back when he was halfway to the top and saw Soraya waving at him from the terrace. She looked beautiful in the evening light. The sun hadn't fully set yet but was giving a warm hue to the buildings. Behind Soraya was a vast red and orange sunset. *It seems prettier because she is in the foreground,* he thought.

Finally, he stood about twenty yards from the columns and looked inside the huge open chamber. A member of the Sanhedrin, a young scribe, was walking out and looked at him with disdain.

"Sir, you are not Jewish and cannot enter the temple," said the man. A temple guard quickly approached.

"I am Merak, an emissary of Magus Melchior of Arabia. I am looking for a member of the council, Joseph of Arimathea," said Merak.

"I am Jonathan of Bethany. I am a scribe of the Sanhedrin and know Joseph," he said.

"Would you know his whereabouts?" Merak asked politely. He had moved a little closer to the temple and was looking inside. He didn't know that the actual Temple of Jerusalem was the T-shaped building in the center of the magnificent mount.

"I could probably locate him for you," said Jonathan. "What business should I tell him brings you here."

"It's personal, not business," said Merak with a smile. He was feeling a little uncomfortable and hoping there would be few questions.

"Oh?" said Jonathan. "Visitors from foreign dignitaries usually visit the Roman governor before they visit the Jewish council."

"Is he inside the temple?"

"Probably not. The council is not in session, but I could go look," said Jonathan.

Merak let his gaze shift from one end of the structure to the other and asked, "How long will that take?"

He imagined that it would take hours.

"A few minutes. The temple proper is in the center. That's where he would be," said Jonathan, who arrogantly smiled at Merak's ignorance.

Jonathan turned and reentered the massive structure.

Merak waited.

✝

"I'm suspicious," Jonathan said.

"We don't even know if Joseph of Arimathea is a disciple of this so-called prophet," said the priest, known as Josephus

Caiaphas. His father-in-law Annas was sitting quietly in the shadows watching the two men.

"It's the second group. They must find out somehow that he's a disciple," said Jonathan.

"That's true. He met this Paulinus person who was sent from King Abgar," said Josephus.

"And we know that Paulinus is meeting with Thomas, who is one of the twelve," said Jonathan.

"Okay, have him followed, but let Joseph know that this man wants a meeting. We'll see if your suspicions—that he is looking for the soon-to-be crowned King of the Jews—is correct," said Josephus.

Annas stood up. The young scribe bowed respectfully. Even though he wasn't the high priest he was highly respected and was chief counselor to the high priest.

"It's a mess. We should have put a stop to it when Jesus came parading in on an ass, with people laying palms fronds in is path and singing Hosanna. What a disgrace. They're claiming it's in fulfillment of Zechariah 9:9. That's very bad," said Annas to his son-in-law.

"A direct reference to the Messiah," said Josephus Caiaphas.

"That's blasphemy, isn't it?" Annas asked.

"Jesus didn't say it about himself, so technically it isn't," said Josephus.

"So do we follow this emissary of the Arabian Magus?" asked the scribe.

"Yes. See if he makes inquiries about Jesus of Nazareth," said Josephus. With a nod, Jonathan was dismissed.

†

"I spoke to one of the other members of the council. Joseph is not here. Come back tomorrow morning. By the second hour, we will have contacted him to see if he will see you," said Jonathan.

Merak nodded.

"Do I come right to this spot, or is there a better door of the temple to wait at?" Merak asked.

"This will be fine," said the scribe. He turned and went inside.

Merak never noticed the two young men walking out as he turned to go back down the bridge to the others. He waved at Soraya and her father and then descended the incline swiftly.

They were all waiting to hear what had happened. When he told them, they seemed stuck on the idea that it would take until the morning to meet this man, Joseph.

"Let's just walk around and make inquiries ourselves. There's got to be someone who's seen Jesus. He's famous now," said Soraya. She had a feeling that he was in the city somewhere.

The two men who had followed Merak down the bridge to the xystus and stopped abruptly when they heard the name Jesus. Merak and the others didn't notice.

"Yes, but it is more prudent to wait until tomorrow," said Abdul.

"What do we do and where do we go now?" Soraya asked.

"Let's get something to eat," said Merak.

"That's sounds like an answer to me," said Nemir. He was smiling broadly at the thought of eating a warm meal and then pitching camp in the foothills of the Mount of Olives.

He wanted to turn in early. It had been a long day thus far. He was interested in ending it full, warm, and asleep.

There is a huge market at the end of the temple. It's called Huldah market," said Soraya.

"Let's go get a few things and then pitch camp outside the gates on the hillside. I don't feel like going into a tavern," said Abdul.

"Can we go out the gate over there," said Soraya. She was pointing to Damascus gate. She wanted to avoid going back to Genneth gate and then having to pass by Golgotha to get to camp.

The men understood her concern and agreed. After picking up some small breads, fruits, cheese, and dried sausage, they started walking along the western wall of the Great Temple of Jerusalem.

"My God, it's huge," said Soraya.

"It seems like it goes on forever," said Abdul.

"It gives you the feeling that God himself has built it," said Nemir.

"They were pretty tight with their security," said Merak. He wanted to go inside and look around. He had a hunch that Jesus visited the temple regularly.

At the end of the temple, they came to the north wall of Jerusalem.

"Are we at the Damascus gate?" Merak asked the legionnaire standing at attention.

"No, sir, this is the door to the Antonia," said the Roman.

They climbed on their camels and looked at the huge fortress just outside the walls next to the temple.

"What's the Antonia?" asked Merak.

"It's the official palace and government building of

Pontius Pilate, the governor of Jerusalem. The tribunal and tax department are here, as well as enough soldiers to enforce the Pax Romana," said the young man proudly. There was a tone in his voice that was meant as a warning for anyone who would even consider doing anything that violated the extensive Codex Romana, the Roman Law.

They rode off to the foothills of the Mount of Olives and picked a perfect place to make camp. Others were also camping, and they chose an area where they were somewhat alone higher up. It afforded them a good view.

†

Merak and Soraya gathered some wood for a small fire. Abdul and Nemir set about grooming the camels and chattering about other journeys.

"The city is beautiful," said Soraya. She watched Merak as he carried wood for her. She placed another piece in his arms.

"It's more beautiful today than it has ever been," said Merak, as they walked to the camp.

"Why is that?" Soraya asked.

"Because today you were in the city."

She turned to look at the man who would say such a sweet thing to her. His big brown eyes held her in his gaze for a moment and then he looked down to sort the wood. She wondered if he were shyer than she had suspected or had his eyes just told her something that was so personal that he had to avert his gaze.

He was bending over the small fire and adding a few pieces of wood. She squatted down next to him and speared a flat bread with her knife. She held it over the fire until it

was warm and then cut a chunk of soft cheese and put it on the bread. He took it with a smile.

"So, you've cooked for me, woman," he said seriously.

She giggled.

"I'm trying to set a more serious tone with you Soraya, but you're making me laugh."

"I'm trying to feed my man," she said with a serious tone that mimicked his and he laughed.

Soraya looked at his big brown eyes and her heart softened.

"What?"

"Merak, what were you thinking before when you were looking in my eyes?" she asked.

He thrust his hands out over the fire and warmed them for a moment. Then he took her hands in his and said softly, "I've finally found the woman that God had selected for me."

The words caught her breath and took it away.

Merak stood and then gently pulled her to her feet.

"Let's go for a walk," he said. He was watching her father and uncle who were coming back over to the fire.

"What are you kids up to?" asked Nemir.

"We were going to go for a walk, Uncle," said Merak. "With your permission of course," he added to her father.

"She is my precious little girl. I trust she is in good hands with you, Merak."

"Indeed sir," he said formally.

Her hand lingered in his as they moved away from the camp. They walked off into the night, toward the next higher level on the Mount of Olives. They wanted to climb up to see the view of the city from afar. Off in the distance, the city of Jerusalem was burning gigantic candles. There were

only a few compared to what they had heard about Rome and its candles, but still there were portions of the city that glimmered in the dark from afar.

"It's beautiful," she said. She held his arm in hers and let her body rest against it.

"It is nights like this that we shall remember for many years," said Merak.

"Forever."

"I have never said this before to a woman," said Merak.

"What?"

She was looking up into his eyes.

"I love you, Soraya."

He touched her face with his hands and kissed her lips tenderly.

In that moment, her soul melted and flowed together with his like molten gold in a heart shaped crucible.

✝

Thomas, the disciple of Jesus, was not aware that he had been followed. He entered the inn and looked around. It was crowded mostly with Jews from other lands, but in the corner sat the man he was looking for, Paulinus. He approached his table and the man started to rise. Thomas motioned for him to stay seated.

"I have come with word from my Lord Jesus. He received your letter from King Abgar Ourchama," said Thomas.

"Will he deign to visit King Abgar?"

"I'm afraid not. Edessa is too far for him to journey right now. His ministry is to the Jews in the Promised Land."

"It's only a short distance north of Byzantium. My king is

wasting away. He will surely die. He has leprosy. His country as well as he, suffers," said Paulinus.

"I am sorry," said Thomas.

"I was told to commission a painting if Jesus the Nazarene couldn't come. Did you request that? I have spoken to a few artists and would like to get something done quickly so that my king may have the image of Jesus to gaze upon," said Paulinus.

"Jesus said not to worry about the image. He would see to it that your king received something," said Thomas.

"May I send an artist?" Paulinus asked.

"No, he said not to worry. He would take care of the image for you," insisted Thomas. "He would like you to return to Edessa and said that you should depart before the Feast of the Passover on Thursday."

"I wish to see him one more time," said Paulinus.

"I'm sorry." Thomas stood up to leave.

Paulinus sat still and nodded his head. Neither man noticed that they were being watched intensely by a Jewish scribe.

✝

"We must do something quickly," said Josephus Caiaphas, the high priest.

He was pacing in the antechamber to his bedroom. Another priest, a Pharisee named Eleazar, and member of the Sanhedrin stood still and watched him.

"Everyone in the world is coming here for the holidays. This has got to be when he plans on taking power from us," said Eleazar.

"Don't you think I know that! He's been visited by a letter carrier from King Abgar of Edessa. Now we have this emissary from an Arabian Magus. Next thing we know he'll get a visit from Rome, and the procurator will decide to declare him high priest."

"They can't do that," said Eleazar.

"Yes, they can. Gratus appointed me to this post and has done so every year for eleven years now," said Josephus Caiaphas.

"And you've done an admirable job. The others that he appointed were gone in a year," said Eleazar.

"Don't you think I know that?"

"What do you think Jesus will do?" asked Eleazar.

"He'll get the rabble to declare him the Messiah and then Gratus will appoint him high priest to quell the unrest," said Josephus Caiaphas. "At least that's what I would do, were I in his place. But I think he may be too late."

"What if Jesus declares himself King of the Jews?" Eleazar asked.

"That would be a disaster for all of Judea. The Romans will come down hard on us and destroy our city. They would close the temple and God knows what else."

"Then it is wise to kill him," Eleazar said.

"It is essential."

"Now if only there was a way to do it," said Eleazar.

Josephus Caiaphas smiled and rubbed his hands together.

"We have found a man to betray him, Eleazar. We may be able to eliminate this man Jesus after all," said Caiaphas.

There was a knock on the door and a servant appeared.

"The one known as Judas is here, sir," said the servant.

"Show him in," said Caiaphas. He motioned for Eleazar to sit down and be quiet.

Judas walked in and stood still. Finally, he asked, "Have you accepted my offer?"

Josephus Caiaphas smiled weakly and said, "Yes. The agreed-on price then, thirty pieces of silver?"

"It is agreed," said Judas.

Caiaphas handed him a small bag of silver. "When shall we hear from you?" He watched Judas and realized he wanted to count it but refrained from doing so.

"After the first day of the Passover I will know where he is and will bring you to him." Judas unconsciously weighed the bag in his hand before depositing it into his cloak.

"Good, we shall await your summons. We will be ready," said Josephus Caiaphas.

Judas bowed to the high priest, nodded to the Pharisee, and left.

When he was gone, Eleazar said, "How did you ever find someone to betray him?"

"It was easy. He found me."

†

The fragrance of fresh baked bread wafted over the hillside from the city. It filled the air before sunrise and woke Merak from a dream where he was the guest of honor at a banquet. Just after the host had blessed and broken the bread, the host was forcibly removed by desert wolves dressed as Roman soldiers. Merak rushed forward to help the man who was hosting the meal, but the wolves kept him at bay. He tried to draw his sword and unfurl his net but the man who was being dragged away turned, raised his right hand, and

said calmly, *"Be not afraid, Merak. Judge not by appearances but by the will of God in all things."*

The wolves bound the man and dragged him away. Merak thought it was strange that they could stand on their hind legs and walk like humans. One of the wolves turned toward him. He expected it to speak but it only growled at him. All he could think of was eating the bread that the man had blessed.

"God, I must be awfully hungry," he said out loud as he woke up.

Nemir was in his bedroll snoring. When Merak heard the sound, he realized it sounded just like the growling wolf. He put the dream aside, but the words of Master Melchior came back to him. *"Don't explain away a dream too easily. It may be God communicating your attitude for future circumstances."*

"I see you are awake," said Abdul to his future son-in-law.

"Yes, I…" he started to say something about his dream and then decided, "I am hungry already."

"Me too," said Abdul.

"Shall we head down to the city gates and get some bread, or should we wait?" asked Merak.

"Let's go. You know my daughter; she'll sleep until she has to get up because the sun awakens her. Nemir will sleep until his snoring arouses him."

"We can get some of that bread we had last night," said Merak.

"It's the last day for eating leavened bread. Remember what the merchant said yesterday."

"Strange custom. It can't taste too good if it's unleavened," said Merak.

"Every land has its own customs," said Abdul.

They got up quietly and walked down the hillside. They were actually closer to the Damascus gate and picked up the road close to the city walls.

"There has to be a bakery just inside," said Merak. His stomach was rumbling.

The entire city was coming to life. People were opening shutters to their windows and letting the cool morning air in. When they got to the gate, the huge door was already open and they passed right in.

"I can find a bakery with my nose," said Merak.

It was much easier than that. A baker was bringing fresh loaves out to the stand in front of his shop just down the street from the Damascus gate.

There was a small forum a short distance from the bakery further down the via. Fruit vendors were setting up their stands and making ready for the morning rush.

A tall man with a magnificent steed was buying some bread from the baker. He was obviously not a Jew and was buying enough bread and fruit to last at least three days.

Merak smiled at the man, recognizing a fellow foreigner. The man smiled back, reflecting Merak's recognition.

"Are you Persian or Arabian?" asked the man.

"Arabian. I'm Merak and this is Abdul. He is Persian," said Merak.

"My name is Paulinus. I'm from Edessa, and as you can see, I'm not Jewish either."

"Then I guess you're not here for the Jewish Festival?" said Merak.

"No. Today is a good day to leave Jerusalem," said Paulinus.

"Nice steed," said Merak.

Abdul was looking at the horse too. He was trying to figure out what the man's business was. The saddle was beautifully made, not exactly military and certainly not a merchants. There were no goods on the animal either.

Paulinus saw them looking over his horse and knew what they were doing.

"You're not a merchant," said Abdul.

"No, I'm a letter carrier, a courier for King Abgar. This is the first time I've come this far south."

"Where's Edessa?" Merak asked.

"It's north of Byzantium. That's where I'm headed. What business are you in?" asked Paulinus.

"We're bringing a gift for someone, and then heading back to Baghdad," said Abdul.

"I'd deliver it and then clear out. This place is going to be a mad house in another thirty-six hours. Every cousin of a Jew from two days journey out will try to get in. And they stop eating regular bread tomorrow. I tried some of the unleavened stuff. It's not very pleasant. No wonder they only eat it once a year."

"Merak could eat anything," said Abdul.

"Well, you better buy a little extra today so that you have enough. I delivered my letter and I'm out of here. I'm glad I found him before the holiday."

"It must be easier for the emissary of a king to deliver a letter. Do you go up to the Roman governor and announce yourself, and then he sends someone with you to find the person?"

"Usually, I deliver directly to the procurator or the

governor. It's very simple. This time, it was a little more interesting," said Paulinus.

He broke a loaf of bread. Steam came pouring out and he offered some to Merak.

"Try this fruit. We don't have anything like it in Edessa," he said. It was a persimmon.

"We have those in Baghdad," said Abdul. He reached for some apricots.

Merak was looking at the next merchant's stand. It had dried fruits and nuts. He made a mental note to buy some before they left. Dried goods were essential for their travels.

"So why was it more interesting this time?" asked Merak. He was looking at another stand with cheeses.

"I wasn't delivering to a politician but a holy man, a healer. My king is sick and wanted the gentleman to come visit."

"A physician of sorts?" asked Abdul.

"No, a prophet or a saint. I can't quite figure it out. He touches people and they are healed of their ailments. My king is wasting away and needs his help. None of our physicians can help him."

"So did the Roman procurator help you find him?" asked Merak.

"No, he was useless. The holy man sent someone to me, as though he knew I was coming."

"That is unusual," said Merak.

"Well, they say you can't get to see the Nazarene unless he wills it," said Paulinus. He paid the man for his goods and started walking to his horse.

"Jesus of Nazareth?" they both said.

"Yes, you've heard talk of him too?"

"We're looking for him too," said Merak. He lowered his voice as he walked closer to Paulinus.

"Let me give you some advice. He's not going to see you unless he decides to. I'm convinced he's omniscient. He sent a man named Thomas to find me. I hadn't made more than a couple of inquiries and suddenly this guy shows up saying the master would like my letter," said Paulinus.

"Do you know where he is?" asked Merak.

"No, and I've heard that there are a lot of people who are very unhappy with the Nazarene. So be very careful who you talk to. People are claiming that he is going to declare himself the King of the Jews. The Romans don't like that, and the Sanhedrin is bitterly opposed to it."

"Is he in the city or somewhere else?" asked Abdul.

"Oh, he's in the city. He came in with a big flair three days ago. He rode in on a donkey. People were praising him, singing 'Hallelujah' and some were even saying he's the Jewish Messiah."

"Did you see him?" asked Merak.

"Yes, I saw him, but I couldn't get close to him. Then he disappeared into the temple. I couldn't enter, so I went and sat down at a tavern to have some wine and this man named Thomas shows up. Just like that. He asks for the letter like he knew what was in it. He even knew who it was from."

"How did he know? Did you question him?" asked Merak.

"Yes, he said the master told him to come get it," said Paulinus.

"We have a meeting with a man who is on the council this morning," said Merak.

"I don't want to tell you what to do, but it'll be a waste of time if Jesus doesn't want to see you," said Paulinus.

"Thanks, I think," said Merak with a chuckle.

Paulinus mounted his steed in direct disobedience to the rule.

"Aren't you supposed to walk that beast?" asked Merak.

"I'm an emissary from royalty. Rules don't apply to me. Besides, it's early. Later today you'll barely be able to walk." Paulinus rode off through the gate.

Merak and Abdul looked at each other.

"That was the strangest story I have ever heard," said Merak.

"Unbelievable. Let's get back and tell the others. You have to go to that meeting in about an hour."

"We should find a place to stable our beasts today," said Merak. "I'd like for everyone to be there at the meeting."

They walked off toward the Damascus gate.

†

Jonathan watched Joseph of Arimathea walk through the large antechamber of the temple. He knew where he was heading and planned on following him. He kept a discrete distance because he didn't want to alarm him. He had been following his movements for days now but had been using others to keep tabs on him. He was curious to see what the meeting was about but didn't know how he could eavesdrop without being recognized.

Two other men came over to Jonathan to speak with him. They walked slowly toward the road where the meeting was to take place. Jonathan spoke softly with them but kept an eye on Joseph of Arimathea. He finally decided that he was

going to walk right up to Joseph and wait for the Arabian. When Merak came in, he would try to stay and listen to what it was about. If he was asked to leave, he had a backup plan.

The backup was where the two others came in. They would move closer to Joseph and the man from Arabia. He figured that they would be able to listen. If anything important was said they would immediately report to him.

"The most important thing to find out is where Jesus of Nazareth is," said Jonathan softly.

The shorter of the two men shook his head. "He's not going to tell a complete stranger where Jesus is."

"He'll at least tell the Arabian where they will meet," said Jonathan.

"You hope." His tone was sarcastic.

"Just do as you're told," said Jonathan sternly. He didn't like being talked back to by anyone with less authority than he had. Even though he was young he had status, and he wanted to make sure it was respected. A leader for Jonathan was supposed to respect the pecking order, if not, authority would be undermined. Jonathan claimed his authority from God so it was blasphemy to undermine it. That was a serious offense for any Jew.

He watched the two young men move closer to Joseph of Arimathea and smiled. It was time to make his move.

"Joseph," Jonathan called.

Joseph of Arimathea turned and smiled politely.

I don't like you either, Jonathan thought as he put on a huge insincere smile of his own.

"The hour draws near. Is the man here?" asked the Arimathean.

Joseph scanned the bridge and saw the Arabian walking up the street with three others.

"That's him there. Interesting clothing isn't it. He has three others with him, now," said Jonathan. He wondered what the others were here for. Jonathan's curiosity was getting the best of him. The small talk was making him sound nervous. More people might mean that the two spies would be detected. He tried to put the idea out of his head and focus.

Merak led the way and stepped forward first. Jonathan moved forward to greet him.

"Merak, I'd like to present Joseph of Arimathea," said Jonathan.

He was hoping that he would be able to stay and listen to the conversation, then he would have no need of the spies.

"Thank you," said Merak politely. "It was very kind of you to bring him here. We appreciate it."

Jonathan knew he was being dismissed but decided to stay, just to see how he would handle it.

"I am Merak of Arabia. I am a representative of Magus Melchior, and this is Abdul, his gracious daughter Soraya, and Nemir."

When Jonathan didn't leave after the introduction, Merak said, "Joseph is there some place where we could sit and speak privately. I'm sure you understand Jonathan."

"Let's go sit on a bench at the xystus down below," said Joseph.

They all nodded in agreement. Before Jonathan could start walking with them, Joseph said, "Thank you again, Jonathan. I'm sure I can handle this alone."

Joseph made a face that said, perhaps it's a big deal for them, so let me appease them.

The insincere smile was replanted on Jonathan's face as he turned to leave. He made the briefest eye contact with the two men who were going to eavesdrop.

"So, tell me, are you Joseph of Arimathea, friend of Aaron the innkeeper?" asked Nemir before they had reached the bottom of the bridge.

"If I am not?" said Joseph.

"Then we have the wrong man," said Nemir.

"I am, but what is all the intrigue?"

"We are bringing a gift for Jesus of Nazareth, and we were told that you could help us find him."

"If I could, why should I?" asked Joseph.

"It's a long story," said Abdul who then proceeded to explain their visit thirty some years ago.

"He was born in Bethlehem?" asked Joseph.

It amazed Joseph of Arimathea to find out that Jesus was actually born in Bethlehem and not a Galilean from Nazareth. It proved to him that he could be the Messiah because the Messiah had to belong to the House of David. That meant that the Messiah had to come from Bethlehem, David's hometown.

Abdul waited for Joseph who seemed lost in his own thoughts.

"Moreover, we've come a long way and we want to make certain that the cloth is delivered to the right person," said Abdul.

"All this travel for a bolt of linen," said Joseph.

"Yes, I know it sounds a little odd, but it's what we had promised to do," said Nemir.

"I know and a man's word is his honor, duty, and covenant," said Joseph.

"Precisely," said Merak.

"Jesus would agree. He is a man who is rigorously honest. He said to some of his disciples that the truth shall set you free," said Joseph.

"I think I'm going to like this man," said Nemir.

"You can't help but like him. He is the most authentic person you will ever meet. Every word he utters is profound. He uses every event to teach. He is awe inspiring."

"Hopefully then, you will take us to him?" asked Merak.

"Not exactly. I have to ask around to find out where he is today and then determine if he wants the gift. He doesn't really accept gifts from people, at least that is not what I've seen. If he wants you to deliver it, where will you be?"

"We are camped on the hillside on the Mount of Olives," said Abdul.

"Do you have those colorful Persian tents?"

"Yes," said Nemir.

"Then it will be no trouble finding you…" he paused, "but if I come to you, it may call attention to us."

Joseph thought about it for a moment and then continued, "Perhaps it would be better if you came into the city tomorrow around the noon hour. There is a Roman tavern near the Hippodrome called, Cibum Caelestium, not exactly celestial foods, but you'll be able to get a warm Roman meal. I'll come in toward the end of the meal and let you know. How many days can you stay here?"

"We will stay as long as it takes," said Nemir. He looked at the others who nodded in agreement.

"Where's the Hippodrome?" asked Merak.

Soraya stood up and pointed toward an area just to the south of the temple. Two men who were standing nearby moved out of her way and then walked off.

"We spotted it yesterday," she said.

"What are the chances that he'll receive us?" asked Abdul as Joseph started to leave.

"One never knows the future with a prophet."

"I would think the prophet would know," said Nemir with a laugh.

"Probably true," said Joseph.

He turned and left.

10

THE LAST SEDER

"**M**y feet are killing me. We've walked half the streets of this city in the last two days," said Nemir.

"What amazes me is that we haven't been able to find a trace of him. It's almost as if he were invisible. So many people said that they had seen him or heard him, but no one knows where he is today," said Abdul.

"Well gentlemen, important matters await us," Merak said interrupting them. "We need to head back toward the Hippodrome and find that tavern."

"He's always hungry," said Soraya. It was said with wonder, but her father knew that she was thinking about cooking for him.

"The name was Cibum Caelestium. I can't wait," said Nemir. He was hoping the food was good. It was run by Romans, so there would be a lot of dishes cooked with honey and vinegar and other spices that he enjoyed.

They were very frustrated by what had become a futile attempt to track down this man known as Jesus of Nazareth. They had hoped that a few inquiries in the city would lead them to him. But it was an endless blind trail. First, they visited the upper city. They walked for hours and talked to dozens of

people. They walked from the Jaffa gate to the Genneth gate. At the upper market they casually asked if anyone had heard of Jesus of Nazareth. They were surprised that so many had, yet no one had seen him since his triumphant arrival in the city on Sunday.

They walked to the other end of the upper city and visited the Tomb of David. They followed the wall down through the lower city and visited the area known as David's city. People didn't talk as much there, but at least they were closer to the Hippodrome.

Before heading over to the Hippodrome, they stopped by the pool of Siloam. There they heard a story of a man who was born blind, and his sight was restored by Jesus.

"That was an amazing story," said Nemir as they walked toward the Hippodrome.

"I'll say. When you're born blind there is no cure. That has to be a miracle. The more I hear about him the more wonderful he seems, Uncle," said Soraya.

"I hope we get to see Jesus perform a few miracles," said Nemir.

"I don't think it works like that," said Merak.

They all stopped to look at him.

"How is it supposed to work?" Abdul asked.

"The miracles are his calling cards. He may do them out of compassion and mercy, but more to fulfill the will of God than to delight the curious. I don't think he'll say, 'Nemir, come here and watch me cure this leper.'"

"He could," said Nemir. He firmly believed it.

"Yes, of course he could. But don't you see, he cured that blind man not because the man was blind or even because the man was asking to be cured, but so that people would

understand that it was God who was working these things. Jesus didn't worry about the cause. That wasn't why he cured him. I wish Master Melchior were here to explain it. He would do a better job," said Merak.

"You're doing fine. It's like what the people at the pool of Siloam said, 'Jesus wasn't focused on who was to blame for the blindness,'" said Soraya.

"Exactly. He was focused on the idea that God is the solution," said Merak. He was pleased with how that sounded.

They were passing the main gate to the Hippodrome. Notice was posted that it was closed. Nemir had already informed himself of the schedule of events. There would not be another race until after the Jewish Festival. He and Soraya were both very disappointed.

"I wish I could get on Delia right now and race someone," Soraya said.

"They wouldn't let you here in Jerusalem," said Abdul.

"Your father's right. If you are going to race, it will have to be where Master Balthasar has some influence," said Merak.

Nemir wasn't paying attention. He was looking around for the Cibum Caelestium Tavern, but it was Merak who spotted it first.

The tavern was a typical Roman eatery, couches and all. Merak walked in first as was his duty as their host and guide.

"Your uncle is going to love this place," he said to Soraya.

Merak looked at the large portions that were being served by a very gracious staff and then winked at Nemir. He was all smiles.

The meal was uneventful. Merak wanted to keep talking about Jesus and was getting a little bolder as he spoke. Nemir

and Abdul had other plans. They wanted to talk about the trip home and the announcement to Soraya's mother that Merak had asked for her hand.

Merak finally settled in and played along when he realized that it was important for Soraya. He wanted her to understand that she could trust and depend upon him.

Joseph of Arimathea came in almost unnoticed. Everyone stopped talking at once. The silence was deafening.

"Hi friends," Joseph said lightly.

Nemir followed suit and tried to act nonchalant.

"Hi Joseph. Have you eaten? Would you like to join us?" asked Nemir.

"Yes, the food was good, just as you had suggested," said Merak.

Abdul sat up and made room for Joseph.

"The food is not kosher. We have strict dietary customs given to us by God Almighty through Moses," said Joseph.

"Oh, so you could never try this? And your big festival starts tonight?" asked Nemir.

"That's correct," Joseph said. The tone and rhythm of the conversation had quickly returned to normal. He was grateful.

After some small talk, Joseph said, "I'm sorry I couldn't get you an appointment with your client... because of the Passover meal tonight. I was told that you should have the merchandise ready for tomorrow mid-afternoon. You are to bring the cloth no matter what else may be going on."

He looked at each of them.

They all nodded and smiled.

"Did he say he would meet with us then?" asked Soraya.

"Not exactly. He said that at the third hour after midday

your duty will have been fulfilled."

"He can't see us tonight?" asked Abdul.

"Business is business, but the Jewish Festival must take precedence," said Nemir.

"Is there a meeting place set?" asked Merak.

"Near the door to the city at the northern end of the temple. Do you know where that is?" asked Joseph.

"Near the Antonia Tower?" Merak asked.

"Precisely at the Antonia. We have to finish everything quickly because the Sabbath will be upon us before we know it."

"We'll be there," said Merak.

"I'll be running along. There is so much to prepare for tonight's supper," he said smiling. He left as unnoticed by those inside as he had when he entered.

Outside the tavern, two men watched him leave.

†

John watched Jesus recite the Kiddush, the traditional prayer that started the Seder. He felt a deep love well up inside.

Judas felt a wave of deep resentment. Jesus drank a little more than half the wine from one of the four glasses while reclining to his left.

It is amazing to watch him at a Seder, John thought. He has all the nuances down. Every subtlety of prayer and every step in perfect order. Seder meant order. There was a certain order to things tonight that had been done that way for centuries. There was an order ordained from God himself. That order was the embodiment of Jewishness.

Judas's resentment welled up again. He could have

announced that he was the Messiah. With his enormous powers he could have already thrown off the shackles of Rome, thought Judas. He was fuming about it again.

John watched closely as Jesus washed his hands. He first poured the water from a large cup twice over his right hand and then twice over his entire left hand. The Lord dried his hands thoroughly but didn't say the blessing.

"This is the most perfect Seder," said Judas to his neighbor at the table. Judas was placed closest to Jesus on his right, a seat of honor. John and Simon Peter were next to Jesus on his left.

"What did you expect from the Jewish Messiah?" Andrew whispered to Judas. The love in his voice for the Lord was astonishing.

Jesus dipped a small piece of parsley in salt water and said the Bracha. Again, there was the perfect lean to the left as he ate the parsley.

Judas was distracted. There was something he needed to do, but he kept forcing it from his consciousness. *He has told us repeatedly that he is going to die.* Anger welled up in Judas' heart. He was more than annoyed that the Messiah hadn't declared himself the King of the Jews. He was furious that Jesus was taking his sweet time toying with everyone. He had watched the miracles, the omniscience in action, and the omnipotence calming the seas; and yet Jesus hesitated. He could control the wind, the rain, and the seas; and yet he hesitated to control the Sanhedrin and the Jewish council. And lately, he was telling them that he was going to die. Judas was angry and frustrated. *I will change all of that soon.*

When Judas looked up, he realized that Jesus had broken one of the three matzoth into two parts. The smaller part was

placed back between the other two matzoth. The larger part was wrapped in a small linen napkin and set aside for later. It was the Afikomen. It would be consumed later at the end of the meal.

Jesus is reading the Exodus, John thought. A moment later, he realized that he was reciting the scripture perfectly from memory. Every word, every consonant was perfectly articulated. *Amazing, but of course. He's the Messiah.*

Am I missing something here? Judas thought looking at all the others. A part of him was too terrified to remember. For a moment his mind drifted to money. *I have to take care of the account here,* he thought. Again, the distraction caused him to miss a good part of the Seder that Jesus was conducting. He pushed away the memory of the promised price of thirty pieces of silver for Jesus' betrayal. He pushed it aside and then realized that Jesus already knew. *Of course, he knows. He's omniscient. I wonder if he's scared.* The idea seemed stupid to Judas after he thought it. He looked around the room and realized everyone was having a much better time than he was.

John was looking at Jesus with that same adoring look he always wore. Matthew was watching the Seder like a student at a lecture. He was taking in every word.

Judas envied Matthew's understanding.

Jesus was much further along in the Seder than Judas had realized. He had reached the part where the three large round unleavened loaves are held up. They were moving quickly but time seemed distorted for him. Tonight, was a night he would always remember. He rationalized his actions. He knew most people would accuse him of betrayal, but when Jesus made his response, the walls of Jericho, or

the temple to be more accurate, would come tumbling down. And Jesus would reconstruct the temple in three days. Then, he knew he would be exonerated.

Certainly, I'm a sinner, thought Judas. He was no longer paying attention to Jesus but thinking about the one constant struggle that had never left him. *Sometimes, I love money more than God.* He knew everybody had a weakness. *I'm not betraying him for the money. I'm forcing him to rise to his greatness.*

Jesus was speaking again. Judas wasn't paying attention. He was thinking about his meeting later tonight.

"In truth I tell you, one of you is about to betray me," said Jesus. "One of you eating with me."

The room was suddenly much quieter.

"Here with me on the table is the hand of the man who is betraying me," said Jesus.

Judas lifted his hand unconsciously.

"It is one of the Twelve, one who is dipping into the same dish with me," said Jesus. He looked around the room and didn't seem to be concerned or upset. Nothing broke his serenity.

"The Son of Man is going to his fate, as the scriptures say he will, but alas for that man by whom the Son of Man is betrayed! It would have been better for that man if he had never been born!"

A murmur went up from the apostles.

"Not me," they each said, one after another.

"Not me, Rabbi, surely?" Judas asked. It wasn't obvious to anyone that his was a question, not a statement.

"It is you who say it," Jesus said back.

Why did he call Jesus Rabbi? Thought John. We have

been calling him Lord for the last year. Only the Pharisees call him Rabbi.

Simon Peter moved forward and whispered to John, "Ask who is it he means."

John leaned his head toward Jesus' chest and softly asked, "Who is it, Lord?"

"It is the one to whom I'll give the piece of bread that I dip in that dish," Jesus said softly to John.

John and Peter waited.

Jesus picked up a piece of bread and dipped it in a dish and gave the morsel to Judas, son of Simon Iscariot.

He's giving me such a small gift, thought Judas as he took the bread with a little charoset.

Judas felt the rush of evil enter into him. He knew the feeling well. It was the foundation of his greed and his willingness to betray his Lord. *You need to give me much more than a little bread dipped in traditional Seder trappings. You need to establish the supremacy of Israel. You need to take your place as the rightful King of the Jews with power and majesty!* He could hear his thoughts getting louder, his inner voice ringing with resentment. It was strident, urgent, compelling. He told it to shut up and it laughed at him.

John leaned forward and whispered to Peter, "It's Judas."

Judas Iscariot was getting irritated as he thought about what Jesus needed to do. *I will force his hand tonight. Then the whole world would know power, real power.*

Judas swallowed the bread and thought about what he was going to do. *I'll force him to reveal that he is the Messiah. If he won't do it himself and prefers to preach and heal, rather than lead, I'll force him.*

The evil that entered Judas celebrated its complete

dominance of the man's mind. It was a demonic relish of evil intention consummated. Unlike joy, this pleasure did not lift up or delight. It darkened the man so and cast a somber pall.

Jesus is looking right at me, thought Judas, taking a long look at his face.

"What you are going to do, do quickly," said Jesus.

No one else in the room understood why Jesus was saying that. Evil knew and was ready to act.

Everyone was paying rapt attention as though it were the most important moment of their lives and yet to Judas it seemed out of place for the Seder. *Just a few more hours and then all hell breaks loose,* he thought.

With that Judas rushed out. He was a man on a mission, a mission of evil.

Jesus then stood and took a large unleavened loaf. It was flat and circular. He held it up for all to see. He said the blessing over the bread, broke it, and said, "Take it and eat. This is my body." As he said my body he leaned forward breathing on the bread. Then he passed the bread to his disciples. Everyone was paying rapt attention as though it were the most important moment of their lives. As each apostle ate it, a rush of grace, an enormous consolation of joy and peace entered their soul.

On a deep level they knew what it was but realized that they could not explain or fathom the depth of love that had just entered their being.

A short while later when it was time to drink the cup of blessing. Jesus stood again. This was a special chalice brought to him for this supper. It was used by Melchizedek many centuries ago when he offered bread and wine to Abraham.

Jesus raised the chalice of wine and said, "Drink from

this, all of you, for this is my blood, the blood of the new covenant poured out for many for the forgiveness of sins."

Each took a small sip and again were overwhelmed with a flood of divine love interpenetrating their very beings, washing their souls with immeasurable and incomparable grace.

There was an incomprehensible feeling of awe and wonder in the room for what Jesus had just done.

†

Simon the Zealot watched the other apostles. They are like little children at times, he thought. Now what are they arguing about?

"He's never really told us who the greatest among us is," said James.

"Maybe tonight is a good night to finally find out," said Andrew.

Simon knew that Andrew was poking fun at the sons of Zebedee again. Their mother had actually asked Jesus to let each of her children sit on either side of Jesus in his kingdom. Simon didn't think it was funny, but Andrew was teasing them again.

Mark joined in and now both ends of the table were having a huge discussion about succession. To Simon, it was more like the children of royalty trying to determine the pecking order in the kingdom.

"Who should be reckoned the greatest?" one of the apostles asked loud enough for Jesus to finally put an end to it. Everybody got quiet and waited.

"Among the gentiles it is the kings who lord it over

them. Those who have authority over them are given the title Benefactor. With you this must not happen," said Jesus.

Jesus paused and looked around at them.

"No, the greatest among you must behave as if he were the youngest," said Jesus.

John leaned forward playfully, and Jesus patted his head with a smile.

"And the leader must behave as if he were the one who serves. For who is greater: the one at the table or the one who serves?"

When no one offered an answer he said, "The one at the table, surely? Yet here I am among you as the one who serves."

Jesus got up from the table and removed his outer garments. They all watched in amazement.

He motioned for Andrew to pass him the nearby towel. He handed it to him, and Jesus girded his waist with it. He then took water and poured it into a basin and began to wash their feet. As he finished washing each man's feet, he used the towel to dry them.

James was perfectly still when Jesus wiped his feet. He understood that the doctor ministers to the sick, and the healer is a servant first to those who are his responsibility. It was a powerful lesson, and as usual Jesus was teaching by example and metaphor.

When Jesus got to Peter, the apostle said, "Lord, are you going to wash my feet?"

His voice was filled with incredulity.

Phillip almost laughed at his naive but outspoken friend.

"Right now, you don't understand what I'm doing," said Jesus. "But later you will understand."

"Never!" said Peter, "You shall never wash my feet."

"If I don't wash you then you can't have a share with me."

"Okay then, Lord, not only my feet, but my hands and my head as well!" said Simon Peter.

"No one who has had a bath needs washing. Such a person is clean all over," said Jesus.

When he finished with Peter, he put his outer garments back on and went back to his place at the head of the table.

"Do you understand what I have done to you?" Jesus asked.

Nathanael smiled broadly. The lesson made perfect sense to the him because it had been inculcated into him by years of religious service.

"You each call me Master and Lord, and rightly so because I am. If I, the Lord and Master, then have washed your feet, you must wash each other's feet. I have given you an example so that you may copy what I have done to you."

Jesus waited for the lesson to sink in. There was quiet in the room.

"In all truth I tell you, no servant is greater than his master, no messenger is greater than the one who sent him," Jesus said.

Again, Jesus paused, waiting for his words to sink in.

"Now that you know this, blessed are you if you behave accordingly."

John watched them. He wondered if they had noticed that he had saved Peter until last.

"You are the men who have stood by me faithfully in my trials," said Jesus. "And now I confer a kingdom on you, just as my Father conferred one on me. You will eat and drink at

my table in my kingdom and you will sit on thrones to judge the twelve tribes of Israel."

John wondered what he meant.

It was then that Jesus started his farewell discourses. John couldn't call them anything but a farewell, especially when Jesus said, "I shall be with you only a little longer."

"Lord, where are you going?" Simon Peter asked naively.

"You can't follow me where I'm going now, but later you will," said Jesus.

"Why can't I follow you? I would follow you even to death. I would lay down my life for you," said Peter. There was bravado in his voice.

Jesus smiled sweetly at Peter.

"Lay down your life for me?" Jesus asked.

Peter nodded his head vigorously.

"Simon, Simon! Look Satan has got his wish to sift you all like wheat," said Jesus.

John knew that he meant we all had our weaknesses that the devil had exploited.

"But I have prayed for you, Simon Peter, so that your faith won't fail completely. Once you've recovered it, you in turn must strengthen your brother's faith."

"Lord," Peter answered, "I would be ready to go to prison with you and to death."

Jesus smiled and said, "I tell you Peter, in all truth that by the time the cock crows today, you will have denied three times that you even know me."

Peter started to say impossible but was silenced by the enormity of even the thought of betrayal. Finally, he mustered the words and said, "Even if I have to die with you, I will never disown you."

All the other disciples said the same thing.

"Don't let your hearts be troubled," said Jesus. "You trust God, so trust also in me. You know the way to the place where I am going."

Thomas was as confused as the rest of them by the veiled reference to his coming death and asked, "Lord, we do not know where you are going. So how can we know the way."

"I am the Way: I am the truth and the life. No one can come to the Father except through me. If you know me, you will know my Father too. From this moment you know him and have seen him."

John was touched deeply by Jesus' words.

Philip, on the other hand, said, "Lord, show us the Father, and then we shall be satisfied."

"You still don't know me?" Jesus asked. "Anyone who has seen me has seen the Father."

Jesus told them about what would happen to him and them, and that later the Paraclete would arrive, but it was confusing for all of them.

When Jesus said, "In a short time, you will no longer see me." A murmur went up.

"And then a short time later you will see me again," said Jesus.

"What does he mean by that?" Phillip asked.

Jesus explained in no uncertain terms that they would soon be weeping for him. He used the example of a woman in childbirth who suffers, but when the baby is delivered there is joy. John appreciated the metaphor. Jesus kept telling them things but was speaking before they could articulate their questions.

"Now you are speaking plainly and not using veiled language," said Andrew.

"And he answers our questions before we even put them into words. We believe that you come from God," said one of the other apostles.

"Do you believe at last?" Jesus asked.

Then Jesus started his last prayer inside for the evening with, "Father the hour has come…"

Jesus got up to leave.

"He was counted as one of the rebellious," said Jesus quoting Isaiah. "Yes, what it says about me is even now reaching the fulfillment," said Jesus. He knew at that moment that Judas had reached the house of the high priest Caiaphas. The others didn't understand this.

"If you have no sword, sell your cloak and buy one," Jesus said.

"Lord, here are two swords," said Peter.

"That's enough," Jesus said to Peter, who put one of the swords on his belt and handed the other one to Simon the Zealot.

They left the house and walked through the city streets. Jesus sang a psalm as they processed out. They crossed into the valley on the Mount of Olives and were heading toward a favorite meeting place, the Garden of Gethsemane.

11

DOWN THE VIA DOLOROSA

The Crime of Injured Majesty
Crimen Laesae Majestatis

"Tomorrow is the big day," said Uncle Nemir. He had eaten some sausage, cheese, and bread and was ready to turn in.

"I wonder what he is really like?" Soraya asked. She was looking at the robe that she had set out. It was hanging on the side of their brightly colored tents.

The small fire that they had built was almost out now. Abdul was sitting close to it watching the flames dance in the cool breeze. He was praying silently that everything would work out after all these years. Part of him was excited and yet another part whispered that he should be still and accept whatever the morning brought.

"Sir, may I have permission to walk with your daughter?" Merak asked.

He was standing rigidly at attention, a sure sign that he was nervous about something. All day he had been acting more like their military escort than her lover. It was a role that he slipped into easily, especially when they passed through the gates and by the garrisoned Roman soldiers.

There was respect afforded Merak by the Romans because of his military appearance. It was an unwritten law that soldiers who were not at war respected each other. Perhaps during times of war, they respected each other even more.

Soraya watched him closely. He was asking permission to walk along the ridge where they had pitched their tents in order to look at the city. Normally her father wouldn't give his permission, but they were almost formerly engaged, and he was also her escort and protector for Magi Melchior and Balthasar. She couldn't be in safer hands.

"Don't be too long, young man," said Abdul. He sounded very much like a father.

Nemir chuckled at his friend's tone.

"Take your time. You have the rest of your lives together," said Nemir.

Merak extended his arm and Soraya took it. She felt very ladylike walking next to her handsome gentleman. She felt him relax a bit as they made contact.

There was no light except for the light of the moon. It was a clear, cool night. They could see the path along into the valley and the gardens below that were between them and the walls of Jerusalem.

The city had been quiet for a few hours. The streets which had been overflowing with a million people were empty during the celebration of the Seder. They heard singing from the buildings as people finished their Seder Feasts with rousing songs and choruses of holy hymns. They watched people walking with torches. It gave an eerie appearance to the city on a mount.

A group of men walked slowly through the next small valley below them. Soraya and Merak watched as the main

part of the group stopped at the entrance to a garden. Four of them went inside, and one of them moved on a stone's throw ahead of the others and fell to his knees.

"These Jews are very religious," said Merak.

The other men sat down. A pair leaned against the trees and seemed to be nodding off. The third stretched out and rested his head on his arm.

"I don't think they're that religious," said Soraya.

She clutched his arm tighter against the cool night air.

"Yes, you're right," he said. Something about the one kneeling had caught his interest.

"One is praying while the others sleep. That's about right. One out of ten is really quite devoted," said Soraya.

"They just had a big meal," said Merak. "They need a nap."

"Men really need that?" Soraya asked.

The area below was manicured like a garden. There was a small building that contained an olive press toward the end of the gardens. It was called the Garden of Gethsemane, or the Garden of the Olive Press. Soraya and Merak were watching the scene unfold from a point that was much higher up on the Mount of Olives which was more barren. There were fewer trees and no formal gardens.

They leaned against an ancient olive tree and watched. She rested her head against his shoulder and smiled at him. In spite of the fact that they were watching the scene unfold below, she felt like they were the only two people in the universe.

"It looks like those men are going to have company," said Merak.

He pointed to the path that led to the front gate of the

garden. A crowd of people carrying torches was making its way up the hill toward the front gate.

Merak could make out the swords and clubs carried by the mob. He sensed that something bad was going to happen.

Soraya picked up on Merak's heightened sense of danger.

"What is it Merak?"

"There is going to be a confrontation between those two groups of men," he said.

†

"Father, if this cup cannot pass by, but I must drink it, your will be done!" said Jesus.

An angel of the Lord appeared and strengthened him so that he was ready for the events of the night. He got off his knees and walked back toward the others.

When Jesus returned to where he had left Peter and the two sons of Zebedee, they were asleep again. Peter had struggled desperately to stay awake, but couldn't. His eyes were heavy from the grief he felt. When a man suffered from deep grief and fears of impending doom over which he has no control, then sleep was the only remedy to bide time until the impending tragedy came. It was the same for Peter. He knew the tragedy about to befall the Messiah. He was overcome with a sense of doom and sleep was his only way out.

Jesus walked up to Peter, John, and James and said, "You can sleep now and have your rest."

The men woke up.

"The hour has come when the Son of Man is to be betrayed into the hands of sinners. Get up! Let's go!" said Jesus.

They started walking toward the gate, back to the other eight disciples who were standing guard.

"Look, my betrayer is not far away," Jesus said to Peter.

Peter saw the torches and watched the armed mob as it approached. It was a full cohort. His hand felt for his sword. He wanted to make sure it was in its proper place.

Peter searched the mob for familiar faces. He saw that some of them were from the Sanhedrin. Others were chief priests, Pharisees, and temple guards and their captains.

Judas stepped out from within the crowd and walked right up to Jesus, while the others kept their distance.

"Greetings, Rabbi," said Judas, and he kissed Jesus on the cheek as was customary for friends.

"Judas, are you betraying the Son of Man with a kiss?" Jesus asked.

Peter couldn't believe it. Judas was leading the band of men right to Jesus and had identified him. He betrayed him with a kiss. *What gall, what nerve*, thought Peter.

Peter watched Jesus. He seemed unafraid and looked at the mob with calm.

"Who are you looking for?" Jesus asked.

"Jesus the Nazarene," shouted someone from the mob.

Jesus stepped forward toward them and said, "I am he."

The mob moved back and some of them fell to the ground.

Peter watched them closely for any sign that they were going to attack. His hand grasped the hilt of his sword.

"Who are you looking for?" Jesus asked again.

"Jesus the Nazarene," the mob shouted.

"I have told you that I am he. If I am the one you are looking for, let these others go," said Jesus.

Judas stepped forward again and nodded to the temple guards.

"My friend, do what you are here to do," said Jesus.

The men reached for Jesus to arrest him. Peter saw that one of them started to draw his sword. He swung his blade out and slashed at the man's head.

The man, a servant of the chief priest Caiaphas, named Malchus, ducked away, but the blade sliced off his ear.

Peter's fighting stance told them that he stood ready to fight to the death. He watched in amazement as Jesus bent over and picked up the ear.

"Come, young man," said Jesus. He attached the ear and made it whole.

Jesus turned to Peter and said, "Put your sword back in its scabbard, for all who draw the sword will die by the sword. Peter, don't you think that I could appeal to my Father who would promptly send more than twelve legions of angels to my defense. Am I not to drink the cup that the Father has given me?"

Peter was confused. He thought that he was supposed to defend Jesus. After all he was carrying the sword at Jesus' suggestion at the end of the Seder. *Now I'm not supposed to use it?*

Peter reluctantly put the sword back. His shoulders sagged. He had hoped that somehow, they would fight their way out, but now he was convinced that they wouldn't.

"Am I a bandit, that you had to set out to capture me with swords and clubs?" demanded Jesus.

The temple guards grabbed him and bound his wrists behind him, like a common thief.

"I sat teaching in the temple, day after day and you never laid a hand on me. But this is your hour. This is the reign of darkness," Jesus said. His voice rang with passion in the night air.

With the word darkness a powerful wave of fear overcame the men. Jesus' disciples ran away. Peter ran too. After about fifty yards he turned to watch. Jesus' wrists were bound behind him, but his shoulders where thrust back and head held high, like a king who had been captured.

Peter started to follow at a cautious distance. He knew that the mob wouldn't spot him because of the darkness of the night. He was startled when someone bumped into him.

"Who goes there?" Peter whispered.

"It's me, John," said the young disciple.

They followed in silence.

✝

Merak and Soraya saw the sword flash down below them in the Garden of Gethsemane. Neither of them understood what the man was doing when he picked up the ear and attached it.

"I'd say the one who was praying was arrested," said Merak.

"It seems that way. Somebody was injured and the man who was arrested helped him."

"I don't think he was injured," said Merak.

"I think his ear was lopped off," she said with a shudder.

"If he had been injured, he'd be holding a cloth to the wound, or he'd bind up the area."

"It was as though the man put it back on. Can you do that with an ear?" asked Soraya.

"Hardly. It would take a miracle just to stop the bleeding," said Merak.

She was startled by the idea of a miracle.

"You don't think that the man who was arrested was Jesus?"

They both rushed back toward their camp to tell Abdul and Nemir what they had seen.

✝

Peter and John watched as they brought Jesus to the house of Annas the former high priest and the father-in-law of Caiaphas the current high priest.

"What do we do, Peter?" John asked.

"We wait to see what happens. They can't arrest him and bring him to Annas' house. That's not legal."

"They just did," said John.

The two men waited in the shadows and watched.

"Wait! Someone is coming out," said John with an excited whisper.

Two temple guards stepped out of the front entrance to Annas' house and looked around. They then pulled Jesus out. He still appeared calm and self-assured, not confident but resigned.

"Where are they going now?" Peter wondered out loud. He and John started to follow the mob.

They quickly realized that they were headed for the high priest's palace.

"What do you think they'll do?"

"I don't know, but they cannot call the Council of the Sanhedrin together for a trial at this time of night," said Peter.

"It's also a feast day, so they've got to do something else, but what?" John asked.

"Look at the people showing up," said Peter.

Members of the council were walking quickly toward the

palace. It became immediately obvious that this was planned for, and the council members had been waiting to be called.

"I wish I could go in," said John.

"Would they let you in?" Peter asked.

Jesus was almost at the front door. He was being pushed along by the temple guard captains. The mob milled around for a few moments.

When the door was opened, John said, "I'm going in. I know Caiaphas and his family. They'll let me in."

He boldly strode over to the back of the mob and walked in.

Peter didn't know anyone so he waited outside wondering if he could somehow get in.

A few minutes later the front door opened again. It was John standing at the front door with the doorkeeper, a young girl. John waived for Peter to come over.

"Come on. Let's go in," said John.

"Aren't you one of that man's disciples?" The doorkeeper asked Peter.

He looked her right in the eye and said, "Woman, I am not. I don't know him."

The servant girl motioned for the men to head to the courtyard and wait. A number of the people who made up the mob were milling around in the courtyard trying to keep warm. A few of the men found some charcoal stacked in the corner and decided to build a fire.

When the charcoal was lit everyone was suddenly standing around trying to keep their hands warm. Peter joined in too but tried to be inconspicuous.

Everyone was very quiet trying to listen to what was going on inside the main hall of Annas' house. Annas was

questioning Jesus about his teachings and about his disciples.

"I have always spoken openly for all the world to hear. I have always taught in the synagogue and in the temple where all the Jews meet together," said Jesus.

"I know, but I want to hear you say what you teach. Your secret teachings," said Annas.

"I have said nothing in secret. Why ask me? Ask those who heard me, ask them what I taught. They know what I said," Jesus said calmly, but with great authority.

A guard slapped Jesus in the face.

"Is that the way you answer the priest?" the guard demanded.

"If there is some offense in what I said, point it out. But if not, then why do you strike me?" Jesus asked.

It was illegal for an indicted man to be struck in court or during a hearing. Annas frowned at the guard and realized that he had to send Jesus to the high priest before things got out of control.

"Take him to Caiaphas at once," said Annas. The palace of the high priest was across the courtyard and connected to his father-in-law's home.

Jesus was still bound, and the guards grabbed him by his shoulders and turned him around. They marched Jesus out of the room and across the balcony where everyone could see him.

Peter looked up, his heart breaking at the sight of Jesus bound and being escorted out.

A man next to him said, "Aren't you another one of his disciples?"

"I am not, my friend," Peter said. This time he avoided the man's eyes.

More of the Council of the Sanhedrin were now in Caiaphas' palace.

The guards were told to wait with Jesus. They stood outside the door to the council chamber and waited.

One of them, a tall thin man with a nose that looked like bird's beak, had an idea.

"Hey, he's a prophet, right?"

The beak-nosed man placed a cloak over Jesus' head as a blindfold. He motioned for one of his friends to hit him.

The friend struck Jesus.

"Prophesy! Who hit you?" the beak-nosed man yelled.

Another struck him.

"Do you not know who that was?"

They continued to taunt him until the door suddenly opened. The man pulled the blindfold off and the guards escorted Jesus in.

Everyone strained to listen to what was going on before the Sanhedrin.

"Can they really find someone guilty of a crime at night?" Someone in the crowd asked.

"By law they can't, but they can do whatever they please."

A witness was brought in who accused Jesus of sedition. By law, they needed a second corroborating witness. When the mob heard the second witness, they realized that he was giving false testimony because it didn't match the first.

John realized that both men were lying.

Men were marched in to testify, but none of the testimony was convincing. It was rather difficult to make up convincing lies in front of the embodiment of eternal truth.

A man's voice rang out loudly. Perhaps he spoke in a shout because he was afraid.

He said, "We heard him say that I am going to destroy the temple made by human hands and build another, not made by human hands."

Another man said, "That's not how I heard it. I think he said destroy this temple and in three days I will raise it up."

"Have you no answer to that?" screamed Caiaphas. He was indignant that Jesus could have made such claims.

Now the group was peering inside to watch.

Caiaphas put his face close to Jesus and said, "What is the evidence that these men are bringing against you?"

Jesus didn't say a word. He stood before the high priest, hands tied but looking even more majestic than ever.

Caiaphas paced back and forth for a moment and finally asked the question that was on everyone's mind.

"I put you on oath by the living God to tell us if you are the Christ, the Son of the Blessed One?" Caiaphas asked. He knew that putting Jesus under oath to God Almighty as the high priest would oblige him to answer.

"I am," said Jesus, "and you will see the Son of Man seated at the right hand of the Power and coming with the clouds of heaven."

It was stated as a matter of truth, calmly and sincerely.

The high priest was incensed. He tore his robes and shouted, "What do we need witnesses for now? He's under oath and you just heard the blasphemy."

"We need witnesses because it's illegal to force a man to testify against himself," muttered one of the men standing by.

"What is your opinion?" Caiaphas asked the council.

"He deserves to die," they answered.

"We can't pass sentence on him now," said one of the Sanhedrin. "It is against our law to hold a trial at night."

The council members muttered their dissatisfaction.

Take him out and return him to us at daybreak," Caiaphas ordered.

The temple captains walked Jesus out of the assembly room to hold him for the three hours it would take for the sun to rise.

Walking out with Jesus was Malchus, the servant of the high priest. His ear was back on his head and look perfectly normal. Peter couldn't help staring at it as he walked by.

Malchus stopped and looked at Peter.

"This man is a Galilean. Didn't I see you in the garden with him?" Malchus asked.

"My friend I don't know what you're talking about," Peter said.

At that moment a cock crowed, and Jesus turned and looked back at Peter.

"Oh God. You said I would deny you three times before the cock crowed." Peter gasped and rushed outside.

Hot tears wet his face and beard as he wept bitterly.

John was torn by his friend's grief but stayed to see what they were going to do.

There was a lively discussion at the fire as the men waited the short time until daybreak.

"I don't think anything will happen," said one of the men, a scribe with judicial training.

"You think you're so smart," said another man. "Tell us why nothing is going to happen."

"He was arrested at night, bound as a malefactor, beaten before his arraignment, and struck in open court during the

trial. That's enough to invalidate anything they did," said the man.

"The council will do what it wants. Why do you think they're waiting to pass the final sentence on him?" The second man said.

"Because he was tried before sunrise and that's illegal too. Besides, it's a feast day and trials are normally suspended on feast days."

"He admitted his guilt," the man retorted.

"You mean he was compelled to incriminate himself under solemn judicial adjuration," said the lawyer scribe.

"Whatever. He's going to be convicted and sentenced today. That's the bottom line here."

"That's illegal too. I have a bad feeling about it," said the scribe.

John listened to it all and was amazed at how unfair the whole process was. The men went back and forth arguing to pass the time.

Jesus was then led out by the guards and brought back in front of the Council of the Sanhedrin. He was not bound but was roughly led by the guards. The room was filled with more people now, various scribes, chief priests, and elders.

Caiaphas wanted to establish the crime of blasphemy and decided that he would simply ask the last few questions again. He knew that Jesus wouldn't change his testimony.

"If you are the Christ, tell us," Caiaphas demanded. He looked around to the other people in the room for a nod of approval.

"If I tell you, you will not believe, and if I question you, you will not answer," said Jesus.

Caiaphas looked at him.

"What is that supposed to mean?"

"From now on the Son of Man will be seated at the right hand of the Power of God," said Jesus.

"So, you are the Son of God then?" demanded Caiaphas.

"It is you who say I am," said Jesus calmly.

"Why do we need any evidence?" Caiaphas asked.

"We heard it from his own lips," they said.

"Bind him and escort him to Pontius Pilate. The penalty for blasphemy is death," said Caiaphas.

The guards took his hands again and bound them even though he made no effort to escape. Some of the Sanhedrin, including Caiaphas stayed behind to await the decision by Pilate. The rest escorted Jesus to the Praetorium where the governor lived.

†

The temple guard captains pulled Jesus roughly up the steps at the Antonia where Pontius Pilate was in residence.

Normally Pilate lived in Caesarea, but during the Jewish Festival he came to Jerusalem to make certain that the peace was kept. This involved bringing extra legionnaires who would viciously enforce the law at any sign of disturbance. With the city filled with a million pilgrims, however, Pilate's ability to quell civil disturbances rested more in his authority rather that his capability. The soldiers with him were nervous about crowd control. If a full-scale revolt or riot broke out, they would have to barricade themselves in the Antonia and send to the Legio for help. The Jews in Jerusalem knew that the Romans would come down with a hard fist if this happened.

"Wait. We can't go inside a gentile's home. It would defile

us," said one of the chief priests who had accompanied the mob over to the Antonia.

"Pilate is going to demand that Jesus be seen in the Praetorium," said a scribe.

The Praetorium was the judgment hall of the Roman Prelate. It was the official court house for the governor who was the only one who could pronounce a death sentence on someone. The Romans demanded that all capital punishment cases appear before the Roman procurator.

"Jesus has to go in," said a priest, "but I don't. I won't be able to celebrate my Passover tonight if I enter."

The priest stepped back to emphasize his point.

The unruly mob was making a lot of noise by this point and the Roman guards had already alerted Pontius Pilate. He came walking out to the Gabbatha or pavement at the top of the stairs to the Antonia. Across the courtyard from the Gabbatha was the Praetorium. Pilate instructed his men to bring his chair forward. It was a symbol of his temporal power in the Roman Empire.

The crowd grew silent as Pilate took his seat.

The two temple captains handed Jesus over to the Roman legionnaires standing to Pilate's right side. He looked at Jesus and then the crowd.

"What charge do you bring against this man?" Pilate asked.

"If he were not a criminal, we wouldn't have handed him over to you," shouted a man in the crowd.

Pilate frowned. He didn't like being played with.

"Take him yourselves and try him by your own law," said Pilate.

"We already have and found him guilty," said a chief priest.

"So, what is he guilty of?" Pilate asked.

"We found him guilty of blasphemy, sedition, forbidding to give tribute to Caesar, and that he is the Christ, the King of the Jews," said the priest.

"Why didn't you simply stone him for the blasphemy?" Pilate asked the priest.

"We are forbidden by Roman law to put a man to death without first presenting him to the procurator."

Pilate smiled. He knew that they wanted a rubber stamp on their conviction, but he was a man who hated to be pushed into anything.

"Sedition, you say?"

"Yes, he has tried to incite a riot."

"Has this riot taken place? I should send my soldier to quell it," Pilate said.

"Not exactly, but by failing to give tribute to Caesar…"

Pilate indicated for the man to stop and turned to Jesus.

"Would you like to answer that charge?"

Jesus indicated that he wouldn't, and Pilate smiled.

"You have two witnesses who will testify to this and understand that by your law false testimony is punishable with the same punishment that the accused would get."

Pilate sat back and waited for someone to come forward. His statement was a clear threat that anyone perjuring himself would be dealt with severely.

"He pretends to be King of the Jews," said a priest.

"That is a more serious crime. Laesae Majestatis," said Pilate. "A crime against the dignity of the head of state, Caesar."

"Exactly," said the priest. There was delight in his voice. He secretly hoped that Pilate would accept the charges and order an execution without further inquiry.

"Crimen Laesae Majestatis," said Pilate out loud to himself. "Yes, that would be a more serious crime, punishable by death."

A murmur went up from the pleased crowd. They waited for Pilate to pronounce sentence.

Pilate stood.

"Return my sedulae to the Praetorium." He was referring to his chair. He turned and started walking toward the judgment hall. A few steps later he paused and turned back to the Roman legionnaires.

"Bring the prisoner to me inside the Praetorium. The seriousness of the charges requires a hearing," said Pilate.

A frustrated groan went up from the mob.

Pilate walked quickly to the Praetorium, forcing the soldiers to hurry with his judicial chair. He sat in it and waited for Jesus to be brought before him.

"Now, young man, do you understand the charges?"

Jesus nodded.

"Well, are you the King of the Jews?"

"Are you asking me this of your own accord or have others said it to you about me?"

"Am I a Jew that I would be concerned with these things? It is your own people and the chief priest who have handed you over to me. What have you done that has angered them so? Have you tried to create a new Jewish kingdom?"

"Mine is not a kingdom of this world. If my kingdom were of this world, my men would have fought to prevent

my being surrendered to the Jews. As it is, my kingdom does not belong here in this world."

Pilate was enjoying himself and intrigued by the young man before him.

"So, then you are a king?" Pilate asked.

"It is you who say that I am a king. I was born for this. I came into the world for this: to bear witness to the truth. All who are on the side of truth listen to my voice."

"Truth?" said Pilate, "What is that?"

At that moment a messenger from Pilate's wife walked in. The messenger told him she was upset.

"My wife has need of me? I am in the judicial chair," said Pilate. He wondered what was wrong now.

"Your wife has had a dream," said the messenger.

"Yes," demanded Pilate. He didn't like to be interrupted. "What is it I should know?"

"She told me to say, 'Have nothing to do with that upright man. I have been extremely upset today by a dream I had about him.'"

And I was just wondering about truth, he thought.

Pilate realized that after examining Jesus that he couldn't possibly find fault with the man. Now that his wife's dream had come as a warning, he wanted to put this mess behind him. He stood up and walked out of the Praetorium.

"Bring the prisoner along," he commanded.

Pilate walked out to the steps in front of the Antonia. The marble glistened in the early morning sun.

Pilate waited as the chief priests and scribes hushed the crowd.

"I find no case against this man," Pilate announced.

A murmur went up from the crowd. The faces of the accusers showed their anger.

"But he is inflaming the people with his teachings all over Judea. He has been preaching all the way from Galilee where he first started to Jerusalem itself," said a priest in a loud, strident voice.

"Are you a Galilean, Jesus?" Pilate asked politely.

Jesus nodded.

"Nazareth," Jesus said.

Pilate smiled.

"Since the man is a Galilean he comes under Herod's jurisdiction," said Pilate.

Herod was the Tetrarch of the northern provinces, which included Galilee where Nazareth was located.

"Take this Nazarene to Herod," said Pilate. He turned his back on Jesus and walked inside.

†

Judas stood still outside the palace of the high priest. His body felt an inertia that he had not known before. When they led Jesus off to the Praetorium he decided he would go in and provide new testimony. Jewish law allowed for a retrial if new evidence of innocence was brought forth. He was frozen and feared entering.

"Why didn't he just deliver himself from them?" Judas Iscariot asked out loud.

His hand unconsciously slid inside his tunic and fingered the money bag. In it was his payment for betrayal, thirty pieces of silver. The Sanhedrin had been careful to pay him with coins that bore no image of the emperor, no craven

images. His payment was with money that was pure. It belonged to the temple treasury.

"Surely they will have to retry him if I plead his innocence," Judas said out loud to himself.

He was distraught. His anguish was deepening as he began to realize that not only was Jesus found guilty of some sort of crime, but Jesus wasn't intent on announcing himself as the Messiah by delivering himself.

"I am doomed. I will never be allowed back into the inner circle," he muttered.

A passerby saw him mumbling to himself and hurriedly crossed over to the other side of the street.

What should I do? he asked himself. He didn't have very many options. He could go inside and plead with the council of the Sanhedrin, but he didn't know what they had convicted Jesus of.

Slowly he moved forward toward the door of the luxurious palace.

"What is it you want?" asked the young girl who was at the door.

"I have come to speak with Caiaphas the high priest," said Judas. Unlike his earlier visit, this time his head hung in shame.

"Who shall I say is calling on the high priest so early in the morning?" asked the door keeper.

"Judas Iscariot. He'll know who I am."

He stood at the door while she went inside to announce him. A few moments later he was allowed in.

Judas walked along the grand corridor and across the balcony where Jesus had just stood. He was escorted into the council room where some of the council still milled around

and discussed the events of the night.

What should I say? he asked himself. The question reverberated in his head as he looked around the room.

Caiaphas was speaking to another man, a scribe. They were laughing about something. When Judas caught his eye, he stopped talking and excused himself.

"Judas Iscariot, what can I do for you?" Caiaphas asked politely.

With the name Judas, the priests and scribes stopped talking. Most of them knew who he was and what he had done.

"I need to talk with the council," said Judas. His voice cracked and his throat sounded dry.

Caiaphas smiled weakly and said, "Well, speak. We are the council of the Jewish people. We will hear you."

A few of the others smiled at Caiaphas' feigned dignity.

Judas reached inside his tunic and pulled the purse out. He felt the weight of the money in his hand and frowned.

"We had a deal, young man. We are not going to pay you any more than what we agreed upon," said Caiaphas.

The fool thinks I want more money, thought Judas. He was getting angry with Caiaphas. He thought about what he did, and the anger quickly turned to shame.

"I have sinned, sir." He looked around. Everyone had stopped talking. "Sirs," he added clumsily.

"What do you say?" Caiaphas asked. He was confused because he thought he was going to be extorted for more money in front of everyone.

"I have betrayed innocent blood," said Judas. "He is innocent and by Jewish law should get a retrial."

"You betrayed innocent blood? What is that to us?" said

Caiaphas. He looked around the room for support from the others. They were nodding in agreement.

"Don't you have any regard for justice and Jewish law?" demanded Judas.

Caiaphas frowned and turned his back. Some of the others laughed.

"How stupid, is this one?" a scribe asked his friend and then turned back to his conversation.

"I have betrayed innocent blood!" screamed Judas. He took the purse and threw it at the feet of Caiaphas. It burst open and the silver pieces rolled noisily on the ground.

The sound of the money caught everyone's attention.

"I have to get out of here," said Judas as he stormed out through the front door. He was talking out loud to himself, no longer muttering or mumbling, but having a full volume discussion.

"Do you know what you have done?" he said as he crossed the courtyard and headed toward the street. He was heading to the Damascus gate.

"You just sold the Messiah, the long-awaited King of the Jews, for money. You just sold your soul and your salvation for thirty pieces of silver."

Judas was talking out loud to himself. Caiaphas watched the spectacle and smiled.

The some of the priests stooped to pick up the money, while the rest of the council smiled to each other and shook their heads.

"Be careful," said Caiaphas.

"It's good silver," said one of the priests. "We minted it ourselves."

"Should we put it into the treasury?" asked another as he

handed the pieces to Caiaphas. The chief priest was putting the money back into the leather pouch.

"It's against the law to put this money back into the treasury," said Caiaphas.

"Why is that?" asked a scribe as he turned the piece over in his hand to examine it.

"It's blood money," said Caiaphas.

"Of course. We can't use it in the temple because it has bought the death of a man."

"What do we do with it? Any ideas?" Caiaphas asked. He pulled the strings tight on the purse and put it inside his tunic. He smiled and patted the purse.

"Let's by a potter's field for the burial of foreigners," said a priest. "Thirty pieces of silver should get a nice size plot."

A potter's field is an area that was no good for farming because it was full of the clay which was used to make pottery. Once the field was used up, it normally sat sallow and unused.

"Pretty cheap price for this so called precious one, this prophet," said a priest.

The others laughed at the thought. Only one scribe standing off to the side shuddered as he remembered the prophet Jeremiah who wrote, *"And they took the thirty silver pieces, the sum at which the precious one was priced by the children of Israel. And they gave them for the potter's field."*

✝

The walk from the Praetorium to Herod's Palace went smoothly. There was much less taunting done than during the walk to the Praetorium. Since Jesus was a prisoner of

Pontius Pilate, the Jews from the Sanhedrin knew that they were not at liberty to harass him.

Jesus still walked with his head held high and his hands bound behind him. The square of his shoulders and his height added to his dignity. He was half a cubit taller than most men. The Roman legionnaires who led him had the distinct feeling that they were dealing with royalty and a man of supreme authority.

Pilate watched the mob from his balcony. He would be able to see them for a short while as they walked by the temple. The ploy by Pilate to send Jesus to Herod Antipas, the Tetrarch of Galilee, was going to fail, but it was worth a try. Pilate was glad to see Jesus leave. He wanted no part in the killing of an innocent man but would do so to keep the peace. The warning dream from his wife bothered him.

The mob, with Jesus in the lead, escorted this time by Roman legionnaires and not just the temple guards, passed by the Hasmonaean Palace. Pilate sometimes stayed there but during the Jewish Festival he preferred the Antonia. From the Hasmonaean, Herod's Palace was visible.

Herod Antipas was one of the three sons of Herod the Great—the man who tried to kill Jesus when he was a baby. He was staying in the family palace, a massive structure, larger than the Hasmonaean and the Antonia combined. Only the temple itself was larger.

When they passed through the outer walls into the courtyard of the palace, the Roman soldiers were stopped and questioned by Herod's personal guard.

"What business do you have here?" one of the guards asked.

"We bring a prisoner from Pontius Pilate who is a Galilean from Nazareth and therefore falls under the jurisdiction of Herod Antipas," said the legionnaire.

The Romans and the mob knew that they would have to wait while the guard announced them. They knew better than to try and walk in. Herod Antipas, though not as cruel as his father Herod the Great, was nevertheless a man whose temper was legend. For a long time, he was not on good terms with Pilate either. He resented the Roman rule and the fact that the kingdom had been divided among the children of Herod the Great.

A few minutes later the guard came back out.

"The legionnaires may escort the prisoner in," said the guard.

"But we want to present our charges," demanded a chief priest who started walking in with Jesus.

The whole mob started moving at once.

The guard frowned. Herod had said nothing about allowing the man's accusers in; he had only said, "Bring me the prisoner."

It was too late to stop them, and the entire mob entered the palace. They were brought to the great hall where Herod sat on a huge chair elevated on a platform.

"Ah, you have brought me Jesus the Nazarene," said Herod. His voice revealed his delight.

"He is guilty of sedition, Crimen Laesae Majestatis, and blasphemy," shouted a priest.

Herod frowned. No one shouted at him in his court.

"Clearly, you're the one everyone has been talking about," said Herod.

He smiled warmly at Jesus. He had secretly wanted

to meet the prophet that everyone was talking about. He wondered if this truly was the Jewish Messiah.

Jesus said nothing.

"I hear that you can perform miracles. Would you be willing to cure my cook. He has a burn from the kitchen," said Herod. "Or maybe you would prefer a few lepers?"

Jesus said nothing.

"He has been found guilty of blasphemy. He claims that he is the Messiah," said one of the priests. The man was excited and speaking quickly. He started to recite a litany of accusations.

"Now tell me, can you really raise the dead. I've heard stories about a man from Bethany who was allegedly dead for three or four days."

Jesus said nothing to Herod.

"If I execute someone right here, would you bring him back to life? I really would like to see some sort of miracle. If you perform a miracle, I will let you go," said Herod.

"He's been found guilty by the council and judgment has been passed by the high priest Caiaphas himself," said one of the priests.

"Stop interrupting me," said Herod.

Herod turned to Jesus and said, "You must have something to say to all these accusations. They are very serious."

"He says that he's the King of the Jews," said another priest who was unable to hold his tongue any longer.

"I really do think you should say something in response to that. You know, Jesus, I'm the ruler of the northern portion of the kingdom of Israel, and I take it seriously when someone claims to be the king of all the Jews," said Herod.

His tone had taken a sharply sarcastic quality. The ruler was losing his patience and not having any fun. He was convinced that Jesus was not going to perform a miracle for him, and this annoyed him greatly.

"Do you think that you are so superior to us that you can ignore me? Answer me!" said Herod.

He was angry and frustrated by Jesus' silence.

"Get me my cloak. I want to dress this man like royalty before I send him back to Pilate," said Herod.

He waited for a luxurious purple cloak to be placed over Jesus' shoulders. Purple was the color of royalty.

"Tell Pilate that I have not found any grounds to condemn the man, so I am returning him to his jurisdiction," he paused for a second. "And mention to him that I am grateful. I had wanted to see the famous Nazarene named Jesus. I owe him a favor."

Before this Pilate and Herod had not been too friendly, but now Herod reconsidered their relationship.

"Take him back," Herod ordered. He got up and left the room.

†

Judas was walking quickly now. His hand felt the rope that held his tunic in place.

He walked with a purpose out through the Damascus gate. He knew where he needed to go. There was an area where olive trees grew over the edge of a sharp incline down the side of the Mount of Olives. Below was a rock encrusted ravine. He wanted out of his misery and wanted it done quickly. He figured that hanging himself would be painless. He wouldn't have to think about what he had done for long.

He would be released from his wretched fate.

As Judas Iscariot walked out along the road leading from the Damascus gate north, he looked to his left and saw the quarry and Golgotha or the Calvarium, the skull. The stanchions were in place for a crucifixion, but nothing was going on at that moment. It would take more than an hour for him to get to the spot he had chosen. He was still rehashing the events of the past week, talking out loud to himself, not caring if anyone saw him. He walked slower now, knowing that these were the last few moments of his miserable life.

†

Pilate was disappointed to see Jesus returned to him. He was annoyed that the mob hadn't been satisfied by sending Jesus to Herod. The fact that Herod had found no evidence of a crime should have persuaded the crowd, but it didn't. Their high priest had pronounced him guilty, and they wanted blood.

Jesus was led inside the Praetorium again, and once more the Jewish council refused to enter the house of a gentile.

Pilate came outside and called the chief priests and the council elders.

"Look, you brought this man before me as a popular agitator. Now I have gone into the matter myself, in your presence, and I didn't find any grounds for the charges you have made," said Pilate.

"He deserves death," a voice from the crowd shouted.

"Herod Antipas has not found grounds for any of the charges you made either. He sent him back to me. He would have kept him if he were guilty," said Pilate.

"Death to the blasphemer," said another.

Pilate was losing his patience, but an idea was starting to form in his mind.

"According to your custom I am supposed to release one prisoner at the Passover. Would you like for me to release the King of the Jews?" Pilate asked. He was hoping that they would take their king and he could be done with it. It would be an acknowledgment of Jesus' guilt and a merciful thing at the same time.

"Away with him. Give us Barabbas," said the crowd with one voice.

Bar'Abbas meant son of a father. It was a name that Pilate hated. He was a common agitator who had committed a murder and incited a major riot. Pilate was looking forward to watching him hang on a cross.

Pilate tried another tact.

"As you can see, the man has done nothing that deserves death, so I shall have him scourged and then let him go."

Pilate turned and left.

"Scourge him. Castigate him. I want him striped by the whip, so that these animals are satisfied. Maybe if we make a mockery of their king, they will think him punished enough, and I can let him go," said Pilate. He was hoping that the humiliation of the flogging would satisfy their anger toward Jesus the Nazarene. While Jesus was with Herod Antipas, Pilate had had time to talk to his wife personally. Pilate definitely didn't want the blood of this man on his hands.

It was unheard of to scourge a man and then crucify him. Men were whipped on the way to crucifixion, but that was generally to motivate the person to keep walking. They were never scourged beforehand. They would be too week to carry their cross up to Calvary. A man would rarely get more

than thirty lashes when scourged because more sometimes resulted in death. Scourging was the punishment of choice to make a visual example of a person. The Roman scourgers used whips with three cords on the end. Small pieces of lamb bone were tied to the end of the whips and left long welts that looked like stripes if done properly.

"How many lashes, sir?" asked Pilate's scourger.

"I don't care. Castigate him front and back," said Pilate.

"Jewish law permits no more than forty," said the scourger.

"These priests haven't followed Jewish law with this man yet. Use two men and make a pattern on his back and legs that will satisfy the disgusting people," said Pilate.

The scourger looked at his centurion with a doubtful eye. "We'll have to scourge him front and back," he mumbled.

Good, thought Pilate. He hoped that the gruesome appearance of Jesus after the scourging would calm the crowd. He didn't want to see an innocent man hung on a cross just because the mob was bloodthirsty.

The Roman legionnaires took Jesus up to the courtyard inside the Antonia, in front of the main entrance to the Praetorium. There was a small pillar with iron rings attached to each side. Two men, both experts with the whip, came forward to relieve the legionnaires of their prisoner. Jesus' hands were unbound and then tied to the rings.

One of the men was the scourger that Pilate had talked to.

"Be careful," said the first scourger to the second.

"Why is that?" the second asked.

"We have to keep him alive," said the first.

"So, we do that all the time."

"Yes, but front and back…" said the chief scourger.

"Front and back and he wants him alive?" said the second, shaking his head in disbelief.

"He wants him striped like a zebra to make a fool of him."

The lashing started.

"What's his crime?" the second scourger asked.

"He's the King of the Jews," said the first.

After about forty lashes the scourgers were breathing hard. They were concentrating on making the welts line up evenly. To them it was a game. They knew that if they dug into the flesh too deeply the man would die even with as few as thirty lashes.

"We have a lot more to go," said the first.

"I say turn him over and do the front," said the second scourger.

They proceeded to stripe his torso and the front of his legs.

"You missed a spot," said the first scourger. He pointed to a part of Jesus' back where the welts were uneven.

"You're right, but I did a better job than you on the legs," said the second. He was sadistically admiring the work that he loved. He was a cruel man who didn't think of prisoners as human beings. Once a man was convicted, he was relegated to the status of animal in the scourger's mind.

They were almost finished now. They released one arm and turned him around and made their hideous work perfect.

A centurion came over to inspect their work.

"Magnificent, the King of the Jews only needs a crown," one of the scourgers said.

"You are both sick," said the centurion. He had been following the life of Jesus for some time and thought that this was truly a shame.

The second scourger, who was finished, said, "Hey, I've got an idea."

He walked over to a hawthorn tree and started cutting branches and twigs. He made a large bundle and tied it with some cloth.

"What do you think it is?" asked the second scourger.

"It looks like a bundle of thorns," said the first. He was untying Jesus' hands from the iron rings.

Jesus had nearly passed out in pain and didn't stand up when his hands were unbound. He simply continued to lean on the pillar. His body was on fire from the lashes. A guard pulled him up roughly by his shoulders and told him to stand.

The second scourger smiled and said, "It's a bundle of thorns until it is place on the head of a king. Then it becomes a crown."

He placed the bundle of thorns over the head of Jesus. It sat like a giant helmet.

"Hail, King of the Jews," said the second scourger.

"Here hold this," said the first. He handed Jesus a reed and pretended that he had handed him a royal scepter. "Hail, King of the Jews."

The second scourger came back over with red military robe. It was the sign of the commander of the legions. He placed it on his shoulders.

"Now he is dressed like king in battle," said the second scourger.

The captain of the guards, Longinus, who was partially blind from cataracts couldn't see all their antics. He wondered what was going on.

Both scourgers went down on their knees to pay homage to the newly crowned king.

The men mocked him.

The first scourger said, "Hail, King of the Jews," and slapped him in the face.

The other soldier took the reed from Jesus' hand and struck him with it.

"Here's something you've never done before royalty," said the Roman soldier. He spat at Jesus.

"We have to be ready to bring him out," said the captain. Two more guards stepped forward and grabbed Jesus.

✝

Pilate came out of the Praetorium to see if they were finished and then walked out to the pavement in front of the Antonia. The mob was still there. Their faces were angry.

"Look, I am going to bring him out to you to let you see that I find no case against him. He has been scourged and punished adequately," said Pilate.

Jesus was then brought out wearing the crown of thorns and the crimson robe.

Pilate looked at Jesus and then to the guards. He was shocked at his condition. "I said castigate him not kill him."

He turned to the mob to present Jesus. "Ecce homo, here is the man," said Pilate.

Pilate's soldiers held the back of the robe up so that they could see how much he had been scourged. Jesus was a horror to behold. His entire body was covered with welts that lined up like a zebra's stripes. It was hideous. Pilate expected them to be satisfied with the intensity of the scourging.

They let the robe back down to cover the wounds.

"Crucify him! Crucify him!" shouted the chief priests and temple guards.

"Take him yourselves and crucify him. I find no case against him," said Pilate. He knew that they couldn't carry out the crucifixion themselves. Stoning was the traditional method of execution by the Jews. Capital punishment under the Romans could only be carried out by the Romans.

"We have our law. According to that law he ought to be put to death because he has claimed to be the Son of God," said one of the chief priests.

"You must carry out our sentence," shouted another.

Pilate was alarmed because he knew the law and was in a bind. He was not supposed to overturn a local conviction if it followed their law. He was supposed take control of the execution. It was symbolic of the fact that Rome held the power of life and death over everyone in the empire.

He turned and went back inside the Praetorium and asked for Jesus to be brought before him again.

"Who are you and where do you come from?" the frustrated Pilate asked Jesus. He knew he was a Nazarene but was referring to the mystery of Jesus. He wanted to know if he was really the Son of God.

Pilate waited for an answer.

Jesus made no reply.

"Are you refusing to speak to me? Surely you know that I have the power to release you and I have the power to crucify you," said Pilate.

He thought the power of life or death would be something any man would kowtow to.

Jesus smiled and finally replied.

"You would have no power over me at all if it had not been given to you from above. That is why the ones who handed me over to you have the greater guilt."

Pilate understood that he was referring to Caiaphas and the chief priests. He didn't want any part of the guilt and wanted to free Jesus.

"Bring him outside and bring my chair," Pilate said to the centurion in charge, Gaius Cassius Longinus. This centurion was an expert in Jewish affairs who was stationed permanently at the Antonia. Longinus barked orders and the men followed them immediately.

They grabbed Jesus, who was still in the crimson robe and crowned with thorns. Two other men picked up the chair and started walking it out front again.

Pilate had the judicial chair set on the Gabbatha, but this time he placed Jesus in the chair. The crowd was more unruly and agitated now. It was approaching the noon hour, and the mob wanted the situation resolved quickly.

"Here is your king, and I have Barabbas the murderer who will be put to death today." said Pilate. "Which of the two do you want released? Don't you want me to release the King of the Jews for the Passover?"

"Release Barabbas!"

"But in that case what am I to do with the man you call King of the Jews?"

"Away with him! Away with him! Crucify him!" they shouted.

"Shall I crucify your king?" Pilate shouted back.

"We have no king but Caesar," a chief priest shouted.

The mob started yelling and it appeared that a riot would ensue. Pilate looked at his soldiers. They were thinking the same thing.

The crowd was chanting, "Crucify him! Crucify him!"

"But what harm has he done you?" asked Pilate.

"Let him be crucified!" they shouted. They were getting louder by the moment.

Pilate gave up. He was making no headway with these stubborn people and was going to be facing a riot in a few more minutes.

"Bring me a basin of water," Pilate ordered.

When the basin arrived two servants held it in front of him. Pilate reached into the basin and washed his hands.

"I am innocent of this man's blood. It is your concern," said Pilate solemnly.

"Let his blood be on us and on our children!" the mob shouted.

Pilate turned to Longinus and said, "Release Barabbas and crucify this one."

Pilate walked inside disgusted with what had just taken place.

They brought out two other men who were scheduled for death that day. One was named Dismas and the other was Gestas. Each man was given his patibulum or the transverse portion of the cross. It was placed over their shoulders and tied at the man's wrists.

Jesus' robe was removed, and his own garments were put on him. He was given his patibulum or cross.

When more than one man was being led to the Calvarium or place of the skull, the Romans would tie them together by attaching a rope to the right hand of one and them run it to the left hand, thus securing the patibulum on the man's shoulders. From the right hand of the first, the rope went to the left foot of the next. Thus, if the prisoner tried to run, he would be dragged down, and if he tried to strike someone by swinging the patibulum or crossbeam he would be held

back. It was a simple but effective method of getting people to Golgotha.

When the three men were bound together, with Jesus second in line, Longinus sent word to Pilate that the titulus needed to be inscribed. A titulus was a small board that was placed above the head of the crucified man. Written on it was the charge for which the man was being executed.

The other two prisoners had been convicted days earlier, and their titulae were already complete.

The three prisoners started walking along the path from the Antonia to Golgotha, on the outside of the city along the northern wall. It was called the Via Dolorosa or Via of Pain.

Meanwhile, Pilate wrote a note that he wanted the titulus inscribed, 'Jesus the Nazarene, King of the Jews.' It was to be written in Latin, Greek, and Hebrew.

✝

Nemir and Abdul were saddling the camels. The tents were completely folded and packed. They had decided to ride down the Mount of Olives to the Antonia Tower to deliver the cloth and were ready hours before they needed to be.

"We can get some food at a tavern near the meeting place and then wait to deliver the linen," said Merak.

Soraya was braiding her long hair and making herself look presentable.

In a few minutes they were mounted and heading down the hill toward the gate next to the Antonia Tower.

"Halt!" barked the legionnaire. He was about twenty yards up the road from the gate. There was some sort of commotion, and he wasn't allowing any travelers near the gate.

"What's the problem, sir?" Merak asked politely.

Three criminals are going for execution. They will be exiting momentarily. No one on an animal is allowed on the Via Dolorosa until after they pass," said the guard.

Three men started walking out with crossbeams over their shoulders. Merak and the group looked in disbelief at the three men, their crossbeams, and the length of rope securing them all together. The second man was bleeding from his scalp and forehead, a crown of thorns upon his head. Blood was dripping down his face.

The men were followed by four soldiers, two of whom had whips. The others carried large mallets, two titulae, and a bag of seven-inch roofing spikes. As the prisoners came through the gate, the Roman executioners flared their whips. The first and last were struck and suddenly picked up the pace. The middle man's left arm was pulled forward throwing him off balance. He fell with a thud. The crossbeam added to his unbalance and the extra weight caused him to fall hard.

His face made a crunching sound as it hit the ground.

Soraya turned her head away in horror.

"God, that's terrible," she said.

"That man looks awfully weak," said Merak.

"That's Jesus the Nazarene. He's been scourged and is so weak he can barely walk. I think he's going to die before he gets to Golgotha," said the guard.

Another guard shook his head. "They'll get them to Golgotha. They always do."

Merak was off his camel in an instant.

"Are you sure it's Jesus… from Nazareth?" Merak asked.

"Yes, I was inside listening to the trial myself," said the

guard. "It's a pity. I don't think he really did anything wrong, but once Pilate speaks, you're a dead man."

Jesus was helped to his feet by the soldiers. His nose was bent. The cartilage had separated from the bone when he fell directly on it. Because his hands were bound, he couldn't break his fall even if he wanted to.

Everyone dismounted.

"Merak, we have to go see Pilate and ask for clemency or a pardon," said Nemir.

"We don't know what he's done," said Merak.

"You heard the guard. He's done nothing," said Soraya.

"Can't you ask the ruler for a special favor because you represent royalty?" Abdul asked.

"I suppose I can. I better hurry," said Merak.

The guard had been listening and said, "Pontius Pilate is inside the Antonia, probably in the Praetorium hall."

Merak and Nemir rushed off immediately.

There was a pool next to the Antonia and the guard nodded that it was okay to hitch their camels at the posts near the pool.

Abdul and his daughter started following the three condemned men as they walked down the road. They were heading toward the Damascus gate. A gathering of people was pouring out through the gate to see what was going on.

Mary, Jesus' mother came running out of the Damascus gate. She pushed her way through the crowd.

"Let her through. It's his mother," a woman said with urgency. The women who gathered to watch stepped aside.

Jesus kept moving to keep up with the others but they stopped when they saw her approach.

Mary ran up and touched the bruised areas of his cheek and his crooked nose. Her grief was so deep that she was unable to speak. She touched his face for only a moment, and then he was pulled by the others to keep walking. Mary remembered the words of Simeon in the temple many years ago, *"You too, a sword shall pierce."*

She felt like she was going to die as the meaning of those words penetrated her soul.

The Roman soldiers snapped their whips. Gestas, the thief, started walking while Dismas looked back to see if Jesus was ready. He pulled to slow Gestas down, but eventually had to start. The rope pulled and Jesus was forced to keep walking.

"They're so vicious, father," Soraya said. She was on the verge of tears.

"Don't worry. If anyone can intercede it's Merak. He knows about these things," said Abdul. His voice rang hollow as he spoke. He didn't believe it for a moment. They walked along with the crowd now.

Right after the Damascus gate, the Via Dolorosa took a sharp left-hand turn and continued to run alongside the walls of Jerusalem.

Again, the lashing of the men caused Jesus to stumble and fall. Again, his face was unprotected, but he tried to turn his face before he hit the ground. His right eye took the brunt of the fall. An area above the they eye and around his cheek started to swell. The soldiers lifted him up by his cross this time. The pain on his back where the cross piece rubbed the whip marks was excruciating.

Women from Jerusalem, who were still pouring out through the gate, started to wail.

Veronica, a follower of Jesus walked right out into the middle of everything with a cloth and wiped the face of Jesus.

The Roman soldiers glared at her, but defiant and loving, she did what she knew was right. Jesus gave her a tender smile of thanks.

The whips cracked and Jesus stumbled for a third time. He almost broke his fall by bringing his left leg forward, but he tripped and came down on his knee so hard that he started limping.

The soldiers stopped the procession of the three condemned men and started untying the cross beam from Jesus.

The women now were mourning and weeping. Their lament made an enormous noise.

Jesus turned to them and said, "Daughters of Jerusalem, do not weep for me. Weep rather for yourselves and for your children. For look, the days are surely coming when people will say, 'Blessed are those who are barren, the wombs that have never borne children, the breast that have never suckled.'"

Jesus continued to speak as the beam was set down and his foot retied. "Then they will begin to say to the mountains, 'Fall on us!' To the hills, 'Cover us!' For if this is what is done to the green wood, what will be done when it is dry."

"Save your breath," the soldier mumbled to himself. "You still have a long walk to Golgotha, and we have to get you there while you're alive."

The soldier looked around and then grabbed a strong looking man named Simon of Cyrene who happened to be in the city for the Feast of the Passover.

"Here Jew, carry this for the King of the Jews," the Roman

soldier said. He motioned to the man to pick up the cross beam.

Simon was a bulky thick-chested man. It was considered a disgrace to carry a cross. He tried to protest, to refuse to carry the cross, but the Roman soldier motioned to his sword, and Simon realized that he had no choice. He easily picked up the patibulum, placed it over one shoulder, and started walking. He wondered how he had ever gotten into this situation. He had come from Cyrene in North Africa to spend the Jewish Festival in Jerusalem. It had been the dream of his lifetime. It was turning into a nightmare. He knew it was right to help this poor fellow but felt deeply ashamed to carry the cross and did so unwillingly.

Soraya and Abdul followed along. There was a large crowd now. Most of the people were women, though some in the crowd were priests and scribes. Two women and a young man stood by and helped Mary walk toward Golgotha.

When they got to the top of the hill where the stanchions had been set, Simon dropped the cross beam. The four soldiers looked at him and then went about their business. The soldiers didn't thank him, but he got a tender smile from Jesus. From a short distance off Longinus watched. He was partially blind from cataracts and didn't like to interfere unless there was a problem. His four men knew what they were doing and had no trouble hanging a man on a cross.

The two thieves were dealt with first.

Gestas was offered the wine and opium and greedily swallowed great gulps. He knew it would stupefy him and ease the pain. He wanted to be intoxicated when he died. They started to nail him to the wood, and he cursed his executioners. His language caused many of the women to

blush and turn their faces away. The soldiers smiled. They liked it when a man fought with pride all the way to his death. The nastier the man, the more justified they felt. Gestas was very nasty.

Dismas took a long drink of the wine and opium too. He wailed in pain as the nails were driven in. He cried like a little child and called out for his mother who was not present. One of the guards rolled his eyes.

Then the soldiers turned to Jesus who was standing by, still as a lamb ready for slaughter. They stripped him of his garments. They would divide them presently.

First, they offered him a drink of the wine mixed with opium. It was an act of kindness. They brought it to his mouth, but he refused to drink.

The two thieves were crucified and hung on the right and left. The soldiers were reserving the center stanchion for Jesus.

The procedure was simple. The upright part of the cross or the stipes was set firmly in the ground. There was an indentation where the patibulum was to be attached. Once the arms were nailed to the patibulum with seven-inch roofing spikes, they lifted the patibulum and set it into the stipes. Near the bottom of the stipes was a step of wood and the feet of the victim would find it and support himself.

The metal pierced Jesus' flesh just below the palm of the hand in the wrist. It was known as Destot's space where eight bones come together. It was an area strong enough to support the weight of a man's body. The Romans had plenty of experience in these gruesome affairs. The last thing that they wanted was for a limb to come lose before a man died.

As the soldiers drove the nail in, Jesus looked up to

heaven and said, "Father, forgive them, for they know not what they do."

Longinus heard the prayer and wondered how the Nazarene could be so composed that he could pray for mercy for his executioners.

They swung the cross piece up and set it into the groove of the stipes. Then they nailed Jesus' feet into the step.

Now the soldiers turned to Jesus' garments which were by rights theirs. He had on four outer garments. It was the prerogative of the crucifying soldiers to divide up the property of the man being crucified. Usually, it simply meant a garment or two, nothing more.

They each took an outer garment, but the inner garment was a seamless wool weave and couldn't be cut or it would be ruined.

"Let's cast lots," said one of the soldiers. He organized it.

The men quickly cast lots to see who would get to keep the woolen garment. They didn't miss a beat. A second later, one of the men was rejoicing at his good fortune.

A number of the priests and scribes watched to make sure that Jesus was executed. They stood by the rest of the crowd but jeered and taunted him.

The Roman scribe arrived with the titulus for Jesus. He had written in Latin, Greek, and Hebrew, 'Jesus of Nazareth, King of the Jews.' The Hebrew inscription was written backwards from left to right because Hebrew was read right to left.

When the chief priest saw the sign, he had a fit. The Hebrew portion said simply, 'King of the Jews.'

"That's wrong. The titulus is wrong. It should read, 'I am king of the Jews,'" said the chief priest.

Some of the scribes looked up and saw what he was really angry about. The translation had been made from the Roman to Greek and then Greek to Hebrew. The Hebrew was shortened to four words. The problem with 'King of the Jews' was that it implied a hidden message. A sentence in ancient Hebrew was written without vowels and without breaks in between the words. Most scribes looked at a sentence and pulled down the first letters of each word to see what it spelled. There was a superstitious belief that said God or Yahweh, as the Jews called him, hid secret messages in the first letters. Yahweh in Hebrew scripture had no vowels and was spelled YHWH or backwards HWHY.

The first letters of the four Hebrew words were HWHY. The chief priest looked at the inscription on the titulus and saw that it held a secret message that Jesus' crime was that he was Yahweh! That verified that he was the Son of God. The priest was furious. He marched off to Pontius Pilate to demand an immediate correction.

†

Judas arrived at the place that he had chosen for his death. A cool breeze moved clouds over the horizon. He looked down on the city of Jerusalem and saw the men being crucified one by one.

"There can be no forgiveness for a man like me," he said out loud. "I shall rot in hell for what I have done."

A still voice inside him said, "Judas, God's forgiveness is greater than man's ability to sin." He spat at the voice.

What dung, he thought. *I am a condemned man. I am condemned to the fires of hell for all eternity.*

When he looked across the valley at Jesus being nailed

to the cross his soul retched on his unforgiven sins. He felt regret but not penitence. He was sorry for what he had done only because of what it meant for him.

I shall be remembered in the annals of history as the one who betrayed the Messiah, Judas thought as he reached down for his belt which was a thin braided rope.

He took it into his hands and tested it. It felt strong enough.

He looked down over the mount at the scene on Calvary. Jesus' feet were nailed to the stipes.

Judas Iscariot had seen enough. He swung his belt over the limb of the olive tree. The branch hung out over the ravine. Sharp rocks below jutted upwards like teeth from a giant demon waiting to swallow its next victim. He fixed the belt around his neck. He pulled on the belt and tested to see that it was well attached.

"I may go to hell, but at least I don't have to witness the rest of this miserable crucifixion," he said as he stepped off over the ravine. He was still looking at Calvary, a visual description of his deceit and betrayal as he entered the air.

Judas felt the belt go taunt as his full weight was absorbed by the limb of the tree. It wasn't a long enough drop to snap his neck, so he dangled with his legs kicking in the air. For a moment, he regretted this foolish decision too because he was still awake, and he could still see the crucifixion, but he knew that in a moment he would pass out choked by the belt.

"I don't have to witness this misery, nor will I suffer as long as..." He couldn't bring himself to even say the name Jesus. He waited for the darkness to come.

A moment later the limb broke. He felt himself tumbling

through space and then his body ripping open on the jagged rocks. Judas moaned as he moved his limbs and felt the broken bones. Some of his intestines pushed through the large open wound in his belly.

It would be hours before he finally died. The birds would watch and wait while the jaws of the giant demon slowly devoured one of its own. The birds would fight desperately for the flesh of his unwanted body, but when men found him days later, he would be already partially consumed by wild dogs.

†

Merak and Nemir ascended the long staircase to the entrance to the Antonia Tower.

"We would like an immediate audience with Pontius Pilate," said Merak.

"And who would you be?" asked the guard politely.

"I am the official emissary of Magus Balthasar of Baghdad and Magus Melchior of Arabia," said Merak. His tone exuded royal authority. The soldier sensed it and hurried off to announce him.

While they were waiting, a chief priest of the temple came running up the steps. He stopped when he got to the top step.

"I demand to see the Roman procurator," said the priest.

The second Roman legionnaire knew who the man was and headed back across the central court in the Antonia. Before he got across the court, Pontius Pilate came walking out.

Merak stepped forward when Pilate came out.

"Excuse me," said the chief priest.

"What is it," said Pilate. He was not hiding the irritation in his voice.

"We have a major problem with the titulus for Jesus the Nazarene," said the priest.

"What's wrong with it?" demanded Pilate.

"You shouldn't have written 'King of the Jews,'" said the chief priest.

"Really? And what should I have written?" Pilate asked sarcastically.

"I am king of the Jews," said the priest.

The 'I am' would have changed the Hebrew text and gotten rid of the word YHWH from the sentence.

"What I have written, I have written," said Pilate. He frowned at the man and with a wave of his hand indicated that he was dismissed.

The furious priest almost bumped into Merak and Nemir as he stormed down the stairs.

A couple steps down the priest paused and said, "Tomorrow is the Sabbath. We want to perform crucifragium so that he's not on the cross on a holy day."

Pilate nodded reluctantly.

"It's been a trying morning. You must be the gentlemen from Persia and Arabia," Pilate said with great dignity.

"I bring you greetings from Magus Melchior of Arabia and Magus Balthasar from Persia," said Merak.

"What business do you have here in our city?" Pilate asked as they turned to walk into the Antonia.

"We have a gift to deliver to a man named Jesus of Nazareth," said Merak.

Pilate stopped walking.

"Really? How unfortunate. His own people have de-

manded his death. I am afraid you are too late," said Pilate.

"We would like to request a stay of execution," said Merak.

"Even a formal request for clemency would come too late," said Pilate. He now faced back toward the entrance.

"Couldn't you stop your men?"

"By now he is already raised up on the cross as they say," said Pilate. "Even if we took him down the poor man would die from his wounds."

"Isn't there anything you could do?" asked Merak. He was quickly becoming frustrated.

"No. I might be able to help you find his family for condolences, but at this point most people who knew him will not be available to speak. There is—how shall I put this—a certain shame when a family member has been crucified. It would be better to let his relatives be."

"I see," said the disappointed Merak.

"He's probably close to death by now."

Pilate looked up at the suddenly darkening sky. The weather had become ominous.

He continued, "And in any event they won't let him stay on the cross too long. They'll break his legs and get him down before sunset because of the Passover Festival. These are a strange people. Their customs leave me confounded most of the time. Thank you for your visit, and again I am sorry."

Pilate turned and walked away.

†

"What did he say?" Soraya asked.

She knew from the look on his face that Merak had not been successful.

"It's useless," said Merak.

He saw the tears of disappointment in her eyes. Her father reached out to comfort her with his embrace.

"My daughter. These things happen. Sometimes they are not just. Good people have bad things happen to them," said Abdul.

He looked over toward Mary whose pain was written on her face.

"No mother should have to see the death of her own son," said Abdul.

"They make it such a spectacle," said Soraya. "You should hear some of the nasty things they have said to him."

"People are cruel sometimes," said Abdul.

"Hey, King of the Jews, we heard that you were going to destroy the temple and in three days rebuild it. Save yourself if you are God's son. Come on down from the cross!" yelled a man near the back of the crowd. A few of the people laughed. Others cried.

An elder from the temple said, "He saved others. He can't save himself. If you're really the king of Israel come down so I can believe in you."

The elder looked at some of the scribes and priests and nodded his head, proud of the insult he had given.

"He put his trust in Yahweh. Now let Yahweh rescue him if he wants him. Didn't he say, 'I am God's son,'" said one of the priests. His voice was dripping with sarcasm.

"These people are incredibly arrogant," said Nemir.

"The poor man is dying, and they are mocking him," said Soraya.

"I thirst," said Jesus. It was said in a loud enough voice that everyone became silent.

One of the soldiers who was still annoyed that he hadn't won when they cast lots had some vinegar in a cup. He put a sponge on a hyssop stick.

He went up to the cross and offered the sour wine to Jesus.

The Nazarene tasted it and refused.

The sky darkened and the soldier looked up. He was frightened but pretended to be brave. As his eyes came back down, he read the titulus and said, "If you are the king of the Jews, save yourself."

"What a fool," said Merak.

"The jerk on Jesus' left is a bigger fool," said Soraya. "You should here the language."

"Aren't you the Christ," said Gestas. He spat out the words as if the word Christ had created a disgusting taste in his mouth.

"Let him be," said Dismas.

"Come on, if you're the Christ save yourself and us too," said Gestas.

"Have you no fear of God at all?" said Dismas. "You got the same sentence as he did, but in our case, we deserved it. We're paying for what we did. But this man has done nothing wrong."

"Yeah, so let him get down," said Gestas laughing.

"Jesus, remember me when you come into your kingdom," said Dismas.

Jesus lifted himself up to take a deeper breath. Whenever he did this, he had to either pull on his wrists or push on his feet. Both were excruciatingly painful.

"In truth I tell you, today you will be with me in

paradise," Jesus said to Dismas. He sagged back down after he had spoken.

"Has he been this dignified throughout?" Merak asked softly.

"Yes. Earlier, with the sweetest tones, he asked one of his friends to take care of his mother. It broke my heart to see it. All the women were crying at once." Soraya could barely tell the story and then burst into tears again. Abdul hugged her and was crying too.

Suddenly Jesus cried out in a loud voice, "Eloi, Eloi, lama sabachthani!"

"What is he saying?" Merak asked a woman nearby.

"He's calling on the prophet Elijah," she said.

Someone ran to get the sponge and reed to offer him wine.

"Wait," yelled a priest. "Let's see if Elijah will come to take him down."

"What does he mean?" asked Merak.

"I think you have it wrong," said a scribe. "The so-called king just started praying a psalm of lamentation that ends up with a joyful victory. He'll have no victory tonight."

Jesus again raised himself up to take a breath and said, "It is finished. Father, into your hands I commit my spirit."

He breathed his last.

Suddenly the earth trembled.

Off at the temple, the veil of the sanctuary that protected the Holiest of Holies was torn right down the middle from the top down.

Longinus was next to the crucifix when this happened and looked up and said, "In truth, this man was the Son of God."

Merak, Abdul, Soraya, and Nemir watched as women started to walk away. Many of them were beating their breasts.

12

THE CLOTH DELIVERED

Longinus started walking down the hill toward what appeared to be some sort of a disturbance. He was having difficulty seeing who was causing the problem, but when he reached the spot where his horse was tethered, he heard a voice that he knew well. It was the same chief priest who had asked Pilate to change the titulus.

Longinus disliked the man intensely. He knew him to be arrogant and contemptuous. For the past three years, since Gaius Cassius Longinus' eyes had gotten worse, he had been assigned to keep track of Jewish unrest. Longinus was stationed permanently in the Antonia but had traveled to Galilee several times to listen to reports about Jesus' activities.

The chief priest had been questioned in the past at his own and not Longinus' request. What he had tried to do is influence Longinus' opinion about the man from Nazareth. The two men disliked each other deeply.

"We represent the Jewish council and the Sanhedrin," the chief priest announced loudly. He was holding a spear and standing with a group of temple guards.

"I know who you represent," said Longinus.

"By the authority vested me from Caiaphas, the high

priest of the temple this year, we are here to perform crucifragium on the Jewish men who were crucified today," said the chief priest.

Crucifragium would ensure that the men died in a few minutes. Once their legs were broken, they would no longer be able to breathe and would suffocate quickly. The priest wanted to make certain that the men were not still on the cross at sunset. They had to have them off the crosses at least a half hour before the start of the Sabbath so that they were entombed before sunset.

Longinus was an expert in Jewish affairs and understood what the priest was really up to. The Sanhedrin wanted to make sure that Jesus' bones were broken in some manner so that the scripture that foretold the Messiah wouldn't have a broken bone would not be fulfilled.

"You may perform crucifragium on the two thieves, but don't touch the Nazarene," said Longinus.

"We were ordered to make sure that they weren't alive for the Sabbath. That would violate our law," said the chief priest.

"The Nazarene is dead already," said Longinus.

"Perform crucifragium on the three men," ordered the chief priest. He raised the spear of Phineas, known to some as Herod's lance as a signal to his men. His temple guards started up Golgotha to the crucifixes.

Longinus grabbed the spear from the chief priest hands and mounted his steed. He turned the horse from side to side and scattered the temple guards. Longinus drove the horse up the hill toward the three crucified men.

He dismounted and took the lance and passed the blade through the right chest wall of Jesus. He pierced his lungs

and penetrated all the way to the heart of Jesus. This was a Roman method for making sure that a wounded soldier was dead in the battlefield. Often the Romans would finish off their own wounded so that the men wouldn't have to continue suffering.

When Longinus pulled the lance from between the sixth and seventh ribs, a great quantity of blood and water poured out onto his face and eyes. At that moment the cataracts on Longinus' eyes were healed.

"I can see!" he exclaimed.

He looked around and saw that the temple guards were clubbing the legs of the two thieves.

"Jesus of Nazareth is dead. Don't let anyone but family touch the body," said Longinus. Two Roman legionnaires stood in front of the body of Jesus and blocked the temple guards who had finished clubbing the legs of Gestas and Dismas.

A young man reached up with a sudarium or face cloth and covered the face of Jesus. It was typically done when a man had died so that friends and family wouldn't have to look at the face of death.

"It is over," said Abdul. He held his daughter who was weeping quietly.

Merak was angry.

"Look it's Joseph, the Arimethean," said Nemir. "Let's go see what he wants to do."

Joseph was talking with Mary, the mother of Jesus. He nodded his head and then turned and rushed off.

The four travelers couldn't get through the crowd to speak to him. He was already on his way back toward the Antonia.

What they didn't know is that the family of the deceased couldn't take the body down and bury him without permission from the Roman authorities. There was a further problem that Jesus was a convicted criminal, and the Jewish authorities would withhold his rights to be buried in a tomb that held the bones of other souls. Joseph had a new tomb that was recently carved out of the rock in the quarry. Since there were no others in the tomb yet, the convicted man's corpse wouldn't defile the bones of others.

Jesus couldn't be taken down from the cross until Pilate had given permission to the family.

Joseph was hurrying to the Antonia so that he could get permission and entomb Jesus before sunset.

Merak was the first to catch up with Joseph of Arimathea.

"Joseph," Merak called.

Joseph stopped and turned around on the steps to the Antonia. He saw Merak and then looked up the road and saw the other three coming along too.

"I'm sorry," said Merak.

Joseph stood there silent for a moment. "I don't know what to say. I have to ask Pilate for permission to remove and bury the body. If you'll excuse me."

Merak nodded and watched as Joseph told the guard to the Antonia what he needed.

Pilate came out immediately and was astonished to hear that Jesus had died so quickly.

"I want to speak with Longinus immediately!"

On Pilate's command Longinus was summoned. In a few minutes he came riding to the Gabbatha.

"Sir," said Longinus. He dismounted quickly and swiftly walked up the steps.

Pilate noticed how easily he managed the steps. He had been aware of Longinus' cataracts. Longinus was a famous centurion who had distinguished himself in battle in Africa, and it was well known that his current command had been given to him out of respect for his service. He normally was careful on steps though, because of his poor eyesight.

"Is the Nazarene dead already?" asked Pilate.

"Yes, sir," said Longinus.

"Didn't they perform crucifragium a little early?" asked Pilate.

"The chief priest wanted to perform crucifragium, but I didn't let him," said Longinus.

"You may have the body," Pilate said to Joseph.

"Thank you, sir," said Joseph.

"What will you do with it?"

"I have a virgin tomb that we can use," said Joseph.

He turned and started down the steps from the Antonia Tower.

"What happened to your eyes?" Pilate asked his centurion.

"When the Jews tried to mutilate his body, I gave the Nazarene a mercy thrust to the heart like we do to a soldier in the battlefield. Blood and water poured forth, and in the instant that it touched my face and eyes, my affliction was lifted."

"Remarkable," said Pilate.

"Let me get back there. They are up to no good," said Longinus.

"What will they try to do?" asked Pilate.

"They are coming to ask you to post a guard at the tomb so that the followers of Jesus don't try to steal the body and

claim that he has risen from the dead as he had predicted," said Longinus.

"That would be an interesting twist," said Pilate with a laugh. He had no doubt that Jesus would stay dead. He was looking down the steps at Joseph, who was talking to the visitors from Persia and Arabia.

"Keep some men posted at the tomb. When they come to ask for a guard, I want the tomb sealed with my official seal. No one enters that tomb without my permission, not even God," said Pilate.

Longinus nodded his head. He understood perfectly.

✝

"May I see the linen?" asked Joseph.

"Certainly," said Abdul.

They walked over to the pool where the camels had been left. Abdul lifted the bolt of linen from the saddle of his beast. He handed the end of the cloth to Nemir who took a few steps back to show him the linen.

"Would you unfold it all the way so that I can see how long it is?"

Abdul and Nemir nodded and unfolded it the rest of the way.

"It is sixteen cubits long and four cubits wide," said Abdul.

"That is the perfect size for a burial cloth," said Joseph of Arimathea.

"All these years of waiting, and this is what the linen is used for," said Nemir.

"It seems like such a tragedy," said Abdul.

"Remember, though, that it was your duty to bring the

cloth, and that you were supposed to bring it at this hour," said Joseph of Arimathea.

"And to this gate," said Merak who had been standing off to the side watching the proceeding.

Abdul and Nemir took the cloth and rolled it back up. Joseph put the bolt on his shoulder and walked back up the Via Dolorosa to Golgotha.

The four travelers stayed back at a relatively discreet distance but went back to see what would happen.

The two thieves were already down from their crosses. No one was there to claim their bodies which were going to be interred in a cemetery for criminals.

Merak watched closely as the men with Joseph worked to get the body down. Jesus' head hung low with his chin touching his chest. First the men released the feet. Then they wrapped a cloth around each foot. Next, they released the nails on each wrist and bound it with a short cloth that they were going to use to carry him to the tomb. They could not touch the body, or they would be ritually unclean.

The body was already set with rigor mortis, so Jesus' head didn't move when they took him down. Mary, his mother, was standing next to the cross with two other women next to her. She sat down, almost collapsing with grief. The two other women stood by to comfort her.

The men tied short strips of cloth to each of Jesus' limbs and lifted Jesus. They placed him in his mother's lap where Mary cradled his head and shoulders and sobbed. After a few moments the men asked permission and lifted the body. A number of other women came back from buying baskets of flowers. They were going to wrap the body in the linen and cover it with fragrant blossoms, as was the custom.

They started walking down from Golgotha to the small trail that led into the quarry where the new tomb had been dug.

Nemir, Abdul, Soraya, and Merak watched from a distance as the small entourage of followers accompanied the body of Jesus to the tomb of Joseph of Arimathea.

"It seems like such a waste," said Nemir.

"Perhaps," said Merak, "but I have the feeling that nothing this man did was a waste. Every word, every gesture had a purpose."

"What purpose could our waiting thirty some years to bring him a burial cloth serve?" Nemir asked.

They were still watching the throng of people at the tomb off in the distance.

"What do we do now?" asked Soraya.

"I think we go home," said her father.

The pall that hung over the four had sapped them of energy and initiative. No one wanted to get started. No one wanted to stay. For them, like most people, this was the end of the story. For Abdul and Nemir it was the end of a thirty-year obligation. Their duty was fulfilled, but their hearts hung heavy with the sadness of lost potential and wasted effort. From their perspective they had delivered a funeral gift, buried with a man that they had not gotten to meet, a king who had not taken his throne.

"You carried out your duty," said Merak. His military training had taught him that duty must be carried out with honor, without concern for the rewards. Sometimes the reward of duty was received immediately. Sometimes it was paid to future generations.

†

Soraya pulled the ribbon off Delia's bit and tucked the colorful scarf into the pack. She was in a state of shock but was even more upset for her father. She watched him sit on his camel and nod silently to Merak.

"I want to go to the Damascus gate and get some dried fruits and nuts before we leave," said Merak.

He was met by a cold silence. Nobody answered him. No one had a comment for him.

Nemir wasn't speaking. He shook his head a few times and then went back to checking his animal.

Abdul started to shrug his shoulders at Nemir but didn't have the energy to finish it.

They all knew that they had a long trip in front of them and weren't in the mood to travel. No one wanted to go back to Melchior and Balthasar and tell them that the king they had patiently waited for was now dead. No one wanted to tell the Magi that the famous bolt of linen was really a burial cloth. It was just too much to deal with.

The party walked their little caravan back to the Damascus gate. Merak left his camel outside with Nemir and walked inside.

He came back out a couple minutes later carrying large pouches filled with a number of treats. He attached them to his saddle and to Jamil. He gave a dried fig to Delia and to Jamil and then got on his camel.

"We have to head over to the Antonia Tower and take the road to Jericho," said Merak.

Soraya nodded.

"It's the road to Jericho, I know," said Abdul.

"We need to go back to Filadelphi to pick up the pack animal," said Merak.

Soraya had forgotten and thought they would return to Gabae. In any event she'd didn't feel like going anywhere.

The camels rounded the turn at the Antonia Tower and started walking. The pace was slower than usual, more like a funeral march than a caravan. They had expected so much and were so disappointed. They had wanted to meet the man who many were claiming to be the Messiah, the Son of God. They had spent years wondering only to see it end this way.

Sometimes, life left a person feeling disconnected from God. It wasn't that the connection with God was actually broken. An omnipresent God was always an immanent God. God was not only ever present in every situation but inherent to every situation. Good or bad God's handiwork was the sustaining force behind every event. The dark night of the soul, when one no longer felt the presence and blessing of a higher being, was in itself the evidence of the relationship with God. When man most missed God and was most distraught about the rupture of the relationship with God, that was precisely when the evidence of the love of God and man's love for God was strongest.

If there was no grief in missing God, then there was no relationship with God. It was not reassuring to the travelers that their grief from the day's events had somehow heralded a relationship with the Nazarene, but it indeed did.

†

"They really seem depressed don't they," said Delia. She was being very cooperative out of respect.

"Yes, they are," said Jamil.

"What I don't get is why they are so upset. They didn't know the man. They had no real relationship with him," said Delia.

"Perhaps they did, and that's why they are grieving. It's hard to tell with humans and grief. They are a strange lot. I can tell you though, that the younger a person is when he dies the deeper the grief is," said Jamil.

"What do you mean?"

"I mean that Mary the mother of Jesus was broken hearted because it was her child. He was younger than her because he was her son, but Jesus was also a young man in the prime of his life. The younger death takes someone, the greater the grief."

"I don't think that's always true," she said.

"A really young child is even worse," said Jamil.

"You mean that the family that sold me was deeply grieved?" asked Delia.

"Most definitely. A mother should never have to see her son die. It breaks her heart."

Delia was quiet for some time. Jamil knew better than to interrupt her thoughts.

"I thought they didn't care," said Delia.

"About what?"

"About David dying. They sold me right off. I never saw them again. I never saw them grieve."

"They were probably devastated and couldn't begin to show you their grief," said Jamil.

"It's terrible to grieve," said Delia. The pain in her voice was palpable.

"It's because death is so final," said Jamil, "or at least it seems that way."

"Oh, it's final all right. Once you step beyond that door there is no coming back," said Delia.

"Heba used to say that once you step beyond that door,

you're fully alive. I never quite understood that one, but I figured the right time to understand it would eventually come."

"You know what I don't understand with all of this?" Delia asked.

"No, tell me."

"Why did they punish him so much?" asked Delia.

"Jesus of Nazareth?" Jamil clarified.

"Yes."

"It did seem excessive," said Jamil. "Remember what Merak said. He had the feeling that nothing this man did was a waste. Every word, every gesture had a purpose."

"But he suffered so much," said Delia. "It was excessive. It was as if they wanted to make sure we knew he was truly dead. It was so stupid. All that misery, for what?"

"He wasn't miserable. He suffered. In life, suffering is not optional, but the misery is. He was peaceful and serene the whole time. Surely you saw that," said Jamil.

13

EPILOGUE

Baghdad, One Year Later

It was a glorious night at the Dromidrome. Delia was returning to Baghdad after traveling with her owners for one year. The entire city was going to celebrate the return of the 'Little Lady' as she was now known.

After the wedding of Soraya and Merak, the Little Lady was allowed one race in the Dromidrome. It was a special wedding present to the young couple from Magus Balthasar. He had convinced the owners of the race circuit that it would be a fun time for all and good for business. Balthasar informed Soraya that as a wedding present she would be allowed one race. If she won, she would be allowed to enter another.

Her racing days were to be limited by a loss—any single loss at any given time. That was to be the end of her career. The way it was promoted was that Magus Balthasar and Magus Melchior wanted to see her run. Merak, her 'warrior' husband, would be happy to retire her to raise a family if she lost. Abdul and Zaffira came for the big race the day after the wedding. The crowds were enormous. Some men were upset, but a lot of people wanted to see the little she-camel who was the granddaughter of the great Blaze. The idea

that Blaze would be at the Dromidrome with her excited the public even more.

The owners feared that if she beat men that their business would fall off. If the races were close, she could be hurt, and if she lost, she might get mocked.

Balthasar assured the owners that she wouldn't get hurt. Any sign of trouble and her professional soldier husband and his friends would deal with it.

What the owners didn't know was that she would beat the men by such a large margin that she would never be in danger.

"If I am in front, they won't be able to hurt me by cheating," Soraya told Balthasar.

He had prayed about it and then smiled.

"Indeed, they won't. Moreover, if your spouse and some of his military colleagues are on hand to supervise the races, no one would dare bother you."

Even though Balthasar was old and barely able to get around, the ancient Magus had gone to her first race and was delighted with the outcome. He hadn't seen Soraya and Merak for nearly a year but was not going to miss the event here at the oval. Melchior had come to town with a large entourage to celebrate with them. This would be the last race for Delia and for Soraya. Both of them were going to pursue more creative endeavors. Soraya and Merak were ready to start their family. Nemir was ready to breed the 'greatest racing camels in the world' from Jamil's bloodline.

During the last couple races Delia hadn't been in full form. Soraya wondered what was wrong. When she asked Nemir about it, he simply stated, "It's too early to tell."

Tonight, Jamil, or Blaze as he was called at the

Dromidrome, would take a victory lap. Nemir was worried about him. He had been slowing down dramatically the last few weeks and was barely able to walk to Baghdad this time.

Perhaps tonight was his final show and he would be retired permanently. He had been using the camel to breed and it had made all of them quite wealthy. Ravi, Nemir, Soraya, and her family were now partners in about fifteen magnificent camels. *Jamil would be put out to pasture permanently after tonight*, thought Nemir.

There were a few preliminary races, but the final race was the event everyone was here for. The entries in the race had to have won a race at the Dromidrome in the last six months. The field was a crowded one with eight entries in the race.

✝

"Thus, the seven marks of character are quite obvious to anyone who would look for them," said Jamil to the stable full of racing camels.

"I don't think I had any of them before," said Delia.

She noticed that Jamil wheezed when he talked. He had been doing it for about a month, but tonight it sounded worse.

"Didn't you have peacefulness, the mark of wisdom?" Jamil teased. Even though he was ancient and now very tired, he had not lost his sense of humor or his compassion.

"I was so irritable that I fought with anyone for the sake of feeling my anger," she said laughing. "I might have had a little honesty."

"Right, the mark of realism. You see when you let yourself use the qualities or virtues of the Sustainer, you develop great character, his character," said Jamil.

A strong lean and tall camel from Arabia, named Sadlak, stepped forward. He was expecting to be the only real challenge to Delia this evening.

"Where does confidence come into play in this grand scheme of things?" he asked.

"Confidence is one of the marks of character. When a camel's character has been polished, confidence is the sign of faith," said Jamil.

"I feel confident," said Sadlak. He was a great camel whose strength was in closing the race. He got faster as he ran longer and often won at the very end of a long race.

"You may feel confident, but on a deeper level it's more than that. You draw your confidence from your relationship with the Sustainer," said Jamil.

A horn was blowing, signaling that it was time for Jamil to be ridden by Nemir around the track. It was Jamil's favorite part of the evening. He was playing at being the old Blaze, but barely walking, and Nemir played at being the great jockey. They were both delighted. The crowd cheered. Jamil knew that Nemir felt like a hero when he was in the saddle.

†

When Nemir went to climb on board Jamil, the old camel balked. He had never done that before. He tried again, but once more the animal refused to let him on board.

"I don't think he wants you to ride him," said Soraya softly. She could see that the old camel knew he didn't have what it took to carry his friend around the track.

"Too old for all the pomp? We can walk if you want," said Nemir.

He started the victory lap around the Dromidrome. When they passed the first turn, Jamil stopped. He just stood still, wheezing quietly. Nemir couldn't hear it because of the roar of the crowd. They started walking again, and again he stopped. This time in front of the grassy public area. The cheering was enormous. It was a living legend's last walk.

Jamil wanted to head in toward the stable but dutifully continued to walk to the reviewing stand. Balthasar, more ancient than Jamil, stood and waved. Next to him was his fellow Magus, Melchior. Both were dressed magnificently. Jamil looked up at them both.

"It was quite an adventure old friend," whispered Nemir. "You can thank those two and Gaspar. Too bad he isn't here either."

Nemir waved to Abdul, Zaffira, and their family. It was his family too, now.

They headed slowly to the stables. It wasn't until they were inside that Nemir noticed how much louder the wheeze was.

"You poor thing. You were the showman until the very end. Get your rest. If we have to take you home by cart we will. No more work for you."

Nemir rushed outside. The real show was about to begin.

✝

"Merak, I love you," said Soraya. She would tell him after the race that he was going to be a father. One last race, this one, was all she wanted.

He smiled, kissed her, picked her up, and put her in the saddle. It was a tender moment that they performed at each race. It was their signature movement. The entire crowd

watched and waited. Soraya was the only jockey who was lifted up by a man. When Merak had her in the air, a roar went up from the crowd. No one bothered her either. He had a small squad of military that accompanied him to the races. Everyone was polite. Everyone was well-behaved.

Tonight, with eight camels racing, starting position was going to be important. Soraya had hoped for the all-important inside position.

The track official came by with the straws. Merak drew for them and shook his head. He drew eight and now his bride was all the way on the outside. She would need to take the lead before the first turn. That was not usually a problem except tonight each of the other camels were champions. It would be much tougher. Merak didn't want to see his wife hit the first or second turn in the middle or outside of the pack.

"Hold up your straws," the official said.

When Merak held up the longest a murmur went up through the crowd. The race was going to be much more interesting. More wagers were being placed. The track official made the camels line up slowly. The more wagers placed the better it was for them. They gave the crowd time.

Delia had the curious habit of facing away from the other camels before she ran. Soraya let Delia stand there facing the crowd. She waved and her parents waved back. Her father was worried. No matter how many times he had seen her race, her father worried. *Just like my husband*, Soraya thought. She looked down at Merak and blew him a kiss.

Soraya took a look behind her and saw that Sadlak's rider was smiling broadly. He had the rail. He was in the best position to take an early lead. She knew Sadlak was a strong finisher like Delia, so starting position was crucial. Her hope

was for a terrific start. Delia had an explosive start.

When the starter blew the first horn which was notice that all eight beasts were on the starting spots, Delia turned toward the track. Soraya felt her grow still but tense. It still amazed her how every fiber of Delia's body grew tense and quiet at the same time. She was like an arrow taunt in the bow ready to be released.

Still though, she hadn't run as well over the past two weeks, but this was her last race for a while. Soraya knew that there would be no more racing once Merak and her family found out that she was with child. It is too early for them to tell, she thought. Then she realized the meaning behind Nemir's words, "It's too early to tell."

"You're pregnant, aren't you Delia?" she whispered.

The starting horn blew, and Delia shot out from the rest of the pack like an arrow from an archer's bow. She was in the lead going into the first turn but hadn't moved all the way over to the inside rail.

As she came out of the turn, the others had gained a few steps and were closing in. Soraya let Delia run her race. She stayed ahead of the pack and moved closer to the rail.

Her lead was a camel's length ahead of the fast starters, two camels who were on the inside near Sadlak. They hit the straightaway, and Sadlak, who was three lengths behind, started to move. He was too big for the turns and tried to close his distance during the straightaways.

On the second turn, Soraya had managed to get Delia onto the rail and hold the position. She would need the extra lengths to hold onto the lead for Sadlak's strong finish. He had no blaze on his forehead but was a marvelously fast animal.

They raced by the private boxes and the start-finish line with Soraya opening up her lead on the pack. Only Sadlak sat two full camel lengths behind and kept his distance.

"You go girl," Soraya screamed. It was her favorite form of encouragement. "This is your last, our last race, so you make yourself proud. I know what you're carrying. Run your heart out while you still can." She never hit her with a riding crop, though she carried one behind her for show.

Soraya's eyes were moist from the wind and the emotion. She wanted to win this race more than any other race. She leaned to the inside as they hit the third turn. She was pulling away from the larger Sadlak.

Out of the third turn Delia had built a greater lead of almost three camel lengths on Sadlak. It was even more on the rest of the pack. This was her race.

On the third full straightaway, Soraya felt Delia holding back. She didn't have the same stamina and was slowing down. Soraya looked back and saw Sadlak was gaining on them. He was a length behind when they hit the turn and really pouring it on.

†

"Something's wrong," said Merak. "That camel is not running like she normally does."

"She's pregnant, Merak," said Nemir.

"Soraya?"

"I don't know about Soraya, but in a couple more days I will be able to tell you about Delia," said Nemir.

"She's okay to run?"

"No problem this one time. In a month she won't run hard at all. At least compared to the way she used to run."

On the last turn, Delia couldn't maintain her pace. Sadlak was alongside her hind quarters to the outside and bearing down. There was a shorter distance in the stretch, but this is where Sadlak was awesome. He had an explosive kick that demoralized most of the other camels. Soraya knew this, but she also knew that Delia didn't lose her courage for anyone or anything. She was a pure racing machine.

Both camels were now pushing themselves to the limit. Soraya realized that Delia had held back just a little to have more for the finish. She was pouring on the speed and keeping a half-length ahead of Sadlak. She was also hugging the rail dangerously close.

Sadlak's head was now even with Delia's shoulders. He was running with his body almost touching Delia.

Soraya looked at the other jockey. She knew what he had in mind. A simple nudge by Sadlak and Delia would hit the rail. That would slow her down or possibly cause her injury. She might even fall. It was a dirty tactic, rarely used because if the animal pushing was too far behind, both animals were often hurt.

Soraya saw the look on the other jockey's face. She knew he was ready if Delia hit the rail. He was whipping the camel with his crop and yelling. Then the unthinkable happened.

Sadlak butted Delia's shoulder.

The force of the blow almost pushed Delia into the fence. Soraya grabbed her riding crop. The next time Sadlak tried to butt Delia she was going to shove the crop in his face. Sadlak moved. Soraya swung, but made it look like she was going to hit Delia.

†

"What is she doing?!" Merak yelled.

He had never seen his wife hit Delia.

"She's smart and she's tough. Watch what she does," said Nemir. He knew his niece better than Merak and knew exactly what she was up to.

†

Soraya raised the whip and struck Delia. It was a glancing blow, not meant to hurt, but to convince others that she was using her whip on her own camel. She held it down a little on toward the end so that it didn't whip so hard. That was a common thing for girls to do. Soraya knew that there were some men in the stands who would be laughing right now.

"Sorry girl, but I have to make this look good. You go girl," she said softly and raised the whip again.

The other jockey was waiting for the blow to land. He was going to follow it with a huge head butt and drive her to the rail.

Soraya swung and missed completely. Her arm whipped the riding crop around in a vicious arc, and her hand twirled it around so that the hard end would swing out. It came right back down, fast and hard. She hit Sadlak directly in the snout with the hard end.

The crack was loud enough to startle the jockey and painful enough to stagger Sadlak who finished a dismal third.

Merak came running up to the winner's circle to get his wife. Soraya was already off the camel, holding Delia's head in her hands.

"I know girl. I never hit you before, but it was just a tap

so I could clobber that jerk," she said to Delia.

The jockey on Sadlak was off his beast looking to see if his snout was damaged. He glared at Soraya for a moment and then caught a look from Merak.

"You open your mouth to complain, and I'll show you what I would have done to you if she were hurt," said Merak.

The man turned and walked away.

"Let him be, Merak. There is something really important I want to tell you."

✝

When the festivities were ended, Abdul and Nemir decided to walk back to the palace of Balthasar where they were being hosted. They were two old friends out on a clear night, talking about life and how things work themselves out.

"It's all about family and friends, Nemir," said Abdul. "I'm so glad you are a part of our family. You are the best friend I could have ever had."

"We've been through an awful lot together, haven't we?"

"Very little that I have regretted, except perhaps that trip to India," said Abdul.

"Don't start that again."

They both laughed and then grew silent. They were walking through the Jewish quarter. They looked around, and both men's thoughts went back to the memory of the crucifixion.

"I know," said Abdul.

"I just don't get it," said Nemir. "It was as though we waited thirty years to participate in a grand tragedy. All those years I had hoped. Reality didn't match my hopes."

There was a Synagogue, not large like they had seen in Judea, but nevertheless active. A tall, strong-looking man was standing on the steps talking to the people who were present. He was speaking fluently and with great passion.

"I wonder what he's so pumped up about?" Nemir asked.

"I, Thomas, one of the original twelve, swear to you that he is risen and ascended. He laid dead for three days and then on the third rose again," said the man on the steps.

"You're telling us then that this Jesus was the Messiah, and though they crucified him and buried him, he did not remain dead?" a voice from the crowd demanded.

"I put my fingers in his wounds," said Thomas.

Most of the people in the crowd dispersed. A few stayed behind.

Nemir looked at Abdul.

"No, it couldn't possibly be true," said Abdul.

"Excuse me," said Nemir. He walked right up to Thomas.

"Yes?" Thomas said.

"Can we have a word with you privately?" Abdul asked.

"What business would I have with you?"

"Last year we were in Jerusalem for the Jewish Festival," said Nemir.

Thomas excused himself and came down the steps.

Abdul and Nemir explained that they had brought the burial cloth but were astonished to hear the good news that he had risen from the dead.

"Thus, we did not bring the cloth in vain," said Abdul.

"The cloth had the imprint of Jesus' image on it," said Thomas.

"How is that possible?" Nemir asked.

"With Jesus all things are possible," Thomas said.

"Where is it now?" asked Abdul.

"We have sent it to King Abgar in Edessa. Jesus had promised him an image."

"Did Jesus declare himself king and ascend to the throne?" Nemir asked.

"Yes, but not a kingdom of this world. He ascended directly into heaven and is seated on a throne at the right hand of God the Father and Creator of heaven and earth," Thomas said.

"How could that be?" Abdul asked.

"I saw it with my own eyes. I saw and touched him after he rose from the dead, and now I am traveling to Jewish communities spreading the good news. I am heading eastward, one Jewish settlement at a time. I am not sure how far across the breadth of the earth Jews have traveled, but I am going to find out," said Thomas.

"We have both traveled to India, and there were small settlements of Jews there too," Nemir added.

They talked for a few more minutes and then said their goodbyes.

†

"Whether I like it or not I am always an instrument of God's will. Even when I try to do something wrong, God can change it and use it for someone's benefit," said Jamil softly but with passion.

The camels had gathered around Jamil. He was no longer able to stand, and his breathing was getting shorter.

"But it is far greater to practice forgiveness," said Sadlak. "That's a real sign that someone's character has evolved."

Sadlak looked over to Delia. She smiled. She forgave him.

In the heat of the race, he had acted foolishly. She understood and let it go.

A couple of camels in the back of the group drifted off, bored with his preaching. The rest of them hung on every word. Jamil knew that they had to work on tolerance. He also knew it was not going to be his task to work on it with them. His days were coming to an end. His time was marked in hours not days, but he was content. He had lived a life of transformed character and could go to his grave satisfied.

"When you surrender your will to the will of the Sustainer," said Jamil, "that's a real sign of greatness."

"What happens to you. Don't you get stuck not doing what you want, but what God wants?" asked a young camel who was finally listening and getting some of it.

"You fall in love with the world, with all of the Sustainer's creation. You get involved in selfless service." Jamil coughed and was wheezing louder now.

"What's that?"

"It's doing good works for others with no expectation of reward for doing it." Jamil stopped to catch his breath and then went on. "You do your duty because it's the right thing to do. Selfless service is the sign of the love that you have been filled with."

"Sometimes I worry that my character will never change," said the young camel, "That I am destined to have all my flaws."

"You can change your character. It is possible," said Jamil.

Delia watched. He seemed to be slowly fading away. She knew what was happening. Her words of gratitude were stuck. She knew she didn't have to say anything, that it was already understood.

Jamil looked right at Delia. He wanted to leave her with one more thought to hold onto.

"Your character is your destiny. Yes, it's true. If you change one flaw you manage to change your character. If you change your character, you've changed your destiny. Just remember that it's possible. And pray constantly."

"Sometimes I don't even know what to pray for," said Delia.

"Me neither," said a few of the other camels.

"Start with gratitude to the Creator and end with a request to be of service to others and to live God's will," said Jamil.

"I was upset about a bad situation and Jamil told me that it was the right thing and the just thing always and everywhere to give thanks… gratitude in the midst of a dire situation," said Delia.

"And then pray," said Jamil.

"I can't believe that's even possible," said a young camel.

"She didn't believe it either," said Jamil.

"I spat at him when he said it," laughed Delia.

"The Magi at their ceremony in Bethlehem stressed that three virtues are gifts from God: Faith, Hope, and Charity. Remember, change is possible with the grace of God," said Jamil.

"The three infused virtues," said Delia.

"Tell him the prayer, Delia."

"Heavenly Father, increase in me the virtues of Faith, Hope, and Charity, and grant me the wisdom to care for your people," she recited.

Jamil smiled at her, and with his last breath he said, "Pass it on."

About Louis A. Tartaglia M.D.

In all his endeavors, Dr. Louis A. Tartaglia has devoted himself to helping others discover their purpose in life and uncover their hidden potential.

He is a Sleep medicine specialist, creative writer and inspirational speaker. He is the author of several books, including *Flawless*, the *Great Wing*, *Heart to Heart*, and *Last Gift of the Magi*.

He lives in Sylvania, Ohio with his wife Jeanne and in his spare time coaches Fencing.

In the past he has practiced Psychiatry and Addiction medicine, and helped set up a rehab for Mother Teresa in Rome, Italy and Chihuahua, Mexico.

An audio book I recommend:
Thirsting for God: The Spiritual Lessons of Mother Teresa
Contains actual recordings of Mother Teresa

www.ingramcontent.com/pod-product-compliance
Lightning Source LLC
Chambersburg PA
CBHW061507020726
47502CB00006B/1965